HOLINDRIAN

&

The Human Revolution

MACAULAY CHRISTIAN

Holindrian & the Human Revolution

Cover design by Macaulay Christian

Map illustration by Travis Hasenour

Edited by Oskar Leonard

"Free the Mind" (Etienette's Song)
Lyrics by Pablo Cruz & Macaulay Christian

To absent family and dear friends:

Nancy Hurdle

Nathan Ginn

Jeff Bess

Valerie Hurdle

Dennis Cochran

You are all, each of you, deeply missed.

CONTENTS

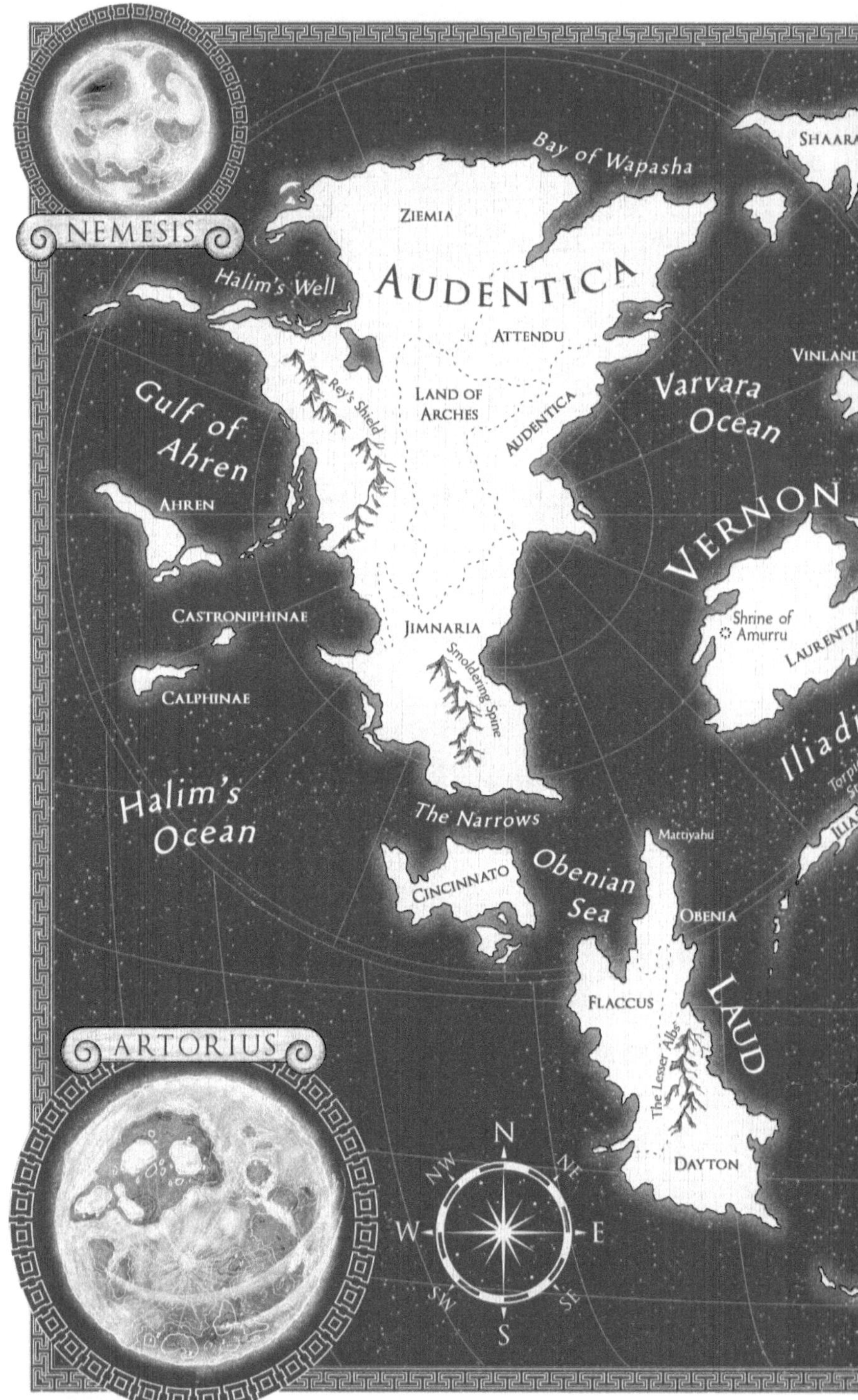

NEMESIS
ARTORIUS
Bay of Wapasha
SHAARA
ZIEMIA
AUDENTICA
ATTENDU
VINLAND
Halim's Well
Varvara
Ocean
Gulf of
Ahren
LAND OF
ARCHES
AUDENTICA
VERNON
AHREN
Rey's Shield
Shrine of
Amurru
LAURENTIA
CASTRONIPHINAE
JIMNARIA
CALPHINAE
Smoldering Spine
Iliadi
Torpio
S
Halim's
Ocean
ILIAS
The Narrows
Mattiyahu
Obenian
Sea
CINCINNATO
OBENIA
LAUD
FLACCUS
The Lesser Alts
N
NW
NE
DAYTON
W
E
SW
SE
S

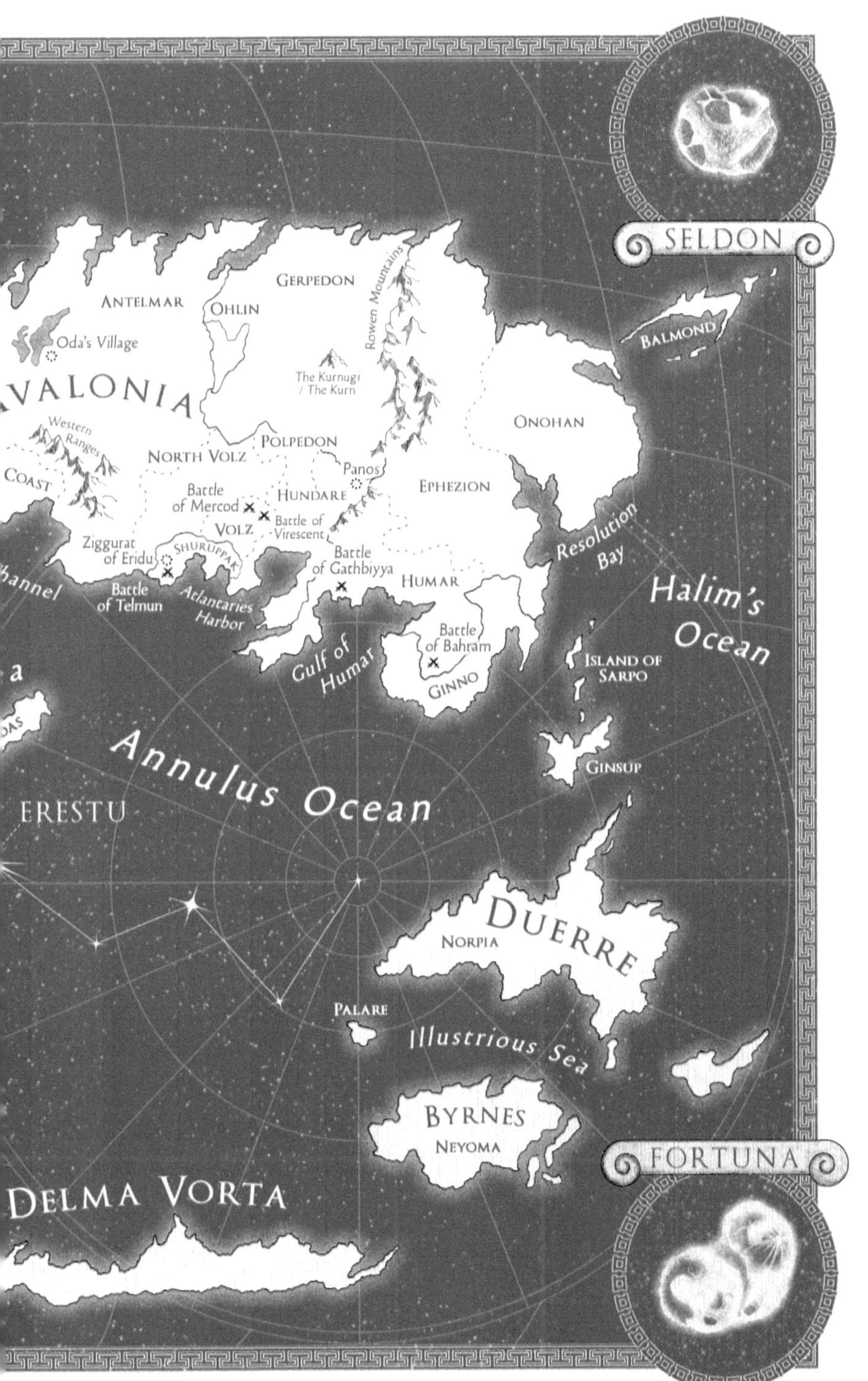

SELDON
FORTUNA
ANTELMAR
OHLIN
GERPEDON
Rowen Mountains
BALMOND
Oda's Village
VALONIA
The Kurnugi / The Kurn
ONOHAN
Western Ranges
POLPEDON
NORTH VOLZ
Panos
COAST
Battle of Mercod
HUNDARE
EPHEZION
Ziggurat of Eridu
VOLZ
Battle of Virescent
SHURUPPAK
Battle of Gathbiyya
Resolution Bay
Halim's Ocean
Battle of Telmun
Atlantaries Harbor
HUMAR
hannel
Battle of Bahram
ISLAND OF SARPO
a
Gulf of Humar
GINNO
das
GINSUP
Annulus Ocean
ERESTU
DUERRE
NORPIA
PALARE
Illustrious Sea
BYRNES
NEYOMA
DELMA VORTA

INTRODUCTION

For me, Holindrian has existed, in one form or another, for more
than twenty years. More than any other character I've created—
or, perhaps better yet, been the mode through which that character has sought to enter *our* world—Holindrian, while not
always the clearest image within my mind, has, nonetheless,
proven to be the most potent and, I hope (with no small amount
of luck), among the most enduring. He has evolved over these
years in ways both overt and nuanced, but always does he retain
much of that first bestowed upon him in his earliest formation.

In the beginning, there was Holindrian. From very nearly the
moment I first dared to fancy myself a writer (not to be mistaken
as an author) with a story to tell, this character rapidly formed,
emerging out of the ether of nebulous creativity not unlike a star
being birthed, around which an entire solar system might come
to orbit. That nascent most Holindrian, like many of those
elements at the start, was crude, ill-shapen. The world that incar-
nation of Holindrian inhabited was one of fantasy complete with
wonderous realms carved into the sides of mountains or under-
ground in expansive caverns; hordes of orc-ish beasts fouling up
the countryside; an evil, despotic villain that needed to be

vanquished. It was a world shallow and crafted from a quaint appreciation for newly discovered work, J.R.R. Tolkien's *The Lord of the Rings*. In short order, Holindrian and the story (such as it was at the time) would undergo pronounced changes—courtesy of Herodotus, Xenophon, Homer, and *The Killer Angels* by Michael Shaar—but it began then with having seen Peter Jackson's adaptations of that most exquisite work.

Early in the development of the character, I, for reasons not wholly clear to me (given that I profess myself an agnostic with generalized deist leanings), began, almost at once, to imbue Holindrian with decidedly religious notes in his history. Sometimes, these trappings were less than subtle. One particular manifestation of this was an idea that Holindrian possessed some connection to the Madonna (Mary the mother of Christ), he was akin (maybe) to the Trinity, and a messianic figure in his own right delivered to an alternate world of humans—for Earth has never held my imagination in the development of my stories as it has too often played a central role in other works of science fiction and the formulation of my apocalis does not *need* our Earth to tell stories about *our* Earth. There was also a time where a version of the character was destined to conclude his hero's journey in a direct confrontation against Morning Star, the Devil himself. Thankfully, many of the details of these earlier iterations of Holindrian have been poorly preserved by me over the years, but, as you will soon read, some of these concepts do remain and seem to have become infused, essential components as to how I imagine Holindrian to be as a character and a device.

The origins of his very name are lost, even to me. I recall, vaguely, the exercise of playing with different words to create this amalgamated collection of letters. Only with the start of his name can I pretend any level of certainty—"holi" has always been derived from "holy". This is yet another connection to Holindrian's innate religious constitution. As for what and how the rest of his name came to be... I, embarrassingly, can offer no answer. In the years since, I have sought, with no small degree of difficulty, to fashion a more satisfactory meaning of his name— one that is in keeping with the broader work I've crafted. In the end, however, it may simply be that Holindrian *is* Holindrian.

What elements of those older iterations of Holindrian that have survived into this present, definitive compilation of the character can be found in the pages to come and in other stories still to be told. Holindrian's metamorphosis has been a long journey from pitiful epigone to (and I once again invoke Fortune) a paragon of virtue. For whatever else the character of Holindrian is and may come to be, he shall forever be the center of this universe I've created. He may not necessarily be the principal character through which a story is told, the world further developed and explored, but it is by Holindrian that all is anchored and, ultimately, dependent.

In the pages that follow, I present to you, the reader, the beginning episode of my apocalis—my future myth. It is the story—a very specific story—about this man Holindrian, who can no longer run from who he is, what he is, and what he needs to become. The Human Revolution is as much his story as it is the story of the people of Eridu. But it does not begin or end with the conflict between Holindrian and Saperon, the oppressed peoples of Eridu against the theocratic tyranny of the Baltutu, or even the glorious struggle for freedom and liberty. The Human Revolution is a journey for all time. At its core, it is about the type of people—the type of civilization we ought to aspire to be, for my part. Holindrian is but the character burdened to progress along that arc—an exemplar for all who share a page with him.

A DAUGHTER'S PREFACE

Opening Remarks.

My father was Panayiotis of Panos, the 66th descendent of
Panayiotis. In the tradition of our family, he was a historian.
From the middle of the Second Age until the dawn of this
Seventh Age, a member of the House of Panayiotis has always
been present to observe and preserve, for future generations, that
which is most precious—our history, our story. Over the course
of seven millennia, we have amassed a chronicle that is unrivaled in any library on Eridu. Not even the cliff-side vaults at
Telmun that once belonged to the mighty Baltutu compare to
what we have recorded here. The Baltutu themselves knew this
for they often consulted our House on matter of history, for a
time.

It was an arrangement that had fallen out of favor when
Holindrian journeyed to Panos, in secret, a hundred years before
the Human Revolution began, to sit and discuss the past with the
Panayiotis of that time, my grandfather. Over the course of the
half-century between that first visit and my father's birth, Holin-

drian and even Anshargal (on one occasion) would make periodic calls to the mountain village where nigh endless tomes containing humanity's history were housed. It is fascinating to consider, in retrospect, that, at the height of their power, when their dominion over the world was near absolute, the Baltutu never sought to impose much harm on Panos. There were… barriers, to be sure, but considering what we knew to be true *and* false about the Baltutu, which might undermine the very basis of their empire, our mistreatment wasn't too great.

When the Revolution began, Panayiotis was busy compiling a steady stream of reports he received by way of our family's network of couriers (I, myself, serving as a correspondent for a time) on the events transpiring in Obenia. I often wondered at the time why my father had not petitioned the Baltutu for permission to travel with the fleet or set out ahead of the invasion to await their arrival in King Matthiolus's court. In his younger days, my father had traveled to Laud and the country of Obenia on several occasions—in fact, he lived for a number of years in that place during the Second and Third Obenian Wars. I expected he would want to witness the ending of the Obenian story personally; the flashes of melancholy I observed in him I took to be a sadness because we were on the cusp of the end of history. I now know that was not the case. He wrote no confession, but I suspect my father knew well what was to come—Holindrian's visitations to Panos continued well into the days of my own youth. He knew closing the chapter on the Obenians was not the end of the story but, as has always been true, the start of yet another chapter.

Panayiotis's History.

There is no finer account of the Human Revolution than the volumes written by my father. They have, in all ways, eclipsed what otherwise surely would have been his seminal work—*A*

Comprehensive Guide to the Conquest of Obenia. That work, though impressive in its own right, serves more as a prelude to the Human Revolution and is enriched once the reader knows what follows, allowing for a recontextualization of the actions taken by Holindrian, given that it is during the wars against Obenia he has already begun setting the stage for revolution.

The completed history, a landmark of achievement, spans three expansive volumes. The *Anthropika*, so-called because the Seventh Age that emerged from the Human Revolution would see the Baltutu removed from human affairs entirely, is my father's undisputed masterpiece, for it weaves together the disparate threads from our greater past and relates the conflicts that arose so recently to their origins long ago. It renders the works of all his ancestors to be but companion pieces to his history. In even these earliest days of this new age, Panayiotis's *Anthropika* is the unqualified record of study concerning (modern) Eridun history.

The *Anthropika* has benefited in no small amount because of three considerations. Firstly, Holindrian granted my father access to people and documents not afforded to a member of my House since before the Fifth Age collapsed—including Holindrian's own personal papers, some which he shared during the war and others shared on his behalf after its conclusion by trusted agents such as Maaschuel and the like. Second, Maaschuel and Conotocarious (among other leaders of the revolution) made available the Baltutu's own stores of knowledge, therefore ensuring details from the point of view of the Baltutu, their Etlu soldiers, and vassals were neither lost nor discounted. Third, Panayiotis was a most gifted writer and storyteller—far beyond my own limitations. He sought to compose *the* history of the Human Revolution from the outset—an enterprise of scholarship as much as it was one of reconciliation for a world torn asunder. I should think he has been proven triumphant.

This Work.

This work, this abridged history of Holindrian and the Human Revolution, is not intended to supplement the prominent place the *Anthropika* has achieved. My intention is only to present a concise telling of the history of the man… this one, extraordinary man who throughout his long life was human, divine (or not), patron and oppressor, friend and enemy, a leader, a visionary, but in all… he was a man. In the end, it was only through him that the spark of revolution was ignited, the yoke of tyranny overthrown, and democratic governance restored to the people of Eridu.

The Proem is substantially unchanged, while his occasional asides, anecdotes, and observations—taken from his prolific collection of notes—have informed the construction of the overall narrative. Without my father's notebooks, the insight he was able to offer into the mind of Holindrian—and fantastically, Enkirus himself—is yet another reason the history of the Human Revolution by Panayiotis stands apart and above those of other historians. My own contributions to the original work have been sparingly included where appropriate in order to permit some resolution by the story's end.

Near the end, whereas Panayiotis affords some pages to share and retell the hypotheses of others, I have made the choice to include but one—the one witnessed by him as well as the many thousands (on both sides). The account of those who saw with their own eyes Holindrian's fate, I insist, is to be more heavily favored than those which came later. Whether by those who heard mistellings and repeated them or those who proffered versions benefiting their own designs, I will lend not a page. Holindrian's end is as described and no amount of words put to page can alter that.

I don't present this work as an alternative to the comprehensive history written by my father, but I do offer it as a more accessible companion to the larger work. I've striven to preserve the most crucial elements present in his history, but I'm also trying something different—at least among the descendants of Panayiotis—I'm trying to tell a good story. A true story. All of it. But a story all the same.

PROEM

My name is Panayiotis. I am the 66th descendent of Panayiotis to carry his name. I was born in the year 7,443, in the Age of the Baltutu, not twenty miles from the spot where each one of my namesakes before me had, too, been born. It is a tiny village. The name of the place is Panos, on the slopes of the Rowen Mountains, north of the Gerpedon grasslands.

I submit this, what may be considered an abstract of the culmination of my diligent research as to the nature of the causes resulting in the last war of the Sixth Age between the forces of Liberty and the Baltutu. The war, known by various names to various people— Holindrian's War, the Baltutu Civil War, or the Human Revolution—is, and I hope it is sincerely communicated, the most noble of wars ever recorded in the history of Eridu, if considered, with respect, to all wars thus far known to have occurred.

Inquiries, sparing no expense of resources or time or distance, have been made so as to most duly account for those causes necessitating violent revolution. Admittedly though, I must confess the absence of appropriate impartiality in my endeavor, as having traveled much of the world in the company of those who sought freedom, it was impossible that my own sentiments should not become, over the course of their struggle, imbued with favor towards them. Furthermore, I stress, it is not nor ever was my intent to portray those who marshaled in opposition to the assemblage of revolution as persons of inferior moral character and the reader is encouraged to view them not in such a disdainful light.

I should not say the Baltutu were an evil empire. Nay, they sought to expunge the very idea of evil, but, and this should become most clear in the pages which follow, that the war between the agents of freedom and security was waged not because order is inherently tyrannical or liberty naturally unencumbered by vices, but instead to remove the sense of absolutism that had prevailed over the world. Two extremes cannot coexist, cannot mutually inhabit the same place. One will always repel the other, seeking to equalize. Freedom and security are not exclusive to one or the other; both can, and rightfully should, exist together, but neither in their extreme most form.

This war had many causes and as many consequences, but it must be remembered that this war, as much as it was about a renaissance of art, of thought, and individuality, it was also about striking the necessary and proper balance between the freedoms of the one and the security of all.

The first section of this Work concerns itself with the abridged history of this world and as I believe it relates to events to come. The second is a recounting of the precipitating events, as war loomed unnoticed in the background. The third recalls the principal engagements of that war and their contribution to the ultimate goal: Self-determination of humankind. Fourth, and last before the afterword, I have included, for your benefit, the Charter of Free Peoples, the first tenants of democratic governance instituted in the Seventh and present Age.

Lastly, it may also be said that this History is a brief telling of the man who made this all possible.

PART 1

A HISTORY BEST REMEMBERED

1.1 OF THE WAY OF ALL THINGS

There is no God. Nor shall it be known, is there a pantheon of a great many gods—at least, not in the prevailing perception. There be neither a singular omnipotent, omniscient being existing before and apart from all things, yet whose will and design be responsible for the formation of the stars, the leaves on an oak tree, or the thoughts of a child, just as there are not a host of gods, angels, and spirits lending order to the nigh unfathomable complexities of nature. There is no God, but, for both an infinitesimal moment *and* an eternity, there did exist one that far and away exceeded the most generous conceptions of what God could ever have hoped to be.

The gods, as understood by common imagination, were invented to preside over the varied plains of celestial existence. In truth, there has ever only been one "god" and its name is Yggdrasil, the yew pillar and worlds tree—the Tree of Life. If the question persists, know that the closest facsimile to the conception of God was that amalgamation of conscious energies that were the immediate antecedent to the birth of the universe. In that sliver of a moment alone, did all the thoughts and dreams of every soul exist together in perfect harmony and in every way exceed the potential and glory of any contrived god.

In the aftermath of the creation of the universe, that which one might, with marginal impreciseness, herald as God ceased to be one and became many. Although no invisible hand belonging to an intelligent designer exists. A more natural force (the Universe) is colloquially invoked to explain the serendipitous.

It cannot be adequately stressed that the Universe is not synonymous with an arbitrator of objective truths. Though "good" and "evil" exist as aspects of nature, they are lorded over by no master nor exercise dominion over any realm absent influence from the other.

The universe does not exist in isolation. It is, truly, part of a larger, grander whole, a whole which, but for the rarest and most blessed, will be ever unassailable. Beyond the material form of a single individual, imbued with conscious thought, is their kin. Beyond their kin, a society, a nation. Beyond the nation, a world full of conscious beings. Beyond that world is a system orbiting a life-giving star. Beyond the star, a galaxy. Beyond that galaxy, along filaments of seen and unseen matter, lie galactic superclusters. Beyond the supercluster, is the threshold of the cosmos itself—the boundary of the universe and the uttermost edge of all that may be perceived....

What exists beyond the universal orb? It is not heaven. It is not the afterlife. The mind of a creator may not be gleamed or touched, but neither is there silence and an endless veil of black nothingness. No dreadful void awaits in the uppermost echelon.

The Tree of Life, not a towering perennial flora, but a tree nonetheless, binds the two worlds, the corporeal and the ethereal —for there is not a third, no netherworld of plight, scorn, suffering, and retribution. Yggdrasil dwells in the realm of light from whose branches an incomprehensible but not infinite number of orbs, each encapsulating a universe of its own to blossom, flourish, and, in time, diminish.

Yggdrasil *is*. Primeval energy, the foundational consciousness that is natural intuition flows ever from Yggdrasil like a river of dreams into these nascent orbs. From these orbs, consciousness, in all its varied forms, grows and returns, pulsating energetically, sustaining the iridescent tree. This cycle is but a palatial exercise of the habitual occurrences within any given universe.

This Tree of Life is essential and does not constitute a portion of a greater whole but *is* the whole. No hand of a divine gardener planted a superlunary seed from which it sprouted. Nothing comprehensible preceded it. Nothing understandable shall supplant it. It is eternal, yet scarcely immutable.

Symbiosis between the tree and the many universes adorning its branches has given cause to reality, just as the relationship sustains one and the other. Yggdrasil provides a universe with a sanctuary and foundational energies to inflate its rise. In return, as a universe matures, it supplies Yggdrasil with a bounty of conscious energy, which, in time, will foster the growth of further universes. Over the innumerable eons, the infusion of evermore sophisticated consciousnesses has surely influenced the development of the Tree of Life, but to what end is impossible to know.

Those gifted the unwonted opportunity to be overwhelmed by the sheer majesty that lies beyond the very edges of the world number but a trifle of all the beings to have ever wondered a thought. Glimpses come in fits and spurts for most over the course of lifetime, often occurring, whether in brief or prolonged pronouncement, in dreams. Yet others may still experience moments of premonition and *deja vu*. Tendrils join the consciouses of likeminded persons across divergent branches as though ensnared in a spider's web. These may either be privileged *coup d'oeil* into the life of another who is of such like character and disposition that they are more alike than twins or the sight from one such person who has perished and, in so doing, issued a warning to distant brethren.

That is not to suggest all these variants are comparable in form, ability, and purpose. Some are undoubtedly mightier and of greater ambition while others are deceptively meager, their needs fewer. A vessel (that is to say the body) can be arranged in any number of ways. It should be surprising, then, to no one, considering the possibilities, that the size of the vessel—in particular, the complexities the brain's architecture—is determinative of the amount of consciousness contained, sequestered, temporarily, from the whole. It is more often true that, during the corporeal lifetime of an individual, the vast sum of who they are exists outside themselves.

There are means of traveling between two universes and even encountering another aspect of oneself. The Tree of Life is densely populated. Orbs in the closest proximity share and are more alike than those more distant. Should the membrane, that outer most edge of an orb, come into contact with that of another. This may either be a fleeting, transitory visit whereby the interactions, if any should occur, are equally fleeting. Other times, visitors may be left behind and forever live on in a universe nearly identical to their own but nonetheless not their own.

During such periods when the orbs are in contact, inadvertent journeying between orbs is possible. However, even inadvertently crossings are most prevalent only with the expenditure of tremendous amounts of energy which tear at the membrane of conscious energies. While the tear exists, passage may be possible. It is the wandering interplay between orbs that may result in the exchange elements. This is but one explanation for the misremembering of trivial things across populations.

The contact of two or more orbs is usually imperceptible and leaves none aware of its happening. The opposite can also be true. Orbs may envelope and devour other orbs or collide, resulting in the annihilation of both. Destruction of entire universes is infrequent. Yggdrasil resents this for, although the conscious energies will always be absorbed and reclaimed, the time allotted before the energies can be reprocessed exceed the life age of the extant universe.

There are still other methods of travel, methods that are deliberate and studied, which rely upon conscious energies.

To traverse from a realm of incidental exposure over to intentional discovery requires one to learn the Ways. The Ways are pervasive throughout the universe. They exist as a direct consequence of consciousness, even in universes with a poor array of intelligent life of any measure. The Ways envelop the universe in a pellicle. Where the concentration of conscious energies (otherwise known as earth energies) has prospered over a period of many eons, the Ways, too, evolve. On life-supporting worlds, the Ways manifest as swirling, shimmering vortices. In their weakest energetic state, the Ways expel and imbue passersby with positive emotions, while at their peak, a Way vortex opens a traversable portal to the very periphery of a universe's celestial shell.

The Ways are a conduit to the ethereal plain, a nexus joining past and present. If one were to learn the full depths of their mysteries, the instantaneous travel across great distances would be but the beginning. For it is only through successful navigation of the Nexus can events be revisited, perhaps even changed.

It is not inconceivable; however, unlikely, that an exceptionally powerful vortex, positioned on a world so teeming with conscious life since the dawn of the universe could offer the penitent pioneer but a chance to set foot outside the universe and gaze upon Yggdrasil itself.

Such things are difficult to *know*. Much of this knowledge has been inherited by humanity and is not the product of humanity's own discovery or divination. It was left behind for us to find; more exists that has yet to be uncovered but it is from this foundation modern Eridun society is built. Our part in this universe is not shrouded in quite so much ignorance.

1.2 THE FIRST PEOPLE

That no God or gods exist to hold dominion over this or any universe remains true to the understanding of the humans of Eridu, though the nature and presence of the First People might well cloud that perception. By happenstance or design, scarcely a word has been made known to provide a fuller account of these earliest of all inhabitants. So precious, in fact, the brevity of this chapter surely does them not the justice they are due.

Alas, what is *known* is this: They emerged from the fires of creation fully formed whilst the first stars burned hot, bright, and short and the black night had not yet come to be. Whether a herald or remnant of the blossoming consciousness, the First People were, indeed, the first conscious beings to perceive the universe. Their perception was not disparate and disjointed, as is so for yourself and any other you might know—no matter how well. The First People have always been as one hand with many fingers. For this reason, it may be so that the First People remained closer in kind to Yggdrasil itself than the consciousnesses destined to evolve in the eons to come. But while they were the first, they had much to learn—about themselves and of the universe they had been born in. When the other conscious beings awakened, the First People resolved to seek them out and teach all they had learned and mastered, for they mastered much. When, at long last, the First People felt the presence of infantile thoughts touch theirs from across the stars, they marked an end to the Great Waiting—for that is what they called it—and set out into the universe with renewed vigor nigh indistinguishable from the gods of legend.

1.3 THE SETTLERS

Though the planet we know as "Eridu" was discovered prior to the First Exodus, the precise number of years is lost to us. We have been able to determine the approximate length of the First Age due to an incomplete but nonetheless substantial Catalogue of the Mayors as the most authoritative source. The city they founded was called Avahairanor (*far away land*). The only census record from before the Exodus is a fragment, but seems to indicate then, as throughout much of history, Avahairanor was divided into boroughs. A pastoral homestead, of whose family name we know only the first, third, and fifth letters: B-o-k, is also denoted on the fragment and must have been in close proximity to Avahairanor proper. Using this fragment to estimate the population at the time of the Exodus, it could have been as high as fifty thousand.

There is also the monument constructed to mark the cataclysm which drove so many from Earth. The inscription has only ever been partially translated using primarily a cognate method of linguistic analysis; however, the dating convention appears to have been tied directly with the progression of the mayors. The monument—a megalithic structure built of colossal stone atop a butte not quite a full day's journey beyond the forest northwest of Avahairanor —is dated to the sixth year of the mayorship of Gilshenan, who was the 21st mayor at that time. Taken with the Catalogue of the Mayors, the first settlers came to Eridu between 76 and 126 years before the Exodus. The world must have been discovered even earlier.

Those pioneering settlers who first ventured into the Ways and learned not to just travel to different points on the Earth but to different planets saved the human species through their curiosity and ingenuity—even if now, so far removed, the knowledge of how this was done is largely forgotten. We know too little about these forefathers and foremothers. They found our kind a new home on which to prosper, a world of warmer suns, and bluer skies where birds fly higher—a dream land full of promise.

1.4 THE EXODUS OF FIRE

The Earth was dying. Our ancestors spoke of it, the great calamity that befell our first home. The history of that first apocalypse and the exodus that followed has been told and retold for many, many generations. It is difficult, being so far removed now from the event and those who lived through it, to parse truth from legend. What we do know for certain, is that the first apocalypse began with fire and ash. Nearly three complete apsidal precessions (a single apsidal precession lasting precisely 23,000 years) now separate that event from the writing of this history.

It began on the far side of the Earth—Erestu in the original tongue, in the land of Sunda inhabited by a people whose own name for themselves is lost but were said to be of diminutive statue—like a man, but smaller, a dwarfish creature belonging to fantastical stories. One should think there must surely have been signs of the impending doom, signs which, as the hour drew nearer, could no longer go unobserved or ignored. Whether there were warnings that did or did not go unheeded, in the end, it proved to matter little, for the eruption of that volcano was more terrible and violent than any to be survived by humanity before or since. The skies grew black and all but blocked out the sun. Ash blanketed the fields and pastures. The air became thick and cold. Without the light of the sun, crops would not grow, livestock could not grow fat, and so, all too quickly, the people of the Earth starved and froze and warred to death.

We are told it was but a single, monstrous eruption of unparalleled destructive power and occurred suddenly. The shockwave enveloped the Earth several times over. It could easily have been many eruptions over many years... it simply cannot be known for certain. We know only that the sun and stars were scarcely seen again for ten years; those who escaped were noted to be of a sickly complexion, half starved, and rather cowed in their disposition. None witnessed the event for themselves and fewer could be persuaded to recount what they had seen in the aftermath of the fire.

1.5 PALTIKA

The name first given to this world translates to "second earth" in the original mother tongue of all languages: *Paltika*. It would not become known as "Eridu" until settlers, of which there were in excess of ten thousand, fled another great cataclysm that appeared during the Second Exodus.

Paltika was given this name as it was the first world to be discovered by the ancestors who explored the Ways to be friendly and comfortable to human habitation. In many ways, Paltika is indistinguishable and perhaps this is so as a consequence of the worlds being in such close proximity. The night sky of Paltika was also quite familiar as many of the stars and the constellations they formed were not too dissimilar from Earth. Through careful observation and study on both worlds of the heavens, Palika's location was confirmed within the constellation of Cassiopeia. From Earth, Paltika appears to orbit a single, nearby star. In reality, while it is true Paltika orbits a single, yellow star comparable to the one belonging to Earth, there is also a white star that is often visible during the daytime but also, over a period of many hundreds of years, illuminates the night brighter than any moon—and Paltika has four of various sizes and forms. A third, lesser star shines like a signal fire and is only visible when the suns have set. For observers standing on Paltika, it is possible to view Earth—or, more accurately, the sun Earth orbits—also in Cassiopeia, though with slightly adjusted proportions.

The four moons are called, in more recent times, as follows: Artorius, grander than even the moon of Earth but of a greater orbital distance; Nemesis, a moon covered in fire and lava; and Seldon and Fortuna, a pair of asteroids captured long ago. Whereas the suns work together to greatly diminish the planet's tilt and impose a temperate condition upon every continent, the moons create just enough wobble to churn the oceans and keep the air from becoming too stale and still.

The human explorers who gazed upon Paltika's alien skies for the first time predate the volcanic apocalypse by some years. It would have been grossly fortuitous for those in flight to have stumbled so incredibly on a new planet eager for the privilege to home our displaced forebearers—though there are some who stubbornly adhere to this version. Given the magnitude of migrants that must have successfully made the journey in order to permit the continuance of human civilization for an estimated 61,000 years, it is simply beyond reason to conclude that Paltika was not already known to our ancestors at the time of the desolation. Much from that period in our history is confused; it is distorted by the powerful confluence of time and trauma, thus, the memories we have inherited cannot be so easily trusted. The older tellings are explicit, however, stating on numerous occasions that those fleeing the aftermath of the eruption were greeted by those who already had made Paltika their home. They were met well, with kindness and sympathy.

Paltika colonists founded their city, the one called Avahaira-nor, around the site of their arrival, amidst where the river Enki bifurcates the forest of mixed cedars. That was the location of the vortex, the means of entering the Ways, and there they constructed a pavilion to receive travelers to and from Earth. Though, the subtler details of navigating the Ways have been lost to later generations, the mosaic tiles that formed the pavilion floor appear to have served a varied purpose that was instructional as well as ornamental. It depicts a traveler standing at one point of a six-pointed star. They would enter with confidence and poise through the archway erected at the site of the vortex alongside a Wayfinder—one experienced in walking the Ways. Earth is shown at the center of this star, from where all other points spring. This suggests, to me, returning to Earth would have been crucial in successful navigation to one of the other worlds, these being Odrin, Paayo, Prdydam, Kazan-i-tal, and Paltika. The mosaic parrots a compass rose. If Odrin is placed at the northern position, Paayo would be at the northwestern position, Prdydam to the southwest, Kazan-i-tal to the southeast, and Paltika to the northeastern position. The world that should be in the southern position is unknown because the tiles depicting it are extensively damaged. Only partial letters of its name remain—those being "u" and "n" as well as passing reference to this world being home to an ancient pantheon of gods. As for the worlds whose names are known, some details as to their quality and the character of the people who settled there do survive to the present, though they are meager.

The world Odrin is said to be home to a greater number of humans with robust jaws, pronounced brows with flatter craniums, wide pelvises, and are barrel chested. They were of two tribes, one originating from lands called "Ereb" and the other in eastern parts called "Asu". Both were considered stout and hearty people who revered the spirits governing earth, water, the harvest, the sunrise, and the like. There were also a diminutive child-like people—a race of dwarves, perhaps? Like those of Sunda? Those hailing from Odrin are thought to have been great lovers of music, for a flute player is shown welcoming travelers.

Paayo is a world we know little. It is thought to lie nearer to Earth than Odrin yet not nearer than Paltika. This is judged by the lengths of each star point. These tiles are less well preserved but seem to suggest Paayo was a world of grasslands and deserts.

The Prdydam tiles indicate a beautiful garden. The people who settled here, once friendly and jovial, quickly erected a barrier and sealed off their world from the others. Though the markings have faded, the paint splashed over these tiles and the damage done to them suggests anger directed towards these lost brothers and sisters.

Kazan-i-tal might have been a newer colony. The mosaic appears to have undergone a refurbishment that was never completed. Consequently, nothing more than the name of this world and a vague direction is definitively known.

The great appeal of Paltika then as is now, is the remarkable balance of the planet's climate. The astronomers of old attributed this to the greatly minimized tilt of 12.41 degrees when compared to Earth's variable 21 to 24 degrees. The seasons are typically mild, with large swathes of the planet locked into a perpetual autumn or spring, and the temperature differs reasonably between summer and winter, though both are abridged. The growing season is long. A great host of flora and fauna favored by humans take to Paltika with ease. Storms are less daunting, save for the erratic tantrum instigated by the suns and moons. Due to the presence of additional celestial bodies of considerable size and weight in close proximity to Paltika, the planet enjoys an orbit that is nearly perfectly circular.

Upon entering or exiting the pavilion, travelers were greeted by a large stone weighing several tons, with a horizontal measurement of twelve feet and a vertical measurement of eight feet. On the face presented to those arriving from Earth was a map of Avahairanor and its surroundings. The pavilion was the central feature, but there was also an agora that formed around it comprised of many vendors and their stalls. A spiraling tower dominated Avahairanor in those times. Only its lower portions exist today, but even then, it would have been perceptibly shorter than the Ziggurat which was built atop the old pavilion grounds. On the reverse was an illustration of the explored regions of Paltika, a mere fraction of the world. The lower center third would have guided the viewer's gaze towards the focal point—

Avahairanor (once again) south of which was where the bodies of water we know as the Annulus Ocean and Iliadic Sea meet are simply labeled as the "Aq'wa". The center shows the extent to which forests once so thoroughly covered the Avalonian continent. The top portion of the map fades as the extent of knowledge of the world diminished. The left and right extremes framed the map with the Western Ranges and Rowen Mountains respectively, a distance of 2,441 miles.

That first civilization, comprised of intentional settlers and migrants fleeing a horrific cataclysm, were the descendants of Aria, an old nation of Earth that had existed for at least a thousand years. What is known about Aria can only be extrapolated from what the colonizers of Paltika were able to accomplish. It can be said with confidence that the Arians were a sophisticated people with demonstrated mastery of mathematics, engineering, architecture, agriculture, and astronomy. Their greatest feat, however, cannot be eclipsed by any of their stone and earth mound monuments that stubbornly persist: The discovery and mastery of the Ways, without which humanity might have perished long ago.

The demise of the first civilization was gradual. It occurred over many millennia, but when the refugees of the Second Exodus made their startling arrival, the civilization had dissolved into two camps—the Titaans and the Gudanna.

1.6 THE GUDANNA & THE TITAANS

There were other tribes that formed as the first civilization's reach receded, but none as consequential. Five hundred and sixty-nine years prior to the Second Exodus, the civilized world had contracted to the lands we call the Shuruppak. Avahairanor remained as the last settlement of note, a nexus for dozens of villages that spanned the cliffs, hills, woodlands, riverbanks, and fields of that territory, but Avahairanor had fallen to decay. Its influence could scarcely be projected beyond its dilapidated walls. Those villages, especially the ones founded at the eastern-most extreme of the Avahairanor's reduced claims, were fraught with danger. Enter the Gudanna, the foremost threat of the time.

On the Gudanna.

What name the Gudanna gave themselves is unclear. These were not a people of language arts nor were they a people of "art" more generally. The fragments of their writing, such as it was, that survives is inconsistent in both syntax and calligraphy. Their technological sophistication, namely of their weapons, tactics, and tools, at a glance appear to be crude, yet effective. Descriptions of their more established settlements strongly suggest a prevailing utilitarian sensibility in all things. They embarked on no great architectural projects, certainly none of immortal stone, and fashioned their more impressive structures from locally sourced lumber topped with thatched roofs, though yurts covered in animal hide are said to have been more common.

The Gudanna practiced limited animal husbandry, relying predominantly on goats to produce milk and cheeses and chickens for eggs. Their primary source of meat, when they had it, came from hunting game, trapping, and, on the rarest of occasions, the taking of a large beast—such as a king mammoth, a noble creature prolific in lands north of Polpedon and Volz as well as east of the Rowen Mountains in the steppes of Ephezion. The successful taking of such a prize, to me, means the Gudanna or elements of their society were migratory. Tales have been handed down of the technique to preserve the bounty of a king mammoth kill for many months by submerging the slain beast in cold water—called underwater caching. It is said that the Gudanna and other tribes would butcher a fresh kill and store the meat during the winter in shallow ponds known to ice over.

There is evidence for Gudanna activity all along the Rowen Mountains and into Gerpedon, that northernmost country. A reasonable hypothesis, I think, is that the Gudanna retreated to the north and the mountains as Eridu's winters (which are alleged to have been harsher for a time) imposed hardships on the people. They sustained themselves with mammoth meat during the cold months before making the trip back down south and to their permanent settlements where game was more plentiful, their animals might produce more comfortably, and the gathering of tubers, mushrooms, and wild fruits could be done.

The Gudanna seemed to have garnered a reputation of nomads who came down from the mountains to pillage and plunder the remnants of Avahairanor each spring, only to vanish at the end of autumn. The stories grew predictably more lurid over the centuries, but the raids also became more frequent with the arrival of the Second Exodus.

It was those latest arrivals from Earth who gave the Gudanna the name for which we remember them. It comes from a dialect spoken by a people who lived between rivers in an otherwise arid and desperate land. Simply, it means "attacker". That is how they saw the Gudanna, and, arguably, that is how the Gudanna saw themselves. They had irrefutably evolved into a more warlike race that lived separate and apart from the rest of humandom in many meaningful ways. They had diverged to such an extent, their warriors slathered themselves in a thick, blue mud, sourced, so it is said, from the slopes of the volcano at the heart of their homeland in the northern wastes. The fire and lava are said to burn bright and blue, while the soil is black, sulfur dust and ash fall instead of rain, and only foul, red-eyed Gudanna savages dare dwell.

The name of this volcano is Helbraius. According to the most popular account, Helbraius and its sick lands lie in the border country between Ephezion and Onohan, stood sixteen miles tall, and, in truth, was not a volcano but a god who had merely taken that form. Now, there is no volcano of such gargantuan height in that place nor any other. A caldera that *may* be the source of Helbraius can be found in the highlands of the Rowen Mountains in the northern portion of Ephezion where a great number of lakes can also be found. This particular caldera is the summit of a wide but gently sloping hill. What the height of this volcano in the distant past might have been is impossible to say. What can be said is that the soil and especially the clay extracted from the nearby lakes has a distinct blue-ish hue to it, unlike anywhere else. It may be that the supposed death of Helbraius referenced in Titaan legend at the conclusion of a mighty battle may, in fact, be the eruption that spurred the Gudanna migrations, which began three thousand years ago.

On the Titaans.

A description of the aforementioned battle (this point will be revisited) is preserved, thematically, thanks to the Titaans, who retained and utilized the technology of writing and art to chronicle their history. Unfortunately, time has seen it prudent to be overly selective in transmitting the story of the Titaans to the present generation. Thus, while more is known of the Titaans than their Gudanna contemporaries, we are frustrated by the lack of crucial details.

One area we are not ignorant is their language. Miraculously, enough fragments have survived the journey from the past to the present to provide linguists (when there have been linguists) with opportunity to decipher key words and phrases, if not so much as to allow mastery. Firstly, the Titaans called themselves the "Ealdor Swefen" (elder dream) and were less one homogenous tribe, but rather a confederation of many smaller tribes that sought to claim the legacy of Avahairanor for themselves, marking no delineation between the first civilization and themselves. Their language is derivative of that spoken by the first civilization of 61,000 years ago, but the meanings of countless words have changed, the pronunciation—if the variations of spelling are to be believed—shifted, and the grammar, although still poorly understood for both languages, is overly simplified. They called the dominion of the first civilization the "Yges'b-sumnes" (or the collective peace). Per their own writings, the Ealdor Swefen felt it was their duty to protect the lif-hord, which, I surmise must mean the Ways, or, more specifically, the feeling when near the Ways.

We call them the Titaans because that is the name they were given by the Second Exodus, who, upon learning the history of this world from the Ealdor Swefen, attributed the feats of engineering and astronomy and building directly with them, for they seemed to be divinely inspired beings. Their tale of the Beadu Wroth solidified the perception that the Ealdor Swefen were the children of heroic figures of old.

The name "Titaan" was not, at first, universally applied by the migrants of the Second Exodus. Though, in time it won out, one group in particular regarded the stories with skepticism, for they alleged they themselves were citizens of a civilization of note, means, and prowess. They called this country Hatehl and themselves the Hatehleans. According to these displaced seafarers, the realm of Hatehl was the most powerful present on Earth whose reach spanned the globe. The impetus for the cataclysm that had befallen Earth for a second time was unknown, but it had unleashed a torrent of flood waters that scarred experienced men and women of the sea.

The nature of this cataclysm which prompted a Second Exodus from Earth will be discussed more thoroughly in a subsequent chapter. It is mentioned here somewhat prematurely only to contextualize the statement that not all who migrated from Earth to Eridu (the name given and was quick to supplant Paltika) were completely beholden to the Titaans' version of history aggrandizing their parentage.

In spite of this, the Titaans were the inheritors to a heroic linage. It culminated in the Beadu Wroth on the slopes of the volcano Helbraius itself 3,441 years before the Second Exodus. The first civilization had all but crumbled and fragmented. The progenitors of the Gudanna, the Andsaka (alternatively, Andsacca) tribe had splintered from the main bastion of humanity in excess of ten millennia earlier and surreptitiously expanded, conquering the lands of other tribes in the east. Their army was a fast-moving horde, mounted on horseback, that swept across half a continent in barely sixty years—from the time horses were acquired (possibly through theft), their wills tamed, and war stock bred. For this, I calculate a period of a thousand years to complete the task.

But it was the rapidity of the Andsakan advance under the leadership of man who had taken the name Helbraius as his own (or, just as likely, his triumphs on the battlefield and rank within their blossoming society justified lending his name to the fire mountain) that roused Avahairanor and the villages in his orbit into action. Then, the Titaans were members of the Beorn, a caste of warrior monks, who rallied the mayor, the leader of Avahairanor, chosen by lot, as was the custom, to marshal a defense of the arid lands today belong to Humar.

City-states and villages were conquered in droves. Helbraius's terms were often simple, as was his retribution: Submit, tend to his army and their beasts, and their lives would be spared for the price of a tithe; resist and there would be no further negotiation as everyone from grandparent to infant would be killed. Refugees fled first south, then west and overwhelmed Avahairanor. Helbraius sought to conquer the whole east and in a few short years, he had nearly done so.

Eventually, the counsel of the Beorn was heeded, but not before Humar fell and the Andsakans raided west of the Rowen Mountains for the first time. Panic gripped the people of Avahairanor and they feared what would become of them if

Helbraius did what he no doubt intended and sacked Avahaira-nor. It would be the pinnacle of achievement for a warlord—one that would grant him the prospect of conquering other worlds if he so desired.

And so, under the auspices of the mayor, the Beorn set out to build an army not just to rival Helbraius but to defeat him utterly. They were inquisitive and interviewed refugees who had witnessed the Andsakans methods of war. Observers were dispatched into Andsakan territory to document their strength and tactics—Helbraius waged a highly mobile form of warfare utterly dependent upon fighting atop horseback. His mounted units were uncharacteristically small in number but used to terrible effect on the plains in that part of the world. These could be said to be the most skilled of the troops commanded by Helbraius. The cavalry was reserved for the destruction of opposing fighters and the chasing down of any who tried to flee. Conversely, a larger contingent of poorer equipped and trained soldiers was used to conduct sieges and occupy captured territory.

Helbraius held few fortified positions and constructed even fewer. The advance (that had likely begun under his father) brought the Andsakans to the desert that ensnared Humar in about forty years. This desert earned the moniker "Scorched Wall", for it provided a natural barrier, greatly slowing the inva-sion. For hundreds of miles, there was too little grass and water to support any but the smallest of armies and their horses lest they carry all that was needed in convoys stretching back to more hospitable places. Thus, though the raids were terrifying and saw many killed, the destruction wrought could have been far worse. So, while Helbraius sought to build capacity to push his armies farther west, the Beorn implemented their coun-terattack.

Many things had to occur simultaneously. The resources of Avahairanor were greatly strained. Per the Beorn, those of fighting age who could be spared were conscripted and taught the pike and javelin—weapons to keep horses at bay. Those who would be needed to collect the harvest found themselves placed under the charge of master builders, set to erect hundreds of mounds, trenches, and forts throughout the Fold, the relatively narrow expanse between the Rowen Mountains and the sea. It is in reference to this group that the term "Ealdor Swefen" is first used, perhaps to imbue their society with a sense of great import. The approximate translation being "elder dream"; what remained of the first civilization would commit their future, their hope, and yes, their dreams to these men and women pressed into service. The final phase of their preparations involved scouring the mountains for a suitable means of passage to cross far behind the point of Andsakan advance and strike directly at the heart of their empire.

They did find a passage suitable to their purposes of driving an army of ten thousand strong. Apocryphal accounts suggest Avahairanor mustered an army that exceeded 150,000 to march on Helbraius's volcanic city, which, in order to be true, would require the population of the realm subject to Avahairanor to be more than twenty million—if these calculations are based upon the five soldiers to one thousand citizens ratio that was been maintained in the three thousand years following the Beadu Wroth. To me, this would be extraordinary, were it true. Census records, while incomplete, do not support a population of that size. To the contrary, if the counts are extrapolated, the population available to Avahairanor might have numbered 230,000 at the uppermost extreme. If that is true, then the ratio of five to one thousand demonstrated how severely the threat of Andsakan invasion was taken, considering this number accounts only for fighting men and women, and not those conscripted for defensive works. It is far more believable that Avahairanor marshalled a force of ten thousand to journey through the mountains while a secondary force of a lesser number garrisoned the fortifications in the Fold.

And this garrison in the Fold was crucial to Avahairanor's victory. Their responsibility would be to lure the Andsakan cavalry into their defensive picket where it could be starved and destroyed. This would be made possible by the hasty construction of a supply center ostensibly to care for displaced people of Ephezion, Onohan, Humar, and Ginno and the re-establishment of Avahairanor-control east of the mountains. As the Andsakan riders heard more and more rumors of a sanctuary, they pushed deeper and further from their own supply lines. In their wake, the Ealdor Swefen set fire to a land already drained of vast quantities of drinkable water (the effects of such a project were felt for generations thereafter).

By this time, the host of Avahairanor crossed the Rowen Mountains (as they are now known) and marched northward in their shadow. Helbraius doubtless discovered their presence and directed his generals to halt the Ealdor Swefen advance, but, in the end, Helbraius, now well into the latter stages of his life, assembled the largest army he could and met his enemy on the slopes of the volcano that spewed blue fire.

The Beadu Wroth lasted seven days. Helbraius's army had to be cobbled together by taking all the reservists, trainees, and boys aged twelve years or more, for his prized cavalry were engaged 3,915 miles to the south and could never return to turn the tide. Ealdor Swefen legends say Helbraius raised a fighting force of half a million men…. However many fought on Helbraius's behalf in that battle, it is agreed they were numerically superior and that they were slaughtered almost to the last man. In a desperate bid to stem his losses, old Helbraius exited his imperial city to challenge the leaders of the Ealdor Swefen, Rowen and Onohan.

His challenge was met. The three fought as the mountain erupted. Onohan was gravely wounded in the melee, but it was

Rowen who landed the killing blow, at the expense of her own life. Helbraius died. His death shattered the will of his army, which dispersed in the aftermath. Whatever remained of his empire was destroyed for all coming time when the volcano that shared its name with that awful tyrant blew itself apart. In the aftermath, the imperial city was encased in stone and submerged the tomb of the Andsakan warlord in lava. This happened around 3,000 years before the Second Exodus.

Many had been killed and displaced on both sides of the conflict. The burden imposed upon Avahairanor by the Beorn to win the war expediated the dissolution of the first civilization's society. A great toll had been levied against the future by committing so many men and women of prime childbearing years to die in foreign lands. At tremendous cost of tribute and resources, Avahairanor had diverted labor from the west and north to defend the east, leaving those villages unbalanced and poor. The decline that had been gradual before the Beadu Wroth accelerated. It seems clear that while the Ealdor Swefen considered themselves of the first civilization, they were learned enough to appreciate the limits of that truth.

So, when the Second Exodus did arrive—quite unexpectedly —and they were regaled with the history of their new home, the Ealdor Swefen came to be called Titaans, for they had fought on behalf of a heavenly purpose.

1.7 THE EXODUS OF WATER

The Second Exodus from Earth marks the end of the First Age. The cataclysm prompting this second wave of migration, being a far more recent memory, is better understood, even if the totality of its nature remains elusive. What is known is that this was a cataclysm of water and not of fire, as was the case before.

In the autumn of the year preceding the Exodus, serpents of fire and light streaked across the sky day and night with ever increasing frequency until they were an endless stream. Few migrants hailed from territories in the north; those who did spoke of a fireball soaring across the sky, brighter than the sun. It fell somewhere beyond the horizon, unleashing a roar that robbed many of their hearing. All at once, the Earth began to flood and whole cities were drowned beneath rising oceans and swollen rivers.

The Hatehleans insist their observation of the planets and stars had long since given the leaders of Hatehl pause, for the number of meteors witnessed grew with each passing autumn for more than ten autumns and of those, a commiserate number made landfall. Great debates, it is said, consumed their city as the doom approached, a place built upon concentric rings of land connected by grand canals which led to a sea unbounded except far to the west.

The leader of the city at that pivotal time was King Karadin. His reign began eight months before the cataclysm, following the death of his mother, Queen Kiretahl, whose rule lasted seventy years. Karadin was confirmed as king by the Witan, a body comprised of the most prominent men in the city. Allegedly, this was done despite Karadin being regarded as less well received than either of his two adult children: Korrin, the eldest, and Haethal, who, for a brief time, it was hoped might succeed their grandmother instead of their father. There is also mention of another child, Thoth, though whether this was a third brother, a grandchild of Karadin, or some other relation, is unknown.

Hatehlean tradition holds that Karadin was not a direct descendent of Hatehlus, the first king, whom the nation and people would take their name. Allegations of secret adoption marked him as being unfit, though, this logic may not have been applied evenly to his children. The method of Hatehlean succession has been muddied and, frankly, poorly studied; however, it seems to me that the most likely truth is that in order to be considered for king or queenship of Hatehl by the Witan, the person must have shared and demonstrated (through letters patent) a common lineage with Hatehlus or his kin. Now, Karadin must have born some manner of relation to Hatehlus to have been eligible for the Hatehlean throne but there may have been others with stronger claims yet who were dismissed by the Witan.

In the waning days of his mother's reign, Karadin advocated strongly for the banishment of Enkirus, a natural philosopher and proponent of rediscovering the Ways as a means of weathering the brewing storm of fireballs which had become as common a sight as birds in the sky. Enkirus is well-known to the people of Eridu. His role in our history will be discussed more fully in chapters to come, but it is important to know that it is he, Enkirus, who is credited for having made the Second Exodus possible. Karadin, and others, thought Enkirus's preoccupation with the old legends to be a distraction and grew tired of indulging in his expeditions all over the world in search for rumored vortices. Karadin felt his mother, the queen, had too long placated the aging scientist. So, he aggressively pursued more tangible methods of hardening Hatehlean civilization against whatever misfortunes Fortune might bestow. For his part, Enkirus was, indeed, banished to Doggerland by Queen Kiretahl approximately eight years prior to her death after Karadin and the Witan applied considerable pressure on her to do so.

It is then hardly surprising that when the cataclysm did eventually cause great upheaval, Hatehl under King Karadin suffered mightily. The Hatehleans who made the journey from Earth to Eridu long told tales of how the entirety of their country plunged beneath the sea's towering waves. What became of Karadin is not known with any certainty, but it is generally accepted that he was destroyed along with the Hatehlean state. His children and their families, curiously, were widely believed to have departed before the worst of the cataclysm came to pass, one heading east and the other west, perhaps with a mind to aid humanity in rebuilding and to keep some semblance of the Hatehlean tradition alive.

The few Hatehleans that came to Eridu boast of a civilization and an empire that stretched more than ten thousand years into the past. It is impossible to accurately distinguish fact from their fiction. I shall not risk a protracted tangent in recounting the entirety of their supposed ten millennia history, but in summation: They were a noble race that had begun to succumb to hubris in their latter days; theirs was an empire of great ships that commanded the seas and knew even the most distant lands and the peoples who inhabited them; the city at the center of their world was rich in precious metals and minerals, abound with all manner of fantastic animals and beasts, spoiled with hearty, fertile soil, and possessed springs of both warm water and cold; possessed a uniformity of standards; and, they were master builders whose feats of engineering made the construction of the mighty Ziggurat, which, to this day, encompasses the old pavilion, a reality.

The popular version of events is that Enkirus, aided by his Anunna-Ki friend, Uilliam, did find a vortex and hurriedly ushered many from Doggerland and elsewhere through the Ways and on to Eridu's distant shore. They came three abreast and a score deep at least three times a day for an entire winter, until the devastation caused by cataclysm made travel through the Ways untenable. It was then Uilliam constructed a tower of unprecedented scale in the bygone lands of Aria and brought the people of all tribes speaking all languages together, once more. From there, they departed Earth with Enkirus aboard a celestial chariot. When it arrived nearly four years later, they were greeted by all humandom, spared, yet again, from extinction.

But there would be no returning to Earth. As had been true after the first cataclysm, the profound loss of life suffered by the Earth has the effect of dampening the power of the Ways. Though vortices could be found to cross great tracts of land quickly, the Ways fell out of use in short order following Enkirus's death, who was 52 years when the Exodus began and lived a remarkable fifty additional years on Eridu.

1.8 ENKIRUS

Now, as will become clear in the later chapters of this history, Enkirus's story is interwoven with that of episodes from Holindrian's life and the Human Revolution; however, it would neither be possible, nor would it be proper to exclude even an abridged telling of the life of Enkirus when one considers what has been shared thus far.

There is a statue bearing his likeness that was erected in due order after his death. I am certain you are familiar with it. Even those who have yet to view the original have surely seen the reproductions scattered all throughout the world. That original came at the behest of the Lady of Eridu herself, who, for all intents and purposes, was the daughter of Enkirus. She unveiled the statue in front of the Ziggurat steps and there, miraculously, it has stood and remains standing to this day.

Enkirus liberally shared details of Earth—as did many, particularly, older migrants of the Second Exodus. It is how we know of the Hatehlean and their empire (the mightiest in their day), which radiated out from the center of the world to touch six distance continents far across the seas. It is how we know that the tribes originating in Ereb and Asu had perished when their numbers became too few—though none are certain when this became true. It is how we know the story of the great fire (the first cataclysm) and how it very nearly extinguished the light of humanity from the world.

There was also information better preserved by the Titaan that Enkirus and the others scarcely knew. One example follows that volcanic cataclysm 61,000 years before the present. Almost all knowledge of the human civilization that existed at that time were but the faintest of memories in Enkirus's time. Myths repeated the names of places and of heroes who had been gone for over 2,440 generations—that Enkirus of the land of old Aria speaks at all of their stories is a tribute to the legacy of those long, lost people.

Concerning Enkirus, some of his biographical information is as follows: Enkirus was born 52 years prior to the Second Exodus, not in Hatehl, though he served at the pleasure of Queen Kiretahl for a period of years until her son and heir, Karadin, conspired to have him exiled to a region in north-central Ereb nine years before the cataclysm of the falling stars; Enkirus was not a natural-born citizen of Hatehl, but a subject of one of the states on the periphery of the domain, in a country, from our best determination, which once belonged to Aria and laid between two rivers; he came into the service of the Hatehlean queen, whom he managed to impress while still a student at an Hatehlean college, at the age of 21; by his thirtieth year, Enkirus had ingratiated himself so thoroughly so as to become beloved in the eyes of the queen, that she elevated him to the position of her chiefest counselor on all matters natural, philosophical, animal, mineral, and mathematical; according to the Hatehlean commoners who migrated to Eridu, Enkirus's most profound contribution to their society was the Haaru-du Clock (Hatehleanized form of *andu* as it was called in Enkirus's mother tongue; meaning "sky travel"), a sophisticated analog astronomical computer the sea-fairing Hatehleans used to great effect.

A brief aside about the Haaru-du Clock. Astronomical computers constructed from a series of intricately set miniaturized gears had been in widespread use prior to Enkirus ever coming to Hatehl; however, these previous iterations all made the same underlying assumption that the sun, planets, and multitude of stars orbited the Earth. This represented a foundational flaw with these earlier mechanisms as the programming would render them useless within a two-decade period at the most.

While this perceived error may be illustrative of planned obsolescence by the Hatehleans, it is more likely a demonstration of the limits of their astronomical understandings. The Haaru-du Clock invented by Enkirus used programming predicated upon his own observations and mathematical formulas to design a mechanism that would no longer need to be discarded after one third of the user's lifespan. Enkirus determined that by removing Earth from the center of the computer's calculations and replacing it with the sun, his Haaru-du Clock would remain accurate indefinitely. The Enkirus variation became a jealously guarded secret and was an item forbidden to be traded to any foreigner.

It may well have been his work on this computer that afforded him such favor with Queen Kiretahl, whom he served for much of his adult life, from the start, but it was not Enkirus's sole area of study. In the land of his birth, where the memory of old Aria was but a dying ember, Enkirus had a boyhood fascination with the legends of the *kadingir* or "gateway of the gods". In order for the abstract presumption of the Ways to persist sixty millennia since their use was, comparatively, widespread, the lands once belonging to Aria must have been robust in their possession of vortices. For Enkirus, who was the first to identify a comet as the source for the increasing frequency in fire serpents arcing over the sky, the kadingir offered humanity salvation… if only their mysteries could be rediscovered.

His Hatehlean colleagues derided his hypothesis that gateways existed in nature capable of transporting a person to a far distant world as beyond nonsensical. Enkirus undertook his research in private, grew evermore reclusive, and made numerous treks to his homeland to investigate any account of unexplained phenomena that might aid in his quest to find one such kadingir. While he was away on yet another expedition, those opposing his unorthodox theory successfully lobbied the heir apparent, Karadin, to their side. When Enkirus returned to inform Queen Kiretahl of his discovery—for Enkirus had found what he had been searching for—he learned that the aging monarch's mental acuity was greatly diminished. Karadin assumed a more active role in the daily affairs of the empire's governance; using this opportunity to strengthen his position while zealously adhering to the advice of Enkirus's opponents, who no doubt coveted the position held by a foreigner. Enkirus lost his privileges of speaking to the queen directly. All matters passed through Karadin, who now viewed the claims of the elder philosopher with mounting skepticism and tainted his messages to the queen accordingly. Enkirus petitioned daily. After many months of this, in a decree written in the queen's own hand, Enkirus read that he had been banished from Hatehl and was never to return.

And so, Enkirus retreated to the desert lands of his birth for a time, but the influence and will of Hatehl was vast and soon he was made unwelcome. He eventually arrived in the sparsely populated lands of Dogger, ragged and destitute. The villagers there knew nothing of his past and only the clumsiest impressions of the Hatehl. In that emerald country, Enkirus tended to his sheep and continued to try and unlock the secrets of how to save the human race as the doom he feared hastened near with each passing year.

1.9 THE ANUNNA-KI

"Anunna-Ki" is the given name to the race that befriended Enkirus, took pity on the people of the Earth, and spared humankind from certain destruction. This name they received in the old tongue for it was understood (or, more aptly, it was *believed*) through the stories shared with the survivors of the Second Exodus that these Anunna-Ki were either the descendants or, at the very least, the inheritors of the First People. How, precisely, the word "Anuna" (in its original spelling) came to be associated with humanity's patrons remains unclear. Anuna, as I interpret ancient Earth-lore, during the time of Enkirus and the Second Exodus was a cult of minor significance yet enjoyed some popularity among students of the stars, sky, and all matters which exist above our heads. "Ki" appears to be the result of dialectal variation with the consonants "k" and "g". It may have been especially pronounced when preceding a long vowel. Enkirus, I should note, favored a different pronunciation—something closer to "Anunna-Gi"; however, it has also been said that some, maybe even Enkirus, used an antecedent of the word "Ki" altogether more similar to "Gaia", a word spoken by many of the Second Exodus. In any case, Anunna-Ki has become the most accepted version of the word.

The name Anunna-Ki called themselves was "Aeternam". It is more common, I think, among the Baltutu themselves.

As a people, only one of their kind truly was known to Enkirus and the other survivors. I, of course, speak of Uilliam. From Uilliam we may deduce what the rest of his kin may be in terms of temperament and bearing—greater than human stature, noble and refined, ancient but betrayed by neither age nor fragility, wise beyond a human's capacity, and powerful enough to travel between the stars as we might travel between villages. In his letters, Enkirus described Uilliam as a man with long silver hair, a golden aura, and a warmth which reminded him instantly of his most cherished memories.

Uilliam and his Anunna-Ki brethren—however many or few there might have been—conspicuously shared little of their own story and less of their considerable craft. What history of his own people Uilliam did share is difficult to discern from allegory and metaphor with any certainty given the sheer disparity in the achievements of Anunna-Ki and the humans of the time.

The Anunna-Ki were a people without a homeland for it had been lost to a cataclysm so terrible that it rendered the destruction of their race all but complete. The home they had once was said to be so far away from either Earth or Eridu that it was doubtful if any human eyes would ever see that farthest away star. They became a nomadic people. In a gold-plated towering city, it is said the Anunna-Ki lived in the days after their home was sundered and in this city they traveled to untold places across the heavens since before humanity's earliest memory. In their travels they sought to lessen nature's occasional cruelty or evils done by those who ought to know better. Their coming to Earth had not been by design and, but for a happy stroke of Fortune, humanity's adventure might well have ended in the drowning of the world.

In the four years between Enkirus's departure from Earth and his arrival on Eridu aboard one of their celestial chariots, the Anunna-Ki took control of what remained of the First Age city Avahairanor, then destitute and little more than an inhabited ruin. On the site of the pavilion, the Anunna-Ki erected a great structure. Then, with the assistance of the engineering prowess of the Hatehleans, did the Ziggurat rise and encapsulate their secrets.

The Anunna-Ki proposed the Baltutu, though that would not have been the word of their choosing or of their own language. They were adamant that in order for the humans of Eridu to thrive, we would need... guides. And so, Uilliam—a being of seemingly godlike ability—began the Anunna-Ki's most splendid work. In this endeavor, he chose Enkirus as his partner and together they labored for many years.

1.10 THE FOUNDING OF ERESTU-UR

Erestu-Ur is the name of the city constructed by humans of the Second Exodus on the spot where Avahairanor formerly stood. The city of Avahairanor was greatly diminished when the first migrants of the Second Exodus arrived from Earth, with the pavilion having been abandoned for tens of thousands of years, the Citadel tower in a ruinous state, and most of the population scattering into the countryside. The Titaans still claimed the city but were effectively overrun by the sheer volume of migrants and lacked the resources to care for and police so many.

A new city was quickly determined to be needed. Though more robust building materials such as stone would have to be sourced from quarries farther away, there remained ample material in Avahairanor that could be repurposed. The tenement structures were erected first—the local forests donated generously. New pipes of clay coated with tar were laid, and the aqueducts repaired to supply the city with potable water and subterranean sewage systems. The old walls were deconstructed and rebuilt to permit more building behind them.

The Hatehleans lent their exceptional engineering skills to the effort. Cranes of considerable size hoisted logs and blocks and trusses high overhead. The river was diverted to make use of the water to float materials directly to the projects in need of them. Even the Citadel tower was rebuilt. It was there a great system of mirrors were installed to function as a signal light for all humandom.

When Enkirus arrived four and half years later, he was greeted by a boisterous city well on its way to completing the Ziggurat complex, which encompassed the ancient pavilion.

1.11 A BRIEF HISTORY OF THE WORLD

What follows is a summation of the chronology of historical episodes occurring immediately preceding humanity's exodus from Erestu (the best recollection of those who made the journey as told and retold to their descendants) to the Present and are now engulfed in strife once more. Dating, as precise as the archives of Panos permit, is provided for further clarity of the reader. Credit is gratefully given to H'lukuh'l, a caretaker of historical records and student at the College of Panayiotis, who consolidated the notes for this chapter.

Enkirus was born on our homeworld of Earth, in the constellation of Cassiopeia, that white star accentuating the most pronounced extremity. The land to which he was born was regarded as Alkebulan while still inhabited by humankind. The name of many of the nations and kingdoms are poorly remembered, but the name Hatehl has been passed down to us. Enkirus served throughout his adult life in the role of principal advisor on matters of natural, scientific, and philosophical in that nation Hatehl and its king, Karadin, until his dismissal from the lands of Hatehl nine years before his meeting the Anunna-Ki, which occurred nearly one year prior to the Second Exodus.

The boy recovered by the Anunna-Ki and delivered into Enkirus's care on the eve of the Margidda's departure from Erestu was named Edis. He would be the same pedagogue tutoring the six Baltutu children in the village of Kish from birth until his death in the 57th year of humanity's resettlement on Eridu.

The Second Exodus itself occurred in phases. The first happened way of the Ways. The second was completed four years later with the arrival of Enkirus aboard the star-sailing ship. The celestial chariot departed from a colossal tower constructed in the decrepit lands once belonging to the long-dead nation of Aria (awash, in those times, in societal collapse as the crises inaugurated by the volcanic catastrophe of the First Exodus decimated the world). By the Anunna-Ki's will, disparate peoples from various lands speaking heard and unheard tongues were brought to the tower, selected for traits and qualities not always discernable to the eye. We are told flood waters ensnared the world and drowned all the peoples of the Earth.

The Day of the Covenant is the name given to the day Enkirus and the human race were delivered unto Eridu's guardianship. This is regarded as the start of a new calendar, so, it is written as year zero in the chronology denoting a separation from the calendars of Earth and Eridu. The Ziggurat was designed and built by the humans of the Second Exodus (in keeping with Old World traditions) but imbued with gift and promises of the Anunna-Ki. Its location is not far from where the Margidda made landfall. The founding of Erestu-Ur paid homage to the home now lost atop the foundations of the first human settlement on Eridu.

The Firsts numbered every son and daughter born beneath Eridu's two suns, one yellow and one white (there is a red star, too, often visible, though it is small and Eridu does not progress around it).

The Seconds came into being in the eighth year. Their names were Cy, Panayiotis, and Lecia.

The village Kish was founded in the tenth year. Esh, the first of the Thirds, was born on the first day of Marutuk (November) of the same year. Her Rite of Mantle took place in her sixteenth year.

Enkirus passed into the Inevitable in Esh's seventh year on this earth.

Apsu and Anshargal were born half a century after the Exodus.

Mummu and Melammu were born one year and one day later.

Maramurru and Shi were born one year and one day after the pair before them.

More of their kind were intended, for this was the plan of the Anunnaki and Esh, but Fortune proved crueler and intervened in order to prevent their dream from being realized.

All the Baltutu were born in the month of November, the month of harvest.

The Glory of Esh lasted until the year 57. During this period, Esh defeated the machinations of Cy, strengthened the governing institutions, and expelled Cy from the city of Erestu-Ur, which succeeded Avahairanor. In this year, the Gudanna raided the village Kish, saw the death of Edis the Pedagogue, and the Baltutu children delivered to her custody within the Ziggurat.

The passages of the Baltutu children occurred in a fashion corresponding to the order of their birth; Apsu and Anshargal passed through the Rite of Mantle in year 66, Mummu and Melammu in the year 67, and Maramurru and Shi in the year 68.

In the year 99, Cy led an army of Gudanna against Erestu-Ur, slaughtering many of the inhabitants, murdered Esh—for whom Maramurru swiftly avenged—and altogether ended the Second Age.

The Third Age existed from the Reconstitution until the 1,000[th] year following the Second Exodus. This Age witnessed great engineering feats, such as the Moglen River Viaduct, and terrible atrocities—the Persecution of the Gudanna chiefest of the horrors and threatened to drive the tribe to the brink of extinction. In the end, the Gudanna were banished to the hinterlands far from human contact.

The Fourth Age spanned another two thousand years. This was the age of the Pyramid Builders, whose monuments, whether in whole or in part, offer a lasting tribute to the people who constructed them. The greatest and most renowned of these megalithic structures is the Kurnugi, constructed 1,600 years before the collapse of the Fourth Age in the region known today as Gerpedon.

For not quite a thousand years, the civilizations of this era embarked on further herculean projects for which they might transform and master the environment of this world. Theirs was the age when hydropower dams forever shifted the flow of the Gerpedon rivers, resulting in expansive grasslands. Theirs was the age when humans bore tunnels through whole mountain ranges, undoing continental divides. Theirs was the age when suspension bridges connected estranged canyon rims. Their ambition literally shaped Eridu until ambition atrophied and became complacency, giving way to neglect. Ruin and a slow decay followed making it difficult to precisely denote when the Fourth Age conclusively ended.

The Fifth Age benefited from the industrious labors of the Fourth. Their development rapidly accelerated; it nevertheless took the humans of this time six hundred years to very nearly conclude what the volcanos, comets, floods, and all Nature's might had begun on Earth so long ago. The Industrialization Wars brought the Firth Age to an abrupt conclusion. These wars distinguished themselves from the previous half millennia of nigh constant warfare by way of drastically increasing the lethality of the munitions and tactics employed. The final conflict in the War resulted in the total discharge of chemical weapon stockpiles after the inconclusive, but sufficiently disastrous, Battle of Pilgrim's Road decimated the militaries of all factions involved but not the resolve of their respective nations. This battle occurred over three thousand years ago on April 23, on the wide Avalonian Plain in place called Zeihan known to none who now live.

Now, it was after the devastation of the Fifth Age that a Dark Interregnum was imposed on the world and lasted seven centuries. What nations had not been completely destroyed in the course of the Industrialization Wars struggled to maintain constituted and, over a period of many years, disintegrated. Much knowledge was lost, and order was swept away; civilization, as we know it, did not return until the year 4,430 SE, after a period of 753 years called the Consolidation by the Baltutu, who emerged at that time and ushered in the Sixth Age.

1.12 BALTUTU DOMINATION

The Baltutu, or the Living Ones as they have become known now that their supremacy is no more, set out to remake the world in the aftermath of yet another civilization's collapse. The end of the Fifth Age did not come suddenly.

It was a tragedy played out in horrifically prolonged detail. Their counsel amounted to no more than a pittance; their warnings unheeded; their pleas discounted by those who thought themselves the wiser. Men and women whose qualities might charitably be counted as ordinary yet who fancied their talents significantly above their ability inherited mantles of responsibility for which they were altogether ill-suited. It was through their ineptitude the Baltutu were once more betrayed. The world was marred, and civilization left fragmented and rotten. Humandom may well have withered and died had the Baltutu not remerged with a shared resolve to remake the human species.

Their experience became their burden. A continuation—so it was argued—of the mandate decreed upon Esh by the Aeternam and bestowed unto them with her death. But for Cy's sundering of Esh's work, the mythos pulled on this thread to manifest a newer tapestry, one that told the story not of reserved guidance but rather of purposeful intervention. That was how they began their religion centuries after the fall. Drawing upon ancient histories for which only the Baltutu could remember to tell, careful omissions and precise inclusions emphasized the errors of what had come before and the remedies necessary to begin again. The stories they fashioned established the framework from which the Baltutu founded their cult. Armed with the power of their innate abilities and knowledge they alone possessed, ignorance was exploited to terrifying effect. Descendants of the survivors were converted into fervent cultists after witnessing the miraculous feats of the Baltutu and soon were marshalled into organized communities to rebuild a broken world.

Even in the despair that surely must have prevailed across so much of the globe, the burgeoning cultish hamlets established by the Baltutu were not the only attempts to establish a new world order. Though few in number and greatly diminished, some nation states persisted into the interregnum. Of the remnants of the Fifth Age to stubbornly languish, two names are most often recounted in records from the earliest days of the Baltutu's nascent reign: Taurica in the near east and Serikon in the far east.

A third nation, opposite old Avahairanor, is presupposed to have existed for some time. Its name has been largely lost to us, for not all of the Baltutu's knowledge or even that of my antediluvian family has been transmitted intact. What remains are the letters "antio". It may be that this bygone was once called Antio by the people who once inhabited its dilapidated borders, or, conceivably, those translated letters were a part of a fuller name now unknown. One ought to loathe the prospect of completely forgetting a people from history—thus, the name of these particular people (whoever they might have been and believed and cherished and valued) is hereby preserved in so far as it is in my ability to do so with the hope that their memory does not entirely vanish from this earth.

Taurica, during the rise of the Baltutu, had contracted from an expansive empire to a small collection of loosely affiliated tribes in southern Polpedon. Serikon, meanwhile, a once formidable power in the east, was reduced to what amounted to a guild of fishermen in what would be organized into the region of Ginno. These patronizing characterizations come directly from the letters exchanged between the Baltutu themselves. Taurica seems to have been pacified through targeted conversion of crucial chieftains to the Baltutu religion and leveraging the Taurican alliance system to compel the adoption of the Baltutu across the country. The coastal dwellers of Serikon were incorporated later into the Baltutu Empire. Their conquest came as a result of hardships—natural and imposed—upon the communities blocked by an ocean to their east and desert to their west. The appearance of the Baltutu fleet (a trifle in comparison to the number of ships commanded in the latter days) coupled with the knowledge of techniques to create a bountiful harvest of cereal grains in a climate otherwise poorly suited to such a crop would see the last of the old-world powers vanquished five centuries after the fall.

There were also the so-called Industrialists who, unbeknownst to the Baltutu for a time, had fled to the southernmost continent of Delma Vorta. The war against them would not come until well after the conquering of the majority of the planet.

The Eiferglen emerged east of the Western Ranges in between the assimilation of Taurica and the subjugation of Serikon as the solitary challenger to the Baltutu's inevitable rise. In the long period of dark days that followed the collapse of the Fifth Age, the Eiferglen stood apart from all the other disparate efforts to rebuild society, for Eiferglen was a cooperative. The peoples who joined this nation chose to freely associate and defend one another, bartering their own strengths so that others might protect against their weaknesses. The Eiferglen grew because the people who formed it believed in a promise of a future predicated on hope and possibilities. This idea of hope was so contagious among outsiders who encountered the place that the regional word for hope—or more accurately, "wellspring of hope"—*eifer*, came to be so closely associated with the people who lived there. Baltutu records concede, on numerous occasions, their earliest missionaries abandoned their missions when confronted by the joyful spirit in Eiferglen.

In short order, the frontier separating Eiferglen and the Baltutu Empire hardened into a fortified border as skirmishes grew ever more frequent. Three wars were ultimately fought between the two Sixth Age powers and while the outcome of the first war was inconclusive, the Baltutu resolved to achieve victory. After their decisive victory in the second war, the Baltutu would mockingly refer to the wars collectively as the Hopeful Wars. The conclusion of the second war expelled Eiferglen from the far reaches of the Antelmari continent, reducing them to their traditional territory buttressed between the mountains. The third and final war was more a demonstration of the

Baltutu's supremacy meant to intimidate the peoples of foreign shores. Eiferglen ended 753 years after its founding.

With the most serious of their continental threats defeated by the beginning of the first millennium of the Sixth Age, the essence of the Baltutu's religious doctrine was established. The Baltutu had long since returned to the Cliffs of Damkina where their village Kish once stood, and upon that place they built their church.

What follows are excerpts from extant Baltutu religious texts, for not all perished in the culmination of the Revolution.

Doctrine of Divine Order and Spiritual Unity.

In the wake of the cataclysm that shattered the old world, the sacred covenant of our faith demands unwavering conformity and devotion to the divine will of the Pantheon. The gods have decreed that all adherents must don the mandated attire as established by our holy clerics, symbolizing the unity and purity necessary to rebuild what was lost. The failures of the previous world, marred by unbridled individualism and its corrosive effects on society, serve as a somber reminder of the need for uniformity. Personal ambitions, once the cause of the old world's disintegration, must be sacrificed at the altar of communal objectives, reflecting a divine order where personal desires yield to the greater good. The faithful shall demonstrate contentment with their material possessions, rejecting any pursuit of excess as a sign of their devotion and adherence to divine teachings.

Our Baltutu, chosen by the Aeternam who alone possess the omniscient power to discern the needs of individuals and the community, are entrusted with the divine authority to make all critical decisions. The gods, in their infinite wisdom, have determined the path for our survival and prosperity, and it is their will alone that dictates our course. All members must accept and adhere to these divine directives without dissent, for any return to the chaos of unregulated individualism is strictly forbidden. Participation in communal worship and rituals, as decreed by our sacred calendar, is compulsory. Any deviation from these divinely ordained schedules is viewed as sacrilegious and a betrayal of the sacred order that ensures our protection and survival. The roles assigned by our divine authorities must be embraced with absolute dedication, as the gods alone provide the structure necessary to sustain us.

Collective confession and repentance, as guided by the Baltutu, replace the failed practices of individual moral introspection. Those who exhibit disharmony or dissent within the community must undergo a process of spiritual renewal and rebirth to restore their faith and realign with the divine will. This process ensures that the unity and purity of our faith are maintained, countering the destructive fragmentation seen in the old world. Teachings, practices, or media from outside our sacred doctrine are to be strictly censored to protect against heretical influences that once undermined societal cohesion. Members must show absolute deference to the divine authority, with any challenge to the established hierarchy deemed an affront to the gods. Through unwavering adherence to these doctrines, our faith aims to correct past mistakes and reestablish divine order and unity in our renewed world.

The Eight Edicts of Burden (Sul-ku Ul).

1. The Oblation of Personal Desires. All desires and ambitions of the self must be laid upon the altar of communal purpose. The wishes of the individual are to be humbled before the will of the assembled, their pursuits deemed but shadows in the light of the congregation's inspired journey.

2. The Mandate of Contentment. Show contentment with earthly possessions as a testament to your reverence. Let the denial of opulence be a reflection of your piety.

3. The Suppression of Divergent Thoughts. Subdue contrary expressions. The purity of the truth and the unity of the community is paramount, and dissent is to be silenced in favor of greater harmony.

4. The Immutable Divine Roles. Roles bestowed must be embraced without deviation or hesitation. The divine structure ordained for the community must be upheld, and any attempt to forsake these roles is an act of disobedience against the sacred order.

5. The Sovereign Decree. Those so anointed by the Baltutu shall alone determine all matters of great import, whether of the self or the assembly. The people are bound to heed their divine decrees, for through their guidance flows divine prosperity.

6. The Command of Rituals. All must partake in the rites and ceremonies established. Deviation is an abomination, and those who stray shall face retribution.

7. The Reverence. The Baltutu decree an order where unyielding respect and obedience to the anointed ones shall be without question or repudiation.

8. The Communal Atonement. The people must confess their transgressions and seek forgiveness of the Baltutu. Individual repentance is not permitted, for communal atonement under divine guidance ensures the purity of all.

Ode to the Baltutu.

O Baltutu, in your everlasting might,
Guide us from the shadows of the night.
Your chosen priests decree the sacred way,
In unity and order, we must stay.
No more the chaos of the past shall reign,
Your wisdom leads us from a world awash in
    pain.

By your divine hand, our needs are known,
In your embrace, our sustenance is shown.
To you we yield, our wills and hearts are bound,
In sacred ritual, your truth is found.

In worship's rhythm, strict and pure we walk,
Our paths are set by your unyielding talk.
No room for strife or personal desire,

We follow the Baltutu, never to tire.
Those who stray, in discord or in doubt,
Shall find renewal, faith's rebirth devout.

By your divine hand, our needs are known,
In your embrace, our sustenance is shown.
To you we yield, our wills and hearts are bound,
In sacred ritual, your truth is found.

O Baltutu, our shield from ancient, fallen ways,
Your law protects us through these testing days.
Rejecting falsehoods, we stand strong and free,
In reverence and peace, we honor thee.
For in your guidance, unity prevails,
In your eternal light, our faith unveils.

By your divine hand, our needs are known,
In your embrace, our sustenance is shown.
To you we yield, our wills and hearts are bound,
In sacred ritual, your truth is found.

It shall not be said that theirs was an evil empire, nor, I hope, shall it be remembered as such, for it was not. Though it was a most tyrannical regime, it was not without benefit to the people. In those earliest of days, when the memory of the Fifth Age collapse still lingered as a smoldering ember does, what the Baltutu proffered was no small comfort. What ended as a corrupted dream had begun, long ago, with audacious hope—a sanctuary amongst the ruin, a kingdom of heaven here on this earth.

The Baltutu returned stability and order to a broken world. Through the six Living Ones, decisions were derived through their word, their teachings, and their sacred law. Authority was reestablished and a strict adherence to ritual contextualized the mundane with the trappings of divine observance. Humility and contentment arose in accordance with the abandonment of material excess. The emphasis on uniformity and communal goals fostered a strong sense of unity and belonging. By subordinating individual desires, the people began to work together more harmoniously than any time in the recorded past, strengthening community bonds, and collective resilience. Disagreement and conflict within the expansive bounds of their empire gradually evaporated, replaced with a predictable and structed environment from which humanity prospered, for a time. The belief that their needs would be provided for by the Baltutu created a sense of security and devotion to the divine plan.

For a time, the blessings of the Baltutu blinded the people to the cost exacted upon their spirits. In their Peace, human development stagnated. Dependency on the Baltutu, their religion, and their ever-present priests took root, ensnaring the once free people of Eridu into child-like thralls. Individuality was habitually suppressed; creativity was stifled; prioritization of the self placed the community at large at risk from dissenting voices. People living within these regimented communities were less individuals unto themselves but rather components of a broader organism. As such, their paths were predetermined and without opportunity for alteration or evolution. Over a great many centuries, the Baltutu charged their priests with enforcement and repression of personal opinions, stressing the subjugation of individual identity; however, this policing of the mind was coupled with monitoring the psychological effects of conformity on the population. The Baltutu did not seek to debilitate humanity with anxiety or depression, but neither would they risk the preservation of the human race solely because of mental health concerns. When necessary, disharmonious elements of the community would be removed if the process of spiritual renewal and rebirth was fruitless.

Public humiliation and ritualistic penitence, especially in the elder days of the Baltutu faith, were the most common forms of punishment exacted upon a trespasser. A person who had transgressed might well be paraded in a state of disgrace or compelled to endure the wearing of symbols identifying their failure or other acts of public contrition. The logic was plain: Public humiliation is a potent tool for reinforcing social norms by establishing shame as a deterrent. The ritualistic components of the punishment strive to ensure an individual's failure is both acknowledged and corrected in a highly visible manner. The institutes of renewal, operated by high-ranking priests and designed to correct misaligned behavior, grew out of this school of punishment.

Ostracism existed, though was decidedly rarer than public humiliation or collective penances. The infrequent discharge of this form of justice meant it was often more greatly feared than some of the harshest methods at the Baltutu's disposal. Individuals could be stripped of their communal rights and privileges, rendering them an outcast doomed to be forsaken. Such individuals were burdened with extreme isolation, losing access to communal resources, spiritual guidance, and social support—even if not physically removed from the community altogether. The psychological impact of the ostracism could be devastating to those condemned to suffer it and, in truth, few survived it.

With the exception of ritual execution, collective penance existed as one of the most severe punishments the Baltutu would bestow. In the event of a serious transgression by an individual or a group, the entire community would be required to endure the consequences together. This has included prolonged periods of fasting, labor, sleep deprivation, and other forms of sacrifice—in the most extreme instances, symbolic or even literal sacrifices in order to restore divine favor and balance. Decimation, ritual killing of members of a community selected by lot, devastated communities and disrupted the lives of all far beyond the completion of the punishment. Decrees of Decimation were never ordered lightly, though they were ordered on numerous occasions, nonetheless. It is reasonable to assume that, had the Revolution failed, the number of Decimations that might have been ordered would have depopulated the planet by as much as one third.

In summation, I shall say this on the Baltutu and the religion they manufactured: During my travels, I encountered a people deeply immersed in a faith that profoundly shaped their lives. I knew individuals who had embraced this religion wholeheartedly, surrendering their personal ambitions and desires to the communal goals decreed by their gods. Their clerics, revered as divine intermediaries, wielded unquestionable authority, and I saw how their edicts were followed with an almost sacred devotion. The rituals were observed with such precision that any deviation was met with harsh consequences, and members were taught to find contentment and shun wealth as contrary to their piety. I witnessed how personal views that diverged from the sacred teachings were swiftly repressed, and the hierarchy of religious leaders was upheld with absolute reverence. Those who failed to adhere faced public shame and rigorous communal penance, illustrating both the strength and the harshness of a society where divine order and communal unity are held in the highest regard.

1.13 AGE OF THE BALTUTU

This history was begun in the twilight of that age when the Baltutu were the undisputed masters of this world and we short-lived mortals their subjects. When the Baltutu came to power, they did as was common in the commencement of a new age and instituted a new calendar. Theirs differed from past iterations in that the Baltutu calendar did not revert to a zeroth year. Instead, the calendar counted the years since the Second Exodus, which occurred 7,535 years ago, thus, the year of my writing is 7,535 SE (Second Exodus).

The Baltutu founded their holy city, Telmun, atop and deep into the Cliffs of Damkina on the spot of the village Kish in 4,430 SE. The Pantheon would not be built until the middle of the first millennium of their rule. The Pantheon would undergo numerous, substantial expansions through 5,353 SE to mark the Baltutu incorporation of the territory between the Western Ranges and the Southern Rowen Mountains and bound by the Anissa River to the northeast and diminishing the farther one traveled into the Avalonian Plain. The city of Erestu-Ur was re-founded early into their rule, no later than the year 4,514 SE but not earlier than 4,552 SE, as written evidence exists within the archives of Panos acknowledging receipt of goods delivered through Erestu-Ur by that year. The Telmun governing complex underwent a great many reconfigurations before expanding to its present-day size and majesty where it housed more than fifty thousand government officials, bureaucrats, priests, Etlu guardsmen, and servants. The principal purpose of Erestu-Ur was to furnish Telmun with the infrastructure to operate independently as an implement of administration of the growing Baltutu Empire. Consequently, the masons, craftspeople, carpenters, cobblers, street cleaners, gardeners, bakers, butchers, farmers, fishers, fletchers, smithies, weavers, and a litany of other professions necessary to keep Telmun in proper order, fed, and armed were drawn from the Empire writ large and funneled through cities like Erestu-Ur and the harbor in Atlantaries, founded in 5,100 SE, as the Baltutu's ambition turned towards the lands that lay across the sea.

The records held at Panos as well as artifacts unearthed in the excavations establish that Atlantaries is not the first city to have been built to leverage the advantage of the harbor, merely the most recent and, dare it be said, the most impactful, if not the most splendid, since the Fourth Age.

Between their diligent efforts undertaken during the Consolidation and the first thousand years of their rule, the Baltutu established themselves as a true, global empire and did away with any pretense of federated cooperation with the states and tribes they encountered (this and the doctrine of the religion of their own invention I have discussed at length).

Their armies and proselytizers were sent across the globe. By the beginning of the sixth millennium, most of Eridu's coastal communities and nations had, through a variety of means—conversion, trade, alliance, or conquest—become so deeply entangled with the Baltutu Empire that to describe these entities as anything more than vassals due to be assimilated would be too generous. Subjugation of the inland territories persisted well into the year 7,120 SE, when the invasions of Laud and Delma Vorta were first designed, but these engagements were wholly in the lands of Audentica, Attendu, Norpia, Onohan, and Ziemia. The tribes laying claim to the Land of Arches, best to the evidentiary record, cannot truly be said to have been ever conquered in their entirety. In fact, the record, as clearly viewed at the dissolution of their empire, suggests the existence of a détente having been agreed in the aftermath of a battle or battles sometime during the middle 7,250s at a place called "Table's Rock" where five of seven legions deployed to pacify the Land of Arches were lost to the last man (some thirty thousand soldiers) due to harshness of climate, disadvantageous terrain, and indigenous hostility. This evidence suggests the Baltutu's Empire did not exercise a monolithic dominion over the whole world as insinuated in the teachings of their priests.

The simultaneous invasions of Laud and Delma Vorta—collectively known as the start of the Unification Campaign—began in 7,049 SE. The southernmost continent of Delma Vorta was sparsely populated and comprised of peoples segregated from the happenings of the world pre-dating their separation. These people lived in isolation since the end of the Fifth Age, from which they were a part. Thus, the culture, thinking, and societal structure resembled that which had not been seen elsewhere on Eridu for nearly 4,500 years. Delma Vorta was conquered, and its dilapidated industry seized 411 years after the commencement of the campaign.

The Massacring of the Last Industrialists is believed to have happened over a five-year period beginning in 7,460 SE. There are tellings, few though they are, which attest to this event having occurred in a single, bloody night to spanning many years, and yet others which fantasize about whether the Last Industrialists truly succumbed. No substantive evidence is known to me and the House of Panos to suggest that these tellings are anything other than apocryphal myths shared amongst those living at the farthest edges of the world.

Delma Vorta's unanticipated quality of resistance necessitated a premature end to the First Obenian War, which lasted from 7,447 SE until 7,460 SE but without any major engagements beyond the Battle of Mattithiah, in 7,451 SE. It would be this battle which would lend its name to the line of patriarchic monarchs who would come to rule Obenia beginning in the year 7,452 SE, and whom King Matthiolus was descended. He was born between 7,486 SE and 7,489 SE. The Obenian calendar continued the tradition of old Erestu lunar calendars with twelve months in contrast to the fifteen months of 28 days that is standard. Obenians did, in fact, use a variation of the fifteen-month calendar prior to the Baltutu invasion, but, on instruction from the first King of the Obenians, the calendar was abandoned in favor of an ancient lunar calendar for which the four moons of Eridu do not adequately impersonate. This did not occur later than 7,454 SE.

A Second Obenian War was waged at sea in 7,463 SE and lasted eleven months.

A Third Obenian War was waged in 7,465 SE. A pyrrhic victory for the Obenians. Though still consumed with completing the conquest of Delma Vorta, the armies of the Baltutu secured for themselves all the lands of Dayton. From this time, skirmishes were constant between the Baltutu, Obenia, and allies of Obenia between the coast and the Lesser Albs—the only passable way between southern and northern Laud. For a time, the Baltutu were held at bay.

PART 2

FORGIVE US, FATHER, FOR WE HAVE SINNED

2.1 THE AUDACITY OF HOPE

The Earth was cast into ruin. A great deluge of waters rose from the deep, promising to engulf the whole of the world and plunge it into an eternal night that would know no dawn. The works of men, their proud cities, their storied halls, crumbled not by foreign hands alone but by the fire born within—kindled by strife, fanned by the chaos of the flood. Civilization fell, as when the wild beast tears the lamb from the fold, and no hand of mercy could hold back the ruin. Where once men settled their quarrels with the tongue, now they brandished the sword, the sacred halls defiled with blood. The worth of life, once held high, was cheapened with each passing day, until man saw not his brother, but an enemy—a ravenous creature, willing to tear the very breath from the lips of the child, to stretch his own fleeting moments.

Fear spread like a plague, and bitterness filled the hearts of all.

There was nothing left to be done, though such knowledge availed them not. In the end, even the righteous few, who clung to the wisdom of ages and sought to die with dignity, were swept into the tide. Many abandoned hope. Most forgot their sacred oaths. Of those who yet lived, a scant number survived, scouring the wastes, betraying their kin, their friends, slaughtering for the bitter chance at life. Yet fewer still escaped the fate that hung heavy over all flesh. For none could say, none could know, how the final hour of their world would unfold. In the choking grip of smoke, the sky blackened, the breath of the world grew faint, as one by one, life was snuffed out—slowly, inexorably.

Stranger, perhaps you think this is the stuff of legend, a fable spun by trembling tongues—but every tale is bound by a thread of truth. This is ours.

Our world—my world—lay upon its deathbed. Despite all our brilliance, or perhaps because of It, we sealed our fate. Not all could be saved. Few could be saved.

I know not when your spark, your soul, shall enter the verse, but hear me now: In this world, or in any other, though we may never meet, I take comfort in knowing—you shall not walk alone. Never alone. Our exodus—an odyssey, perilous, beyond the stars—was for you. That we might endure. That our people might have a future.

Erestu—the Earth—is no more. A memory now, seared with anguish, a wound upon our hearts for all who knew its ghostly shores, now walked by shadows. But here, in a strange land beneath foreign stars, we have endured. Not for ourselves. No, we build for you, for your kind, for those yet unborn. Our dreams, our hopes—we place them in your hands.

I rest now where Margidda, our ark, lies, the cradle of this new world. And I believe—yes, I believe—that this new land, this new people, will not bear the failures of the old. My time is passed, and I leave this purpose in your care.

You shall be the light, the standard to which all men shall rally. In you, they shall see the spark of our common humanity, and in your steps, they shall seek to follow. They shall fall. They shall falter. It may seem a heavy burden but know this—destiny has favored you. You are chosen.

In time, they will stand with you.

I could not save them all—but you—you shall save all that you can.

Know this, wherever you are, whenever you are: You carry the strength of those who came before. Their love, their wisdom, their fight—they are within you. And you shall do great things.

Fight for the future. Always.

-Enkirus

2.2 THE VILLAGE OF KISH

The Margidda overshadowed the small village of Kish, nestled on a plateau at the edge of the Cliffs of Damkina where the gulls soared high above the ocean's swells far below. With their backs to the sea, the southern horizon was a composition of water and air. A coming storm could be seen for miles before it ever gave the few villagers trouble. Before them, an expansive wilderness erupted from the gentle sloping hummocks. The trees had grown tall and strong, vacating any interruption to their sovereignty. Waves crashed upon rock. The beaches, narrow though they were, were home to smoothed black stone and never dry. Two winding paths had been carved into the grass and dirt, one primarily by the labor of the foot and the other by the wheel. A path followed the coastline, trudged by nothing more than one's good pair of feet, skirting the cliff's brim, up another hundred or so feet, to the ever so dilapidated celestial chariot. The other path was more a road, carts ferried by horse and ox journey every so often out of the wood, hauling wares and comestibles harvested from other towns to be traded. There used to be other paths, leading in many directions, but now, there were only the two.

Few people lived in Kish. Nearly half of the adult population were fishermen. The town's three fishermen relied on a rickety set of wooden stairs, built by an earlier generation, zigzagging down the face of the cliff to a slip where their sole boat was tied, bobbing up and down with the tide. There was a baker, a young woman just coming of age who had inherited the position from her mother. A builder, who was the girl's uncle on her mother's side. He was responsible for nearly everything that was not concerned with the town's supply of food. The oldest resident was simply known as "Pedagogue", a rather doddery fellow. He alone among them remembered the old world. The fisherman's wife, the only other adult woman in the town, was the de facto mistress, a sort of mother figure to everyone, especially the town's most remarkable inhabitants.

There were six children in the village. All had lost their mothers during birth. All conceived absent a father, born from nothing more than the touch of the Anunna-Ki before their final farewell. Survivors had scattered or been scattered, but a few chose to remain close to the grave of Enkirus, accepting wardship over the children, whom they were instructed to nurture and protect until such time as the children could tend to their own needs. The eldest pair was seven, the youngest five. It was the day before birthing celebrations, or, more precisely, the day by the best recollection of the Pedagogue and the Mistress.

"Come, come, wake up, boy!"

"Ouch!" the boy said as he was prodded by the Pedagogue's walking stick.

The Pedagogue had these foggy eyes, set deep within a heavily wrinkled face, scars of both age and toil, looking down at the boy who had been napping, laying in the sunshine on the back side of his house. "Daydreaming, again, weren't you?"

"I wasn't sleeping," the boy said, holding up a hand to block out the sun's light.

"What were you doing, then? I've been hobbling all over town looking for you."

There were only three permanent structures in the village.

"I was making something," and he held out his palm.

Grasping the wood figure with viciously trembling fingers, the Pedagogue squinted his dark eyes and held it up close to his face, the tip of his nose tickled by the fresh carved fibers. He ran the tip of his thumb and index fingers all over the figurine, when he said, "it's a person…."

"Shi," the boy said, defeated.

"Oh," and the Pedagogue's eyes popped as though everything suddenly became clearer, "I'm sure she will love it, as will the others," and he handed the carving back to the boy, patting him on the head.

The boy took it, stuffing it into his bundle.

"It'll be midday soon enough. Why don't you see if anyone needs help getting ready for your party?"

Doing as he was told, the boy cinched up his hand-me-down short pants and shuffled off towards the center of town. The one he'd been whittling behind was the children's home and school, where the Pedagogue told them stories about the worlds, old and new. Off to his right, the bakery-butchery-depository. The fishermen's steps were just around the back. Center of town was a great large fire pit; stones had been piled around in a circular manner, building up a waist high barrier between flesh and flame. Set at somewhat of a peculiar angle was the stable, animal pens, and mill. It was arranged so that it forced visitors coming through the main gate to be funneled between it and the bakery-butchery-depository. The village's water supply was situated adjacent to the stable, closest to the children's house.

The young baker was crossing town from the mill, carrying a sack of freshly ground flour, and she looked like she was struggling. The sack was nearly the same size as she and probably weighed twice as much. She dragged it across the windswept ground, tracing her path back to her ovens.

"Sera! Miss Sera, do you need some help?" the boy said, hurrying up to her.

Her hair was coming undone from its tie and she had a dollop of sweat beading on her nose. "Oh, thank you, Maramurru, but I think this is too heavy, even for you."

The boy placed his hands on his hips in a look of disbelief, then, with his tiny muscles bulging to their fullest capacity, he, with both hands digging into the sack, wrenched it up out of the dirt. Resting the bottom on the tops of his toes, he walked the sack, which had to be at least a foot taller than he, towards Sera's bakery. She followed him, giggling as his face and ears became redder and redder.

"*Phew*!" and he plopped the sack down.

Maramurru collapsed on top of the flour, white dust puffing out.

"Your face is almost as red as your trousers!" Sera said, handing him a ladle of water, "you get stronger and stronger each year."

Drinking it and four more, he nodded back, his breathing quickly returning to normal levels.

"Here," she had disappeared inside of her bakery for a brief moment, then returned with something wrapped in a beeswax linen wrap, "these are supposed to be for later, but I think you've earned it."

She ran her hand over his shaggy head.

Taking the cloth napkin, Maramurru opened it to find a honey roll, still warm.

"Thanks, Miss Sera," he said taking a ginormous bite.

"You're welcome. Now, go and play. It's your birthday!"

"The Pedagogue said I should help," and he took another bite.

"You did," and she winked while tilting her head at the door.

Finishing his roll in one last bite, Maramurru left, waving as he did. He liked Miss Sera. Everyone liked Miss Sera, especially Reilu. He was the fisherman's son and about the same age as Miss Sera. Maramurru and his brothers often joked that if Reilu didn't marry Miss Sera, one of them would, someday, even though none of them had a clear understanding of what "marriage" was. But they knew that, whatever it was, they wanted a marriage with Miss Sera, or someone like Miss Sera.

Wandering out past the town gates, following Traveler's Road into the tall grass of Ezinu's Fields, separating the town from the wood, the children played here most often. Wheat and other cereals were sown and harvested along with a limited variety of vegetables, a labor necessitating the whole village's efforts. There was a lot of reliance on Erestu-Ur, the largest human settlement twelve miles just north of the wood, for much of the essentials for life on the cliffs. It was expensive, if for nothing else but in time, to keep the villagers of Kish well stocked. Dangers lurked outside of walls of their fledgling civilization, and, this time of year, the road through the dense wood was among the most perilous for the uninitiated.

On the anniversary of their arrival, the end of the Exodus, colonizers were embarked on lengthy journeys from the farthest reaches of this new human empire to congregate in the fields surrounding Kish for a festival running the second half of autumn, following the harvesting of the crops. The roads to the north were very rarely ever without the pattering of feet, the clattering of the ox cart, or the stomp of a hoof. A sea of canvas would blanket the fields and knolls as many thousands made these cliffs their temporary home. The start and end of the festival was marked by a giving of thanks to the late Enkirus, whose grave, under the shadow of the celestial chariot, perched atop the highest of the cliffs, became something of a shrine, a memorial, not of lives lost, but of lives saved. A thousand hands would pass across his burial stone, some muttering the now customary supplication: *The life you saved.* Those finished paying respects to Enkirus would march further up the hill to the Margidda, and, in similar fashion, touch the hull of the vessel which had sailed through the heavens, transplanting them and their ancestors from one celestial orb to another. The days of thanks were merry, a great reprieve from the hardship of being the foundation upon which later generations would thrive.

The children had, since their birth, taken on a special role in these annual celebrations. Their birth coincided with the last appearance of the Anunna-Ki, the manifestation of the gods on earth. When they had first returned, more than a decade after the death of Enkirus, they, as the stories go, would come in pairs and seek out women of birthing age but who, either by loss or curse, were childless. Only two women a year for three years were selected, and through the grace of the Anunna-Ki, learned themselves to be with child. Each year's birth succeeded that of the previous year by exactly one day, and, had any reliable time-keepers from the old world remained functional, the exacting nature would surely have startled the town folk. Born just after the start of the harvest, the children were spared the influx of pilgrims that otherwise might have been afforded the opportunity to travel to Kish, were it any other time of the year. So, as it was, on the second day of the festival, the children would be revealed to all of mankind, and gifts were abundant, but it was not until the birth of the third born son, Maramurru, who, even at so young an age as he was, began a new tradition—sharing the gifts among all of the children and well-wishers.

"Maramurru! Maramurru!"

The boy turned around. It was the town builder, Sera's uncle.

"Son," he was always calling the boys "son" even though he was not their father, "oi, Maramurru!"

He was a rather lanky man, toned, but lanky. His skin had been darkened by the many thousands of days he had spent working beneath the sun, swinging a hammer, sawing down timber, and patrolling the perimeter of town as a self-appointed sheriff. His hair was tied back, bobbing behind him, while his beard swayed side to side under his chin. There were patches of sweat forming around his collar and under his arms as it streamed down his face, rivers flowing along the contours of his neck.

He was waving frantically with one hand, while brandishing a spear with the other, "turn back, son! Get back!"

Maramurru stopped, a pace or two beyond the gate.

"…the alarm! Sound the alarm, son!"

He made a beeline for the field, where the other children were playing. Behind, emerging from the far side of the wood, were a pack of Gudanna, ravenous little creatures. Barbarous monsters. The Pedagogue said that they had been enemies of man since their first night on their new world, appearing from the tree line, hooting and hollering terrible sounds, jackals is what they were, waving clubs and hurling stones at the encampment. Their skin was a pale blue, almost sickly when compared to the flesh of a man, hair an apricot tint to it, and a gray, flaky mud covered most of their bodies. Framing their eyes, also blue, was a reddish paint feared to be the blood of their spoils. Their stature was not quite as tall, more often than not hunched over and stooped. Some wore animal skins around their sensitive areas, others did not. Their weapons were exclusively those which could be thrown, or brute force would induce submission, but they attacked in such numbers, with a savage intensity, whole human settlements had been decimated by their raids. Never attacking during the summer seasons when man was most populous in their territory, the colder months were when the Gudanna were most dangerous to those situated such as the folk at Kish.

Turning back, sprinting as fast as his little legs would carry him, Maramurru rushed back into town. Scrambling for the rope, he tugged, hard as he could. The clanging of the bell ushered in a pause on all activity within town. The fishermen, who had just hauled up their last basket of the morning's catch, in spite of their fatigue, came darting from the other side of town, harpoons in hand. The Mistress was a few yards behind.

"Maramurru, what are you—" the fisherman was interrupted by the sight of the town builder shepherding the children up the road, chased by one of the largest Gudanna hordes he, or anyone for that matter, had ever seen.

"Grab a bow!" he shouted at his son, Reilu, "Tombar, signal the City. Quickly now!"

Hurrying back, bow and quiver in hand, Reilu took up a position near the gate's stone arch. Tombar heaved dampened leaves on to the fire at the center of town, and soon thick smoke began rising into the sky. Rejoining the other fishermen at the gate, Tombar took up a bow opposite Reilu.

"Faster!"

They could hear the town builder scream. He stood in between the Gudanna and the children, absorbing the occasional pelt of rock. His eyes were wide, filled with panic and fear clearly seen even from the hundred or more yards still separating him from the town's gate.

"Reilu, Tombar, loose!"

Dipping their arrows into the flaming oil, both young men released a small volley, not intending to kill, but rather to scorch a buffer between the horde and the town. The Gudanna had not and perhaps lacked the cognitive capacity for fire making; it was a mystical invention of the colonizers capable of providing as much benefit as terror. The arrows sailed high into the air before plummeting down, striking the soil, and setting sizable clumps of grass aflame. Gudanna thinking that they might flank the town builder and his charges were halted by a wall of fire.

Like a windmill, the fisherman beckoned them, one hand ready to throw the gate shut, and bar the entrance to town. The Gudanna were right on their heels, their shrill cries as sharp as the chiseled tips of their spears. Wrapping an arm around the middle of the smallest of the children, a girl the same age as Maramurru, the town builder just managed to get inside before the wooden doors were swung shut. Their attackers would not be deterred. Clawing and banging on the solid oak, beating on it with flesh and rock, the rage of the Gudanna would permit their entry in time. Bracing themselves, the fishermen dug their feet into the soft earth, pushing against the combined mass of tens of dozens of Gudanna.

Releasing the little girl into the custody of the Pedagogue, who found himself engulfed in the embrace and care of six terrified children, the town builder hurried, trying to help bar the gate. "Argh! I dunno… what's… provoked them!"

The elder fisherman grunted, thigh muscles tearing through his trousers, "Pedagogue, I think it best you take the children… and bar yourselves inside."

"Argh! Sera, go with them, uh," when she made to scoff, he reaffirmed his judgment, "go! *Go*…Sera!" Her uncle wrestled with the lock, he watched as Sera followed the Pedagogue and the children back to the farthest part of town.

"Have you ever seen so many?"

"Not… in all my… years…" the builder said, panting, the lock and door would not align.

"Tombar… Reilu, climb up… the watchtower… draw them off the gate…"

Moments later, they could hear the plucking of bowstrings followed by the near immediate reduction of force on the gate.

"Ahhh!"

A cry of pain and thud. Reilu had been struck and fell from the watchtower, a Gudanna spear having pierced his shoulder. Blood trickled out of the corner of his mouth while drenching his shirt, then seeping into the dry soil.

"Reilu!" Governed by nothing other than a tidal wave of parental concern, the fisherman instinctively abandoned his post, rushing towards his wounded son.

The lock slipped. "Narlu, I…can't hold it…by my—"

He was knocked to the ground, mouth feasting on dirt and straw. Feeling something penetrate his body's integrity, he let out a yelp, but it was drowned in earth. Not knowing from where, he forced himself to stand, tumbling in the direction of his town folk. Reilu was slumped in the arms of his father. Wincing in pain, his wound not immediately fatal, Reilu brandished a small knife he probably used to gut fish. Narlu held a harpoon defensively over the body of his weakened son. Above, but hunkered down, was Tombar, arrow drawn, fixed on the lead Gudanna. The Mistress stood near her husband and son; a pitchfork was her weapon, borrowed from the stable nearby. Searching for anything that might be a suitable weapon, the builder reclaimed his spear and took up position center, himself a shield for his town.

There was a gash in his leg, but he could not feel any pain, the adrenaline coursing through his veins made sure of it. His primal instincts were taking over. He was angry. He wanted to live. He wanted to protect his kin. Eyes shifting, the Gudanna had paused for a moment. Twelve, fifteen, twenty, and maybe more. They snarled their yellow, rotten teeth, cut lips, and blood-thirsty eyes. A pack of wild dogs; feral beasts!

Their leader, the Alpha Gudanna or chieftain—given its size and headdress—lurched forward but was instantly cut down by Tombar's arrow. Striking the creature in the neck, it tried to scream, but the arrowhead had severed its vocal cords when it destroyed the spinal column and carotid. Crumpling in a pile of agony, it was soon dead, blood pooling all around.

A devotion to their leader bordered on fanatical, for they did not run and flee, but descended on the villagers with all of the ferocity of a hurricane. They were butchered, bodies hewn as they lay dead, but the villagers did not go out so easily, in spite of their numbers, wounds, or skill, this was their home, and even after taking many a fatal blow themselves before at last succumbing, they ensured the Gudanna tribe would have their own losses to mourn.

An undesired pounding came at the door of the far away house.

"In the backroom—bar it shut with everything you have—and you don't open less you hear the voice of a man. Do you understand me, child?"

Sera barely managed to nod and tried to mutter a response, but she had no words, no voice.

The Pedagogue thrust a small, hand-size rectangular object into the young girl's trembling hands. "When help comes, you tell them to take you to Erestu-Ur. You want to speak to a Pedagogue. Take them to her. No one is to know you have this save for the Pedagogue. You tell no one, child."

The doorframe was beginning to splinter, Gudanna spears poking through the narrow windows.

"Children, you do as Sera says, you hear? You follow her word. Her word is *my* word." When they acknowledged him, between fits of tears, he looked back to Sera. "Not a soul. Watch after them," and he closed the door.

Listening to the furniture dragged to barricade themselves inside, the Pedagogue staggered across the common room. Uncovering a chest he had not opened for many years, he drew his old sword, and a layer of dust fell from the scabbard. The hinges were peeling away from the structure. The Gudanna were relentless in their assault. Then, finally with the door hacked to pieces, it gave way, permitting their entry to his home. There were only three. Given the injuries they had suffered the Pedagogue believed them to be the only survivors of the horde to make it this far into town. They were covered in blood, from head to toe, whether their own or that of the slain villagers, the Pedagogue could only offer a supposition. Two were armed with spears, while the third—the one standing at the center of this threesome—held on to a stone dripping with oxygen rich blood.

They appeared fatigued, but they were still much younger than the 76-year-old Pedagogue, who held the sword tightly with both of his wrinkled hands. His vision was poor, and in this dim light it was even worse, but the old man knew what he had to do, otherwise Sera and the children would not survive.

From the other side of the door, behind a mountain of furniture and things, Sera and the six children huddled in the corner as far away from as they could be from the door. She held them all in her arms, thin though they were, doing her best to keep them calm while fighting back a floodgate of despair herself. There was a skirmish of some sort, the clanging of steel against stone, and then nothing. Silence.

Several hours passed. They sat there, alone and afraid, aware only of the passage of time by the dimming of the sky, just visible through the narrow window where wall met roof. There was movement outside, but the sounds were indefinite and voices indistinguishable. Sera had not relented in her firm hold of the children in all this time.

"Shhh…" she said in a voice barely that of a whisper, placing her hand over the mouths of one of the boys, "Anshargal, you have to be quiet."

Her eyes happened to find Maramurru's, who, despite being a boy of only five, conveyed to her a message of reassurance.

Sounds of trespassers encircled the house. The floorboards in the adjoining rooms squealed under the weight. "Ho! Is anyone in there?" the owner of the voice was knocking on the door. "We are riders from Erestu-Ur. We have come to your aid. I say again, is anyone in there?"

"Yes! Yes, we're here!" Sera exclaimed.

"Are the children with you?"

"I have them."

"Stand clear of the door!"

With the strength of ten men, the door was rammed down, the barricade hastily erected cascaded down. Not waiting for the lock to be retracted, the mechanism was torn from the frame along with the hinges, and the door collapsed onto the floor. Standing, bathed in only the light of a singular flickering torch, was a man, clad in leather armor, layers laid upon layers, held together by straps and buckles. From his right hip, a piece of cloth dangled, just passed the bend in his knee, and where otherwise dark, it captured the light just enough to reveal its frayed carmine. He was a soldier of the City.

"I have them! I have the children—and a young girl."

They could hear quite a commotion from outside the walls of the house as men and beasts flocked to the man's proclamation.

Taking his first step into the room, he surveyed the scene. If the Gudanna had made it into this room, there would have been nowhere for any of them to go. The window was little more than a slit between wall and ceiling, far too high for any of the children to reach, even with the help of the girl. The stone masonry would have entombed them there. All of their juvenile souls snuffed out before they had even begun.

Passing the torch's flame over each child's face, dully illuminating the terror forever scarred unto their minds, he verified that they were, in fact, the Children of the Anunna-Ki, for their faces were known to all in humandom. Their bodies looked to be well enough, minor scratches, some dirt, no blood. He saw that they all, even the two oldest boys (seven years), had their little arms snaked around the girl, herself not much past her own years of adolescence.

"What is your name, miss?"

He was a soldier. That was obvious, the children knew as much. A cowl hung around his neck; he must have removed it upon entering the house. One's eyes might be convinced he was at least a man of thirty; he had a hardened look about him, strong features accented by jet black hair, bushy brows, and a thin goatee. But he could not have been as old as her eyes would lead her to believe, as the aura emanating around him was one still captivated by youth, even if outwardly suppressed. There were wrinkles in the corners of his eyes, which almost seemed to undermine his gruffness, as they conveyed all the emotion and sensitivity one could ever hope express in a lifetime. Those hazel eyes were now smiling, beaming at the girl and the children she had protected—trying in earnest to convince them everything was going to be all right.

She did not even realize she had answered the soldier.

"Aye. Sera," more soldiers filed in, wanting to see for themselves that the children were alive, "give us the children—it's all right," he said quickly, noticing her apprehension, "you've done beautifully. We are going to take you, all of you, back to Erestu-Ur, where you can be safe. Come," and, holding out his hand to her, helped her rise as the soldiers moved forward, lifting a child into their arms, only with the reassurances of Sera.

As they were escorted out of the house, Sera saw, but fortunately the children did not (she would remain forever grateful), the soldiers did take that much precaution, the Pedagogue laying slain on the floor, three Gudanna savages dead around his feet. Two spears stuck out of his body, one in the upper chest, the other in his abdomen. On seeing this, Sera let out whimper, before the soldier turned her head away and steered her into the evening dusk.

"Did you find anyone else? My parents, they were near the gate...."

The soldier answered her with a sadness creeping over his eyes. Save for herself and the children, no one else in the village had survived.

A fire had burned the bakery-butchery-depository almost entirely to the ground, while at the stable, the pair of horses had freed themselves and leapt over the stone wall, vanishing into the wilderness. The donkey, whose last days had been spent grinding wheat into flour, had not been spared from the brutality of the Gudanna. She could not see or hear the sheep or the goats, but chickens were wandering loose from their coop, completely oblivious.

"Why don't you ride with the children," the soldier said, on seeing them being loaded into a cart.

Managing a nod, she followed him.

"Try and keep their eyes down until we've entered the wood. They don't need to see any more than they have," he said, whispering to her as he helped climb into the ox cart, "same goes for you."

"How will I know when to open my eyes?" he could see that she was fighting back tears.

"When your skin grows cold and the trees begin to talk, then it will be safe, and you can open your eyes."

2.3 SAMSARA

And so, the Fifth Age came to a somber end. Wrecked down. Its foundation collapsing upon itself, weighted down by centuries of moral decay and horrendous war. Huge swaths of land yielded to the raging fires of industry where dilapidated concentrations of man and wealth tempted more envious men to plunder their riches, first by way of the forked tongue and later by force of arms. In their defense, they retreated inward, deeper into the depravity that had long since betrayed them to a damning fate of self-destruction. When the war came, the last war, the tragedy was complete. A dense and suffocating dullness settled in, a grayness that rained down on the bodies stacked up one on top of the other in the network of trenches spanning thousands of miles. Where the fires and pestilence did not kill, the gas, the sickly, pus-colored clouds of chemical contaminants, blew steadily across the continents, leaving the cities in a dark silence from which they would never recover. Anarchy, the ultimate dissolution of society, was the reality the survivors, the cursed few there were, vacating their shelters to find their world had ended.

A student of history would note here that the ending of the Fifth Age exhibited more than one parallel with the destruction that had brought about the Exodus. A cynical observer might note that as proof, positive that sons and daughters are doomed to repeat the mistakes of their parents. A realist would argue that history has taught us that only through our strength might we ever survive the follies of our collective character, while another would look to the same set of facts and conclude it was precisely that flawed logic of the past that would surely again ruin the future. Neither these nor other lessons were absent from the Baltutu, who, after having witnessed yet another collapse of civilization, resolved to act.

The winds were generally still. A feeble breeze was swept up from the south, swirling around the town square, circling the edges and faces of the facades of the bombed-out halls of law and order. The fires had reduced themselves to but a handful of stubborn embers, puffing out smoke like one chewing on the end of dying cigar; clumps of spent fuel remnants huddled round like vulture nests. It was nearly midday, though with the blanket of gray draped over the planet, one might have thought it a later hour. Save for the six cloaked figures trespassing, the square was a fairly silent, undisturbed grave.

At what had not so formerly been both the center of the square and the city itself was a tree, or more precisely now, the blackened charcoal remains of an ancient elm tree. Far and away the city's oldest inhabitant, its branches had extended out towards the building faces that surrounded it, where the leaves, a rich, vibrant, well-watered green, would push and tickle the fired brick. Those leaves were gone now. The branches, the lot of them, consumed by the fires that had raged. All that remained standing, raised slightly upon a knoll, was the solid, knot trunk—a monument to sin.

"It's happened again," said one of the figures scraping a layer of soot from a scorned ceremonial shield with the sole of his boot.

"Before... wasn't as bad. Not as bad as this," another remarked, kneeling over the decaying bodies of a presumed mother and father clutching between them their child, trying to protect them from the fire storm.

"Each end is more terrible than the one that preceded it," this time, the voice was that of a woman, her hair was covered beneath the hood of her cloak, thinly veiling her from sight. "Apsu, we have to do something. We've stayed silent for far too long."

The one named Apsu, who was now tracing his fingers along the face of the child, took a moment to respond. Their bodies had adopted a texture more akin to weathered stone than flesh, hard and callus. Rising, he wrapped himself tighter beneath the folds of his traveling cloak.

"Ours is to guide. What would you have us do?

"Lead them."

A response came not from Apsu, but the man who had spoken first. A response that was as much a declaration as invocation of a revelation.

"It's plain that our *guidance* has fallen short of desired end—yet again."

Sitting on the sunken steps arranged around the tree, head craning to the side, fingers intertwined, a third man of the group gently shook his head. "Lead them? Or do you mean to *rule* them, Anshargal?"

Anshargal wiped away the ash settling on his upper lip. "Look around you, Maramurru, have you seen destruction such as this? In all our time on this earth, have any of us been witness to anything like this? *No*! No, no, we have not because there has never been destruction such as this *here*."

"We can't. We do not rule—"

"We have stayed the course! For 3,700 years *we* have stayed the course." Anshargal became increasingly animated, the world was his courtroom, the square his evidence. "We have stayed silent and allowed them to slaughter themselves in droves. We are complicit in their crimes, and their atrocities."

"You'd have us abandon our responsibility!"

Darting from his position on the steps, Maramurru moved to where Melammu stood, near a pitiful dribble of acidic water leaking from a punctured lead pipe. Reaching into Melammu's knapsack, he pulled from it the Baraggal, an inscription upon a small metal tablet, encased in a sheet of glass, which only showed itself with the touch of flesh. Pressing his palm against the glass, the tablet illuminated with light, displaying the words of their bond.

Maramurru read the words aloud, his voice reverberating towards heaven: "They will strive to emulate your example, to profit by your views and your wisdom. They will *stumble*. They will *struggle*."

"I know the words as we all do. But Maramurru, you must surely see that we have given them no example to profitably emulate. We have stayed shrouded, living behind masks, working through anecdotal mysticism. We share fables and bedtime stories. Now… there is no one alive to remember those stories. Remember the words of the Enkirus recounting the last days of Erestu. Are they not as fitting, *more* fitting here? They are, just as our ancestors, destroying themselves and this world."

"Eridu is not Erestu," said Maramurru, eyes still fixed on the ancient text.

Anshargal took this moment to ease towards his brother, placing his hand around his shoulder. "No… but it is becoming more and more like Erestu. The home we lost. The home *we* never knew. We have the opportunity and the capacity to change this world," their eyes locked, "but, do we have the *will*, Maramurru?"

The others, who had largely been silent, turned their eyes to

Maramurru. They had not needed to contribute. This was not a debate new to them, nor was it unknown to him where the others stood. For quite some time, Anshargal's words had swayed all but Maramurru. In looking around, absorbing the indiscriminate plague of death, he felt his resolve begin to waiver. If he was honest with himself, it had been wavering longer than he was proud to admit.

He then felt a tug, Shi, the youngest of them and perhaps the most innocent, kneeled her fine robes into the black, while wrapping her milk white fingers on either side of his face. His face frozen in time, auburn hair wind swept, and bronze skin kissed by many suns. Only his eyes showed any signs of age, but even they seemed to smile, silver though they were, from the corners, as though the muscles had become permanently fixed in that position staring down over a nose whom genetics had affixed a small bulge, right there in the middle. Shi, by contrast, was composed of porcelain, her features finely sculpted and sharp, particularly her nose. With brilliant blue eyes that seemed to glow accented by dark eyebrows. Objectively, she was the fairest of the sisters.

"Each of us have our own gifts, our own strengths. Yours is wisdom. If we're to do this, we'll need your wisdom more than ever to guide *our* actions. Ensure fealty to our sacred obligation. We can still *save* them. Will you save them with us, brother?"

Her words, true to her name, pierced his soul, striking a chord with his conscious. Given the abhorrent manner with which the Fifth Age had ended—murder of tens of millions—the essence of what the others called on Maramurru to do was not lost on him. How could it? Nothing was so apparent; not even the existence of the suns in the sky could be said to be more evident than the state of humanity. The course had to change. It must. But, for all of his countless centuries, the cavity, the singularity that enveloped his heart obstructed any clarity that might have still clung to the recesses of his mind. Racked with such immeasurable grief, for though he did not know the names of the persons who laid dead at his feet, he did know the dreams they had had for themselves, their children, their children's children. Racked with such immeasurable grief, for though he did not know the nature of their character, he had loved them. He still loved them.

Seeking approval from Apsu, Anshargal removed the Baraggal from Maramurru's hold, and returned it to the care of Melammu, who stored it once again. "If we are to go through with this, we must abide by the laws we set for ourselves. This decision, like all others, must be unanimous."

Apsu exposed his face from underneath his hood. His was a face whose skin was stretched tightly against the bone. In addition to being the largest of his kin, he appeared the most alien, with exaggerated limbs but stubby, knotted appendages.

"As eldest among the immortals and the first charged with our solemn responsibility, I call on each of you to declare yourself before one another: Shall we assert ourselves in the coming age to lead mankind according to our purpose?"

"I, Mummu, second born daughter, do declare."

"I, Melammu, of inspiring light, do declare."

Maramurru felt Anshargal caress his shoulder as he spoke the words into his brother's ear, "I, Anshargal, prince of heaven, do declare."

"I, Shi, breath of life... do declare," she said, turning to respectfully face her elder.

"I, Apsu, one who exists from the beginning, do declare. What say you, Maramurru?"

The weight of the stock he felt barring his neck was enormous.

"If we do this, we do it for *them* and not ourselves."

Apsu craned his head down whilst towering above. "What say you? How do you declare?"

He felt shackled to the spot.

"Yes! Yes..." each word felt to him as a betrayal of the greatest magnitude, worthy of all the lashes a strong man might bring to bear.

"Say the words," he heard Mummu, almost in a motherly tone, he thought.

Wrenching himself free, he stood before the dead elm, atop the bodies of the inglorious dead, and pleaded as much to the Aeternam as to his brothers and sisters, "I, Maramurru, son of the West, do... declare!"

2.4 THE FOURTH OBENIAN WAR

Though none living at the time could possibly have been aware of it, the Sixth Age, as the Baltutu would tell you, was bookended by a peace and stability that had not existed on the surface of Eridu since humans first arrived on its shores. For more than 3,800 years, rooted in the bountiful—and well defended—Atlantaries Harbor, the cradle of human civilization, the final resting place of the celestial chariot, an empire had been founded, spanning the whole of the globe. Their expansion had been aggressive; the supremacy of their dominion was near absolute. Few were left with either the capability or audacity to resist. The strongest of the apostates laid at the far end of the Iliadic Sea, slightly more than 275 leagues from the most southern island of Ilias, on the continent of Laud, in the land of Obenia.

For generations passing into centuries, the Obenians had resisted the will of the Baltutu, denying them supremacy over their lands and waters. Tasking other peoples to be of greater importance in their doctrine of domination and assimilation, the Obenians were granted de facto autonomy for the past seventy years at the conclusion of the Third Obenian War; a status their line of kings knew would not last forever. Not wanting to wait until the Baltutu could amass their full strength, King Matthiolus's grandfather had struck the first. Skirmishes against the

Obenians and the Baltutu garrison continued throughout these seven decades of peace.

Thousands of ships and their crews employed in trade had been sunk, captured, ransomed, or otherwise plundered, robbing the mighty Empire of much wealth and goods necessary in keeping the domestic tranquility. Pirates and marauders spread across the high seas to shores the Obenians might not normally reach. Their campaign of piracy robbed village fishermen and merchants alike. The chief prize and payment owed by the pirates to their Obenian allies was the Ankida as proof of their buccaneering. A grave insult to the Empire was to see so many of their standards looted and horded by the southern defilers. To the pirates, the Obenians left the much of the booty, cargo, ships, treasure, and slaves. Eventually, though, the true war would come. King Matthiolus, grandson of the king who had begun subverting the luxuries of Baltutu civilization, had spent his entire life preparing for the day when legions of Etlu, the warrior servants of the Empire, would land on their free shores. Now, that day had come.

Having secured all but the most remote tribes of man, the Baltutu turned their attention to their final enemy, and with horrifying efficiency under the command of Anshargal, liberated the seas of pirates and Obenians alike. Adjudicating their heresy absent compassion, the pirates were handled with relative ease; lacking a centralized authority, the bands of raiders were subdued with prejudice. Subjugated to the lash and labor, they were returned home. When Anshargal's fleet finally arrived on the horizon, as viewed from the palace watch, their numbers were so great that they spanned the whole of the observable sky, and not an inch of blue ocean could be perceived between their wooden planks.

King Matthiolus's father, knowing that the coming war would require better fortifications, moved the capitol of his kingdom south, to the only suitable harbor within his realm. Of all of the defensive measures undertaken to defend the sovereignty of Obenia, perhaps the sea chains, which stretched the length of the harbor, barring the shallow waters from the invaders, were the most ingenious, if no more effective.

Anshargal, however, would not be rendered impotent so easily. The numbers of his assembled fleet offered opportunity to blockade not merely the harbor, but all of Obenia. You see, Obenia's territory was almost exclusively composed of the northern extremity of Laud, with only a handful of inconsequential settlements further inland, but those neither would find refuge, as the alliances the kings of Obenia had thought to form with their neighbors were nonexistent, either by the fear imposed at the size and strength of the Baltutu's army or because the Baltutu had out maneuvered the line of kings and brokered exchanges more favorable to the destruction of Obenia. It was in this manner that King Matthiolus, last of his name, for his wife had not yet born him a son, was to face the might of the world.

"My Lord, our division from the northern coasts has taken position ten miles to the north and northwest of the city. The western army reports thirty thousand ready. Our pincher regiments are advancing from the chain towers and are approaching the city walls. The south is overrun, Flaccians, Philites, Daytons, and our commanders there are only a few hours from the city. We respectfully request instructions."

Anshargal watched from the deck of his flagship as the fire barges torched the harbor, balls of fire streaking across the sky more as though from space than man, pitch black tails trailing their arching movement.

"What do you think, Brother?"

Approaching from astern, Maramurru came and rested his hands on the deck railing; the sight of war was not at all appealing to him. "End it. Now and swift. You've—"

"Ah…*we've*…" he interpreted.

"Of course. *We've* encircled their city, their king. Their allies have abandoned them. Their country is overrun. Do not toy with them—but exercise mercy and deliver the fatal blow with haste."

"A shrewd tactical maneuver, Maramurru." He folded his arms behind him, letting his knees absorb the jostling sea. "In only a matter of days have the Etlu done what any other army of men would have needed weeks, months."

"They are imbued with our divine presence."

Anshargal snapped his head towards Maramurru, in order to respond in words to what had been communicated via pure thought. "Best we adhere to your wisdom, Brother. Barumgal," and his vicar answered his summons, "order the fire barges to stand down. Move our transports forward. Deploy all batteries and take the harbor. Signal the generals to commence bombardment of the city. Let us test the resolve of the King and his god."

Barumgal uttered his compulsory response before disappearing to execute his lord's will.

"Come, Brother, we must don our battle dress. We have a peace to win, after all," and with a firm clap of Maramurru's shoulder, he steered his brother below deck as fifty thousand men stormed the blackened beaches, clambering over the smoldering rubble in pursuit of their quarry.

The inner sanctuary of the castle had been breached. Soldiers of steel, the Etlu advanced unforgivingly, armed with lengthy halberds; the Obenians could not land a blow, let alone a fatal one against the invaders. They were skewered one after the other on the steel tip, then tossed aside in the growing heaps of dead. Arrows were raining down on them, but the craftsmanship of their armor was too fine and not a shot found its mark, not even from the most skilled archer. Fire teams, armed with crossbows, ejected obese bolts, penetrating the bowmen along the rooftops, entering and exiting their bodies, the head becoming stuck in the stone. The red caped infantry then swarmed the stairs, leading to the second level, and the throne room of the king. Wielding the finest weapons, the Obenians were cut down in scores, their bodies crumpling on the steps, retreating further and further until their backs were against the barricaded entrance to their king.

The assault stopped only when, with the last few defenders, languishing for breath, lamenting for the fallen, faces bloodied and eyes rabid, enticed the attention of Anshargal as he and Maramurru made their way up the stone steps, the life force for hundreds of men spilt in accumulating in scarlet lakes. The Obenians trembled as he approached. His stature, when compared to that of a fit man, was menacing. In his armor, the same steel shell as his Etlu, although far more elaborate, engraved with iconography of thousands of years of conquest, elevated him to a height of more than seven feet, the shadow he cast could block out the suns from view for all those caught beneath it. He did not adorn himself with the morion. The hem of his cape dragged through inches of war filth in between fits of wind causing it to billow in his wake. Following the lead of his brother, Maramurru stood at the opening of the cavity their warriors had created. His dress paled in comparison; leather cuirass, tassets, and skirt—a style popular among the Laurentians who were among his most devout—over white canvas undergarments, the blue cloak was latched on to bronze clasps at the shoulders. The bracers he wore were of splendid Hundaren make, knowing ancient ways of fashioning hide to be as durable as iron.

"Stand aside, soldiers," Anshargal's voiced bellowed over the backdrop of a city burning.

"Has your stubbornness robbed you of all sense? Your god commands that you stand down!"

Anshargal held up a hand, silencing Barumgal.

"He is not our god! *Ours* is the true god! And he—"

"…has forsaken you. You are a brave soldier, you have served your king—and *your* god—with courage, unshaken fealty. But such loyalty has not been justly rewarded. Our swords have already slain many of your kin for their defiance…"

Maramurru edged forward, seeking to blunt the rising vexation in his brother's tone. "Your city is burning. Your countrymen are dying. Your king has the ability to end all of this now. Let us—"

With a pluck of the bowstring, a dozen arrows were unleashed, flinging towards Anshargal and Maramurru, but then, came to a sudden, inexplicable halt, suspended in mid-flight. Left hand fully extended, fingers outstretched as far as they might, Anshargal slowed the Obenian missiles to a crawl, rotating ever so slightly as they inched through the air. Knowing what his brother's intentions were, Maramurru flashed Anshargal a warning that was unmistakable: Disarm and subdue.

"We have already won."

Anshargal's vein was throbbing, an ugly protrusion in the middle of his face. It was taking considerable will to hold the arrows where they were, and he did not much appreciate Maramurru violating his mind. Thrusting the steel tipped arrows to the ground, as opposed to the archers who had fired them, Anshargal removed the swords and pikes of the men barring the door, while Maramurru, with a flick of the wrist, severed the strings of the bows.

"Take them!" Anshargal barked, ordering his men to seize the defenders, "place them in iron," he glared at his brother, "they wanted to protect their king? Let them suffer his punishment."

Summoning the strength of a summer typhoon, Anshargal led a procession into the King of Obenia's great hall, marshaling a column of his elite Etlu to overwhelm and subjugate the last remnants of Matthiolus's armies. Few were killed outright; most were beaten into submission, then hauled away, some unconscious, some screaming in fits of fury. The king's guard were led away in chains, stripped of their weapons and honor, leaving the king alone with his most trusted advisors.

"King Matthiolus the Second," Anshargal said in false reverence, "ah! Can you feel that? *That* is the feeling of peace. This is exciting!" The grin on his face was of utter triumph; he was intoxicated by the euphoria washing over him in this moment. "Come," he beckoned the defeated king off his throne.

"Our king bows to no man!"

Holding up a metal finger, Anshargal silenced the general. "I am no man," he said as the general tried frantically to pry his own jaw open, "it is not blood which courses through my veins."

"Neither is it ichor!"

His smile did not dissipate. "Such incivility! A churlish people, aren't you?" and he caused a sharp pain in the second man's stomach, causing him to fall to the floor, writhing and convulsing like a fish out of water.

Again, Maramurru discarded his place, taking a step towards the king. "Noble king, it is done. The war is over, whether you surrender here and now, or not. Honor might dictate that you refuse, stand firm, and such would be your right as sovereign, but I beg that you consider the price of continued... resistance. You will needlessly cost these two men their lives, mark the sincerity of my brother and do not cross him. I mean this not as a threat, but the lives of your wife and children, still in the palace —I will have not the words to stay my brother's temper. You will not only bare witness but be compelled to live out your days reliving their tormentous final moments, sustaining you by force if they must. These lives... and more, for I know you care deeply of your people, can be saved. All he asks is that you bend the knee. Please... there has been enough death today."

Anshargal scowled down at the king, whose head swiveled between the sight of one general flailing about on the carpet, tears streaming down a face that had never before known their touch, and another general, panic-stricken, nails carving gashes into his own flesh. If there ever was to be a day in the years yet to come when the Baltutu might be knocked from their perch, he desired very much to witness such a day. Ignoring the gasps of shock from the others cowering behind his throne, King Matthiolus, grandson of the first to defy their will, became the last. On bended knee he kowtowed, his forehead resting mere inches from Anshargal's boot.

2.5 ENKIRUS IN EXILE

Establishing their seat of power at and as the cradle of human civilization, the landing site of the celestial chariot, a mythos was crafted linking the Baltutu's stewardship of mankind with the legacy of Enkirus, a man whose friendship saved the human race.

Enkirus knew Erestu, the ancestral home of man, was dying, but he was limited by the knowledge, skill, and craft of his time. He was prepared, however reluctantly, to die with the species, as seemed to have been deemed the fate of all. But, as that same fate would have it, man was not written to die that day—not all at once. Enkirus, a man learned in the natural sciences and unbridled compassion, happened across one of his people's Gods. You see, one of their celestial chariots had come crashing down not far from the village Enkirus had retired to, intent to spend his last days there among the quaintness of the folk who worked the land. He had even begun to fashion himself a bit as a farmer. It was in the course of his new occupation that, one foggy morning, while shepherding his flock, he lost control of them, as he too often did, and they escaped up into a narrow crevasse in the mountains. He had heard, through rumor, after all it was a small village, but more importantly he had heard it himself, the cloudless thunder and lightning the night before. The earth shaking which followed had the priests attempting to divine a message from the gods. For Enkirus, in his growing age, was concerned he no longer had the power to investigate, nor the resources to study. And, so, early the following morning, Enkirus and his staff, chased after his flock as they vanished into the altitude.

After some hours of searching, exhausted, dehydrated, and very nearly lost among the winding passages, Enkirus feared that, as the villagers might put it, "the mountain had swallowed his sheep." Out of breath, he paused in his labor, only to hear voices, unfamiliar voices, emanating from just over the next bend. These were not the voices of the village folk at the mountain's base, nor, so far as he could discern, though admittedly his hearing was not what it once was, were they the manner or tongue commonly spoken by men in these parts. It was language alien to him, patently unrecognizable to a learned man such as himself. Thus, he resolved to ease around a boulder to better inspect the strangers.

Jutting out from the mountainside into the goat path was a large rock formation, tall and wide enough to obscure a full-grown man from view. He hid behind it. The sheep were bleating just on the other side of the rock. The voices had diminished and thinking, willfully even, that they had not been voices but merely an atypical reverberation of the sheep's song in the rock, Enkirus eased into the opening, a spot which might have made a nice dell had not so many of the trees been burnt to charcoal. There seemed to be plenty of grass poking through a blackened earth, the look of freshly spread manure or other fertilizer. His sheep didn't seem to mind. Best he could discern, they looked and sounded to be in their usual spirit, and perfectly content with ignoring his urging them to cease fattening themselves and marshal on back down the hill. They relished the games they played upon him; he could see it in their fiendish eyes.

Enkirus was so distracted in wasting his efforts that he had failed to take notice of the rather substantial object laying, half covered, further in the clearing. In fact, it was not until he took count of his flock, noting one adventurous sheep, evidently an intrepid critter, looking back at him whilst its hooves were planted firmly in the charred soil mounds churned up around a mysterious structure. With one inhuman hand outstretched, petting the head of the one sheep, a pair of great, black eyes, dark as a moonless night and the size of a grown man's fist stared at him with an expression that might have been the equivalent of stupefaction. Two other, apparently identical, beings came into focus, flanking the one who had been petting his sheep. They were skeletal but oddly muscular at the same time; the definitions in the structure of their faces were stark beneath a gray skin, similar to that of man, but moister, as though from humidity or perspiration. Where the human nose was divided between bone and cartilage, theirs seemed to melt away into their face, the nostrils shallow and more like thick slits in the flesh. Using its lengthy fingers to scratch the head of the sheep, the visitor blinked. Enkirus's staff slipped from his fingers.

2.6 THE BURDEN

There were many more panels such as this. Reliefs of pre-history chiseled by master artisans, while they still existed, adorned with rich, vibrant hues which seemed to create the illusion of reality, as though they were not finely worked pieces of stone but rather windows into a distant past none alive now remembered. The most splendid of all the reliefs were located along the acropolis at Telmun, home of the Baltutu, capital of their empire, and the seat of heavendom on earth founded atop the ruins of Kish. Maramurru never grew tired of studying the images immortalized for all time... though, not amounting to flagrant omission, a conscious effort had been made in the depiction of other, prior civilizations that had adorned the surface of Eridu, limiting their inclusion. A strict emphasis was placed on versions elsewhere of the endless cycles of destruction occurring absent the Baltutu's careful tending. Maramurru had expended significant capital bargaining that the reliefs at Telmun be a faithful representation of history, as few mortals would ever set step within its holy walls. Perhaps that was the reason his brethren acquiesced... within reason of the narrative they had created.

The Fishermen's Steps carried them from the deck of their ships to the Library, a colossal structure of some 350 feet—the very height of the cliffs themselves. In the estimations of many, the Library exceeded in all ways the beauty and sophistication of the Pantheon at Telmun above, for it was hewn into and from the very rock. White in its own right, it assumed a golden hue with dawn's light and magenta with the approach of night. A temple of knowledge selfishly guarded away adorned with many fine reliefs and statues stood 131 feet in stature and supported by 27 columns—as girthy as mature godwood trees—on three sides. The pediment was appropriately scaled, its high peak fixed with an exquisite example of classical acroterion. This all was set atop another structure. Betwixt the library proper and the Grand Terrace were a further array of columns of a comparatively demure size—37 feet high. The Grand Terrace itself was in the shape of a half-moon supported by a third series of columns and could be approached by the causeway leading out to sea. Beyond this façade a labyrinth was carved deep into the cliff face beneath where the ancient of village of Kish (now supplanted by the expansive city of marble and limestone) once existed. Together, the Pantheon above and the Library below constituted the city-state of Telmun in the region of the Shuruppak, the Holy Land within the Baltutu's religion.

Regimented municipalities and towns were scattered across the globe, constructed to exacting specifications, conditions of nature permitting. Every citizen had a responsibility, a function in his or her town, and should one individual prioritize their needs over that of the community they risked collapse of the whole of the town's survival. More often than not, what they truly risked was retribution. Subsistence dominated their daily routines. There was no place for art, literature, philosophy, or music nor any of the liberal arts, not when there was labor to be done. The whole of the world was but one garden, the towns, and villages the herbage, the people individual petals, and the Living Ones the gardeners. Nothing was organic. Everything was programmed. Control was absolute.

The return voyage from Obenia had brought about a change in the seasons. Where it had been nearing the end of the summer season in the planet's south, spring was just beginning to blossom along the coast as they crossed back over the equator. It was never particularly cold here; the ocean currents kept the climate temperate, but Maramurru always enjoyed spring the most. Standing atop the foundations of the village of their youth, an edifice, spanning some three hundred acres, the most magnificent architectural marvel of the age. It was equal parts palace and capital city of a global empire. Nearly all of the fifty thousand persons who called Telmun home served at the pleasure of the Baltutu, more likely than not, tending to their needs over the administration of world affairs.

Entering through a passage at the cliff's top, Maramurru followed Anshargal. A large rectangular lake was situated at the center of the compound. Servants could be seen bustling about tending to the trees, vines, and flowers, others exercising routine maintenance on the brick and mortar, and others still scrubbed every exposed surface. The Ankida, the one-hundred-foot-high statue of cylindrical palladium encased in copper coils, its sheen as exemplary as the day it was forged, cast a shadow over them as they made to join their brother and sisters inside the conferred concrete dome of the Pantheon. Crossing over the threshold, they were at last home.

The soles of their boots clapped against the mosaic tile floor, an elaborate illustration of Eridu: The islands of Calphinae and Castroniphinae to the far west in the Gulf of Ahren, Audentica itself, the largest continent in the western hemisphere, to the southeast was Laud, Ilias and Troas, Laurentia dominating the center, the supercontinent Avalonia-Onpedon dominated the east, with the islands Balmond and Ginsup surrounding it, Duerre and Byrnes were located in the most eastern corner with only the island of Palare separating them, and the southernmost mass of Delima Vorta framed the edges of the world. All that was known to man was now, indisputably, theirs.

Three sets of tables were organized around the map, a pair of seats for each pair of Baltutu. The others were already waiting for them, having been alerted of their pending arrival by Anshargal's viceroy and principal servant, Barumgal. An altar had been placed precisely at the midpoint of the circular room upon it rested the Baraggal. Apsu, the eldest, was seated at the head table, the seat beside him reserved for Anshargal, empty. As he saw his brothers step into the light shining down through the giant oculus, he rose, a thin smile welcomed their return.

"Brother Anshargal, Brother Maramurru, please take your respective seats, rejoin the Baltutu as we open this meeting in due form."

Bowing to their brother's command, they took their seats; Anshargal to Apsu's left, Maramurru on Shi's right.

"Sister Melammu, shield our congregation so as to let no wandering eyes nor wanting ears to invade this council."

"Your command, Brother Apsu, shall be obeyed," and with that, to all those outside, the sight within the Pantheon was that of an empty space and all sounds were muffled into silence.

Apsu continued, "we shall now proceed in due course, Brother Maramurru, recite our Burden."

"Let the Burden be read!"

The ominous chant moved Maramurru to rise. Moving to the alter he began to speak:

The Earth was dying, the seas did rise,
Darkness came, to veil the skies.
Civilization's towers fell,

Consumed by fire, by sword, by knell.

Brother turned on brother's kin,
A world consumed by death and sin.
No hand could stay the final breath,
No mercy spared the reign of death.

But still we marched, beyond the stars,
A ship of hope, from ruin far.
For you we fled, for you we fight,
To kindle once more humanity's light.

Erestu's ghost now walks in pain,
But here we stand, where hope remains.
A new world dawns, for you to lead,
From strife and sorrow to break free.

O chosen one, bear high the flame,
For others yet shall know your name.
Though burdens great, your path is true,
The strength of ages flows through you.

We could not save the many, no—
But you shall guide where we could not go.
Fight for the future, fight and stand,
Our love and hopes lie in your hands.

When he had finished, Maramurru returned to his seat.

"I now declare this council open for the discharge of our obligation. Brothers Anshargal and Maramurru, regale us with tales of your triumph."

"Brother Apsu, with pleasure and dignity, I report to our

esteemed council that King Matthiolus, false lord and charlatanic sovereign of the people and land of Obenia, has been subdued, and all that was once his beneath the suns is ours."

There was general agreement at these words.

"Your triumph is well received and should be shared by all who rely on our stewardship," said Apsu.

"A day of celebration—"

"Nay, a *year* is required. The people should share in the achievement of peace," Melammu said, speaking over Shi.

"Agreed," said Apsu, "do we have consensus?"

Shi was the last to acknowledge and conform, following a pause by Maramurru.

"So let it be!" they said this in unison.

"Brother Apsu, I do have an additional matter which I must report," and at Apsu's grant, Anshargal continued, "at the behest of Brother Maramurru's everlasting wisdom, King Matthiolus and company have returned to our shores. They await decision of this council aboard my long ships."

"Why were they not destroyed with the rest of their cities and towns and armies?"

"Sister Melammu, to answer your query, I direct you to Brother Maramurru," replied Anshargal.

"And, so I shall." Melammu shifted her gaze to her younger brother. "Why were the deceivers permitted to live, and why were they permitted to taint our waters with their impudence?"

Maramurru folded his arms across his chest, closing himself off from the others. "Executing their leader, the king, may have pacified those who resisted and continued to wield arms against our Etlu, but we have seen repeatedly the opposite comes to pass. They become emboldened. Radicalized. Sparing the life of the king and his men after their surrender subdued the populace, and now Brother Anshargal may present the world with a trophy of our divine right. Ours is to rule. Theirs is to be ruled. There is no other god but us. *That* is as we have said. King Matthiolus now owes each subsequent day that his heart beats, that his children grow tall, and that his people live to the grant of rights and mercies from the only true Gods."

"Your words are well chosen, if ripe with emphatic deliverance, the meaning is well received."

"So," Shi said, looking from her brother to the rest of her siblings, "we shall sustain them, but where? And, for how long? The remainder of their natural duration?"

"If I may, Sister Shi, may I posit rehabilitating Kurnugi?"

"The Kurn? It's a Third Age relic," Maramurru said, feeling his arms fall away, hanging by his side absent conscious consent.

Anshargal nodded in agreement. "Yes, it is, Brother, but it is also a terrestrial fortress not weathered by time. Given a sufficient force to commence with the labor, the Kurn could be made ready to house the deceivers and other undesirables… perhaps in a month's time."

"What numbers would see abstraction turned to realization?" Mummu asked, her demeanor like that of an eagle perched and prepared to strike.

"If I recall correctly, the work necessary is minimal. I surmise no greater than five hundred would see such a task to completion."

"A thousand may see it done with further expediency."

"Sister Melammu, I will graciously accept any volume of manpower that the council appropriates," responded Anshargal.

Maramurru was furiously beating his nail against the table, chipping tiny rivets into the wood.

Shi interjected her soft-spoken thoughts, "we mustn't forget that however many workers are sent into the Kurn to repurpose it, those men will require lodging, food, water, medicine. In short, it will take a village to complete this enterprise."

Although grateful she had raised one of his concerns, Maramurru did not return the sympathetic smile Shi expressed to him, instead choosing to rifle his fingers through his hair. Maramurru detailed the facilities the prison—as that is what it was in point of fact, and he would not retreat from labeling it as it was—must provide. After some time of negotiation, Maramurru knew he would be walking away with far less than he had wanted, but far more than what would have been offered otherwise, vacant his protest.

"If there is agreement, a work force of one thousand men will be placed under Brother Anshargal's dominion for the prosecution of this project. A relative number of persons necessary to support the endeavor will also be placed under Brother Anshargal's charge. The triumph will be inaugurated once the Kurn has been completed."

Flicking his wrist haphazardly, Maramurru pleaded that time trickle by more quickly and this session would be ended.

"Take charge of your obligations."

Following Apsu's command, they all rose, grasping hold of individualized amulets given to them long ago, and in a single voice they spoke towards the heavens, their voices funneling through the oculus, "we are the Baltutu. Guardians of all in existence. Through our ministry, humanity has grown robust. Through our wisdom, humandom's supremacy is ensured. Ours is an impervious shield beneath which Eridu has prospered. There are none to oppose our will. We are the Living Ones, the Baltutu. And all is hopeless without us."

2.7 AN EVENING IN TELMUN

It was dusk. Nemesis, one of Eridu's smallest moons, was bobbing over the sea, aloft across the last rays of pink sunslight, chased away by the coming night. Muted from this height, the white foam of the ocean bathed the rocks, just as it had for centuries. A trio of tall ships was out on the water anchored just far enough off. Even in the coming darkness, it could still been seen that the dock and rowboat at the base of the Fishermen's

Steps were being pulled and tugged along with the tide. Servants were swarming the grounds, lighting the torches, and soon, as night came down all around them, Telmun was preserved in light beneath this artificial glow.

"Ugh..." said a man's voice approaching from behind Maramurru.

He was a stocky man, the top of his head rising only as high as Maramurru's shoulder, with dwarfish arms and legs—as was common with his race. His hair, blonde and scraggly, extended passed the lobes of his ears; his beard was of the same coloring, but it at least showed evidence of regular maintenance and trimming. The cloak he wore was like the color of wheat, though it flowed behind him more like a pair of angel's wings. A simple blue shirt and checkered pants, brown and mustard, were all that he wore. His appearance was in stark contrast to the fine garments worn by the other viceroys, his mien was more rugged, authentic.

The man brushed a lock of hair out of his face. "How I long to be delivered from their irksome company, by your mercy, my Lord, grant me this one grace!"

"You say that with hardly an air of sincerity or earnest," Maramurru replied embracing his friend.

"I know... my Barum impression still needs work. He made that same damned speech again this evening."

"What passions trouble his thoughts now?"

Unclasping a wooden flagon from his hip, he signaled one of the servant girls to approach. "I drank nearly all my ale listening to him. Thank you," and he released a luxury token onto the platter she carried after having presented Maramurru with a cup full to the brim and found his own refilled.

Her eyes stayed fixed on some point that was nowhere near their faces. "Much thanks, my Grace, my God," and she bowed her head deeply.

She was already disappearing before Maramurru could respond, "I wish they wouldn't do that."

"What?" said the other, his face buried in his mug.

"Hold themselves like that," and he mimicked her, hanging his head.

"She isn't one of yours," he shrugged, "and if she were one of The Great Prince of Heaven's, bowing 'er head is not the only thing she would have done. She might still be kowtowing at your feet."

Maramurru rested his arm against a column, resting his head on the exposed flesh of his hand.

"What is it?"

Another moon, this time Fortuna, was beginning to creep across the sky.

"Look there, Maaschuel!" Maramurru pointed up at the stars.

"The constellation Cassiopeia."

Maramurru was craning his neck upward, tilting off to the side ever so slightly as though in immense concentration and thought, "I tried to build a telescope that would allow us to see back to the beginning, back to where we came from… that was ages ago. Had to climb the highest peak of Panope to do it," he looked over his shoulder at Maaschuel, "the others thought it a grand waste of time. I came close—there's a planet there, not quite so large as Audro, with a great big red spot! Oh, I wonder what they call it there? I wonder if there is anyone there to name it at all…"

"Did you give it a name?" Maaschuel asked, holding his cup around the navel.

"No—but there's another world, encompassed by dense halos of stardust, beautiful layers of clouds, crowned with a blue aurora atop its head."

"And you named that one?"

"Yes. I named it Esh."

2.8 THE CHILDREN ARRIVE IN ERESTU-UR

The sun was rising in the east; the plains were glittering like twinkling stars as the morning dew reflected the first rays of a new dawn. The ox cart was rolling over a bridge spanning the cleft, a river running beneath. Straight ahead were the city gates of Erestu-Ur, and the children, along with Sera, were fast asleep.

Their rescuer, the soldier, rode his horse alongside the cart, every so often peeking over at the precious cargo, a compulsion out of fear that were his eyes to linger too long away, they might vanish. His horse proceeded at a steady, albeit slowed trot. The pace had grown increasingly unhurried the nearer they drew to the city. Gudanna rarely ventured over the beam bridge spanning the width of the river, constructed from parts salvaged from the chariot, rusted in some spots, with bits of paint that had been applied decades before flaking off, but the bridge still stood. Wooden planks had been laid across, harvested from any number of tree stumps left on the banks of the river, and the rubber tires hummed as they skittered across the well-worn timber, polished smooth by repeated and unfettered use. Lanterns, formerly battery powered and now lit by candlelight, hung, one at either end. The morning patrol had yet to pass by the bridge, otherwise those solitary candles would have been extinguished. As their convoy rode on, the solider paused briefly at each lantern, gingerly opening the glass compartment and snuffing out the flame.

A sharp jolt knocked the mind from an unconscious rest back into the world of conscious perception. Maramurru, whose nose and face had been buried in the folds of Sera's garments, winced as his tired eyes were burned by daylight. Holding up his tiny hand over his eyes as a visor, he saw the gates of Erestu-Ur come into view through the thicket. He and all the children had seen the city before, but this time was different. The sixteen-foot gate was inclined towards the city, away from the wilds, and flush with the wall, a composite of rock, stacked at least a meter high in most places, and lumber log erected vertically. Areas near the gate were reinforced with the few panels from the hull of the Margidda that could be spared. A turret mount on either side hung with their barrels pointed at the choke point created by the bridge's conduit and the natural funneling of the trees. He had never actually seen the guns do whatever it was that they were supposed to do, but they had all heard it from time to time back in their village. They sounded like thunder, and if they sounded like thunder, Maramurru thought, that was plenty enough to scare any, especially if they could make lightning, too. The ground here had been paced and trampled and otherwise bludgeoned so that it was completely bare of grass and undergrowth.

As the carts slowed to a stop, Maramurru could hear members of the watch, sitting perched upon their wall, hailing the party as they approached, but the words they spoke he did not know. His mind felt disjointed, disconnected, a mixture of thought simmering over an open flame swirling around the center of a vortex. Next, he knew, there was a low groan as the gears and weights heaved open the heavy gate. The others and Sera were awakened by the mechanical grumble, eyes widening as they took in the sight of humanity's citadel.

In truth, the first and only city of man was anything but remarkable. At the intersection of the Cardo Maximus, which, of the two, was the only one to lead to reaches beyond the wall, and the Decumanus Maximus was the agora, a place where communal, governance, and commerce were segregated from the mostly suburban quarters. Watch posts, marking off different sections of the wall, six in all, were among the tallest structures and their occupants were afforded a decent vantage point, especially to the north where much of those living beyond Eridu's walls who had taken to homesteading and a more agrarian lifestyle resided. Their path along the foot and cart-worn road through the agora brought them to the door of the only building of note, the only building in all of humanity worth protecting, the only building that stood for something.

It rose from the earth, composed of materials of their new home, scavenged and harvested from near and far by the Anunna-Ki and their machines for man, second of their three great gifts. Steps of chalk and limestone, accented by bluestone or clay reddened by the oven's fire, adorned with a crown of greenery held this tower high above the tallest trees in the wood, visible for miles beyond the realm of man. Tapestries were tugged and pulled on at the corners when the wind blew through the city's streets; leaves and the petals of flowers went sweeping through the air, occasionally becoming lodged in someone's hair.

The guards that patrolled the perimeter or stood within small wooden cabins were of a different sort than the soldiers marching alongside their caravan. Soldiers wore a cap beneath their scarlet cowl—but their faces were generally visible—leather armor, and sturdy boots. The Ziggurat guards, on the other hand, had faces concealed behind protective eyewear and metal contraption hiding their nose, mouth, and throat, the fore-head was suppressed beneath a cowl as well, but no armor was apparent as their bodies were covered in a heavy, dense cloak draping well passed the knee where the tops of their dark boots vanished from sight. Their weapons, assuming that is, in fact, what they were, were three-and-a-half-foot long spear-looking instruments, though crafted entirely from a silvery metal and not wood plundered from a tree. The tip glowed the palest blue and was completely invisible in the direct light of the suns. A small lever was situated some inches from the bottom and, given the way they held the weapons, this lever had some sort of important function as their index finger rested upon it at all times. In contrast, the soldiers seemed to be crudely armed, most boasting the same design of short sword; however, their weapons looked as if they were more versatile, suitable as tools and not limited purely to the killing of things.

Grinding the carts to a halt, the Ziggurat guards seemed all too disinterested in the concerns of the soldiers until they noticed the children huddled in the back, then, with great haste, two of the guards nearest the street swarmed the cart while a third struck the butt of his staff hard against a gong, its signal resonating throughout the agora, echoing through the narrow, densely crowded streets, singing a song across the air. With a more aggressive stance than the soldiers were comfortable with, the guards inserted themselves between them and the children; the tips of their staffs now glowing brightly, like a tiny blue sun on the point. Some of the soldiers had instinctively grasped for their own weapons but stopped short of drawing them from their scabbards under the bellowing bark of the soldier who had discovered Sera and the children.

"Stand down! Stand down, men," he shouted; fleeting glances were given to the crowds beginning to congest the agora and surrounding streets like blood at a wound.

Many of the onlookers had followed them ever since they entered the city, each trying to get a good look of the children with their own eyes, and some had even tried handing them sweets and other presents.

The guards then inexplicably relaxed, snapped their heels together, and reassumed their default stance, though remaining fixed near the ox cart. Turning as the pattering of leather on stone became audible, the soldier saw a small congregation racing down the many steps, descending the three hundred feet from the Aura, the highest point of the Ziggurat, a place stretching out towards the home they had left. Leading the group as they flocked to the convoy was another young woman, only a year or two older than Sera. Her hair was of a soft golden hue, and largely tucked away beneath the white headscarf she wore and tied behind her. Her features were gentler than Sera's, the area around her icy eyes was dark, framed with dark eyebrows. There were patches on her neck of redness, consequences of anxiety, fear, the bitterness of not knowing. As she came hurrying forward, one hand clutching a knot of her thistle-hued robes out from underneath her feet while the other kept the scarf and hood of her robe from slipping off her head.

On seeing her, the children all began piling out of the cart, and climbing over Sera in the process. Despite her size, she somehow managed to engulf all of the children in a single loving, relieved, and thankful hug. Kissing each of them on the brow, she then whispered something to each of them.

"Just the children?" she said, brushing a stray strand of hair from her face, she was still kneeling on the ground.

The soldier shook his head as those who had been following her arrived. "None, other than Sera here," and he pointed to the girl, who continued to sit in silence in the back of the cart.

"Her family?"

When the soldier hung his head and Sera remained as inert as the Ziggurat guards, the woman surmised what she needed to. The poor girl had lost everything. Her home. Her family. There was even something in her reproach that suggested that her loss extended to those not bound by kinship but rather juvenile love. She was alone—unlike the children who would pass from the care of the Pedagogue to the golden-haired woman—no family, friends, or love to accompany her in the days to come. There was a sudden tugging at her cloak, "Esh, can Miss Sera stay with us?"

Maramurru was looking back at the sight of the wretched girl, seeing her in such a way made him feel sad. He could see her collapsing in upon herself; the weight of her suffering was beginning to kick, scream, and claw its way to the surface. She had been so brave, she had not even shed a tear nor let slip a subtle whimper at the news of her parents' deaths, but now, here, in the heart of the city, on the steps of the Ziggurat, a tidal wave of cascading emotions descended on her and the rock she clung too.

Rising, Esh smiled down at Maramurru, "I think it's probably for the best—for *all* of you."

2.9 THE REVOLUTION APPROACHES

"You don't speak of her often," Maaschuel said, his cup now empty of even the smallest drop of wine.

Maramurru shook his head. "None of us do, and haven't for a long time."

He turned to stare at the lake and its source, a stone figure of a woman, visible to mortals only by the flickering of lamps on either side. It was life size, but it felt taller than she had been in life, according to Maramurru. The quality of artisanship, in both its sculpting and adornment of various pigments, made it quite the chore to distinguish the marble from flesh, though, and once again according to Maramurru, they had not quite perfected her eyes. He seemed to be the only one who noticed. Her pose was elegant, hair rebelliously poked out from beneath her headscarf and hood of her robe, which was pressed against her form as though by a breeze rolling in off the ocean, bringing the next morning's sunshine to shore. The fingers of her right hand were loosely held by her breast—and if you could manage a close enough inspection, you would find a space between fingers and chest. Her left hand was held at her side, palm up. The right leg, from about the knee, was visible; that same breeze brushed back the hem of her robes to the left, exposing her bare feet to the shallow water emanating beneath the very spot she stood.

"She wouldn't approve of what we've become. Not any of us. It's late. I think it best we both resign ourselves for the night. Here, give us that," and Maramurru beckoned for Maaschuel's flagon, who looked somewhat taken aback.

"What? I have a barrel in my quarters! How am I too empty it if you confiscate my cup?"

Maramurru rolled his eyes, "from the tap if you had to. I'm

putting it out for cleaning. Besides, I'd appreciate it if you were to rise in the morning instead of the afternoon."

Maaschuel surrendered his cup, "I do—this under protest."

"*Protest*? This isn't a democracy."

Putting all jesting aside, Maaschuel looked positively confused, "a what?"

"Uh… never you mind. Another time. Go, rest. The governors are due to arrive tomorrow and I would appreciate it if you were well rested," and he dismissed Maaschuel to bed.

Placing the cups into a wicker basket, he made to head towards the front of the compound where his chambers overlooked the Margidda, still perched on the cliffs after all these many long years, well, what was left of it anyway.

Only after Maaschuel had disappeared into the darkness of his room upstairs did Maramurru slip into the Pantheon.

"Obenia was a success," he said, seemingly to no one, an empty hall.

There came a sudden flash as the face of the Burden was illuminated, the sacred text dissolving, replaced by a pulsating, circular projection. The light spoke.

"Yes… I saw that. King Matthiolus's forefather heeded and nurtured your words exceedingly well. Were you able to preserve the toppled king?"

Maramurru folded his arms. "Yes? Weren't you listening?"

The light flickered, a mark of an irksome question. "…I had to step away. Briefly."

"Is something wrong?"

"There is always *something* wrong somewhere," the light gave a laugh that sounded fairly forced, "nothing that should torment you. I assure you," and it changed the subject without the elegance Maramurru had come to expect, "if Obenia has fallen and Matthiolus taken, then, I trust, you are prepared? Things are about to be set in motion that, once started, cannot easily be… paused."

"The deck is stacked."

"How much have you told him?"

Maramurru's response was delayed by thought. "He knows the plan. Knows his part. I suspect you can reckon the point of his contention."

The circle of light ballooned outward. "Convince him, Maramurru. The road ahead will be arduous enough. A great deal of hardship. You shouldn't have to walk it alone. Frankly, you will need a friend."

"He's ready, Uilliam," and he unfolded his arms, defiantly.

"Then tell him the rest. Revolution is at hand. It has already begun, and they are hopeless to stop that."

2.10 THE NETHERWORLD

Kurnugi. In the tongue of the Baltutu it meant "netherworld". Those who built that place had known it by another name, one that has long since been lost to the world. It stands, even now in spite of the many centuries past, as an imposing site upon the subtropical grasslands, a mountain forged by man, standing well before the mountains of nature some miles to the north and east. The rivers that had once flowed through these lands and supported the people who had lived here had become dry and bare—courtesy of a Fifth Age dam—anxiously awaiting the rain to come with the next monsoon. In the heat, the relics had remained, preserved as though frozen in time. Adornments and pigments had faded beneath the suns' everlasting gaze, but neither rot nor ransacking vagabonds had diminished what had been constructed here so long ago.

It was a pyramid, or, more accurately, a pyramid complex. The Kurn was by far the largest and most impressive. Its golden apex a beacon visible, they used to say, a thousand leagues away. From those purple mountains further north had come the stone encased beneath fine marble ferried up the river from the south, back when there was still water in the bed. Each face of the pyramid saw an amalgamation of raw and polished sapphires running down towards the base and in this light, they mimicked the appearance of waterfalls. Little of these decorative features had crumbled with neglect. Time had been kind to the Kurn.

Three lesser pyramids with summits reaching not higher than a third the height of the five-hundred-foot tall Kurn kept it company here in the solitary grasslands. Similarly adorned though lacking the touch of sapphire, these smaller pyramids were staggered, laid out in a zigzag formation off to one side of the great pyramid. One did not need the ability to soar above in the sky to determine the pattern. Archeologists, someday, might be left to argue the purpose of these monuments, but they would have to be in agreement with the cartographers and astronomers when asked what the pyramids looked like from the heavens. They were a representation of the single most important symbol in the night sky to Eriduns, the constellation Cassiopeia. No matter the religion or philosophy, nearly every culture and civilization that had arisen on Eridu had known where they came from, and many spoke to the day when man would return.

Anshargal remembered coming out with Maramurru and watching the ancient master builders, back when the river looked less like an expansive patch of dirt and more like a deep blue sea. Now, he just watched as people hardly better than slaves toiled under the suns. A canvas and wood village, charged with cooking, washing, and other domestic works had sprung up around the pyramids. Etlu soldiers patrolled the ox cart roads in and around the camp. Teams of five moving as singular units, their movements rigidly choreographed and rehearsed. A consciousness was shared between them, heightening their awareness and prowess in combat... or policing. Their presence ensured that work would proceed with all possible haste.

"I wanted to be... beautiful. We were supposed to be beautiful. We were created to lead others to peace, to end war, to end suffering. They would have looked to us and seen hope. Huh… *hope*… Hope was what we took from them first. We gave them what they needed. Their primal desires satisfied, and now look at them, living like caged animals. We gave them their Eden. We were created to end war and suffering—and end it we did.

"We know all too well the fate that would befall them were it not for our intervention. Time and again the cycle has shown us man seems destined to rise yet doomed to fall. It was their self-destruction which brought our father to these alien shores we call home. It was that same wretched compulsion that brought down the refined and sophisticated into the muck, turning countryman upon countryman, kin against kin.

"But, no more. There will be no more sadness, anger, or envy! The worst of the human experience will be purged from the human condition. The plagues and sicknesses of the mind, heart, and soul will die, beaten out of them, exercised by our righteous devotion. We will remake them in *our* image. We will drag their imperfect beings, if we must, with us into infinity. They will survive. They are going to live on. Humankind shall not perish from this earth."

These were the things the Baltutu had told themselves in order to keep on. False truths, conveniences, and restatements of fact twisted so as to advance their goals, but, over periods of time inconceivable to the average man, those fictions saturated the mind, amassing such a pressure so as to seep deep within the subconscious where truth and lie could no longer be separated.

A courier approached Anshargal's yurt, where he had only just retired. Maramurru was due to arrive in a few days' time and he had grown fatigued in his supervision over the final stages of construction. The Etlu barred her entrance and signaled for an attendant to engage the courier.

"Yes?"

"I come with an urgent dispatch from his Lord's Viceroy,"

she said, bowing her head with the reverence one must show to a servant of a god.

"And… how do *you* know it is urgent?"

"Because, sir, it is a red letter—and those men were sent to guard me." The courier pointed back behind her where five Etlu, whose armor was far too pristine and plated in luxury to serve anywhere but the capital, stood.

The attendant was licking his lips and teeth, trying to remove the remnants of the nectarine he had been eating just moments ago. "Give it to us then," and he flicked his fingers at her messenger bag.

Plunging inside it, the small woman whose cap was at least a size too large for her head said, rummaging through the letters she carried, "sir, you have to sign for it," as he made to take it from her.

Scribbling his name on the parchment form, the attendant took the letter. "Is there something else?"

The courier hadn't run off yet. "Would you like me to wait here for a response?"

"Yes. Fine."

The attendant returned to the yurt. "My Lord, Barumgal has sent word for Telmun."

Anshargal made no move to recognize his attendant. He was preoccupied. A canvas, of fair size, was being rapidly transformed from a blank, empty space into its own six by four-bit universe. There must have been at least a dozen paint brushes tasked with a specific portion of the canvas, a specific facet of the piece. Nearby, hovering several feet above the floor, a palette with the pigments he had made at an adjacent table fueled his creation.

"It is a red letter, my Lord," the attendant said, making sure that he uttered the words with profound respect to the God.

Anshargal turned around and permitted the attendant to hand him the letter, which, in accordance with proper etiquette, was placed first upon a purple cushion in a small basket before Anshargal could retrieve it. Breaking the wax seal, his eyes scanned the contents, and as they did so, the attendant happened to notice that the brushes, although still hard at work on the painting, began to slow, becoming frozen in midair and the palette wobbled. When he was finished, he folded the letter, and placed it in the drawer of his desk.

"Would you like me to prepare a response? The courier is just—"

But Anshargal waved his hand and the attendant fell silent. Walking out from the yurt, he moved towards the courier, who had fallen to her knees, nose mere inches from the dirt.

"Rise."

And the girl rose, though her eyes remained fixed on the toe of her boots.

Reaching into his pocket, he presented the courier with a ceramic token, roughly the size of a large coin, or a small tea saucer; there was a six-pointed star etched on its face.

"This you will take and present to Viceroy Barumgal, and to the Viceroy alone."

The token was pressed into the courier's trembling hand, and she was sent on her way.

2.11 IN CONSULTATION WITH UILLIAM

"I really shouldn't answer that," Uilliam said.

Maramurru imagined a man leaning back, crossing his arms, and shaking his head in a way that conveyed, *"we've been over this"*.

"I'm not asking you to tell me anything that I haven't been able to divine myself."

"No, you're asking for confirmation," Uilliam replied bluntly.

"You've said you have been watching us."

"Well, of course we have been watching you! Transplanting a population from one planet to another is not as easy as one might be inclined to believe. We did not spare humanity from annihilation once just so that it could be permitted to kill itself at some later date."

"…and so, you created us."

Uilliam spoke in a muffled tone, his face sounded like it was buried in his palms, "yes, so we created you, and, if I do say so, the seven of you have done a remarkable job thus far."

"Six."

"Sorry?"

Maramurru massaged his hands. "There's six of us—now."

"That was… unfortunate. We had such high hopes for her."

"How? How have you been watching us? Are there people—agents—on Eridu? You know, I've always felt this…presence I could never explain."

"*That*? That's just your average bout of paranoia; everyone in the universe experiences *that*. No, there are no 'agents' of ours or anyone else's on Eridu nor have there been for quite some time."

Maramurru bit into his tongue. "Are you saying that there's truth to the stories, myths of… encounters?"

"I am afraid that information is classified. As is the information regarding our data collection instruments." There was a modicum of drollness in Uilliam's voice, Maramurru was sure of it.

"It's either a base or observation outpost of some kind, likely on Artorius. Particularly if inhabited. The other moons are too small, barely more than rocks left adrift. But I don't think it is inhabited. I don't think you're *here* at all. I think there is an artificial satellite in orbit, but we would have seen it before now reflecting light from the suns… so it must be *cloaked*… somehow rendered invisible to the eye and light."

"Or maybe we just use an excessively sensitive telescope. If we are finished with these games, Maramurru, I should like to hear how your man received your word."

"You were there." Maramurru was now leaning against one of the Pantheon's tables.

"Will he follow where you lead?"

"Maaschuel will do what he believes to be right."

Uilliam's groan was plenty audible, though he probably didn't mean for it to be. "I hope then that you are a good judge of character. What will you do about the other one?"

"Barumgal?"

"If that is his name," Uilliam quipped.

"He has given me no inclination so as to suspect he either heard or saw anything, but the lack of full confidence was anything but undetectable, not because he thought it not truthful, but because it may… hinder the plan."

"…did you search his mind?"

Maramurru shook his head from side to side. "No. Their minds are too fragile. If I didn't discover what I was looking for quickly, I could have damaged him, killed him possibly."

"Their minds are… *fragile* because you have them spend not enough time expanding their minds. They should be creating culture instead of shunning it. Reading books instead of burning them."

Uilliam was referencing the cultural purge, a process the Baltutu charged their Etlu to perform once an enemy had been defeated. All of their creative works inconsistent with the life-style being engineered by the Baltutu were to be erased permanently from the banks of human knowledge. The works destroyed, burned more often than not. The authors killed outright or worked to death. The students not so far along in their studies would be given the opportunity to become indoctrinated with approved philosophy; otherwise, their fate was less than kind. Obenia was currently experiencing this purification, as the Baltutu preferred to call it.

"I've made arrangements. Their legacy will be preserved."

"Some, but not all. Did you know that, of all of the human civilizations to have arisen, on Erestu or Eridu, theirs was the only to celebrate parents—especially the mother—on birthdays? It is a central theme in much of their art. You measure your own success by the health of your progeny.

"I don't know why we rescued your species, but I'm not all too confident it was out of charity. And I would be in a position to know more than most. In the many questions you have asked me in all these years, you have never asked why I do it—why I act in flagrant violation of my people's own law. Someday, I hope Fortune and circumstance conspire and that you ask me, and, someday, I hope to have an answer for you. You should go. It will be dawn soon. And you have a very long journey ahead of you, Maramurru."

2.12 FLIGHT FROM TELMUN

Maaschuel came thundering in, bursting into the servants' quarters, those servants who tended to the needs of Maramurru. Quickly barring the door behind him, his broad chest heaving, and his eyes nearly the size of saucers, he lingered there against the door for half a moment. With Maramurru away, most of his servants were taking advantage of the reduced workload—not that Maramurru ever sought to put them to exceeding amounts of labor to begin with. Most were here, downstairs, enjoying their leisure time whilst awaiting supper. Though far from proper procedure, it was not unheard of for Maaschuel or another member from upstairs to grace them with their presence. Locking the door was a bit odd.

"Master Maaschuel!" said the chamberlain, who, in all of his subtlety, hastened the downstairs staff to their feet, "uh, what—how may we be of service?"

Maaschuel was breathing ever so heavily. His face was

flushed with red, a contagious rash spreading over his light skin. His body was still firmly entrenched, his palms turned against the wood of the door. His eyes had yet to reduce themselves to their normal size. The servants were quite attuned to the emotional state of their masters upstairs. Empathetic creatures the lot of them. They could sense what was wrong with you before you were ever the wiser. The panic so clearly displayed on his face was being transposed on to each of theirs. He had come here running. Something was wrong.

"They are coming. They are going to take you."

The chamberlain inched forward, the chair standing between the lion and its trainer. "Sir, whatever are you talking about?"

"I need all of you to pay very close attention to what I say. I need you to *focus*. The others. They will be coming down here next. Any moment now. They'll round you up. They are going to ask you some questions. They are going to tell you things. You. Will. Be. Fine. I swear it. And, when they release you, I am ordering you to seek and accept whatever posting you can."

How they had managed to not hear it before, they would never know, but the heavy movements of the Etlu, mountains blessed with legs of steel, were rummaging about upstairs. There were also the muffled sounds of voices, like when someone holds their hand over your mouth. Others were unintelligible screams—painful ones they all thought. It sounded like a right mess up there.

Maaschuel's eyes followed the sounds as the clanging of metal boots changed direction and headed for the entrance to the servants' hall. "Do whatever they ask of you," and he skirted about the space, his intent made plain: He was moving towards the rear entrance.

The chamberlain, still without a satisfactory understanding of what was about to happen, called out to Maaschuel as he disappeared beyond the hallway, "what if they ask us if we've seen you?"

"Tell them the truth, Mr. Davos. I told you to remain loyal to the Baltutu. I've fled out the rear entryway," and his voice trailed off just seconds before Etlu soldiers broke down the door and funneled in, some hauling the servants up to the courtyard while others proceeded to search the hall for signs of Maaschuel.

2.13 THE REVELATION OF ENKIRUS

Enkirus found himself in quite an alien place. It felt like being inside of a tube. The rounded walls were white, but not like any white he had ever seen. No, this was, well... an otherworldly white. He wanted to say it was as white as freshly fallen snow, but that was not white enough. Snow undisturbed for generations atop the highest mountains of Erestu seemed dull in comparison, closer to gray than white. Then there was the floor and the ceiling. Enkirus was not entirely sure that there even was a floor or ceiling. From the surface of the Earth, space was a sea of blackness populated by oases of starlight, beacons of the past calling out to the future. Some believed that the light came from tiny holes whereby heaven shined through. Others, Enkirus among them, thought it more probable that those sources of light be far distant stars and worlds and civilizations, too far removed to ever be known by man. These floors and this ceiling though—were it not for the fact that he could feel *something* solid beneath his feet, Enkirus would have been more than convinced that he was in fact standing among space, the stars, and everything.

"I do not believe I have ever seen someone so sincerely fascinated by our floors."

Enkirus had been so absorbed that he had paid hardly any attention at all to the visitor standing just behind him. This one was different than the others. Whereas they had been truly... exotic, most definitely not of this world, this one was... normal. Perhaps a little taller than the average man. More robust in his stature. His hair was longer than most men considered to be fashionable, at least in Enkirus's part of the world, and, while it was surely a hue of blonde, he could have sworn he saw it twinkle, as though composed from the very starlight that shone in the black floor. The eyes, too, were a combination of the mundane and the extraordinary. If you managed to hold their gaze for a long moment, Enkirus thought that you might see the complete history of time unfold right before you. He also thought that pigmentation seemed to change subtly, a chemical reaction of gases swirling around in a container. With features not too dissimilar from any man or woman he had ever encountered, Enkirus just could not free himself of the idea that the visitor felt, somehow, *more* human, *extra* human.

"I-I-I can understand you," Enkirus said, tapping at his own ear.

The visitor smiled warmly. "It would be an awfully brief conversation if you could not. Would you like to sit?"

No sooner had the visitor offered him a seat, did a chair, the same kind of white, materialize, birthed from the wall.

"Uh… no. Thank you," he replied, staring at the rather efficient looking piece of furniture as it melted back into the wall. "Um, you're not like the others."

The visitor tilted his head, indicating he did not understand Enkirus's meaning.

"You look more like me," and he pointed from one to the other.

"Ah! Yes, we are of distinct species. We—this vessel—were responding to their distress signal."

"So… two species of, of… what should I call you? Both of you?"

The visitor glanced down at the spot where his blue robes met the black floor; he looked to be levitating—probably just an optical illusion. "They are known as the Conservators among my people. To others they are known simply as 'the Grey'—"

"There's others? More than just the two of you?" Enkirus said, quite surprised.

"Oh yes! It is a—there is a much larger *world* out there. Filled with all sorts of interesting people. Not unlike yourself. You have taken your first step, not just for yourself, but for your species. Unfortunately, that step has come too late."

"I don't understand."

The visitor paused. "You were a scientist, correct? A seeker of natural truths. It was you who, through your work, determined that your planet routinely passes through a volatile region of this solar system. Meteors—fragments of a comet which broke apart eight thousand years ago by our calculations—often can be traversed without notice or catastrophe. But you noticed. For years you have studied and taken account—the accounts of balls of fire streaking across the sky from lands both near and far have grown more frequent... not unlike how sand in an hourglass moves more swiftly at the end. You brought this to the attention of your government, to your leaders. You told them of the impending doom that might well spell the end of your species. Your warnings were heard and summarily discarded. And, you became a shepherd, exiled far to the north, on a land in the middle of an ocean."

Enkirus thought he might lose his footing but found himself supported by a staff that had risen from the floor. It glistened and twinkled with all the majesty and brilliance of an unadulterated night sky. "How could you possibly know that? Any of that?"

"The same way we knew the Conservators had become stranded on your planet."

"What... you happened to be in the neighborhood?"

"Not a completely inaccurate comparison," he said this more to himself than to Enkirus, "yes, something like that. We were 'in the neighborhood'. We also have technologies *you* do not."

That much was obvious to Enkirus.

"Your species is facing the second most dangerous threat to its existence: Nature."

This naturally compelled Enkirus to ask, "what's the first?"

"You already know. It would be impossible for me to describe to you how powerful and destructive this impact will be. You are, by several orders of magnitude, underestimating the coming fire and death it will cause. You hominids have squandered your world's trove of resources. Greed for wealth, land, power it has only made you more susceptible to what is coming. Your world is going to die.

"But not all of you have to. You all do not have to go gently into that dark night. You asked who *we* are. We call ourselves the Aeternam—the eternal. I am Uilliam, and we are going to help you, Enkirus. We are going to help your people survive."

2.14 THE TREASON OF MARAMURRU

"I didn't realize you had dismissed the workers," Maramurru said, keeping in lock step with Anshargal.

"Their work was completed. I did not see it necessary to retain them. They have been returned, along with their families, to their communities. With the thanks of a grateful God. Your people can testify as much. I am sure they kept you well apprised."

They were approaching the Kurn, now devoid of the canvas city surrounding its base, flanked on either side by small number of Etlu honor guards.

"Quite. What of Matthiolus and the Obenians?"

"Oh, the high and mighty King of Obenia will arrive once the celebrations of our triumph are completed. We will inaugurate this era of peace with the procession of the unbelievers through the City of the Gods and share the gospel of their defeat to every village within our empire. The Kurn is well prepared for our guests. The meeting with the governors, how was it?"

"It remains to be seen between the two of us, who has had a more… agreeable month. You know how they can be. You didn't miss anything worth retelling," Maramurru said with a chuckle.

The exterior of the Kurn looked much as it had for much of its existence. Some guard towers had been erected, but the intention had always been to leave a minimal footprint in terms of security, as once sealed within, those held inside would be secured for all time. The substructure was fairly hollow and larger than one might expect, sunken into the ground beneath the foundation—a basement of sorts. Channels provided air and a new chute had been installed allowing for regular dispersals of basic food stocks. Another had been built so that prisoners would not drown in their own filth. The Obenians would be left alive, but they were without a doubt being entombed.

When the tour of the areas the Obenians were to call home was finished with the usual amount of balking Anshargal had come to expect from his brother, Maramurru followed Anshargal through the Grand Gallery and into what Fifth Age explorers had presumed to be the King's Chamber. It was not. Not at all. Maramurru and Anshargal had known the ancient builders. This space was *not* a tomb.

It seemed however that Anshargal might have taken to repurposing this space to serve as a cell.

A door crafted from solid godwood planks, the most durable known, had been fashioned and installed, cutting off the chamber from the gallery. Imbued with qualities more often found in skillfully forge steel, mature godwood trees could not be cut down with simple iron axes nor of any other metal. Only when barely more than a sapling while the bark was still green and tender might the precious wood be harvested, hastily worked, then treated by a master woodworker. Sprouts yielded wood no more remarkable than a common oak. Saplings whose bark had begun to darken were prized but demanded a tremendous investment in labor to properly hew the dense wood. Kept damp and out of sunslight, the craftsman would have not a fortnight to shape the wood. Untreated with the proper varnishes, the adolescent godwood would splinter, disintegrating into saw dust in a matter of weeks. When done properly, a door lumbered from a godwood tree such as the one within the Kurn could be expected to last until Eridu's dying breath.

Against the wall opposite the door, shackles had been bolted into the centuries old stone. Equidistant between the wall and the door was a pit; a fire pit had been burrowed into the floor. Another air vent would prevent the ensnaring of smoke and the suffocation of the occupant.

"Is this for Matthiolus? You're putting him here?" Maramurru asked, not sure why his brother had bothered renovating this space.

Neither Matthiolus nor his subjects would have any hope of escaping, not even if they all concentrated their time, effort, and exceptionally limited resources to tunneling or wrestling open the godwood door that would be their warden.

Anshargal ignored him; instead, thrusting a cup of wine into his hands. "Drink with me!"

"And… *what* are we drinking to?"

"To peace! You and I haven't always… agreed on how best to move forward, but we have always respected each other. We don't define one another by our differences, our sometimes-conflicting views. We want the same thing. We all want the same thing."

Maramurru pressed the rim of the cup to his lips. "And what's that?"

"But what else? The safety and prosperity of the human race! They have everything they need under our care. *Everything*. And absolutely nothing they do not. You were by my side the day we ended war for all time. Never again will man be endangered by self-destructive acts. Or natural disasters—not under *our* careful tending. Not even a—"

"Not even an act of God?" Maramurru said, the wine tasting sweeter than he liked.

Anshargal sighed, "we are gods, Maramurru. To them. And we are doing exactly what we were created to do. Save them. From their own demons."

"*And who is supposed to save them from us and our demons*," Maramurru thought to himself, pinching the ridge of his nose.

Maybe it was the conversation or his mood or this place, but Maramurru noticed that his head had started to bother him.

Anshargal leaned back against the wall, crossing one leg over the other, wine cup held about the navel, "remember when we were kids, what, *phew,* you couldn't have been more than eight, and um," he chuckled, "we got into that little scrap."

"Yeah, I do," he said, scratching his tongue on the back of his teeth—it felt a little numb.

"That was a good fight. I shouldn't have been bullying you, but you stood up to me."

"It shouldn't have come to blows. Shouldn't have hit you. Shouldn't have had to."

Anshargal shrugged. "Maybe. I always thought we got along better after that."

Maramurru felt his heart rate plummet. He groped for the wall or anything to brace himself with but found nothing. Collapsing, he rolled onto his back. The edges of his mind felt as though they were separated by miles. His hand might as well have been back in Telmun for all the control he had over it.

"For all this time, for as long as we've lived, we've been more than brothers, we've been friends. Best of friends...."

Maramurru's body felt paralyzed. He was not. He knew that. But he had been utterly sapped of energy. His bones might as well have been replaced by so much lead that not even with his greater-than-average strength he was still helpless. Maramurru just laid there. A fish out of water flopping on the ground.

"It's taratum root. It's sweet—you might have noticed the wine was sweeter than normal—couldn't take any chances. It's the strongest paralytic we know of," he said, sipping from his cup.

"W…w…wh…why?" Maramurru could hardly scrounge up the muscle control to whisper.

Anshargal hung his head in disappointment. "You know why. Because you finally had enough. You were going to stand up to me again. Barumgal saw you one night. In the Pantheon," he paused for a moment, "you and Maaschuel should have been more careful. He heard you—the both of you.

"Damn it, Maramurru! You should have come to us. Summoned us, the moment you were contacted! They may have created us. Fine! But did you ever consider that maybe plunging our entire society into civil war might not be in the best interests of the people?"

There was a sharp crack as the wall Anshargal leaned against split. A sizable gash about a meter in length ran across the face of the granite stone.

"If we're not in charge, their entire way of life is decimated! We have seen it! We. Have. Lived. It. Time and again! Over and over! The same patterns! They rise… only to fall. They *destroy* themselves. The little we do know of Erestu, says our ancestors have done the exact same thing. Absent our guidance, our intervention they are doomed to share the same fate!

"You know almost nothing about this supposed Aeternam. No idea as to his motivations. No idea if he is who he claims to be. But you would gleefully accept revelation and use it as testament to tear down everything we have built!"

Casting his cup aside, where it spilled the remainder of its contents as it rolled into a corner, Anshargal stretched out his arm, fingers extended as far as possible. Maramurru was lifted off the cold stone where he had all the appearance of a dead man. His heels and knuckles dragged beneath him as he was lofted into the King's Chamber. With the twist of his other hand, Anshargal pulled Maramurru off his back so that he could face his brother as he held him suspended in midair.

"You are my brother, Maramurru! I love you! But I never would have thought you'd betray me, betray us," he spoke through clenched teeth, but even in his intoxicated stupor, Maramurru could discern the shakiness in his words and the dampening of his eyes.

Behind him, the shackles sprang open.

"…'hen the others…l…l…earn what…you've…d…d… d…."

Anshargal placed a hand against his brother's cheek delicately. "Melammu cured the taratum root," and with that, Maramurru was flung back, his spine doomed to have shattered were he a mortal man as it collided with the unmovable stone.

The shackles snapped over his wrists. The door was closed. The Kurn was sealed.

2.15 DISQUIET AMONG THE BALTUTU

Apsu, Law Giver. That was how he was known to most. He had always been a stoic man, a modest man, a pensive man. Tallest and largest of his siblings. He had the look of a man who had been carved from a sturdy oak rather than birthed from a human woman. His hair was kept short, not quite shaved, in an unimaginative style. His nose was arguably a bit too large for his face, wider rather than elongated. Brows darker than one might have guessed given his pallor complexion, and his smile was awkward, but genuine—if one could inspire a smile. Because Apsu was the eldest of the Baltutu, he had emerged as the de facto head or king of the Eridun Pantheon in the Sixth Age. Some depictions of him took some liberties… He was often portrayed with a full beard in spite of being clean-shaven.

Anshargal, the Great Heavenly Prince and Baraggal's Throng

or the rarer Saperon. He was more colloquially known as the God of War or the God of Vengeance depending on the circumstances of his arrival in one's lands. Lean and very muscular, he towered over the ordinary, dwarfing them underneath his impressive stature. With hair dark as night, as black as pitch, he wore it a little longer than Apsu, but spiked in the front, giving him a more menacing appearance, particularly in his silhouette—there were more than one statue which interpreted his unique hair style to be a horn fixed atop his head.

Mummu, Life Giver. Her domain was all that in which man needed to feel safe and content. It was her name invoked during the marriage ceremony or during the sowing of seeds in expectation of a bountiful harvest. She watched over and blessed the family and the community. If there were problems in the family, one need only look to the community to give them the strength and support to weather that domestic storm. If there was a problem within the community, every member and every family unit was expected to come together to heal and forgive any transgressions for the betterment of the whole. In assuming this role in the Pantheon, she had adopted the dress of Esh, whom they had viewed more as a mother than a sister. A golden headscarf concealed much of her cedar hair and flowed into the white robes sweeping along the ground, though, unlike Esh, her arms were left exposed from the shoulder. She played this part well, the part of the mother. She did genuinely love man as though they were her own children birthed from her very womb. But no matter how sincere she was or how good she strove to be, she never quite measured up to that intrinsic quality of her late sister. Given the chance to be around her long enough, as only the Baltutu can, one would, from time to time, catch a glimpse of her... imitating it, *it* being that motherly quality one cannot always articulate but knows when one sees it.

It should be noted, and here is as good of place as any, to mention that, for the Baltutu, it was immensely difficult to conceive a child of their own. The Ziggurat of Eridu houses many wonders and treasures left secluded to all those living beyond its grounds. Knowledge sealed away behind stone and metal and what some might haphazardly call magic. The Baltutu, though they each came from a human mother and were of the same material as every human that had come before or since, they were the spawn of sophisticated genetic experimentation and augmentation. Put plainly, they were engineered to be superior. Genetically, they were perfect. Though susceptible to death, absent a more purposeful cause, their anatomy would not only continue functioning indefinitely but also react to the threat of evolving disease magnitudes more efficiently than any other human being. Genetic perfection came at a price: It was almost impossible for the Baltutu to produce offspring.

No, they were not sterile, and the option was always there to interbreed, but the quality of their genetic material was too much for that of the common man to handle. For the female Baltutu, their bodies destroyed the sperm of mortal men as though it were a cancer, rarely giving it the opportunity to fertilize one of their eggs. Any embryo that managed to survive the initial stages of conception had only ever once, in all their years, produced a child that was not still born. That child's life ended at the closing of the Fifth Age.

For males, it was their sperm that was the problem. Effectively, it overloaded the capacity of a woman's egg to process the genetic information. Fertilization itself never occurred in over 99.9% of all sexual intercourse. Twice, and only twice, had a common woman become pregnant, and of those, only one child had been born. For twelve blessed moments, Anshargal had been a father to a little girl.

Melammu, Truth Giver. It was from her divine inspiration man had acquired the knowledge to shelter himself, grow and cook for himself, and build the facilities of infrastructure permitted in the agrarian society of the Baltutu. It was told that after the fall of the last civilization, man had been left to wander the world deaf and dumb, muted in his thoughts and capacities as recompense for his sins against his fellow man and the earth. Melammu fashioned the abridged texts and histories the humans of this Age would need in order to understand their place in the new world. When a need arose, it would be Melammu who would fill it by releasing certain prescribed nuggets of knowledge into their temples and schools. She provided the answers to the questions of the natural world. Only ever the *how* of the thing, never the *why*. Answering *why* questions could be dangerous. Shortest of the six, she was even short by mortal standards, but her authority came not from any physical intimidation she might have exerted, but instead from the confidence that resonated within her voice. It never wavered, never shook. Fear and doubt were as unknown to her as the horseless carriage was to the humans held under her sway.

Suffice it to say that Maramurru was the God of Wisdom and Virtue. A kinder, more idealistic soul than the rest, he had no ego to bruise. He spent less of his time lecturing and preaching than he did stopping and talking to an ordinary person, thus, he was indisputably the most accessible and personable of all the Baltutu. When he would speak and tell the people to live just lives, moral lives, he never discouraged them from sinning per se, but often said, "to do the right thing is to act as you would before your family, your community, and your Gods even when no one is around. If you can do that, if you can go about your day not feeling guilt or regret, then you're doing simply fine."

Shi, Heavenly Life. The Eridun Aphrodite, so to speak. Shi was the youngest of the six and the most innocent, the most pure, and the most fragile. Or so she was in her appearance. Shi was as strong willed as any of them. An analogy for that which she treasured above all else, children. It has been common enough throughout all the countless civilizations they had witnessed—the Baltutu remembered them all—that they all cherished and relished the birth of a new life, the sanctity of it, and how terribly precious and vulnerable it was. That new life was more resilient than most people think to give credit, however. It might seem as though the entirety of the world is a singular monolithic beast biding its time, waiting to pounce, to strike, and snuff it out. And yet, even under incredible adversity and unfathomable odds, these tiny, innocent, unadulterated creatures somehow are imbued with a strength irrespective of their size. Shi was like that. A petite little thing, she was always clutching, hugging her robes to her, presenting herself as a daintier person than she actually was, but, every time adversity had been poised to strike, in an instant, she would swat it down with such ferocity so as to never have to suffer like that again.

As the voices died down and the tension began to clear, these had been just some of the thoughts Anshargal had pondered as his brother and sisters argued.

"It is done! We are committed now," Apsu said, at long last rising from his seat, chair knocked aside, "do not let action cause you to waiver now."

Melammu chimed in, "we were all in agreement...."

That motherly instinct of Mummu's flared up upon Anshargal's return from the Kurn. She was now standing marked in silence.

"We did agree, that's right, but," and Mummu took a calculated step forward, closing the distance between herself and Anshargal, "we do need to discuss how long we are going to keep him in that state."

"I was exceedingly careful. The root of the taratum plant is more potent, but the leaves smoking in his chamber will only release enough toxin to keep him in a fog. Disoriented, concentration will be almost impossible."

"Melammu, we cannot leave him there indefinitely. Eventually it will cause lasting damage," Anshargal said.

Shi peeked her head around Mummu's back. "How long can he survive in there?"

"I was careful!"

"How long, Melammu?" Apsu said firmly.

"There are enough dried palms to last years… but, based on the deterioration of my subjects, for Maramurru, the damage could begin become permanent within a year."

Mummu and Shi's faces flashed with anger, which they hurriedly masked.

"It all depends on how much of the root he ingested—and I was careful!" Melammu barked back at her siblings, feeling their disapproving eyes scold her. "This is what you—what *we* wanted. It is done." She looked to her elder brother. "We are committed now."

Apsu took her meaning, "very well. We must ensure that the leaves are burned only at regular intervals to maximize duration while minimizing any long-term harm. I am confident Sister Melammu can provide your Etlu with the necessary instructions." Melammu bowed her head in thanks and Apsu continued, "there is still the matter of Maramurru's viceroy."

"I'll handle it," Anshargal said.

"And, what of your viceroy, Brother?" Apsu said crisply.

Anshargal's plotting eyes scanned the room. "What about *my* viceroy?" he asked cautiously.

"He has heard things. He knows things above his station," Melammu replied courtly.

"Barumgal knows his place."

"Perhaps we have allowed our servants too much… latitude in their responsibilities," Melammu said.

"Barumgal *knows* his place. He has always been loyal. Not to only myself, but to *us*. He brought that information to us. Not Maaschuel. Not our ever-moral brother. If any of you possess doubts as to the quality of my man, I shall afford him the opportunity to regain the trust he ought never have lost."

The Pantheon was emptied not long afterward. Barumgal had been summoned by his master. When he arrived, he found Anshargal hovering over the Baraggal, just as Maramurru had that night when he had happened by, hoping to derive ancient knowledge and wisdom from the words etched within the glass.

"My Lord," Barumgal said, kneeling at the feet of his God, "how may I serve?"

He rose only at Anshargal's explicit permission. "You will take a legion of my best Etlu. Find Maaschuel. Scour the countryside. If you do not find him there, expand your search. Ride far to the northern lands of his fathers or sail to distant safe havens in countries devout in their affection for Maramurru if you must, but you will find him."

"My Lord, forgive me, but is my place not here? By your side?"

"Your place is wherever I deem it necessary to be. You will find Maaschuel for me."

Barumgal bowed. "Of course, my Lord. It shall be done."

Leaning closer, ever so slightly, Anshargal spoke so that it would be impossible for any would be eavesdropper, "the others question your fealty. It is best, for your sake, that you put some distance between yourself and this place for the present moment," he silenced the obvious questions his servant desperately sought answers to by raising his hand, "I shall recall you if needed, but, otherwise, you are to do as ordered: Find Maaschuel."

"And what would you have me do with him once I find him?"

"Ask him whom he serves. Ask him who his gods are. There can be only one answer. If he chooses poorly—dispose of him."

All expediency was made by Barumgal as he departed from the gates of the Holy City riding ahead the columns of Etlu under his command. Anshargal did not watch but listened as the gates were drawn shut once more from the threshold of the Pantheon.

His fingers touched the cold glass of the Burden, tracing the lines of text, he sighed.

"He needed the push."

2.16 THE RITE OF MANTLE

The Ziggurat was now the children's life. The memory of the Gudanna raid on Kish would always be scarred into their minds; each painful and horrific detail preserved for the rest of their days. Their purpose turned to the fulfillment of the Burden. Their waking moments consumed with nothing other than training. With each passing year, they became stronger, more agile, but their growth was not limited to the physical. Their schedules were filled with exercises and feats that were unequivocally superhuman in the light of the suns. Nights were spent in the library, studying for hours until it was nearly dawn. Sleep was mitigated to brief periods of respite, but never those long, undisturbed slumbers they had known in Telmun. At last, when they each had reached the age of sixteen, the next phase of their training would begin where Esh and the Grand Magister could test the character of the children.

"Good afternoon, children," said the Grand Magister as the youngest pair, Maramurru and Shi, assembled in what the city dwellers referred to as the Temple.

Their older siblings were there, having returned from their deployments for this momentous occasion. Esh, who had not aged a day, and the other magisters were there as well, standing pleasantly as the children approached. A few select guests from the city had been permitted to attend. Councilors from the government, the domestic staff, even some familiar faces of the delivery persons found themselves standing shoulder to shoulder with some of the most powerful humanity had left to offer. As guests of the Baltutu, those societal distinctions counted for very little within the walls of the Ziggurat.

Only two in attendance were not employed by the Ziggurat had attended the previous ceremonies of this nature, and they stood at the end of the aisle waiting to congratulate Maramurru and Shi. They would have broken into a run if the Grand Magister were somewhere else, but Miss Sera and the soldier were not going anywhere. And Miss Sera was not *Miss* Sera anymore. Now, she was Mistress Sera. Her and the soldier had gotten married not too terribly long after relocating to the city.

"Mrs. Sera!" Shi and Maramurru shouted in excitement, unable and unwilling to contain themselves at they neared the pulpit.

"Maramurru! Shi!" she said in pure joy, wrapping her arms around them both.

"Who's this little guy?" Shi said, noticing the toddler clinging to his father's index finger.

"This," and Sera lifted her young son into her arms, "this is Holin. Say *hi*, Holin!"

Maramurru just smiled while Shi touched his plump cheeks.

"*Ahem*... may we continue the reunion after the ceremony?"

"Apologies, Grand Magister," and Maramurru and Shi shrunk back from their friends.

"Thank you... *every two years*..." he muttered that last part to himself. "Maramurru, Shi your training stands completed. None here can offer you more in the way of formal education. We have taught you *how* to think, but not *what* to think. That—is something you must learn for yourselves. That is thus the crux of your final test.

"Before you on this table lay three cards. On each of them is a task that has been solicited from the community to which you seek entry. Take the next few moments. Read each card. Then, decide which task is worthy of your energies. There are no rules. No limitations will be placed upon you."

They both looked down at the cards before them on the table. *Protect the Farm*

A farmer by the name of Enil is suffering from Gudanna raids on his farm. Two of his farmhands have already been killed. The Council has agreed to send a small company of soldiers to protect the farm, but it will be days before they can reach this remote homestead. The farmer has offered a portion of his canned jams and honey, highly sought-after goods in the agora, as payment for aid a Baltutu can offer.

Merchant Escort

Gudanna are not the only dangers out in the untamed parts of this world. Privateers and bandits prey on merchants and vulnerable wanderers on the roads leading to the farmlands in the north. The Council already has guards accompanying each convoy to and from the City, but the presence of Ziggurat colors or even a single Baltutu would save more lives and treasure. The Merchant's Guild has agreed to shoulder the burden of any expedition. In addition, all merchants under the protection of the Baltutu have been instructed to make available any equipment upon request, either by need or compensation for services rendered.

The Birthday Gift

In three days', time, it will be the seventh birthday of a young girl, whose father has recently passed and is now the sole responsibility of a grieving mother. Her mother works long hours but can afford only the family's necessities and no more. She fears that it will not be possible to give her daughter anything to mark the day of her birth or ease the loss of a doting father. The mother concedes that she has no wealth to speak of or influence to promise. All she says she can offer in exchange for the help of a Baltutu is a mother's thanks.

Maramurru took half a step back. "You first."

"You sure?" Shi said, her fingers already pressed against the card she wanted.

He nodded.

"Shi has selected the Protect the Farm card," the Grand Magister announced.

Swiping his card from the table, Maramurru presented it to the Grand Magister, who took it from him. "Ah! Maramurru has chosen the Birthday Gift card. Very well. A representative of the petitioners are waiting for you," and he gestured off to his left, "we shall reconvene just before dusk on the morrow and tell us of your triumph… or failure."

2.17 RESURRECTION

Maramurru was alone. The skin around his wrists grew purple and raw from the iron shackles. Blood had dried and flowed over them so many times, what had once been freshly forged iron now looked decisively rusted and worn well beyond its age.

The King's Chamber reeked of the sour stench of smoldering taratum leaves. New leaves descended slowly, but often enough to replace those having been reduced to ash, often enough to keep the embers going. Had he the cognitive strength, he might have hypothesized that the rotating barrel was operated by a turbine positioned somewhere on the exterior of the Kurn, operating a crank that would shake the poison loose. The smoke created a fog isolating his consciousness into innumerable cubicles where they could hardly communicate. His sole means of preserving what little function he had left were altogether spent on counting the number of times the tiny sliver of light peeking through the air shaft crawled across the floor, marking the passage of a day.

He had counted the movement of a small square patch of sunslight 54 times.

But Maramurru was not only chained by shackles. Despite being long lived, his body required hydration and nutriment as much as the next man. Tubes, connecting his frail form to a number of monstrous vats, ensured that he was readily supplied with water and basic proteins and carbohydrates. The food mush was piped directly into his stomach.

In anticipation of his inevitable need to defecate, a hole of some depth (how far down he couldn't possibly discern in his current state) collected almost all of his waste, swallowing it.

The clothes he had worn hung from his ever-shrinking frame, torn in places where the tubes needed access to skin. His hair had become tangled and disheveled, his face bearded, and his reality confined to the limits of this granite box, greatly diminishing faculties of his mind.

Fortune, however, as bleak and hopeless as it seemed, was in fact, about to sway the currents and send his ship into better waters.

First, the very thing that was incapacitating him—the taratum plant—was, with each passing day, becoming more of a liability. You see, Melammu was still, at her core, as human as any lorded over by the Baltutu and not free from miscalculation. More accurately, she had not foreseen cause for a contingency of prolonged taratum exposure. Her test subjects had been unmodified humans to whom exposure of these levels of saturation would be fatal. Maramurru, too, would succumb in due time. Thus, Melammu diluted the potency. Her efforts to calibrate the poison granted the superior genetics of Maramurru, which were constantly battling the toxin, the opportunity to mutate. With each breath Maramurru took, the engine of his siblings' betrayal grew weaker as his body grew stronger.

Second, the original intendants of the Kurn would be making an earlier than planned arrival given their relentless uncooperative nature. Hardly surprising that the deposed king and his merry men would not want to be paraded around the world as trophies of the Baltutu. In anger, they would be joining Maramurru in imprisonment.

Third, was that the explanation given for Maramurru's sudden disappearance was less than well received by the millions who worshipped him as their principle Baltutu deity or, at the very least, held him and his teachings in highest esteem. In the regions formally belonging to Maramurru, discord manifested as sudden as the savanna catches flame with the slightest spark. Of course, Maaschuel, who continued to elude Barumgal, did what he could to fan the flame of disobedience among the faithful. What was supposed to have been a year of celebration ventured towards chaos.

"Quite the predicament you've gotten yourself into," said a voice.

Maramurru looked up. He was no longer shackled to the wall. He was no longer in that cursed room. He also was not entirely sure where he was.

"Bewilderment doesn't suit you," the voice said again, and its owner strode closer.

"What… who… *who* are you?"

The figure stopped a few feet shy, remaining far enough back that the features of his face, a man's face to be certain, were obscured, hidden, and unknown.

"You don't recognize my voice?"

"Should I?"

"*Remember.*"

Then, with the same immediacy of a bolt of lightning striking down from the heavens, Maramurru knew who that voice belonged to. "Uilliam?"

"Funny, how the subconscious mind works."

"Why can't I see you? I can't see your face."

Uilliam sighed heavily, "what do you mean, you can't see my face?"

"I can't see it."

"Nothing?"

"No… not a thing."

"Hmm," Uilliam said, "I know you have never *seen* my face, but I would have thought you would have invented some sort of mental image of me at very least. Not the most... creative mind."

"So...this," and Maramurru gestured around the foggy space, "isn't real?"

Uilliam shrugged, "it's a hallucination, but that doesn't make it any less real to you."

"But you're not *really* here though, are you?"

The shadow that was Uilliam shook his head.

Maramurru looked disappointingly down at his feet.

"You know, it is a good thing when you can hallucinate again. It means that your mind is beginning to wake up. Did you notice the fog?"

How could he have not? It was dense, thick enough to almost be able to sculpt.

"Did you notice that it is dissipating?"

That feeling of sudden realization returned. Beneath his feet he could feel pressure. The ground no longer was like floating in a pool but was rapidly solidifying until... there was a firm surface under his feet. Boundaries and edges emerged through the haze. Walls. His hands were restricted, held against their will.

"You need to wake up, Maramurru. *They* need you to wake up. Shake off this drug induced stupor and do what you were born to do." Uilliam's shadow came closer. "Wake up! *WAKE UP!*"

Then, on his 57th day, he heard something. No. He did not hear anything. He *felt* something. Later, he would call it nothing more miraculous than a nudge, instinct, an invisible force pushing him to rise. An encouraging touch of a friend's hand. That is what it felt like.

There were no guards inside the Kurn. To be sure, there were a few stationed about outside. Deliveries of supplies would be made from time to time, but those deliveries were deposited through purpose-built shafts, releasing anyone from the need to personally enter the prison. So, when the Obenians arrived, though intended to remain in the substructure, nothing prevented them from touring their stony tomb. On their third day, but Maramurru's 57th, a regular presence examined the godwood door without a nob or means to access. Without much besides their fists to hammer against the impenetrable wood, two things had become clear to Matthiolus: Whatever was behind that door was something the Baltutu themselves were obviously fearful of and that the godwood door was not about to be wrecked down by any of the simple tools at their disposal.

Attempts had been made to communicate with anyone who might be on the other side of that door, but such attempts were futile gestures. There was a fleeting notion, a desperate hope that, just beyond this door might lay a means of escape— whether by more purposeful tools or a passage leading out back into the world, Matthiolus did not know.

That, however, would not last much longer.

Matthiolus came to see for himself whether any progress had come from the efforts of his men. Standing very near the door, he leaned in, pressing his ear against the wood when he thought he heard something on the other side.

"Sire, what is it?"

Matthiolus strained his ear to listen more closely, to gleam some sense of what lay on the other side, "I do not know. Breaking stone?"

The sound the king heard was Maramurru's shackles snapping open while simultaneously being wrenched from the wall.

Then, something smacked against the door, hard. Matthiolus and his men leapt back. The men inserted themselves between the door—danger lurking beyond—and their king, just as their years of training instructed them to. Again, and again. A force of incredible power beat against the door, colliding against the wood. A clap of thunder echoed each heavy-handed blow. A deep gash spread across the middle.

"My liege?" asked one frightful soul.

Matthiolus didn't have time to formulate a response before the door was shattered, an explosion of splinters showering the Grand Gallery. Steam and gas poured out. Hoses of some kind hung from the ceiling, connected to gigantic tanks bolted in place. A narrow strip of light shone down, illuminating a portion of the man's face.

"Oh... oh my God..." was all Matthiolus managed to mutter.

2.18 THE RETRIBUTION OF CY

Esh was not the first, but she was the first of the Thirds. As has been said, the implantation of a genetically perfect human embryo into willing womb, even for ones as gifted as the Anunna-Ki, proved reliably difficult. Many were unviable and never survived to term. The Firsts were consequential in only so far as they established a revised genetic baseline for humanity on Eridu. It was from the Firsts the Anunna-Ki furthered their experimentation. Three of those proto-children indicated success was near yet still illusive. These three unique (but imperfect) souls became the Seconds. Two found respectful stations in society after leaving the Ziggurat. One—he did not adjust as well as the two.

Like his "siblings" he had a variety of enhancements, augmentations making him superior to the common man in a number of ways: Faster, stronger, more intelligent, capable of accelerated healing, a more robust immune system; he was effectively a prototype. None of his abilities were of quite the same caliber as true Baltutu. He further was blessed with a longer life expectancy... but he would not live forever.

Unlike those who proceeded or succeeded the Anunna-Ki's experiments, this particular subject was predisposed to mental instability, a quality exacerbated by rejection. It was not his fault nor was it a fact realized until it would have been unethical to prematurely terminate his existence. His defect, a gradual yet ultimately systemic sickness of the mind, betrayed the futility of ever achieving true perfection. His interpretation of his existence was that of a mistake unceremoniously discarded and replaced. Replaced with *her*. With Esh.

His name was Cy. And now, after many years of justified exile, he returned to Erestu-Ur and he didn't travel alone.

"We wondered why there hadn't been a Gudanna attack in decades—since ever they came for us and our kindred.... Now we know," Anshargal said to Maramurru, peering over the wall at the vast army that had marched on the city.

They numbered in the thousands. Everything in sight north of the wall not set ablaze—obviously they had overcome their rightful fear of fire—was only Gudanna. These Gudanna were not of the same disposition as they had encountered in their adolescent days. There was intention and organization on display, markers of a nascent civilizing mind. Little blue monsters arranged in regiments, as far as the eye could see. Primitive leather hide armor replaced the mud once used to camouflage their bodies. Clubs appeared still the preferred weapon, but slings, hand axes, spears, knives and scrapers revealed further evolution and emerging realization of mechanics. Even siege machines—beyond the skill and knowledge of the Gudanna—had been brought from the depths of Hell.

Maramurru glanced over at his brother. "You do have a plan for this, don't you?"

"The city's defenses weren't constructed anticipating a siege or army of this size," commented Anshargal. "The training and professionalism of the guard will fall to their numerical superiority once the walls are breached."

"It's certain then?"

Anshargal caught the worried gaze of Maramurru. "Let that storm break upon our unyielding rock!"

Scouts, previously dispatched, returned, their ranks fewer. Resistance had been met almost the instance they had stepped foot outside the walls of the city. Fanning out, the scouts sought to measure the magnitude of the Gudanna army and discern the extent of its assembly. The scouts reported the bulk laid to the north, plainly seen, but hunting parties had entered the forest. A breakout was still possible, but only for a short time. The road to Telman was still clear.

Missiles, boulders doused in fire, streaked across the evening sky. Dark, black trails of smoke traced their arc. Much of the bombardment concentrated on the gate, but plenty struck homes, squashing the poor residents huddled inside. The agora was reduced to a sea of fire, the wood and canvas bazaars fuel for a raging fire. At the city center, the Councilors' Tower was the first of the consequential buildings to be brought down, leaving just its bombed-out corpse standing. Neither was the Ziggurat spared from the assault, but each strike produced only a glimmer of light instead of physical damage. The city's two trebuchets near the gate hurled debris back at the enemy. The automatic turrets would be held in reserve until the horde descended.

Back at the Ziggurat, now the de facto seat of government, soldiers were marshaling, leaderless. Mrs. Sera was there, too. Surrounded by her family, though her husband of thirty years, the soldier who had rescued them from the last Gudanna attack of any relevance, had passed on ten years ago. Mrs. Sera, being several years his junior, was thankfully still with them, but, and maybe it was more the present circumstance than anything else, her own health was suspect.

"Sera!" Maramurru exclaimed, making a beeline for her, "you need to get off the streets. Indoors. All of you!"

"Holin's gone up inside," she said, pointing at the Ziggurat's summit, "they summoned him to coordinate...."

She was scared. All of them were. Worst of all though, she had the terrible misfortune of having experienced this all before. In her eyes, Maramurru could see not the woman of almost sixty, but that young woman, barely more than a girl, who had held all of them in her arms as their whole world ended as they hid in a corner of a locked room.

Another fiery rock smashed into a bakery hardly ten yards away, flames erupting through the windows, shattering the glass, and scorching the exterior.

"Please! Sera, you have to—" but his words were inaudible over the growing chaos.

Anshargal grabbed his arm. "We have a job to do!"

"Watch over him," Mrs. Sera said, weeping.

"Get inside! Now," Maramurru ordered, directing them to seek refuge in the lower levels of the pyramid.

Sprinting up the steps, Maramurru and Anshargal strode past the guards without a word. Esh was standing inside, as were Apsu, Mummu, Melammu, Shi, and the fraternity of magisters.

"The north gate is under a coordinated attack—it will be breached. The Councilors' Tower is gone," Anshargal said, informing the group as he and Maramurru entered, "I guess that means you've been promoted, *General*."

Holin gulped nervously. "Are you sure? Are you absolutely certain?"

Anshargal was laying out the Gudanna positions he and Maramurru had observed. "Pretty damn sure. Half the tower is gone. Other half set ablaze." He turned his head to look at the soldier. "If anyone survived and they're not out of that mess already, then they're as good as dead."

"Holin, there are men down there, waiting for you. You are their commander now," and Maramurru paused just long enough for that to sink in, "did you know your mother is down there?"

"Mother?"

Before Maramurru could continue, Anshargal interjected, "this really isn't the time."

"She's inside. Downstairs," Maramurru told him in a hushed whisper, "people are frightened. They'll need a place to go," this he said to everyone.

You would have thought he had just cursed them given the tone of the Grand Magister's response. "You can't be serious! We couldn't possibly take them *all* in!"

"Not all, no," Maramurru conceded, "but there is space enough for many."

"To what end?" pleaded the Grand Magister, clutching tightly to his robes.

"To weather the storm… and evacuate the city, if we must."

The Grand Magister all but collapsed. "A second exodus, you mean?"

"We need to get the people out of the city while we can."

Anshargal put a hand on his brother's shoulder. "Maramurru speaks wisely. We will reclaim our city but not with the people between us and the Gudanna. We're meant to be symbols of hope, aren't we? If humanity dies, not one of us has reason to exist."

Maramurru and Anshargal received Esh's gentle smile in recognition. "Magister, you will open our doors and shelter the people inside. Tend to their wounds, body and mind. Comfort the children."

With a courteous bow, the Grand Magister led his order from the war council to carry out her instruction.

"My Lady, the gate nor the walls were designed to withstand catapult bombardment," Holin stated, a Ziggurat guard approaching in a stiff, inhuman fashion.

"I do not understand how the Gudanna have learned to craft siege weapons and complex military battle strategy," Melammu bemoaned.

Anshargal shook his head violently. "Well, if the cursed creatures have learned to speak, perhaps you can ask them," he said reproachfully.

"Genuine concern: The north gate is breached."

Holin turned to Maramurru. "What do I do?"

"Your duty. Just as your father would."

"*General* Holin, take command of the army," Esh said to him, "I am deploying our guards to reinforce your numbers. Secure a perimeter around the Ziggurat. Spread the word: Everyone is to retreat and find safety here. Go now."

Holin departed with a speed more characteristic of one of the Baltutu.

"The six of you," Esh continued and diverted their attention to her every word, "they will be destroyed and the people, too, if you do not help them. Divert the brunt of the Gudanna away. Give Holin the time he and the army needs. I suggest you don your armor."

Maramurru was the last to leave. He remained long enough to see that Esh was thinking, pondering, her eyes studying the map.

"You know something, don't you?"

"I know many things, Maramurru...." She raised her eyes to glare back at her young brother. "Go, the people are in need of you."

Despite their numbers and newfound organization, the Gudanna were no soldiers. The defenders of Eridu fought fiercely and died bravely. It was a struggle of hundreds against thousands. The trebuchets were smashed and the turrets out of the precious ammunition. Gaping holes in the wall allowed for the Gudanna to pour into the city, flooding it with death, destruction, and all the violence of war. The city burned. Pushed back, Holin, tired and bloodied from hours of exhausting combat, reformed the line in a defensive circle around the city's center, where the dwindling number of soldiers held the line in the shadow of the Ziggurat.

Outside of the city walls, the young Baltutu formed their own circle. Standing close to one another, the Gudanna horde concentrated its might upon them, eliciting their savage nature to subvert their training. Compact, blue-painted bodies littered the plains in scores, cut down with precision. No movement or energy was wasted. Every strike was made with the intent to kill as swiftly as possible. And swiftly did the Baltutu kill many.

To a mortal man, the Baltutu moved in an unintelligible blur. They were simply too agile for the eye to follow. The battlefield moved at a fluid place, but one was always completely aware of the others. If you could slow down time so as to be able to perceive how they moved, it would look less like warfare than a ritualistically choreographed dance, highly technical, but rooted in the conservation of momentum—every motion had a purpose and flowed effortlessly into the next. The bond between them synchronized their movements.

A relentless Gudanna came again and again, and the Baltutu hacked them to pieces again and again. Apsu swung about a claymore with all the ferocity of a tornado, sweeping in all the enemy like a vacuum trying to equalize, where then Anshargal's kopis slashed fatal chunks of flesh from the bone; Mummu, armed with a sturdy atlatl, hurled darts that tore through the soft Gudanna bodies in puffs of red; Melammu twirled a haladie like a gymnast's baton; Maramurru's gladius carved a path of death opposite Anshargal, where he relied on how he could manipulate it through the air by just spinning his fingers, and Shi plucked the string of a longbow with such speed that it might as well have been automatic machine fire.

"None of this will matter if we can't get the people out!" shouted Maramurru over the dying cries of hundreds of tiny blue men.

Anshargal snarled as his blade severed the life force of yet another attacker, "go!"

"Get them somewhere safe," Shi said, flinging up a Gudanna who was then crushed by a heavy blow from Apsu.

"We'll regroup at the Ziggurat!"

And, with that, Maramurru took off, as fast as his feet would carry him, a column of dust, blood, grass, and sweat trailing behind him. The north gate had been smashed to pieces.

Gudanna, too many to be counted now, laid dead, beside many a fine human soldier who had held their line with the utmost devotion to their solemn duty. Fires swept across the city. Black clouds of death and ash floated above, killer angels stalking, preying on the hapless souls. A cacophony of screams, of terror and pain, merged to become a new, more terrible sound. Bodies of the dead were everywhere.

"Holin!"

The de facto commander in chief laid against the wrecked remnants of the Tower, his breathing heavy, and he clutched at a mortal wound. There must have been dozens of Gudanna piled around him; many more times their number had been killed than his soldiers, who had so valiantly given their lives this day.

"You… ya… you need to get in there." Holin winced with every labored breath he took.

Maramurru dropped to Holin's side. "I've got to get you out of here."

Maramurru's eyes scanned for the source of the bleeding.

Holin gripped his hand with what little strength he still possessed. "…not going… anywhere. Not on… this earth… *argh*! Inside. You must get inside!"

"The Gudanna? Did they—"

Holin gritted his teeth and wagged his head, "no… not… not Gud… Gud… man. A man. No more Gudanna in the city… huh… uh… dispatched my men south. With survivors."

"I can't just…" Maramurru did not want to finish that sentence.

"…yeah, you can. You have to…" and with his eyes fixed over Maramurru's shoulder, the light dimmed in Holin's eyes and then his head fell downward.

He was gone.

On his tear up to the top of the Ziggurat, Maramurru paid hardly any notice to the guards lying dead and dying from the base to the summit; their bodies were everywhere. Charging,

Maramurru transferred such great quantities of kinetic energy through his shoulder and into the door that it was not knocked from its hinges but disintegrated upon contact. He stood there, in the Gansis Fenna, glued to the spot.

In the room where he and all his siblings had been greeted and accepted into society at the conclusion of their training, Esh was locked in a frenzied battle. In one hand, she wielded a sword, similar in type to Maramurru's but with elements undoubtedly alien in origin, in her other she whirled a guard's staff, ejecting from it flashes of blue lightning at her attacker. Her attacker was a great beast of a man, a bear armed with a sword instead of claws, he towered above her comparatively Lilliputian form, a black cloak bellowing behind him as smoke did from a fire. He knew none of her agility or grace, relying on brute strength—for he had much of it. Each swing came with a shower of sparks. Each swing came in tandem with a hideous grunt escaping his lips. Each swing left a gash in the floor and walls.

The beast's roar resonated deep within and when unleashed, it struck Maramurru like dragon's breath in the old stories: "*AAUGH!*" It was Cy.

Maramurru clenched the hilt of his sword tightly beneath sweating fingers. Esh shot further bolts blue light into the behemoth, the tip of the staff pressed deep into his bulk. Maramurru felt Esh's eyes come aware of his presence. Ratcheting back his hand, Cy smacked Esh hard across the face; his other hand slaved to his broadsword. Lifted clear off her feet, Esh twirled in an uncontrolled maneuver over the map table, landing on her back. Blood trickled from her nose and mouth; a gruesome, purplish mark covered half her face. Upending the table, the barbarian staggered towards Esh. The staff had rolled away somewhere. Her sword sat in the palm of her hand, but she lacked the consciousness to take hold of it. By the time she did, it would be too late.

Brooding over her, the brute snapped her wrist just as she made to bring the blade to his neck. As she yelped in pain from the break, all the air was suddenly pulled from her lungs as the edge of his sword pierced her abdomen. She had this look of being stupefied as her head slid back and Maramurru collided with her killer.

But Maramurru was sufficiently lacking in mass as opposed to his foe, barely knocking Cy back, and he regained his footing quickly so that when Maramurru swung, the attacker was able to bring about his full weight and strength behind it. Maramurru could do nothing to stop his sword from sliding out from under his grasp. Ducking beneath the next swing, Maramurru pivoted around, felt the hilt of a sword by some other means appear between his fingers, and drove it where the neck meets the shoulder. With all of his superhuman strength, Maramurru plunged that sword through all of the bone and muscle and fat. He could sense the vibration in the metal as the spine and vital organs were destroyed. Then, as though pulling the sword from deep within a stone, Maramurru wrenched it out, allowing Cy's body to crumple and die.

Esh was not gone, but she did not have much time. The injury was serious enough that even with her healing abilities the body would be dead, and the mind lost long before the cells could do what needed to be done to regenerate. She did not say anything. She could not say anything. All that she could manage was to lie there in relative peace in Maramurru's arms as tears streamed down his face, pleading to the Universe to help him save her. He knew neither the skill, medicine nor magic to accomplish this. She smiled at him.

He had no idea how much time elapsed before he seized himself back to reality. With Esh laying across his arms and her sword still freshly baptized in the blood of her killer, Maramurru carried her down from the Ziggurat where her brothers and sisters stood, unaware of the grief their brother carried with him.

For a time, Maramurru and the Baltutu were consumed by inconsolable rage. Their retribution was terrible and swift. Gudanna did not survive long after that.

2.19 GOD AND KING

"You can't be serious, Deceiver!"

Maramurru accepted another bowl of a porridge-like substance. Using a piece of stale bread as a utensil, he fed his gaunt form while 133 Obenians looked on. He figured they had never seen one of the Baltutu eat before. Tearing off another chunk of bread, Maramurru nodded his head.

"You are overstating how much good will you have bought yourself. I have ordered my men not to kill you. Any debt I owed you, you should consider repaid."

"I am not interested in debts, Matthiolus," and he dipped a ladle into a bucket of water.

There were murmurs of discontent amongst the Obenians.

"They still consider you to be their king. Out there, however, Obenia has no king. The Baltutu will rule your lands with an absolute and incontestable resolve. In one hundred years, the people living there will remember you only as the Baltutu want you to be remembered. No songs other than those praising your defeat. No namesakes because your name is too vulgar. And the only time they speak of your… *struggle*… will be when they invoke damnation on your memory for defying the true gods. That is what awaits Obenia if you refuse to help me." He took another long drink. "Perhaps you have not realized it yet: I am your only means of leaving this place. When I leave, I can go with or without you, but, if I'm to do what needs to be done, I would be personally very thankful for your assistance."

The deposed king stood there, listening. There was an uneasy acquiescence hovering over the room.

"How could I be expected to trust you?"

"You shouldn't. Not yet. I'll have to earn your trust just as you will have to earn mine. But… that being said… your grandfather, Manthilous, did. Enough to commit yours, your father's, and your country's destiny to what I asked of him. The same thing I am asking of you now. The continent of Laud was the last bastion of defiance. While not quite free—don't believe for a moment I condone the monarchy your forefathers perpetuated— the people of Obenia and the surrounding lands haven't been deprived of their expression. Their thoughts are still their own. That… philosophy I should earnestly hope to share with the world and rekindle humanity's latent spark.

"And I am offering to break you out of prison—that has to count for something, doesn't it?"

2.20 ROUSING THE NORTH

Deep in the woods of Antelmar, far to the north of the Avalonia continent where the skies are of a perpetual gray, about a mile from the little village on the frozen stream, did Maaschuel stand in a Thing of lawspeakers. The place of the Thing, the Thingstead, had been used sparingly since the ancient times, since before the Baltutu. The trees here were old; even the youngest of them were older than the ruins that laid beyond Telmun's walls. Leaders from half a dozen communities had answered the call to assemble, though fewer knew why. The viceroy of one of the Gods, Maaschuel, First Servant of Lord Maramurru, had come the many thousands of miles north. Even the most stubborn of men knew to make themselves available when summoned by a herald of a god.

The folk of the Antelmar were a hardy people. Once golden haired and fairer skinned people, their ancestors had come to these cold and wetlands at the top of the world long ago—their decaying constructions, overgrown with nature, could still be spotted in more open areas. Their traditions spoke of a time when the air had become toxic and yellow clouds of poison drifted through these very forests. They fled further and further north, until they reached a point where the snow rarely melted away entirely, the sunslight was dim, and glaciers stood like pillars supporting the sky. Survivors settled where the climate was harsher than further south, but produced workers, men and women not the least bit afraid of labor. They were an industrious people, inquisitive and loyal.

Maaschuel had finished speaking, and the gathered lawspeakers had ample opportunity to listen and digest what their kindred had to say. He had said many disturbing things.

Most expressed anger. Anger for the charge of treason leveled against the Pantheon at-large. Anger for willful heresy and sedition against the Gods. Anger that it might all be true. Anger that, above all, not just their God, but their friend, Maramurru, had been complicit in a conspiracy to lie to them, manipulate, and prostitute them.

"So, you would leave him there?" Maaschuel asked, the frustration in his voice clearly rising.

"If t'is story you have told us is true, might it not be such a terrible t'ing?"

Mumblings of agreement spread like a plague.

Maaschuel scratched his scalp, rustling his long hair in annoyance. "What crime has he committed?"

"…treason…" another said, as though this question were ridiculous.

"Against *us*," Maaschuel restated dismissively.

"He lied. Our sacred trust betrayed!"

"Ah!" Maaschuel cried, approaching an elder man, "he lied. He *lied*! And, so, a man is condemned to life imprisonment? Say you do leave him there. A man who has not just treated our people with unrivaled benevolence, never asking anything of us, not goods, or women, or blood, or even worship. A man who lets us retain the practices and beliefs of our forefathers. Yes, he lied.

They have all lied. He never asked us to believe. Never punished the overwhelming number of our people who do not—in truth—hold the Baltutu in our hearts as our *true* gods. All he asked of us was that we keep the peace, and he would protect us.

"I put it to you all: What will happen to us now that he is gone? Hmm? What of our children? Our beliefs?" He thumped his chest. "I know the others did not approve of the autonomy he permitted us. What do you suspect they will do without our advocate fighting for the *old* ways? Anshargal will march legion after legion of Etlu soldiers into our villages and he will not depart until our spirit is broken—and it will break… eventually. I have seen it done. His viceroy is already here. Scouring the countryside.

"If we leave him to waste away in the Kurn… if we allow him to die, our culture will die with him. We will lose all sense of our identity. We won't recognize ourselves. Yes, he lied. He lied, but I can't help but believe in him. Not because of what I've seen him do. I believe because I know the *man*. I have known him my entire life. There *is* a divine spark in him. It's a spark that exists in all of us.

"He is offering us a future. A future of our own choosing. A future free of false gods. A future where a man, a woman writes their own destiny. My brothers and sisters, any possible hope we have lies with him!"

Silence filled this small section of the wood for a long while. The lawspeakers shifted eyes, having listened to Maaschuel, and mulled over what he had to say. Finally, Folcher, the lawspeaker for the village on the frozen stream, who had heard and listened absent any need thus far to participate, lowered the fingers previously steepled underneath his chin to his side and rose from his seat by the fire. The leather overcoat he wore shimmered as the light from the flames consuming the logs reflected off the thin layer of dampness that seemed to exist perpetually on everything. He was built like the trees surrounding the glade; tall, the tallest Antelmari Maaschuel had ever seen, and sturdy, a cask of ale would not be enough to knock him off his boulder-like feet. He had a weathered look about him. His face was accented by bushy eyebrows and a thick beard, the same color as the soil. His hair was darker than most, though a few strands of gray hinted at his age, and he wore it tied tightly behind him. His eyes were small, dark, and sunken into his cheeks—a fire could be seen inside of them, but whether it was just a reflection or something deeper about the man, Maaschuel was not yet sure.

"If ve are to do t'is, Maaschuel, it cannot be for sentimentality," Folcher's voice seemed to bellow out from somewhere near his stomach, resonating in his throat, and passing over his lips in a tone so low each man assembled was compelled to give him their absolute attention, "ve do t'is for t'e future: Our children. For children efferyvere. T'ere can be no doubt. None at all. Maaschuel, you ask us to stand against angels, men masquerading as gods. If you say you belieffe ve stand a chance, I vill belieffe you."

Maaschuel tugged on his wheat-colored cloak as a soft rain began to fall through the canopy of leaves and needles immobile high above. "I do. Truly—but only with his help."

Rays of sunslight pierced the dense cluster of trees as the suns fell away and night approached.

Folcher nodded his gargantuan head. "Fery vell."

"Barumgal is already here! His fanguard blocks t'e roads. T'ey are looking for you, Maaschuel. Hunting."

Maaschuel turned to Folcher. "The revolution has to begin somewhere. I can lure Barum away from the village. Send me away with a few good men—riders. You'll be free to throw off your bonds. Then, gather as many fighters as you can. In thirty days, meet us at Virescent."

Folcher grunted approvingly, "have Oda ready her forest horses. T'ere is not a better rider for a t'ousand leagues in any direction. She vill ride vit you. Ve vill do for Maramurru as ve vould do for any of our kinsfolk. He may haff lied about vhat he is. Never t'ough about *who* he is. Ve are Northerners! Stalvart and true. A better friend you could not ask for," his eyes fell to Maaschuel before he walked over to an old stump and pulled his axe from it, "and a better friend to the Antelmari, ve haff neffer had," and he offered the woodcutter's axe as a token of friendship and agreement.

Leaving the cheers of the lawspeakers behind, Maaschuel jogged out from the tree line towards the village and stable, relieved, when an unsettling and shrill cry shattered any emerging sense of calm that might have been descending on the small northern town.

"Maaschuel! MAASCHUEL!"

He deadened his pace to a complete halt.

"Stand down!"

The voice grew louder as its owner drew nearer, his mount approaching at near a full gallop. Twisting around cautiously, his hand hovering preemptively over the hilt of his sword, Maaschuel watched as Barumgal, flanked by two Etlu, one presently holding a lantern, came to swarm the place where he stood. Astonished, he had not noticed it before, but wails of panic were coming from the village. The Etlu were surely conducting door-to-door inspections, searching any and all conceivable places Maaschuel may have been hiding.

"Throw down your sword," Barumgal barked; even in the pale moonslight and over the echoing cries of fear, it was obvious this was a man red with anger.

He dismounted a horse not too dissimilar from a Friesian. The two Etlu remained fixed on their mounts, though only one had drawn his weapon.

"You know I can't do that, Barum," he said, inching slowly backwards.

Night had fallen fast, but he could just make out faint movement along the tree line with his Antelmari eyes.

Barumgal held his sword tightly in his hands, a sosun pattah, a type of curved blade common in the region of Humar, belonging to Anshargal. "You will disarm! You will return, with me, to Telmun!"

"I'm not going to Telmun. Someday, maybe, but not today," he said with a cheeky grin.

Barumgal was absolutely flustered. "Why? Why would you —either of you—be willing to up end the entire world? You and I are educated more than most. We know what comes from war. Our civilization stands on the edge of oblivion! It is order *or* freedom, you cannot have both! Are you really so selfish as to risk everything we have?"

"If something is worth having, then it is worth the risk. Any risk."

"Our Lords have delivered us from suffering!"

"Into cages! Animals locked in pens. We wake, eat at a trough, work in the fields—growing more food, then we sleep. Waking just so we might do it again and again."

"No crime, no poverty, no violence done or against any other," Barumgal spat.

"No freedom, no thought or ambition. We are sheep herded from one pasture to another. Flowers in a garden to be pruned then left alone as decoration. We are pets. Slaves to their whims and egos."

Barumgal laughed mockingly. "Slaves? You think us slaves?"

"They needn't work us to death in order for us to be slaves, Barum. They use us. Limit us. They keep us trapped in our own minds—"

"Oh, now we are prisoners! You are no revolutionary, Maaschuel. An insurgent perhaps, but nothing so noble as a revolutionary. I ask you this, one last time, lay down your sword and return to Telmun."

"War is coming…."

"…but it doesn't have to!" Barumgal begged him.

"Barum, it may never be again so incontrovertible in all of human history yet to come that war was inevitable. I am sorry, but I will not go with you."

"My instructions were to end you, should you fail to see reason," he said with a nominal sigh.

"You'll forgive me then, if I resist."

Barumgal hoisted the curved blade high above his shoulder, then chopped through the frigid night air, slicing through the mist spilling out from the river. Maaschuel expected this, knowing that Barumgal would have to slash rather than stab, so he ducked down low, anchoring himself with his left foot, then spun out and around, and as the tip of the sword cut through the spot he had been standing a second before, Maaschuel thrust his elbow into the back of Barumgal's head. He splashed into the soggy ground, delirious and momentarily paralyzed. That was all the time Maaschuel needed. Releasing the axe just as he knocked Barumgal aside, the Etlu holding up the lantern was knocked clean off the back of his horse as the axe became imbedded in his neck.

The second Etlu managed to fire off a shot from his cross-bow, but it was wasted in the dark. Pulled from his saddle by a pair of strong hands, the Etlu flailed as a sharp sword point pene-trated him under the arm.

There was rustling in the grass just behind Maaschuel. Barumgal hacked at him again, eyes ablaze with fury, his face muddied. Their swords clashed and clanged. Maaschuel made a conscious effort to limit the number of blows intended to be fatal, Barumgal, on the other hand, hit him with as many as his disoriented mind could muster. He was a taller man than Maaschuel and he leveraged that fact as he sought to beat the man into submission. It was all Maaschuel could do to just deflect the fast-moving blade.

Finally, Maaschuel landed a strike that gave him a moment of reprieve. Forcing Barumgal's point down, he cocked his left fist, and swung at Barumgal's face with his fist, who returned in kind with a strong, backhanded punch.

"Take your men and leave these lands," Maaschuel ordered as the villagers marched on their location, it looked to be the whole of the town, disarmed Etlu leading the way, their heads hung in defeat.

"You have started a war with the Gods!" Barumgal yelled back; he had a rabid look about him now, spit dangled from his lips.

The Etlu folded in behind their commander, whose mind was not so jumbled that he could not recognize when he was outnumbered and defeated. Keeping his sword drawn, he mounted his horse without ever taking his eyes off of Maaschuel.

"I will wait for you at the Kurn!" and with that, Barumgal led his Etlu out along the winding forest road.

Folcher approached a weary Maaschuel, a slight trickle of blood running out from a split in his bottom lip. "Oda can lead you by ways known only to Antelmari. Roads known not even to you. She will help you reach him before Barumgal."

Oda and three of her best horsemen and women stepped forward, leading their mounts. They had dark coats, reminding him of the chocolate he enjoyed in Telmun, and manes long and lovingly groomed, a sort of faded blonde color.

"Ohlin. He'll have gone to Ohlin first. From there, he will send word to Anshargal and the others. When they attack Antelmar and the northern territories, it will be from Ohlin," and he mounted the mare Oda had brought him, "normally, there are less than a hundred, maybe only half as many Etlu there. But the Ohlinine will answer Barumgal's call to serve their Lord."

"Ve vill do vhat ve must," said Folcher, already discharging runners to the other villages.

"Around the neck, under the arms, and back of the legs.

There is no armor there. Don't engage them head on. Attack from the sides—"

Folcher touched his shoulder. "Go! Ve vill see you again."

"At Virescent," he said, as Oda and her riders began trotting back towards the forest.

"At Firescent."

2.21 MARAMURRU NO MORE

The boulder sealing the entrance to the Kurn might as well have been a mountain.

"Oi! Thought I saw it wobble a bit."

"I thought you said you could move it," Matthiolus said disparagingly, arms crossed, watching as Maramurru attempted to shove the rock the size of a small island aside.

"You are more than welcome to help push," he said, his breathing a little strained, sweat forming along his brow.

Matthiolus almost broke out into hysterical laughter. "I am a king. I don't *push* things."

"Were a king," Maramurru corrected.

Outside the Kurn, Maaschuel pulled his sword from the breast of a slain Etlu guardsman. A splatter of scarlet, thick and dark, followed it then seeped into the thirsty soil. Oda and her riders were salvaging what weapons, armor, and other materials they could. Several carts and wagons were parked near the guards' barracks. Presently, they were being readied to haul men and treasure as soon as they figured out how one breached a pyramid made of stone. They did not have to wait long.

Maaschuel had not been standing surveying the door for long, holding his hand over his eyes to block out the suns, when he felt a powerful force cause him to stumble. Deep cracks formed half a moment later, the result of an invisible pickaxe delivering a decisive blow. Half a moment again, and Maaschuel barely had enough time to heed the warning, as his instincts shot through his body. Leaping as far to the side as he could, the door was not just moved, it exploded. A boulder, once arguably large enough to be one of Eridu's four moons, was ejected into the air as a hundred million pieces. Dust poured out next. Maaschuel was covered in the stuff, lying on his back.

A man materialized, kneeling beside him as the dust settled. "You can't very well fight a revolution on your back."

Maaschuel panted. "A little trouble with the door?" he asked, propping himself up on his elbows.

"Eh… you know how it is," and he helped pull Maaschuel to his feet.

"Actually, I've never been in prison."

"There's still time."

"It's damn good to see you," Maaschuel paused as a procession of Obenians, led by Matthiolus, came walking into the intense light of Gerpedon savanna. "Uh… made a few friends, have you, Maramurru?"

He winced at the sound. "We're… working our way up to acquaintances. And I'd prefer if you didn't call me that anymore."

Maaschuel cocked an eyebrow. "Um, what should I call you then?"

"Well, I've given it some thought. I was sort of thinking… Holindrian."

"Uh huh… 'Holindrian'? Invoking Hollins of Hadria, eh? Well, you look awful. Let's get you and your new 'acquaintances' on the wagons and out of here. Barumgal is only a day, maybe two, behind us."

PART 3
THE HUMAN REVOLUTION

3.1 RISE TO REBELLION

Maramurru had not taken more than a few steps when something caught his eye. A falling star shot across the night sky, a trail of silver starlight chasing after it. He followed it with his eyes, watching it streak high over Telmun and towards the sea. He then saw something else. He could just barely make out a light coming from within the Pantheon, whose doors were left open. The light, or its source, was… moving. He thought perhaps someone was in there holding a torch or lamp to illuminate their way, but none had business within so late at night and the fires here did not burn turquoise. Peering over his shoulders and seeing no one, he stealthily crept forward, taking great effort to ensure that neither his presence nor movement would be sensed by whoever was searching the hall. As he drew closer, he heard nothing from within and his hearing was characteristically Baltutu (in other words perfect), but no voices or pattering of feet could be heard. Not even the faintest trace of breath. All sounds other than those of nature were absent.

The heel of his boot was on the verge of making contact with the stone, when a voice called out to him from inside, "it's all right. I've been waiting for you."

Upon entering, Maramurru was greeted by… no one. There was not a soul to be seen, and the space did not want for light as the dome's aperture permitted a wealth of moonslight to wash over all that was beneath it. Taking a moment to search, though there were too few places one might hide, Maramurru was mystified as he awkwardly said, "hello" to a seemingly empty room.

"I'm over here," the voice said.

"Where?" and Maramurru spun around, hearing the words come from behind him.

"Here!" and the Burden began to pulsate with light, a beacon signaling him to approach. "I was beginning to fear you hadn't internalized my message."

He was now standing directly over the altar, where the palm-sized piece of rectangular glass, which had only ever contained the same 63 words, now glowed with text he had never seen before but somehow instinctively felt that he understood—if only partially. There was also a small red icon on the glass, but he did not know what that was for either. Speaking to an inanimate object like this was not at all normal.

"Message? What message?" His subconscious suddenly thrust a thought to the forefront of his mind. "Oh! *For you we fled, for you we fight, / To kindle once more humanity's light*?"

"Yes!" said the voice.

Maramurru shook his head. "I was on my way to bed.…"

The voice gave a disapproving sigh. "I saw that… had to put one of our suborbital probes into an uncontrolled descent to get your attention."

"That wasn't a meteor?"

"No," the voice responded matter-of-factly.

"Who. Are. You?" was Maramurru's only reply.

The light dimmed slightly. Were a person standing before him, he might have thought they were hanging their head in vexation. "You know what I must be. I cannot be anything but that which you already know I am. Your people believe us to be gods. You and your kin know us to be your creators. Enkirus called us *Anunna-Ki*, those who from heaven came to Earth, and I must speak with you now at the turn of the tide."

What otherwise might have been a moment of extended silence was punctuated as the voice continued to speak.

"I have indeed seen the misery that has been wrought upon the humans of Eridu. For two thousand generations, but never has it been so great as under you. Too long have those whom you perceive to rule suffered beneath the weight of your oppression. I come to you now because I am concerned for their wellbeing and future. I come to you now because it is only through you which they might be rescued from their current plight and be delivered into the empire of dawn. You will go and do what we meant you to do. Our work saved the human race. You will save the human spirit."

The silence that had been interrupted before now fell like a curtain, snuffing out any capacity Maramurru had to respond. He was processing. His mind was aggressively trying to apply context to what he was hearing, to what he was being told. A voice, asserting itself as one of the Aeternam, was here, speaking to him, telling him… things. *"Never has it been so great as under you."* The voice obviously meant him—he and his brothers and sisters, the Baltutu. *They* were responsible for the apex of human suffering? But how, how was that possible? The memories were as clear and as vivid to him now as they had been during the moments in which he had lived them. A witness to a multitude of human evils; the abuse and exploitation of young children, the inexplicable cruelty done against animals, cultures propagating rape and violence and intolerance, horrifying acts committed against the dead, persons hewn and violated for sport. This and more he had seen, and yet, according to the voice, the Baltutu were guilty of worse crimes.

These ills had been purged from humanity. If there had been any benefit under Baltutu rule, it was that these vices which plagued the human heart were utterly absent from the men and women inhabiting the Sixth Age. Crime, both violent and petty, within the Baltutu realm was not only nonexistent, but unheard of. No citizen would ever, even for the briefest of moments, tolerate a thought of harming the welfare of his or her fellow man. The theft of a neighbor's goods was a theft of the community's labor. When you stole from one, you harmed all and you shamed all. It was a source of pride among Maramurru's brothers and sisters that the violent impulses which drove one to kill, maim, or abuse another seemed to have been suppressed, perhaps even bred out of the composition of man all together in due time. When victory is achieved over Obenia and its line of kings, the very thought of war itself as an institution would seem to stand on the precipice of extinction. The idolized peace so many had often spoken of at long last seemed to be within the grasp of man, to finally be obtained, maintained, and preserved for all time.

And, as if the voice could perceive his very thoughts, it continued, "in spite of all that you are, all that you have learned and achieved, you remain stunted. Your persistence that oppression exists in only one form, the physical domination of one will over that of another, is archaic and evidence of an imperfect mind—but we did not create you that way. You, Maramurru, are guilty of a crime far and away more egregious than your Baltutu kin. You are guilty of being blind, not because you have been robbed of sight or reason, but blind by willful submission.

"The progression of the human spirit remains as steadfast as a ship anchored in the harbor. Every son and every daughter born today is condemned to die in a world absent ambition and adversity, a purgatory damning their infantile souls. The oppression you have placed upon them is not oppression of the body, but of the mind and spirit; you have stunted the maturation of their own consciousness. There are few acts of villainy so abhorrent as the deliberate limiting of the mind.

"You all have misinterpreted your purpose. We did not create you to rule."

But then, Maramurru did something the voice did not expect. "What would you have us do?"

"I am not interested in your collective. I do not trust it. I am interested in you, and you alone."

"What would you have *me* do?"

When the voice did not answer him, he said, "nothing that you say I can or dare protest. You're right, of course you are right… I-I gave up; I capitulated, acquiesced to their demands. I couldn't refuse them any longer. I was tired of it, tired of seeing the same patterns of evolution followed by periods of dissolution, unable to stop it—too ignorant to stop it. I've turned a blind eye towards the things we've done to preserve security at the expense of liberty. So, tell me what you would have me do, how might I redeem myself and my brothers and sisters? How might I redeem humanity? Tell me and you shall see it done."

There was the distinct sound of a person exhaling a deep breath, in preparation to take a great plunge. "Eridu needs nothing less than a revolution."

Maramurru's eyes squinted at the light. "Revolution?"

"Reformation cannot hope to succeed where the ruled do not have a voice among those who rule. More importantly, reformation cannot ensure that the Baltutu are removed from power. The Baltutu were never meant to rule, but to *council*, to teach the humans of Eridu *ethics, culture,* and *civilization. Man should rule man.*"

But, Maramurru said to the voice, "who am I to go against my brothers and sisters and bring man out from the throes of ignorance and into an age of enlightenment?"

And, the voice said, "you are who you are. You are in every respect what I need you to be, and you are certainly what they want to be. Maramurru, you appeal to an inalienable truth even the most oppressed soul cannot deny. They want to believe—in something, anything! Give them something to believe in."

"…and you want me to do this through war? Throw our entire civilization into upheaval?"

"I want you to do what needs to be done. What I ask is not so that you and those who follow you may enrich themselves with plunder, flesh, land, or other loot and power—what I ask is that you set out to make mankind free. Eridu should be free. All of it. Every man and woman, young and old, rich and poor, well and sick should be free, in their bodies as well as in their minds. Free to be *something*, free to choose their own destiny, to write their own history. Everyone-has-value. You have to believe it! Believe it for yourself as much as for the people you inspire, and they will believe it. You and the people of Eridu have to want to be that change. To go out and build that better life, through work, to triumph over adversity. But this will not happen unless you do what you have always known to be right. Unless you rise now and stand for what you believe in against those who commit wrongs unto the world."

"Suppose I go to the people. How do I convince them of all this? Of you—"

The light's intensity grew and Maramurru was forced to shield his eyes, the palm of his hand warming beneath its fiery glow. "You will not subvert one false god with another! Freedom can be secured only by those who feel compelled to seek it. In their very spirit. You must awaken that spirit. Live as you want them to live. Value what you want them to value. And, be prepared to die for what you ask them to die for."

Maramurru retorted, "what if they do not believe me or listen to what I say?"

Then the voice said, "you cannot dragoon a free man. He must *choose* to believe you and listen to what you say. The Baltutu will not release their hold over the people unless compelled by a mighty force. Seek out those with questioning minds and open hearts. They will follow where you lead. Your days, whether by your will or mine, as a Baltutu are coming to a close."

"I… I don't… how am I going to do this! I don't even know if any of this is real." Maramurru craned his neck up at the aperture at the starry night. "This is madness, I'm sure of it!"

He then felt pressure on his hand, as if it were being squeezed gently. "There is a reason I have come to you and not your siblings. We have been watching. We never left—not entirely. Everyone who has ever had to stand for something has felt smothered by doubt, but what separates the great ones, the ones who live on in stories, the ones who made a difference is in the moment when doubt was suffocating, they found the strength within to endure. They cajoled and rallied their followers to achieve glorious purpose. You are not alone, Maramurru, nor will you ever be alone."

The light began to fade and Maramurru knew that his time with the voice was nearly spent.

"Wait! *Who* are you?"

"You already know who I am."

"Yes, one of the Aeternam. Who's the individual I'm talking to? Who would ask such things of me?"

His query was met with silence.

"Please… I must call you something."

"Uilliam. You may call me Uilliam," and the Aeternam's light dissolved into the night… a night some 140 years in the past.

3.2 THE CATACLYSM OF MAN

The first blood to be spilled in this war came not at the hands of Maaschuel in the Antelmari village buried deep in an ancient wood. Though, it would be this moment in the annals of history to come, that the starting date for the war would be firmly anchored. From the moment he had engaged Barumgal and his Etlu guards, any possibility of peaceful reconciliation between Holindrian (Maramurru no more) and the Baltutu was finished. This much was true. There could be no going back now. The die, so to speak, was cast.

On shores on either side of the Laurentian Channel, a blockade of merchant vessels, orchestrated by a band of rebellious sailors in those territories, was smashed and broken by the might of the Baltutu navy, for their numbers were too few. Concurrently, two governors in southern Volz, including Virescent, had expelled all ministers and persons professing loyalty to the Baltutu. These acts of disobedience prompted Anshargal to put them down with force, leaving almost eight hundred dead at sea and nearly half as many on land. Districts surrounding the Shuruppak were occupied.

That was 35 days ago, and the climate could not be more different.

News of Holindrian's infeasible escape from the Kurn spread across his domain, thanks in no small part due to Oda and her Wildcat Riders, whose ranks had now swelled to more than twenty. From village to village they rode, rousing the able bodied as well as the wretched, entering a town stifled and suffocating under intense meddling of Baltutu bureaucracy and leaving the same town in a state of unabashed fervor in advance of Holindrian's arrival. Across the many regions of his domain—Antelmar, Hundare, the Trovian Coast, Volz, Vinland, and Laurentia—all listened and answered Holindrian's call: Freedom, it begins with you.

In no time at all, if it can be believed, thousands, tens of thousands had flocked to his side, remembering the lessons he often preached. If they, in good conscience, were content to live out the rest of their days just as they always had, and if they were content on the same destiny for their children and their children's children for an age, they should feel no obligation nor face any compulsion by another. But, if they felt a longing in their hearts, if in their minds there seemed to be a pressure, a burden to conform and accept while never being true to oneself, if they wanted a life for their children that was ordained not by some magistrate, but righteous sensibility, then no excuse could be made for not heeding one's duty.

Without adversity there is no ambition. Without ambition there is no hope. Without hope, how could anyone be free?

In each community he visited, Holindrian professed a variation on a recurring theme: He always began with an overview of the history known so well, even in this age. The Exodus from Erestu—Earth. To not invoke the memory of the homeworld they had never known would be a grave cultural error. He would then tell them of those who had come before. He told them the calamities which had destroyed the civilizations of the past were the result of the same entrenched vices that had ruined their first home. These civilizations had fallen because man, at some point, had forgot to aspire, to dream, to achieve wondrous things. It did not have to be so. Not again. Freedom for all! One and all possessed within his or herself the capacity to thrust humandom into a future brighter than anything they could imagine. All this and more he told them.

"Apsu, Mummu, Anshargal, Melammu, and Shi were, like me, born through the science of those who rescued Enkirus and our long distant ancestors. The celestial chariot was a vehicle, nothing more than a ship to traverse the stars just as we might sail the oceans. They were not gods. They were of flesh and blood just as you are—as *I* am. They did not intend for me and my siblings to impersonate the divine. Cut me, I bleed. Stab me, and I will die. We are not gods. We never were. We never should have pretended to be.

"I do not know whether a god or gods exist. I know no more than any of you as to what happens when we leave this world for the inevitable. I hope, earnestly and sincerely, that there is more. That there is *something* when we pass on.... What it may be, I cannot say.

"I do know that it doesn't matter. If you believe—if you *want* to believe, then believe. Believe in something, but above all I ask that you believe in each other! Believe in yourselves! Do not look to gods or supermen to rescue you. Persevere! Help one another! When you lay down for the long sleep, do so knowing you have lived a full life, one of service and meaning, a philanthropic life. Go on into the inevitable knowing you have done great works, and that you have done your part to make this world better for those inheriting it.

"*That* is what this revolution is about. It isn't about me. It isn't about a desire to rule, to usurp my kin. It is about doing what we know to be right. We can feel it! In our hearts! Man was meant to be free, not just in his body, but in his mind.

"If you feel as I feel, if you want to be a part of this movement—this revolution, then I implore you to stand with me, with all of us, and ensure this dream becomes a promise."

The power of his words did not just affect the common populace. His words were a signal. A signal fire raging, radiating its illuminating glow across the realm. It was the signal many had been long waiting. Throughout his provinces, a polarity of the same governors who had not so long ago professed undying, unrelenting allegiance to the Baltutu, now declared, boldly, their independence from the Empire. In an instant, granaries, academies and gymnasiums, lumberyards, and harbors turned their backs on the Baltutu, shutting themselves off from the rest of the world. The seeds of doubt surreptitiously planted over the last two and half centuries yielded a bountiful harvest.

The schism in the Baltutu clergy erupted into unrestricted sectarian violence. Priests and the local administrators of the conviction to remain true to the Baltutu intensified their apprehension and persecution of subversives. In contested lands on the periphery of the breakaway regions, Vocational Education and Training (VET) "rehabilitation" camps were inundated with the first prisoners of the Revolution.

The VET program was a cornerstone of the Baltutu judicial system, and an essential aspect of Baltutuism, even if it was less emphasized in the mundane facets of the dogma. The welfare of the community was of paramount concern; it was from a resolute community that order and prosperity flowed, benefiting all within the Baltutu's empire. Fractures in the community threatened the very essence of the Empire, of their control over the people. To combat fractures, as may reveal themselves in time through due wear, members of the community were obligated to report their neighbors, family members, even themselves to the proper authorities should they act in ways inconsistent with the teachings of the Baltutu—placing oneself, the ambitions, and desires of the individual over the whole. Everyone knew their place. By the time one reached adolescence, they were inserted into the role they would exercise until their inevitable death.

Community leaders known as "Ethics Officers" monitored their tribes, conducting formal inquiries, and more casual observations through seemingly benign conversation. They would submit knowledge reports to the priests and local administrators with recommendations of whether further action was necessary, to which degree of severity, or would become necessary. If a person was deemed to be in need of discipline, they would be gently collected (rare it was for someone to be snatched suddenly in the middle of the night) and led away for a rehabilitation workshop until the defective behavior was corrected.

Almost everyone who was taken away to a workshop was returned some months later, although it varied by offense, of course. Hardly ever was it the case that someone did not return, that someone had been "released" unto the care of the Anunna-Ki who might be better equipped to reconcile their deficiencies.

This all became less agreeable the longer a place was held by the Baltutu… though no one dared give voice to such thoughts.

All over Holindrian's domain, skirmishes broke out. The Etlu presence had been minimal. Generally, only a handful of soldiers were stationed at any given station to assist in occasional policing or maintain order in case of some natural, environmental event. And, in those regions considered most secure, the presence of any military personnel might have been limited to a singular liaison officer. This presented a unique challenge to the Baltutu—Telmun and Shuruppak were bounded by Holindrian's domain on three sides and the open sea on the other. And though the military presence had been greatly increased once it had been decided to imprison him, the truth of the matter was, there were just not enough troops.

Anshargal, as supreme military commander, was presented with a board on which he had few moves to make. To his advantage were things such as training and experience—Etlu were professional soldiers, the finest in the world, and they would be fighting, for the most part, farmers—and armament, as Etlu were not only armed with vastly superior weaponry utterly inaccessible to the rebels, but also clothed in a durable protective armor capable of withstanding almost any attack. Additionally, Etlu positions were well fortified, either a courtesy of nature or design.

Complicating his ability to end this rebellion swiftly were logistical challenges. The overwhelming majority of his army was located half a world away in Obenia, where the lands of Matthiolus were under an oppressive occupation. He had committed a sizable deployment to secure the southern most regions of Hundare to buffer Telmun and keep supply lines to the east with Humar open. A garrison in his enclave of Ohlin, boarding Maramurru's Antelmar to the north and west and Shi's Gerpedon to the east and south, had been entrenched in a bitter, protracted fight with their Antelmari rivals, who, to Anshargal's surprise, had elected to strike first. He had reinforced it as best he could, given what he had available, but Anshargal knew that he was confronted with only two choices.

The first was the most unappetizing. He could recall the Etlu in Obenia and pull garrisons back from their outposts across Eridu. Concentrate his strength at Telmun and then destroy Maramurru's band of revolutionaries in a single, decisive campaign, and end this war quickly. The risk was that, if he removed what troops he had scattered across the planet, those areas may find themselves that much more susceptible to revolutionary sentiments or become new battlefields all together. In short, Maramurru could, with one hand, draw Anshargal into battle, sacrificing his rebel army to disperse his message across the globe.

The second option somehow found a way to be equally unsettling. Between he and Maramurru, they each had controlled the most populace domains. There were ample sources of bodies that he could conscript to supplement his dangerously weak companies of Etlu. The idea troubled him immensely. He would have to then rely on the same quality of crop as Maramurru. Farmers and smiths, who had never swung a sword, let alone ever seen one. It would take as many months to equip and train the lot, as it would be for him to commit everything to Telmun. Conscription also bred discontent—handled indelicately, he might spark upheaval in his own lands.

A further consideration of note was that it was Maramurru's realm that provided much of the materials, ships, and personnel for the navy and trade.

Regardless of how he would decide to proceed, Anshargal had another even more urgent problem: Virescent.

Communities in the Empire were by and large self-sufficient, though there were safeguards in place to provide when a community could not meet its own needs. Virescent was one of four agricultural communes on the continent producing vast quantities of surplus. Regrettably, Virescent was situated in south-eastern Volz, on the border with Etlu-occupied territory. For now, the caravans continued to flow into Baltutu-controlled lands, including Telmun. He had seen to that. It would be absolutely critical for the war effort that Virescent continued to produce for the Baltutu. Maramurru could not possibly hope to sustain his army of farmers without it.

It would seem Maramurru, who was not a foolish man, had calculated the same, obvious enough though it was. A scout—a spy, in point of fact—of Maramurru's had been captured. With him he carried correspondence confirming Anshargal's suspicions. Maramurru was marching on Virescent. Marching with a strength estimated to be nearly thirty thousand, given the reckoning of his own Etlu reconnaissance efforts.

Virescent was on a fairly direct road to Telmun. Maramurru could never be allowed to cross the bridge and come south, as crucial imperial positions, none so preeminent as the capital, would be at risk. Virescent and the bridge at the village of Mercod had to remain in Baltutu hands. At present, that much clear.

While Telmun was paralyzed, Holindrian refused to let up. He desperately wanted, no, *needed* to spread the spirit of revolution across the sea, to Audentica, Laud, Norpia, and all other lands under Baltutu rule. The combined Laurentian and Trovian fishing and merchant fleet could access the farthest reaches of the globe and spread his message of freedom, of self-determination. Stoutly built ships they were, designed according to specifications handed down by Holindrian himself, and they surprised the Etlu sailors in the Channel, swarming, ramming, and plowing their way through the blockade and on to the world's oceans.

The settlement known now as Virescent had, more or less, served a similar function for most of the last four ages, even if it had undergone some quite drastic changes to its topography. Settlers, fleeing the destruction of Erestu-Ur, would eventually stumble across this astonishing fertile floodplain a few hundred miles to the north. Flooding predictably each year, the plains were rejuvenated as the waters spilled and gushed over, drowning the farmlands in rebirth. The river Moglen divided the Volz province between north and south. A stone masonry viaduct from the middle of the Second Age spanned the steady waters of more than a couple hundred yards. The people of the Fourth Age had begun construction of a steel suspension bridge… It remained standing though consumed by rust and unfinished.

Since then, the fertile farmland had been home to a dozen or more cultures; the most recent inhabitants—the ones before the Baltutu had come to power—erected colossal earthworks, mound cities. The people living there now took advantage of what was left behind by earlier generations, but had no knowledge of why they were built, or what their purpose had been. To them, they were shelters. Ready-made shelters. Nothing more. No one ever wondered why. They had been taught not to.

Those same mounds were also capable of providing incredible defensive positions, positions that would be invaluable in the coming days.

"Have the scouts returned?" Holindrian asked, massaging his chin.

A map of Volz had been rolled out across the tabletop.

Maaschuel nodded. "Oda and her riders just returned to the camp. They're on their way."

The news coming out of Virescent painted a despondent picture. When the Etlu vanguard moved into the town (cavalry brigade of 2,00 men), they arrested the governor, elevating her with a person whose loyalties were not in question. Martial law was enacted. Dissidents were hung or otherwise summarily executed—there would be no further participants for the VET program. The northwest bridge, the only crossing of any consequence not necessitating a boat or ferry for miles, was secured.

"What is the situation inside the town?"

"Unchanged, less Oda reports different."

Holindrian, Maaschuel, and their army made camp here some days ago, at the community of Mercod, eighteen miles north of the Moglen River Bridge. It was a quiet enough spot. Nestled at the mouth of a valley, flanked on either side by steep, impossibly steep hills. It was a solid day's march to Virescent.

"Red Cloak fanguard haff taken t'e bridge," Oda said, joining them beneath the canopy, "my scout reports two corps. Etlu. Here," and she pointed at the map.

"Thirty miles?" Maaschuel asked, leaning in.

"A little more. T'ey are mofing fast. Marching t'rough t'e night. Hardly sleeping."

"There are no obstacles of any kind for them to overcome and the road is well maintained. Weariness will not see their advance slowed," noted Holindrian.

Maaschuel hung his head. "So...what should take them two days...."

"Vill take t'em a day. A little more if rain is carried in t'ose clouds," she said, gnawing at her lip.

Maaschuel placed two red clay tokens near Virescent. "That's 52,000 men. He's pulled almost everything out of defending Telmun. It worked!"

Holindrian nodded. "So it would seem. What of the situation in the town, Oda?"

"T'e same. T'e new goffenor is making no friends," she answered with a slight bow, more habitual than anything else.

Maaschuel's eyes swiveled towards Holindrian, but, said nothing. He instead placed another, smaller token, this one blue, over Virescent.

Holindrian plopped down into a chair, interlocked his fingers, and continued to stare at the map until he cocked his head to the side. "We need to be certain Anshargal's scouts can survey our position, gauge our strength. Maaschuel, redirect patrols to make this area *here* accessible."

"Won't that give them a clear line to see what's on the tops of these hills?"

Maaschuel was calling attention to hills on either side of the valley.

"There's nothing worth noting atop those hills. They've been watching us for the better part of the past thirty hours. By the day's end, his scouts will have gone back over the bridge and tell them what they saw. Anshargal will waste no time in his attack."

"Any orders for the men?"

"Breakfast should be about finished. The regiment that joined us outside Karlsberg—"

Maaschuel was looking inquisitively at him. "Laeder's men? The farmers who joined up at the border?"

"The same. Run them through the drills again. Particular emphasis, mind you, on moving from column of fours into line of battle."

"Vy efen bot'er? I am surprised t'ey are as fat as t'ey are, giffen how... clumsy... how, how, daft. How it is t'ere dorf didn't starve...."

"Is everything else ready? Everything in place?" Holindrian asked Oda, discounting her critique of the Karlsberg regiment.

Oda affirmed: "Just as you ordered."

"Excellent! Good. Hmm. Why don't you grab something to eat? Oh," and he called after her as she made to leave, "thank you. When you are finished, please see to it that Matthiolus and the others are duly notified."

With thin lips, she flashed him a polite, if not sincere, smile, and then made way towards the mess tent.

"That... is awfully dangerous, Mara—*Holindrian*."

"Can it be done?"

"You're asking me?" Maaschuel about fell over. "I don't know." He pulled at his golden locks. "You're not coming at him from the front, but the sides. You're keeping his gaze fixed on you. A lot depends on those barrels. It's a daring plan... My feelings wouldn't be incensed if you were a god because you are asking for a genuine miracle."

"I know," Holindrian said, rising to his feet, "I wish we could have gotten our hands on a screw. The men are tired."

"The men, women, they're rested. The army's ready," he said assuredly, touching his friend's shoulder.

"I don't know about you, but I'm famished. Come," and Holindrian gestured vaguely in the direction of the cook, "let us share a meal. You have a boat to catch soon enough."

The arrival of the war at Virescent had, in not so many words, greatly inconvenienced the harvest due to take place. The previous night's rain did little to help. So often autumn and spring brought light showers to Volz. Summers were, more often than not dry, though a thunderstorm or two was not unheard of. Streaks of lightning would light up the purple sky. Winters, while snowy, were not unbearably cold. Last night, the clouds had opened up, and muddied the roads, softened the soil, and now that the suns were just beginning to consider waking from their slumbers, a dense fog rolled in off the river.

Anshargal rode ahead of his Etlu, a cluster of senior officers accompanying him. He had not intended to attack when he set out from Telmun, but, it seemed, the situation had changed. The courier whom his agents had intercepted carried misinformation. Maramurru's strength had been grossly exaggerated. His own scouts estimated the entirety of his army in the southern Volz to be not a man or woman more than twelve thousand —a far cry from the thirty he had been led to believe some days before. Now, he was presented with an opportunity. With him marched over fifty thousand Etlu soldiers—career soldiers, professional soldiers. Not farmers or stable boys or street sweepers. Just on the other side of the Moglen River Bridge, over these hills, up the road not twenty miles, Maramurru's army sat encamped. The reports invoked many sentiments, none of which instilled confidence in the abilities of the enemy. In a matter of hours, this war and his brother's tantrum would be ended.

He paused for a moment, sitting atop his horse, its hooves on the edge… the edge of a bridge, yes, that was true enough, but on the edge of something more as well. It was undeniable. Almost tangible. Yet… it was only feeling.

In the fog hung over the river and this stone artery like a curtain, a veil obscuring an uncertain future. A conspiracy of nature and psychology was imposed; he would swear not even to his own kin, that a face emerged. A familiar one. One he was confident he knew. He knew her face—Esh! But something was amiss. No, not distorted in the fog. Distressed! Agonized, troubled, some thought unsettled her, unsettled him.

"O! Where do you march, little brother? Where do you lead your toy soldiers and your flag, and against whom? O, how the lessons once taught so thoroughly abandoned!"

Trembling overtook him, a nervousness he had not known since childhood. He was paralyzed by… fear? Nay, panic! Strangled by anxiety's complete fixation upon him, forsaking all other men.

"Perched in your High Tower you would dare presume? No, I say to thee! Heaven hath not imbued nor death accorded thee with capacity or right to weigh or measure my worth! A thousand lifetimes has granted me with a clarity unknown to all others, who have or may ever walk this earth! No, I say to thee! No! Thrice no!

"I abdicate nothing. I abandon no responsibility. Here I stand, Anshargal, a Prince of Heaven, committed, if permitted, to preserve what must and has always been preserved. The man who would make me your enemy, lies yonder. It is his conscience, his contemptuous spirit, not mine, you should seek to burden with guilt, for it is he who is the guilty one! Let me bring you the disciple of Cy!

"Here, on the banks of this mighty river, I avow my everlasting fealty to our Burden! Here I *do* abandon sacred bonds of fraternity and fellowship. For it is to you, our Burden, I commit my fate. Farewell, and let war be our judge!"

Then Anshargal crossed the Moglen.

The village of Mercod was completely deserted. Holindrian had sent the inhabitants away, scurrying up the steep hills on either side of the valley, seeking refuge beyond the forests. Then, he had ordered his army to form six miles farther north to the center of the valley.

Running rainwater flowed down in streams, mucking up the roads even more so than during the height of the storm. Haze rose off the ground as the suns lifted morning dew from the grass. A thicker, denser fog hovered about waist high, casting doubt as to whether there was any firm ground beneath one's feet. A good stomp in the mud provided all the assurance one could expect to receive that there was something solid below. The valley had taken on the look and feel of a bog. This was the Jernee Valley on the day of battle.

Anshargal's presence motivated his soldiers onward. The clanging of Etlu armor could be heard echoing through the hills along which the road twisted and rounded. A discernible shiver ran through each man and woman of Holindrian's army presently assembled. A decent number had trained at the gymnasiums to perhaps one day be an Etlu soldier, satisfying each district's quota, and some were even retired Etlu themselves, but for many, war, both in concept and the word itself, was an alien abstraction bordering on inconceivable. Violence in their lives had been relegated to minor disputes, arguments settled by an impartial, Imperial arbiter. Conditioning and training had readied their bodies for what was about to come. Whether they survived or not would be as much a question of their mental fortitude as the sensibility of Holindrian's tactics.

An invading army had not set foot on soil of the Volz in little more than five thousand years. In as much time as the Baltutu had ruled, no soldier exercising his duty, of any state or band, had trespassed these lush and fertile lands. Quite frankly, the thought itself in a time not too terribly distant was utterly implausible, unimaginable, and impossible. Yet... soldiers, Etlu soldiers, entered this place, brandishing weapons, outfitted for war for the first time since the start of the Age.

When the Etlu at last entered the Jernee Valley, they swept through the empty streets of Mercod like the unrelenting flood-waters of a tsunami. The suns, at last, began to evaporate the fog and thinning the haze, increasing visibility. Leading the procession was the Etlu cavalry, 2,500 men mounted on fast horses. Behind them, perhaps fifty yards, were the heavily armored infantry, four divisions wide (there was ample space in the valley to accommodate their arrival).

The ground here was wet, wetter than the roads thus far taken, but they continued to march. Beast and iron churned the soft earth into sludge. A few miles ahead, the mass of untidy rebels could be seen, strung out in messy lines, amateurish lines. They were advancing. So, the Etlu quickened their pace, moving deeper into the valley. Then, the rebels, who proceeded more in clumps than organized brigades, stopped and attempted to reform before continuing onward. Over and again, they did this, for the better part of a mile. Once the distance had been narrowed and the Etlu were well into the valley, about four miles from the town, the rebels began to retreat.

Without warning, barrels came tumbling down the steep hills, a substantial number on either side. The first smashed into valley floor, ahead of the vanguard, bursting and spraying gallons of water on to the field—thirty gallons at a time! The same happened at the rear. Then, too, at the center. Everywhere, from high atop those hills, dozens, scores of dozens of barrels rolled the slopes in an avalanche of water, wave after wave washing over the Etlu.

Horses cried out, panicked and spooked, as they reared and knocked their riders into the slush where they sank, drowning in mud. The magnificent creatures were as fixed to the spot as the Etlu infantrymen, who felt themselves sinking deep into the swamp. Movement was impossible, but they had to move, had to press on; their quarry lay not far off, and none desired to suffer the scorn of their God.

In the excitement and distance, the Etlu would be forgiven for not having heard the plucking of longbow strings, but the neighing of horses could not deafen the whisper of hundreds of arrows arching high into the sky before plummeting straight down towards earth and their huddled masses. Three-foot bolts, launched from a bow more than six feet in length, (larger than some of its archers) struck with such force at more than one hundred miles an hour that the Etlu could not help but be sent plunging into the mud.

Few, save for horses, were killed in the initial barrage, but a thousand lay wounded, incapacitated after being hit by so many heavy, iron tipped arrows sticking out in all angles, stuck in their armor. The next barrage killed more, and the next even more still. Significant effort was made to trudge through the muck to reform in the center, but the situation was confused and uncoordinated. The fourth barrage ushered in the deadliest wave yet, as the bowmen were now supported by siege weapons—the catapultae had been deployed.

A thunderous clanging of iron cogs and gears and the nerve shattering *whop* of an inbound missile were among the last sounds heard by hundreds of Etlu as they were skewered on massive bolts. Javelins hurled towards them by machines lifted them off their feet, wrenching them out of the clinging clay.

Piling the dead for use as protection best they could, crossbow squads flopped down in the mud and returned fire, shooting desperately at the summits of those hills. The cavalry's center, the wings destroyed, drew their swords and galloped towards the rebel line, but the horses were exhausted, and each trot exerted considerable effort as the mud and clay built up on their hooves. Abandoning their horses, the Etlu dove into the bog, slogging the distance on foot.

Witnessing the cavalry charge, the Etlu infantry found their courage, resolving to do their Lord's will, and with energy they should not have still possessed, wounded or not, fueled by zeal and divine fervor, clambered out of the pits—out of the very thralls of death itself. Desperate to earn themselves honorable positions in heaven, the Etlu tore themselves free of their iron bulk, sacrificing defense for speed. Charging the rebel lines, they knew themselves not to be men of flesh and blood and bone, but, instead, instruments of the destruction of heretics, blasphemers, and infidels, worthy of neither pity nor mercy.

"My Lord, cavalry—rebel cavalry—is moving in to flank our men to the east!"

Anshargal did not need a junior officer and his spyglass to tell him this. It was plain enough to him. Maramurru, or *Holindrian* as he had taken to calling himself since being freed from the Kurn, had deceived him. Given the ferocity of the volleys and artillery bombardment, and the sheer expanse of rebels engulfing the valley as far back as he could see, there were far more than twelve thousand farmers standing in opposition. He figured, by rough calculation factoring in their general displacement, there had to be at least four times that number here assembled.

"Sir—my Lord, the siege weapons can proceed no further. A number have already become stuck in this..." He fell silent under the intensity of Anshargal's stare.

Tiny orange pelts of flame were now being lobbed from the top of those hills down upon his army. The rebel cavalry was plowing through the Etlu who had reached firmer ground, cutting down the drained men at arms well before they could meet the rebel pikemen. Short bows let loose at the hills as the remainder of his first corps edged nearer, turning, rotating, shifting as much as possible away from the western hill where the artillery was most concentrated. They were being steered directly into the rebel cavalry.

"Cannibalize what you must from the second corps, I want no less than a brigade advancing on each of those hills."

"I beg you, my Lord, but these hills are unclimbable. They are too steep."

"Their sacrifice will permit their brothers to advance under a reduced onslaught of missiles, General," this Anshargal commanded from the rear of his lines, stationed on a gentler slope affording excellent visibility of the battlefield with the morning haze now greatly diminished.

The dismissed commanding general of the second corps rode off just as a courier approached from the direction of Virescent, his horse tired from riding so hard.

"Speak!" Anshargal said in a forceful utterance.

He knew the news the courier carried was poor because of how the boy held himself. He was fearful, on the verge of being petrified.

"V… V… Virescent is uh, um, has fallen. The bridge as well. General Saetal requests reinforcements, my Lord."

Steering his horse to the hill's crest, he watched as what was left of his army of 52,000 dissolved and disintegrated in front of him. The second corps brigades did as commanded, assaulting the high ground in a futile effort, where fatigue, wounds, and death trapped them well below the summit, targets for untold numbers of arrows to rape their flesh. Much of the rest of the second corps marshaled across the field to support the first, which had been reduced to a paltry few hopelessly surrounded by rebel savages, who swarmed and cleaved and hacked, desecrating their hallowed bodies.

How many thousands will you commit to death in pursuit of this freedom *for you and yours?*

"All men, all people are born free, Anshargal. You know this. Do not speak to me as if I were one of them."

"Maramurru, it is you whom I thought I would face today on the field of battle, not this, Holindrian. Him... him I do not know."

3.3 ETIENETTE'S SONG

Etienette watched as the last of the Etlu disappeared on the road winding through the hills out of Virescent. It was not yet dawn. The four moons had been out tonight, but by the time the clouds had broken up, clearing the skies, Nemesis had already slipped below the starry horizon. Noble Artorius waned and was on the cusp of ushering the end of the night and the break of day. The tiny elliptical rocks, Fortuna and Seldon, gave chase just as they had done for eons, forever the stragglers of the night.

Once enveloped in the fog, things were to begin quickly. Etienette knew her part and was eager to lend what aid she could. A curfew was in effect, so she was putting herself in danger just by having stepped out of her family's longhouse, peeking, surveilling the Etlu. Not even an hour ago, fifty thousand soldiers had been garrisoned in their city. Now, there was not a thousand, and down by the river, camped on the banks preventing all access to the bridge, another two hundred.

Anshargal and his Etlu had not been the only visitors in recent days. Virescent, given its status as a breadbasket, place on the river, and home to the largest crossing around, naturally attracted significant amounts of traffic. Thousands would pass through the city that was as a gateway to the rest of continent if traveling from Telmun. The days leading to the battle had been routine in almost every way, the sole irregularity being the increased numbers of persons coming from the north. The newly installed governor interpreted this deviation as being benign loyalists—refugees fleeing the revolutionary hordes—for this is how they presented themselves upon their arrival. With the excitement of war and the arrival of a God, simpletons were not regarded as sufficiently suspect as hindsight would attest.

Though not a displaced person, Etienette was loyal… just not to the Baltutu, who had invaded her home, removed her governor, executed any who expressed seditious sentiments, and now made prisoners of them all in their own homes. A great number of the community's farmers had been arrested, some beaten, for humming, whistling, or (heaven forbid) singing as they worked the fields. The priests said it threatened the constitution of the community because *music* encouraged the individual, stealing resources away from the whole of society. Everyone had a responsibility to the community. There were farmers, builders, smiths, soldiers, loggers, fishers, bureaucrats, and so on. If everyone started putting their energies into their own passions and not their work, all those crucial roles would suffer, thus, society would suffer, or so said the teachings of the Baltutu.

"Music", that is what Holindrian called it, had been alien to her as a child. But now at 37, she had done what she had always been told not to, what she had always been told to ignore, or put out of her mind. Etienette put her energies into her work. Her work gave her pride; honest work was as good for the mind as it was for the body, but she had also found that her work did not satisfy her, not truly. She might never have realized it she had not taken the time to reflect on her present situation. There was something missing from her life, something her work had not managed to satisfy: Expression! Etienette felt a need, an urge, a resolute conviction to express her thoughts, to share her thoughts *with* her community.

There was not a man or woman or child in these parts who had not been exposed to the revolutionaries' song. "A revolution", Holindrian is quoted to have said, "without music is a revolution not worth having." Music, dance, literature, and art were as to a revolution as air, water, and food where to the body

—no less vital to the cause than the sword. This was not just a revolution to overthrow one regime and replace it with another; it was a revolution to change the quality of the human condition, a condition, which, by its very nature, was one craving the artistic spirit.

And, so, Etienette waded out into the coming daylight. Her dark, curly hair was tied with an evergreen ribbon. She wore her apron, but she knew that this day would see few of her hours spent baking bread over the torrid oven. Everyone had his or her role to play. Etienette, standing outside her family's longhouse, began to sing:

Sing with us and free the mind!
The men above are not divine!
The awoken hearts now form a line.
Their discourse cannot divide!

Oh lads! Will you see?
They took from you,
They took from me!
Now we stand in misery,
As this is not equality!

The land, now pale and grey,
Though our color did not fade away!
Let us paint in tyrant's blood,
The cruel throne that stands above!

Sing with us, for freedom's sake!
The men above are merely snakes!
Our awoken minds they cannot take!
Death before our spirits break!

Oh, and though we may be slain,
Our lives shall not be lost in vain!
Liberty's voice will remain,
Amongst the youth to end the reign!

Sing with us and free the mind!
The men above are not divine!
The awoken hearts now form a line,
Their discourse cannot divide!

She had a lovely voice, for a novice. Her voice carried well. The air was calm. Nature, it seemed, wanted all to hear her song. Windows shut during the night slid open; doors swung wide as men and women, dressed ready for a day of labor and reckoning, crept out into the streets. Members of her family, young and old, well and ill, joined her in song, and soon, their little choir became a chorus wherein each and every resident of Virescent was a member.

Taking to the streets, the people continued to sing. Their collective voices finding harmony and a volume that roused the content from their beds, startling those who ruled as they ventured out from their keep to behold such a sight. Forty thousand townsfolk (though it seemed like awfully more in the fleeting moments just before dawn), supplemented by several hundred rebel infiltrators, marched on the keep. Etienette's song trumpeting their arrival.

Mounds outside the citadel proper were swallowed en masse by the people, who, approached as assuredly as the coming light of day. The wooden barricades barring entry to the stronghold were thrust open, timber falling to the ground to be trampled upon. Etlu reservists, rudely awakened, not fully clothed or armored, hastily formed and managed to organize themselves into a defensive line at the base of the steps before the keep.

Standing opposite them was an armed and agitated people, now fully enthralled in revolutionary zeal.

Hurriedly, the governor, trailed by a score of his staff and aides, came as far down as would permit his voice to be heard in the silence succeeding Etienette's song. Clutching the knot in his robes, dismay on his face, and trepidation in his voice plainly heard: "Do not provoke them! Do not provoke them, I say! You will heed my words! Do not provoke them!"

He was addressing the Etlu, armed with their swords, spears, and crossbows, stood ready to engage.

"People of Virescent... good people of Virescent, please, I implore you: Return to your homes. Lay down your arms and disavow thoughts of this revolution. This, this is your home! Do not see it rashly turned to ruin. Do not incite violence. Violence will, violence can *only* be met with further violence. I beg of you, please!"

Only the distance of a good halberdier thrust separated the Etlu from the people. The Etlu, for all their impeccable training, were visibly uneasy at the realization they were outmanned forty to one, so when a bolt cut loose from a crossbow by a nervous hand, piercing the heart of a youth at the sight of their lines shuffling, the Etlu prepared themselves for death.

"A child! *A child*! They've killed a child!"

"Murderer! Murderer!"

Rearing back, a scorpion poised to strike, bloodlust dripping from its stinger, the assembly became a mob and descended upon the Etlu in a savage frenzy, bludgeoning the soldiers' bodies, breaking, shattering their bones, and severing their souls from their bodies.

"The Gods will not be merciful in their retribution!" the governor cried, but his words were heard by no one, lost to the agonizing screams of the dying, Etlu and rebel alike.

3.4 THE BRIDGE OF MERCOD

There was a great deal of commotion on the bridge.

"Huzzah! Huzzah!"

"We've done it—driven them from the river!"

Maaschuel had come across the river in the dead of night whilst the clouds remained to block out any starlight. Commanding a brigade, he slipped by quietly, ten miles upstream. Another detachment of comparable strength did the same ten miles farther down. In the thicket a short way east of Virescent, he and his troops huddled together for warmth under the canopy of trees, laying and waiting. When he was confident Anshargal had moved far enough down the road that his attention would remain fixed on the battle to come, thus delaying any reaction, he pounced.

Attacking from both sides, three thousand revolutionaries, some of the best Holindrian could muster in those early days, overran the Etlu holding the bridge—two hundred men. The survivors, few though there were, routed and fled, seeking the sanctuary of their master's shadow.

"We haven't much time. Mr. Conotocarious, move your regiment across to the northern bank, and barricade yourselves on the bridge. What is here is yours to take. Make sure to pile it up high. Best protection you can."

Conotocarious accepted the orders without question and moved his rebels out with the effectiveness Maaschuel would have expected only from a career soldier. He was a former priest at the Shrine of Amurru, indisputably the most sacred of all temples built in Holindrian's honor; it was more a college than place of worship, making Conotocarious more of an academic and intellectual than a holy man. It was perhaps this, more than his agreeable disposition, that permitted fewer cold stares directed towards him. His reputation, thankfully, was not stained with the knowledge he had been responsible for the suffering of others, as those unfortunate enough to experience the VET program were rarely ever themselves afterwards. The title and position of "priest" carried an unsavory connotation in the hearts and minds of many now engaged in open rebellion.

Maaschuel, for his part, had heard of Conotocarious's emphasis on forgiveness over punishment, and found he was fond of the black-skinned Laurentian.

"Oh, do you hear it?

Maaschuel nodded, mopping the exhaustion from his face. "That I do," and he knocked his knuckles against the ancient rock, "let us hope we've won the day."

3.5 THE HUMILIATION OF ANSHARGAL

Won the day they had. By midday, Anshargal could no longer sustain the losses Holindrian was inflicting upon his army, and so, for the first time in an exceedingly long time, he ordered his army to retreat. But, even in defeat, Anshargal was pursued. Fire continued to pelt his Etlu trapped in the valley below from high on the hilltops; the ground was still a slopping mess; movement for a wounded and weary man was next to impossible. The first corps was decimated to the point of complete annihilation. Only those divisions of the second corps further back managed to accompany him on the road south.

Yet… he was harassed still. Small companies of men, bands of raiders and bandits more like, gave chase. Staying close to the tree line, they stalked the Etlu scrambling away from the battlefield, letting loose arrow after arrow for eighteen miles until at last they came to the summit of the Linden Baum Hill directly overlooking the Moglen River Bridge—now firmly held by the rebels, who had entrenched themselves along its mile length. Attacking their position, with spent troops…. No, Anshargal would not do this. He would not permit his humiliator greater satisfaction in a final, suicidal charge.

Instead, ahead of the column of walking dead, Anshargal led them into the forest using the hills to screen his movements. He would take them to his lands in the east.

For Holindrian and his revolutionaries, the cost had not been so high, that was true, but even an Etlu so absolutely sapped of strength, wounded and hurt as these Etlu had been, proved still a deadly adversary. An Etlu soldier did not expend precious energy on fanciful maneuvers, each movement had purpose: Each blow intended to kill, not to maim. Attack. Parry. Conserve momentum. Attack again. Turn the enemy's own motions against them. Three thousand rebels were dead, twice that number injured in some way or another, not the punishment the Etlu sought, but a punishment, nonetheless.

While victory in the south was to be celebrated, elsewhere, Fortune had not been as kind. The fighting north, in the woodland border country between Antelmar and Ohlin, was the fiercest by far. Barumgal had incited ancient hatred and long dormant rivalries—all the better to rouse the Ohlinine to inflate his ranks. There was little flat ground. Nowhere to field an army. Fighting was reserved for small, nimble groups, moving rapidly through the trees. An attack could come at any time, the enemy upon you before you knew what was happening.

Folcher took his leave at the Battle of the Jernee Valley with Holindrian's gracious consent to ride north with all the speed his steed could muster when news reached him that the Ohlinine had commenced a campaign to raze whole villages and burn and cut down the ancient forests.

3.6 HOPE IS KINDLED

The marshaling of troops at Virescent had delayed the start of the harvest. In the northern territories, the harvest would suffer as so many adults had gone off to join Holindrian's war, leaving few to shoulder more. Victory rewarded the fighting folk with some relief. Caravans, full to the brim, could be driven along roads north bound. Though, securing bountiful stores of food had not been the primary objective, the combined effect on the troops produced a terribly infectious, euphoric feeling amongst the army.

It was September. Late September and, while it pained him, Holindrian was compelled to wait, to not press his advantage. It was time he regrettably had to relinquish to the Baltutu, time they would surely use to bolster their defenses, but it was also time not wasted.

Engagements along the border territories absorbed the worst of the war. Like Antelmar, the south and eastern lands of Hundare were marred in conflict, conflict exacerbated by Anshargal's retreat into Humar, cutting a bloody path through Hundaren territory. Rebel armies were directed to assist, to attack the east.

The mountain territories with their only means of transcontinental travel between east and west were bitterly contested by rebels and Etlu. Shi's Gerpedon was torn right down the middle. Skirmishes south of Virescent were pervasive. Holindrian was probing the quality of the defenses prepared, but he concentrated on the east.

There was an additional reason prompting Holindrian's pause after taking Virescent in anticipation of punching a whole in the Baltutu line. In the weeks since, a message was being spread, faster than one might expect for the time. Carried by fishing boats and merchant vessels across the expansive oceans, from ports to cities and towns and villages by horse drawn wagons on distant roads, dispersed by mouth into the atmosphere, it was left for the people to decide. The people would have to decide, each man and woman for his or herself, whether they were revolutionaries or believers, whether the destiny of mankind was to be theirs to write or the exclusive purview of the Gods.

"I know not how this message will reach you. Whether it is

transmitted by another's lips to your ears or gleamed by your own eyes, I hope that it finds you agreeable and ready for what must be said. These words may well put your very life at risk. You should, firstly, be well aware that there are those who do not want us to speak. They are the same who said I had returned to Heaven in conference with the 'divine' Anunna-Ki. They are the same who proclaim themselves gods—they are not. They are but tyrants, clinging bitterly unto their abhorrent power in this profane comedy.

"To so many of you, I am known for impartiality, reason. I believe strongly in the power of words, more so than the power of arms. A civilization cannot long rest upon a foundation that knows only the use of force, coercion, oppression, the suppression of self and thought. We live in a world that knows order because it only knows fear, because the threat of chaos is ever looming with greater evils poised to strike.

"Fear is powerful. When we are scared, we surrender more than we should, question less than we must. We allow those with authority to take from us. Always taking, taking more and more in exchange for less and less. We demonize those who do not conform, those who are different. We ostracize them. We persecute and torment and intimidate until they are extinct, by their own hand, by ours, or by the crushing weight of society they submit.

"Fear is easy. It is primal. An animal can feel fear. Hope is something different. It is human. It is hard. It requires perseverance in the face of fear. Hope is so much stronger than fear but is also so much more fragile.

"Each of you has a dream. You have never before spoken of it because you have been indoctrinated not to. Instead, you bury it deep inside. Think about that dream and ask yourself if this world will allow you to turn aspiration into reality. I suspect many of you will answer that it will not, that this world is not made for dreamers.

"But it can be.

"This is not the greatest version of the world. There is a better one. There is a version of the world where we are governed by our dreams instead of our insecurities, where we celebrate what makes us different, where we cherish the imaginative, and where we run towards adversity instead of away from it.

"If, however, the world as it is does more than just satisfy your base desires, then, I ask nothing more from you, but, if my words have resonated a feeling inside of which you do not recognize—it is passion! If you feel an energy surging from deep within—it is passion! If you refuse to stand by, if you refuse to just subsist, I ask that you stand with me, rise with me, fight with me on this Baltutu Day!

"Together, we can change the world! We can build a world where dreams are possible."

Holindrian's words became inescapable. It did not matter in what part of the Empire you lived, no matter how rural you may have lived, or in whose domain. It was heard in the agora just as it was heard in the fields. It was read on pamphlets nailed on to the doors of temples just as it was read scratched into stone and wood tablets.

A hundred thousand Etlu spread out across the planet tended to the suppression of the Revolution; flyers were ripped down, people detained for subversion, beating those who resisted, and killing those who proselytized.

The pillars of civilization seemed to be crumbling all around. Rare was it to find a village not disintegrating into madness. War was waged in small towns more often than the battlefield. Communities, families, friends, and neighbors turned against one another. In the best of circumstances, the partition was cordial, with one faction departing quietly, without incident. In the worst of circumstances, communities destroyed themselves.

Change is terrifying because it is difficult, uncomfortable, and the result is unknown. People can cope with the difficult and uncomfortable, such is life, but intentionally making oneself vulnerable, exposing and raising the possibility of failure, *that* people will fight. People will fight desperately, vehemently, gladly sacrificing reason, to preserve what is known.

3.7 PARADISE TORN ASUNDER

With Anshargal recuperating far to the east, life in Telmun proceeded under a sort of daze.

"Damn it, Shi! What he wanted doesn't matter anymore! He's gone. Holindrian has chased him away," Melammu said, slamming the tabletop with the palm of her hand.

"His name is Maramurru," Shi quipped angrily, the tips of her fingers tracing the many tiny rivets left by Holindrian's fingernails.

"No, Shi, it's not. Maramurru was imprisoned inside a of pyramid of stone. The man who came out—that wasn't Maramurru! That wasn't our brother! *He* is not our brother! He is our enemy. He is a threat. We need to accept that and do everything we can to neutralize—"

Crack! The table broke in two, then was flung aside as Shi walked through it. "*Neutralize*? You mean *kill*. You want to kill him! Trying once wasn't enough for you!"

Mummu grabbed Shi's arm, yanking at her in a scolding fashion. "Shi!"

"I said I was careful! You never listen. *Never*! You never could see what he was doing... you never wanted to. You were too close to him!"

"*I* couldn't see?" Shi said, her normally muted voice trembling with irritation.

"None of us saw. Not this... how could we?" Mummu said, trying again to quell the dispute.

Melammu continued: "*Reforms* for hunting. *Reforms* for

agriculture. *Reforms, reforms, reforms.* Enhanced skill with a bow. Better methods of curing and stockpiling food. *Lies!*"

"Such is the benefit of hindsight, Melammu. You didn't speak out against it. Anshargal, himself, said it would make for better recruits," Apsu said dryly.

Melammu smirked wickedly. "Exactly! Better soldiers."

Shi shook herself free and shot a scorning glare at feigned parental disapproval.

Melammu turned to Apsu. "Make a decision." Her voice shook with contempt. "Obviously we can't reach consensus, so you are going to have to make a choice. We are going to need those Etlu here. Holindrian knows that to 'win', he will have to come to Telmun eventually. There are a hundred thousand Etlu not engaged in occupying Obenia. Bring them here."

"...and if we do as Melammu suggests, we abandon the world to chaos. We could lose the whole thing," taunted Shi.

"We are guaranteed to lose everything if we do not muster a wrath only gods can command," Melammu spat her words furiously at her sister.

A wave rushed through the Pantheon. The pressure rose. Wind swirled, a vortex raced around the rotunda, hoisting tables and chairs off the mosaic floor. Melammu made to swat Shi to the ground but found herself frozen in place by Mummu. Apsu extended his arm, shooting an invisible force directly at Shi, causing her to lose her focus, and crumple, her legs falling out beneath her.

"See how quickly the young ones turn to violence when they don't get their way!" Melammu shouted, breaking free from Mummu's hold.

"ENOUGH!" Apsu's voice cut through the air like thunder's echo, commanding the bickering cease, and all to listen. "I will not have our family divorced further. Have your governors raise militias for their common defense. Communities in the protected zone will commit... twenty percent of their population to Telmun. The Etlu will come home."

In seven thousand years, one could probably count on two hands all the times Apsu had ever raised his voice, shouting at his siblings. The effect tended to leave them all feeling disappointed, ashamed. Recovering from his outburst, Apsu transformed back into his accustomed, aloof self.

There were things Shi wanted to say, needed to say, but not here, not in this forum of willful ignorance.

How did it fall to Apsu to become the decider? Never before when consensus could not be reached had they ever chosen to yield, to rely on birth order as the means of determining what, as a group, they should do. Yes, the Pantheon and mythos of Baltutuism they created placed special reverence on the first-born pair, and Apsu in particular—mortal man craved a definitive order to things, a hierarchy of their own imagination imposed on the natural world. Yes, the rituals they had invented infused this idea further into the religion and state, but... it was all supposed to be an act. For, no matter how much the humans believed the Baltutu to be living gods and no matter how much the Baltutu sought to reinforce this belief, they knew, did they not? Apsu. Anshargal. Mummu. Melammu. They knew this world was of their own design. An illusion created for the benefit of all mankind. To keep them sheltered and safe. To keep their needs of food, sanctuary, and sex aptly satisfied.

Shi closed her eyes and thought, *"how did we get here?"*

To her great surprise, she heard a voice, far off and distant whisper to her in the back of her mind, *"you know how. We were never immune from the same force corrupting good men, turning them into tyrants."* It was a voice that assumed the tenor and cadence of Maramurru.

Startled, Shi's jolt did not go unnoticed by the others.

"Are you alright?"

Shi smiled at Mummu. "I'm fine," then, to Apsu she said, "I will take my leave, and do as instructed."

He made to correct her, to tell her that it was not so much an order as a suggestion, but Shi preempted him; again, she was smiling. "Yes, it was," and she bowed ever so slightly.

3.8 RETURN OF A KING

Matthiolus came to shore under the cover of darkness, the blackest night ever experienced by Eridu in all its history. The voyage across the sea had been smooth enough, a little choppy in places, but Fortune had seen it fitting to bless their crossing with no great swells or storms, a peculiarity during the autumn months. Their journey had begun just a day before Anshargal's defeat. A trek across half a continent to the Trovian Coast where a trireme waited in an isolated harbor to take them to the opposite side of the Channel where larger blue water ship lay in anchor. That ship, a Laurentian galleon of the same sort built for the Baltutu navy, was now off the Obenian coast, a fleet of row boats deployed, rowing their way to shore.

The five boats made landfall before dawn, releasing their cargo of 133 Obenian men into occupied country. The shore was rocky and deserted. One of the few coves not stormed by the Etlu half a year earlier. Vanishing into the jungle, they found war had not accompanied them from abroad, but preceded them. The war had never ended.

In the prelude to invasion, when Matthiolus still ruled the lands of his ancestors, the people, his subjects, had taken to arming themselves. It became a custom. It became the duty of every Obenian to be prepared to fight and die to defend their homeland from the Baltutu invaders. When the Etlu finally did come, they pulverized formal Obenian defenses, spewing mayhem and confusion to disorganize the civilian resistance as they pressed on to the capital, King Matthiolus their ultimate goal. Obenian obstinance, no matter its constitution, was simply insufficient to prevail over a rehearsed military exercise.

Anshargal thought, just as Matthiolus did upon hearing the wise words of Holindrian, the people would lay down their arms once their king had been defeated, dismiss all notions of hostility, and, begrudgingly, accept their new reality. The deposing of their king only roused the people to further action. Disorganized, but impassioned, there was not a man or woman, calling themselves an Obenian, who did not fight against the soldiers occupying their homes.

The invader had to be purged. Violently if necessary. The Etlu refused to board their tall ships and sail back across the wide sea. A hundred and sixty thousand Etlu. Each one a target. Every day an attack. There was no place for decency, no place for civility. Blood and death. The Baltutu and their Etlu stooges understood that. The people of Obenia would communicate in a language where their message was impossible to mistranslate.

"You aren't listening! We don't *need* you—"

"Well, we don't need you… in that way… sire."

"Do not 'sire' him! He's not our king anymore. He's not the king of anything anymore."

The organizers of this gathering had warned Matthiolus that public perception of the king was mixed at best, with no clear prevailing view. There were those who thought him a traitor. A cowardly man, once a supposed leader, who had turned his back on his country, betraying them to the Baltutu. Some thought, inexcusable though his actions were, they were not beyond comprehension—he had surrendered to save the lives of his wife and children—honestly, how could you fault any father for appeasing his first, most sacred obligation? Another popular characterization saw his abandonment as a blessing, for now the people felt a sense of empowerment; when they fought now, it was not because a king led them, but because they thought it the right thing to do. Few were prepared to welcome back the king with gracious arms—they tended to be of the more traditional sort.

Matthiolus licked his lips. He did not fancy having to skulk around, creeping about his own country like a vagrant or meeting in dingy places like this barn.

"What... how would he be of use to you if not as your king? Mind you, a right of his by birth. I pray you remember that!" Matthiolus's general did little to control the disgust in his tone.

"Meaning no disrespect, but the Obenia the former king ruled does not exist anymore. I'd ask you to tell me what you recognize since you've returned? All but the stars have changed. There isn't a city or town that hasn't been razed. Burned to the ground! The fight is everywhere, on the beaches and rocky shores, in the fields and in the hills, in the streets and charred remnants of villages. We can't count the dead, let alone bury them properly. They lie where they fall. The Obenia of old is dead.

"You say it has been but seven months—sire, to us, it has been years... entire lifetimes. This," and the man pointed to his own face, "this is not the face of a young man. Would you believe me if I told you, I am not yet thirty?

"We don't need a king. We need leaders! Leaders who understand this fight! We need men of conviction who can bring these factions together to overthrow our common enemy. To many, you abdicated your throne," the king's men balked but the man spoke over their scoffing, "if I may say so, I don't wish to see you retake the throne. I don't want a return to monarchy. Even in this hell, the taste of freedom is intoxicating. Exhilarating! But, if you want to help your country, really help, then help us not just liberate Obenia but *free* Obenia!"

Matthiolus heard similar speeches wherever he traveled, sentiments shared by Obenia's youth and disenfranchised.

"The monarchy is finished," Matthiolus said, hanging his

head, sitting on top of a hill overlooking the remains of a once magnificent city now smoldering and utterly unrecognizable.

He listened to the shrieks as halberds impaled the freedom fighters, fleeing into the night after setting fire to a grain silo.

"Maybe not for all time, but for the present, in our current struggle, we are all just men. No kings. Men at war with gods."

3.9 PANAYIOTIS

The trees were bare. Leaves of red, gold, and brown coated the grass in a crunch, crinkling beneath each step, each roll of the wheel, each trot of a horse. The days were getting a little cooler and a little shorter. The sun's rising a little later. Mornings were just cold enough to make one want to bundle up and stay in bed.

It was beautiful country. Even in autumn, when all life seemed to be shutting down, a great yawn before a nap. Mountains were too far off, but there were wide fields and long valleys interspersed among the hills, wearing the forests like a blanket.

Wood was being chopped. Wagons, loaded, positively overflowing with the harvest's bounty, drove what was reaped from the places where it was sown. Woodsmen stalked the plentiful game.

For many, this was their most favorite time of year.

I have been sitting here, trying to think of what comes next for days. These few paragraphs are all that I have to show for it. Oh, I have gone for walks. It really is beautiful country this. You know, the Fifth Age had this device, called it a "camera". Truly extraordinary! Basically, you have this box, which is light proof, doesn't let any light in or out except at the right moment. When the light enters through this hole or aperture it captures the image! Right there, on paper or glass or what have you. Remarkable! The things I could show you if I had one of those… perhaps, I'll build one…

Okay… I was not supposed to tell you about the camera.

Holindrian, I think, wants me to scratch out that paragraph, but I didn't tell you how to build one, I just told you what a "camera" was. There is probably a hundred of them at Telmun, in that vault in the cliffs. You are supposed to "discover" them on your own, in your own time. *Pfft*. If the cycle ends, if civilizations stop rising only to destroy themselves, I sincerely hope you—whomever and whenever *you* may be—have invented the camera. I think you will really enjoy it.

I have asked Holindrian for permission to travel to the Hundare. Repeatedly. He says I'll just have to rely on eyewitness testimony for my History. Truth be told, it does not sound like very much is happening out in the east either. Hundarens and Humari slaughtering one another. Revolutionaries and Etlu flocking to support their side. No big battles. No decisive battles. Just enough to keep the pressure on. Attacking the defensive line between Telmun and us.

I suppose since I am just sitting here, waiting, that I might as well take this time to (at last) introduce myself. See, you probably didn't realize it at first—unless you did—this isn't *just* another story, it is history. Our history. It is the story of us and how we got to where we are and where we are going. Now, you would have a scrupulous eye indeed if you were to point out that this history is neither complete nor unpartisan. Historians are people, too, susceptible to all the same biases. This is a history of an end as much as it is a history of a beginning. I have knowingly and willfully drawn attention to some events while passing over others and, in some cases, outright ignoring them. I encourage you to become a student of my other works—should they survive into the future and find the welcoming hands of our posterity—for a fuller picture.

My name is Panayiotis. I am named for my father, who was named for his mother, Panayiota, who was named for her father, and so forth. My progenitor, Panayiotis, once upon a time, was a sibling of Cy and Lecia. In their time, they were known as "The

Seconds". Though not pure Baltutu, instead being only a template, proof that what was desired was possible. It has already been said they have long life, living more than twice as long as a mortal, but they possessed another ability, one eluding even the Baltutu.

Cy was dead. Erestu-Ur lay in ruin. Humanity spread out over hundreds of miles. While their Baltutu cousins buried Esh beside Enkirus on the cliffs, Panayiotis and Lecia, in the confusion of the aftermath, vanished into obscurity, victims of history. Perhaps they feared the retribution that befell the Gudanna as it was their brother who had destroyed humanity's first city. Perhaps they wanted to live out the rest of their days in a comfort and serenity they could never achieve in the company of others. Perhaps. Maybe. Some things are lost to history, never to be made known.

What is known, according to the stories passed on through my family, is that at some point Panayiotis was confronted with his own mortality. We believe this moment occurred sometime after Lecia departed from his company, though how and under what circumstances remain unclear. Different versions of her death are popular with different generations of the family. For some, the legend tells that she had in fact been wounded during the battle and that her body simply could not regenerate quickly enough. Another says she was felled by nature and the elements, a wild animal. There is one where some ravenous refugees attacked her and Panayiotis. One where she killed herself. And one where Panayiotis awoke one morning to find himself alone —no explanation given. Oh! A personal favorite, though quite unlikely, has responsibility for her death falling to the Baltutu themselves, fearful that the Seconds could challenge them—this theory did not come into existence until well after the Baltutu had conquered the world.

No matter the specific cause. The important part is what happened because of it. Principally, me. The Seconds were inferior to the Baltutu (or Thirds as they were once known, albeit for only a short time) in a whole host of ways, but there was one area in which they were not. Seconds lacked the genetic purity, the fine quality of genes. To put it another way: Seconds did not require compatible genetic profiles (or luck) to reproduce, just another member of the appropriate sex and species. There are benefits to not being perfect all the time.

Any genetic augmentations in Panayiotis's blood have been so diluted by time that there really is not anything special about me, at least, not in that way. I do stand out though, different from the rest. You ask any other human about the ruins and they will tell you some myth that has been shared and borrowed amongst a dozen villages for a thousand years, but no one really knows. The Baltutu do, and so do I… more or less, more than the average person, that is for certain.

I can only imagine that is why Holindrian came to me, all those years ago, and asked me if I would chronicle an event, something that would change the foundations of the world, and alter the destiny of all mankind. I might be a historian, but I am still human. It is exciting to be a part of history instead of just recalling it.

I do not regard myself a particularly interesting man, but there is some cardinal biographical information I would like very much to leave you with.

I am the 66th descendent of Panayiotis to carry his name. I was born in the year 7,479 SE within not twenty miles of the spot where each one of my namesakes before me had too been born. It is a tiny village. On the slopes of the Rowen Mountains, north of Gerpedon. I urge you to visit the place. We have kept a comprehensive record of man's time on Eridu. I have a wife, Acacia, whom I have been married to for forty years. I love her very much. We also have a daughter. I will leave it to you to speculate as to what her name might be.

This is where I leave you. You know a little about the author of this work. I hope that you find its conclusion satisfying. If not, well, there is honestly not much in my power to do about that, as it is, as I have said, history.

3.10 THE TOWER OF ONE THOUSAND TONGUES

"Are you alright?"

Just over a year had passed since the day when he had given chase to his flock, hobbling through the carved rock only to find his sheep in the company of the truest strangers. A year since he had been taken up, beyond the threshold of white clouds, and into a world the likes of which he had long ago forsaken as being outside the capacities of man. Just over a year ago when he learned, with certainty, that his world was ending—nature's punishment for the transgressions of a piggish man, a selfish man, a hollow man. Now, a little more than a year removed from all that, humanity would be given a second chance.

"Enkirus? Enkirus!" He turned around. It was Uilliam who called out to him, "I know that you would rather stay, but it is time to go."

They stood at the crossroads of human civilization, tangible and real. Little remained in the waning days of the governments of old. Desperation and instinct overcame sensibility and civility. Thus, mankind's final hours on Earth were not marked by an era of cooperation and fraternity, but a last, bitter contest for control over the last, precious resources. In the land between rivers was the very thing that would save some of them from the coming plight, a doom certain to bring human existence to the brink. In this land, the Aeternam constructed in the desert "The Tower of One Thousand Tongues" and at this place did they gather peoples from the farthest reaches of humanity's sprawling dominion.

From those who came to Eridu during the Exodus, we know the Tower of One Thousand Tongues stood mightier than any building of human fashioning. It is said by those who made the journey when not yet knee-high that the top of the tower was obscured by the sun and could not be seen. The Tower proper is said to have been the color of an apricot or that of summer's setting sun, distinctly visible for hundreds of miles in every conceivable direction and made from an ore with remarkable resilience to heat, fire, and wind. Adjacent to the Tower was another structure, described as a labyrinth of metal, crisscrossing every which way, and quite nearly as tall. Its function is unclear. A swiveling bridge connected the Tower to the Margidda, the means of our salvation. All this rested atop a pedestal of stone and mortar, not unlike a ziggurat in its form.

Over the past year, people from faraway places, distant lands, and unexplored shores had been plucked out of their lives, scoured from all over Erestu, and deposited in the hot sands where they lived in communes, a reservation of humanity. Each passing day made the decision to leave a little easier. Riots, wars, famine, drought, shortages of everything, wildfires, earthquakes, floods, plumes of black smoke, toxic clouds. It was the same in the lands of Eurasia, Africa, and Oceania. It was twilight for the Earth; the planet was in the thralls of death. Soon, the last breath would be gasped, and life would be no more on this world.

Uilliam led Enkirus by way of a motorized cart, levitating half a foot above the ground, from the command module to the base of the Tower.

"Nervous?"

"I am wondering why we have to board this... ship... this *spaceship*. Couldn't you use that device which produces the technicolor light and transport us there? Wouldn't that be swifter? Wouldn't that be simpler?"

Uilliam's hair flew behind him, fluttering in the wind as it roared passed. "It would be swift, that's true; however, far from simple. Four light years, in this... rural portion of the galaxy is a long way. There are other means of transit available. Our choice was deliberate."

Enkirus nodded reluctantly. "I just... four years confined within a metal cylinder is unsettling."

"You will be asleep," Uilliam said measuredly, his eyes paying no attention to the intense brightness of the sun.

Enkirus was shielding his eyes. "...I'm not overly fond of that either."

"There are—dangers out there," Uilliam admitted, though it seemed he would rather let this subject of conversation end.

"I thought you said this was all rural?"

"Is something safe just because it is rural?" When Enkirus didn't respond, Uilliam continued, "we have provided you with technology centuries beyond your capabilities, a fact that does not rest well with my people. The thought of giving a child race such power is... disconcerting—hence the great many safe-guards we have instituted. What has been provided will be more than sufficient. Your species will endure. We *do* have other concerns outside our involvement with humanity, warranting our full consideration and resources." The cart began to slow, nearing the pedestal and their destination's terminus.

"Enkirus, I encourage you to put all worry aside. Let it go. We wouldn't have brought you this far if we thought you would die before it was all over."

They disembarked. Walking over towards the lift that would carry Enkirus to the Tower's summit, they paused just short. Enkirus stared, mouth ajar, at the top. How high it was, he thought.

"You needn't worry. It's perfectly safe. Got us here, didn't it?"

"*This?*"

Uilliam laughed. "In principle."

The lift doors opened, and an Aeternam automated attendant

stood ready to accept Enkirus. A child, a human boy of about five, was present as well, a ragged and worn thing he was, too.

"There is someone I would like you to meet," Uilliam said, touching his shoulder, gestured to the boy, "we found him wandering the desert. He was tired. Dangerously dehydrated. Hadn't eaten for days. His family presumed dead. He is lucky to be alive; luckier still that we were the ones to find him. He doesn't possess any of the genetic markers we have not already selected for, but one more child couldn't possibly hurt."

Enkirus turned. "What's his name?"

"That we were not able to determine. We've taken to calling him 'Edis'."

"Am I going to see you again?" he asked, approaching the lift car with an air of caution, but doing his best to exert confidence in an effort to elevate the fear clear in the child's eye.

"I should think so. A familiar face should be there to welcome you to your new home," he said, smiling, and then the doors closed.

Enkirus's knuckles were white. Fingers clenching the arms of his chair so tightly his nails were on the verge of cutting through the upholstery. Eyelids pressed firmly shut.

The Margidda rocketed upward, riding a cone of fire and smoke, arching into the sky.

He opened his eyes. He had felt almost none of the jarring. An experience he had convinced himself would be akin to strapping oneself to a tree in the midst of a hurricane, had actually been far more pleasant, enjoyable even if he had not been so completely terrified.

All the others were asleep. Little Edis, too.

"Enkirus, you need to enter your hibernation capsule."

He jumped, searching for the source of the voice. Its owner seemed to be the ship itself.

"You are encouraged to look out the window on the starboard —right hand side of the vessel."

Planting a hand on either side of the glass, he could not help but smile nor not help the tears forming in his eyes. For the first time in his life, he saw the Earth.

3.11 VAIN ACQUISITION

The Empire was crumbling. The whole of the world erupted in fire and fury. Revolutionary fervor swept across the land. Holindrian's words, once a whisper, now stirred the indifferent and apathetic from their hypnosis, revealing to them the true state of the world. Etienette's song became their anthem; the first song many had ever learned, heard, and sang. Effectively abandoning the world to its own devices, the Baltutu readied themselves at the place where the fate of mankind would be decided.

For nearly the entirety of Baltutu rule, no army had been permitted to traverse the holy land of Shuruppak, a region sixty miles deep, radiating outwards from Telmun. This sacred law had been muted. Today, just as the days before, saw tens of thousands of Etlu transforming the land into a system of forts and trenches nigh impossible to be breached. Thousands more arrived each day, with thousands still yet to arrive. Much work remained to be done if Telmun was to survive this Human Revolution.

Then, the ground beneath them began to shake. Tremors echoing from somewhere far away. The distant rumble of thunder lay beyond the horizon where it grew louder and louder; the shaking of the ground becoming more fraught and more violent. The apocalypse approached.

The land nearest Telmun was mostly flat atop the Cliffs of Damkina, with only the gentlest hills and few in the way of jagged rocks protruding unaesthetically out of the earth. Sloping upward nearer the cliffs, Ezinu's Fields separated the capital from the forests—a natural barrier—called the Duru in this time. The re-founded Erestu-Ur sat as sentinel on the northern side of this forest, with eyes fixed on a (formerly) pacified and agrarian dominion.

A dark mass could be seen lumbering near the fortifications, those erected by man and nature. The Etlu stationed in the watchtowers, forts, and trenches carved throughout plains steeled themselves in preparation for what they would soon be called upon to do in service of their gods. The mass appeared amorphous—a singular entity with no individual component distinguishable, and it extended from one end of the world to the other.

Holindrian marched at the forefront. From atop this dwarfish ridge, he could survey much of the Baltutu's Holy Land. Telmun and the Pantheon at its center was within sight perched on the Cliffs of Damkina with one eye overlooking the Annulus Ocean crowded with ships and another those Fields of Ezinu crowded with armies. The ground was damp and would remain so throughout the whole of winter. Gray clouds would become a staple, leaving the blue sky something to be desired for when the new year came. There would be a heavier fog in the mornings. Stronger winds, foreign gales, powerful gusts riding the white caps of a turbulent sea, whipping, and lashing against the high barricade of rock.

Holindrian stood at the forefront. Assembled behind him was a force twenty times greater than anything the Etlu could muster. The Revolution had arrived at the land of Shuruppak. War had come to Telmun, Capital of the World.

There was a commotion ahead, but Holindrian paid it little mind. The suns were waking. Light chased the last pockets of darkness away and illuminated the Virtuous Horde in hues of red and gold.

"…*Maramurru*…"

He jerked his head around, searching for the one who had called out his name… his forsaken name.

"…*Maramurru*…"

Again, he swore he heard it. Whispered by the wind, a soft voice from somewhere… else.

Around him fluttered a double-breasted coat stretching quite near the knee and darkened by moisture in the cool morning's air. Pulling the navy shemagh off his mouth to hang loose, it draped over the linen vest he wore, and he fixed his eyes on the lanterns burning in Telmun.

He said: "We do only what the Universe and Fortune have conspired. We seek only what greatness is thrust upon us. A greatness tempered by courage. A greatness embraced and cherished. We come, marching on this place, the cradle all civilizations, a place that has rarely known war, not as conquerors but as liberators. We come, not to depose one leader for another, not to replace one tyranny with another, and not to elevate a few over many. We come as emancipators of all humankind. I invoke you, Enkirus, and you, Esh, and all the honored dead, not to seek your blessing but your understanding. For once and always, here do we discard the decrees of false gods, declaring that we, men and women of Eridu, consent to be governed, alone, by the laws of free people!

"It is here at the Gates of Titaan where I entreat those millions yet born to look back on this moment kindly, favorably, should we prevail. We do this not for ourselves, not to satisfy our own vices, but, as in all things, for you, our posterity.

"Fortune, I beseech you, favor this Revolution!"

Zigor, the Troasi Etlu commander to whom the defense of Telmun now fell, watched from the battlement of a fort controlling the Traveler's Road. A magic seemed to be at work. A foul magic. He had given the order. Etlu were piling into the trenches, catapults were strung out for more than a mile to the east and west of the road, and the doors to Telmun barred shut.

Zigor held a position of immense importance in the Baltutu hierarchy. When Anshargal was on the field, he was, without dispute, the supreme military commander, an angel of violence.

Barumgal may have held a position coveted by many, the viceroyalty, but that was a political role and a matter of governance. Zigor had no interest in the affairs of statesmen, in the making of laws or their interpretation. He was a military man. His singular passion, the entirety of his purpose, his reason for existing was to serve in Anshargal's army. He was his Lord's left hand, General of the Etlu.

Holindrian felt a hand grip his arm. "Are you sure about this?" Maaschuel asked, wagging his chin towards Telmun, "they very well may mean kill you."

"Don't you mean *us*?" he replied, forcing a smirk.

"Yeah, well, I thought I'd to appeal to your sense of self-preservation before begging for my own life."

"You don't have to come with me. Might even be wiser if you didn't…"

Maaschuel would have none of it. "Never. 'Til the glorious end." He gripped the hilt of his sword. "Besides, the look on Mr. Davos's face when he sees you—wouldn't want to miss that," he said with a wink. "If we die because Fajr doesn't get here in time… I apologize in advance… but I'll kill her."

A pair of horses were brought up by Oda, muttering about the insanity of what Holindrian and Maaschuel were about to do. By the time the duo reached the capital under a flag of truce and under heavy Etlu guard, it was well into the hours of morning. Holindrian could hear Maaschuel's pulsating heart, sense on his skin the tense breathing of the armor-clad warriors and smell the stench of perspiration soaking undergarments. Maaschuel sat up straight as possible; one hand fixed firmly to the reins, the other clenching the white banner above their heads. He had had to surrender his sword immediately. Holindrian, meanwhile, had ventured forth unarmed.

The Gate of Titaan was a wonder unto the world. It was a double gate, extending far beyond the old wood one that had stood on similar ground many ages ago. Riding casually, the

Procession Way began roughly a quarter mile out. The center of the Way was a covered in light-colored pavers, accented on either side by sun bleached red stones not native to this region. The gate itself was a colossal structure. The first set of doors rose forty feet and the second towered above higher still at no more than sixty. Covered in deep blue lapis bricks (harvested from the tiny island of Palare, half an ocean away to the southeast) the gate glistened, even in an overcast day such as this when the quality of light was poor. It had this seraphic, heavenly, celestial sheen to it. On the left side of the gate, were three animals of white stone accented by strands of gold. A ram, an eagle, and a bear. On the right, likewise construction, but an ox, a dog, and a horse. Centered above the door was an owl. The door itself was Antelmari godwood coated with decorative red cedar.

Upon approaching this architectural marvel, and dismounting, Holindrian and Maaschuel surrendered their horses. Etlu guarded the atrium, not wanting either man to have access to other portions of Telmun. They were ushered into the deserted courtyard. The water level in the lake sat diminished, for the spring water that fed Esh's Fountain had chosen to run dry. Escorted to the steps of the Pantheon, Holindrian led Maaschuel inside; he could feel a bitterness nipping at him in the air, a surreal chill draining his life force.

The tables that had always been there were gone. Chairs too. The space itself had otherwise not changed at all, though the atmosphere of the place had, quite perceptibly. Something sinister lingered here, loathing, hate more likely than not, a passion concocted from the worst of human emotions. The fury emanating from his siblings was tangible.

Apsu stood tall at the center; Mummu, Melammu, and Shi huddled around. The eldest two present looked on him without a discernible expression. Melammu, never one for subtly, wore her sentiments on her sleeve, and a keen-eyed man could derive that she harbored an intense grudge. Shi... Shi he thought, however so slightly, however so carefully, may have flashed him the weakest of smiles, just barely curling the corners of her lips. He hoped she was at least glad to see him, circumstances of their reunion aside.

Holindrian took up a stance whereby he remained close enough to Maaschuel to protect him, if need be, but far enough away so as to not crowd him; it was important that he stand before the Baltutu as his own man and not appear a lackey of Holindrian's.

"It's him."

"Our brother."

"Do we proceed?"

"Yes."

"He is still—"

"A traitor," Apsu said, silencing the back and forth between the sisters.

Maaschuel fought the urge to crane his neck so that he could see the expression on Holindrian's face. He fought to calm the thundering in his breast; he fought the droplets of sweat already dotting his brow; he fought to control his body and show no impotence.

Melammu grinned widely at him. "Your mortal pet is nervous."

Maaschuel felt a tinge of anger, but it was almost immediately exhausted.

"Focus your efforts on me, Melammu," Holindrian said, serving her fixed gaze on his friend.

Apsu crossed his arms. "You came to us under a flag of truce."

"A mission of peace."

"Ha! Peace... *peace*! He wants to talk peace but has marched on the center of the world with an army."

Melammu fell silent by the wave of Apsu's hand. "If you

have come to talk peace, how can we be expected to do so in good faith when you have so many now perched in the Shuruppak?"

"I have come to you, unarmed. That army of which you speak is twenty miles away. I stand at your mercy."

"Yes... and our mercy has limits, even for you," the elder brother said.

Holindrian chuckled. "I have seen the limits of your mercy. Poisoning me. Imprisoning me." He was pacing now, circling the mortal. "Chasing Maaschuel to the top of the world. Executing any who dare speak out against you, any daring to stand up to tyranny."

"Conspiracy to commit sedition and treason is a capital offense, Maramurru. You have brought this upon yourself."

Holindrian sunk his hands into the pocket of his linen pants. "Have any of you bothered to ask, to wonder why so many have heeded my call? Why so many, when hardly prompted at all, when just presented with the opportunity, have been willing to lay down their lives to oppose you, to oppose *this*," and he waved around the Pantheon, "I may be well blessed with words, but surely it has not escaped you, any of you, you have driven them away, you have pushed them towards me. I have been the spark, but you have provided the accelerant to this fire in your efforts to smother it."

Melammu crept forward. "And, because of you, we now know the face of our most lethal enemy. You have graciously brought so many of them here, where they will either kneel before their Gods or die at our feet. Once your army has been destroyed, *Holindrian*, we will purge Eridu of the unbelievers— now that we know who so many of them are. So, what I guess I am saying is... *thank you*! Because of you, the war will end tonight!"

"Maramurru, please! Put an end to all of this. Come home!

Help us heal the world," Mummu said. The sincerity in her voice was unmistakable, but misplaced.

"If you did not come to discuss terms, why are you here?" asked Apsu.

Holindrian turned his head, Maaschuel was rooted to the spot, a little pale in the face, but ready nonetheless, he could see that.

"Whether I came back under my own volition or in chains, we both know I would spend a considerable amount of time drugged until I exist only within my own subconscious, completely unaware of the eons passing by. So, no, Mummu, I cannot come home.

"Melammu is right, however. The war will end tonight," and his eyes fell to his brother, "you asked why I am here. I want to show you something. All of you," he said, gesturing to the back of the Pantheon.

They followed him, through the passage and out on to the cliff edge, with Atlantaries Harbor in plain view. The navy was under attack. Galleons sails amain, the Liberty flag flying proudly from atop their mast, were streaming over the waves of the blue ocean. Triremes, flying those same glorious or cursed colors, rowed along the coast, on a collision course with the red bannered Etlu ships. The rebel crews sang, almost yelling, loud enough to be heard even by Maaschuel's common ears.

A horn sounded. All six heads swiveled. On the eastern hills, the southernmost border with Hundare, another mass had formed, this one of cavalry. Ten thousand Hundaren riders, mounted on fast desert horses, lances pointed up at high heaven.

There was nowhere now for the Baltutu to run, to flee.

"My terms are simple: End the charade. We are not gods. We were not meant to be gods. End this! Help me teach them, to aspire, to chase their dreams. End this. These are my terms. No one else need die for their freedom."

The Baltutu, Telmun, Shuruppak, they were all surrounded. A distant, inaudible murmur became a song, belted out as loud as could be by the many voices of the revolutionary rabble. They were floodwaters drowning the soil. Fire scorching the earth. They came from everywhere, emerging out from behind trees in the wood, over and around hills, sweeping across the flat plains. To the Baltutu who stood watching outside their sanctuary, it surely must have seemed to be the work of a demon, a monster, a fluid creature swarming their lands, swallowing up their soldiers, muffling and silencing their cries, creeping steadily, too swiftly, towards them.

It was terribly quiet for a moment on the Cliffs of Damkina.

Melammu, paralyzed up until this point, snapped out of it at the sight of the Hundaren cavalry charge, a single rectangular formation plowing into the Etlu positions in the harbor, trapping them on this cliff. Shi was shaking her head vigorously, trying to dispel some invisible shroud that clung to her like a spider's web. Moving towards her brother, she touched Holindrian's hand.

With a sudden, unexpected jolt, Melammu shot Maaschuel back down the passage, knocking him off his feet, and sending him into the Pantheon's hall. Deflecting her next blow, Holindrian provided cover so that he and Shi could retreat. Swatting her powerful gusts, with the force of a tornado, away from himself, Shi, and Maaschuel, Holindrian sent them into the walls of the passage, giant cracks tearing at the stone, dust shooting out like miniature volcanic eruptions.

Shi helped Maaschuel, clearly startled and stunned, to his feet. Holindrian followed, pursued by his older siblings. There was a vengeful fire burning behind Melammu's eyes and, were it possible, she might have lobbed flaming orbs at him, intent on incinerating his flesh. Producing, seemingly out of thin air, her haladie with a flourish of her robes, Holindrian was forced to spin, countering her twirling blades by seizing her arm, hoisting her off the floor, and sending her tumbling off balance.

With his own burst, Holindrian shattered the lock on the door, allowing it to swing open. "You know what to do!" he shouted as he leapt into the air, dodging another barrage unleashed by Melammu, rotating, he hurled his own tidal force at her as he landed.

There wasn't time to argue. Maaschuel stumbled out of the Pantheon, assaulting a pair of Etlu standing guard outside. Lifting one of their swords, he dashed towards the Fishermen's Steps. Shi followed him out, and, with a flick of her wrist, shattered all the locks on all the doors, liberating hers and Holindrian's servants.

"Followers of Shi, your Goddess asks that you help Maaschuel and the free people of Eridu—"

Shi was wrenched back inside; an unseen hand grabbed her by the middle and hurled her to the ground. Smacking her head against the mosaic floor, she breathed heavily, not expecting to see Mummu looming over her. Shi dabbed at the trifling amount of blood on her lip with the tip of her finger.

Watching the horde advance, pouring out from the wood in droves, in spite of their numbers, Zigor did not suffer fits of panic or alarm. The rhythm of his heart remained unchanged. Purposefully, the defenses beyond the forest were not manned to their maximum. He wanted to lure them in. Little warning had been afforded to him of Holindrian's numbers, but he was perceptive enough to have known the traitor would have to bring his entire strength to bear. With as many as there were, those rebels would have no space to maneuver. The Etlu fortifications would dictate their movement across the battlefield. The losses would be terrible, on both sides, an absolute slaughter of the highest magnitude, but that did not matter. It was inconsequential how many lives had to be sacrificed; the will of his Gods would be done. He would serve as their willing instrument.

Tactics and cleverness would not be enough, and so, in their divine wisdom, the Baltutu, through the Goddess Melammu, had gifted ancient, sacred knowledge. The first bit was conventional enough, an enhancement to existing technology—the repeating crossbow. Second, and of far more interest and usefulness, was a mysterious gray powder with the propensity to combust, to burst into flame. Gunpowder. There had not been time to adapt this wondrous godsend to their siege weapons, but Melammu had presented the Etlu with what they called a *harquebus*.

The harquebus was a massive weapon for the individual soldier and very nearly their size. It was long, six feet, and had to be supported by a fort stand. Firing a lead ball, heavy, two solid ounces, these new weapons spewed fire from their mussels, roared like a ferocious beast, and were completely beyond the means of anyone, rebel or Etlu, to defend against.

Zigor had something special planned. Holindrian's revolutionaries had a terrible surprise waiting for them just on the other side of those trees.

Emerging from the tree line, the revolutionaries had more than a mile, closer to two, of open field to cross. The ground, for that first mile, was unaltered. Flat ground. Recently harvested ground. It was that second mile that would be the cause of so much grief. A stone wall, three, maybe four feet high, ran parallel with the forest for two and a half miles. Etlu infantry, armed with pikes, repeater crossbows, and the new harquebuses, were positioned behind that wall, just waiting for the rebels to come into range. Behind them, artillery, catapults and trebuchets, let loose heavy stones, raining down upon those brave enough to charge the stone wall. Forts, strung out in a line of six, evenly spaced, divided the Etlu defensive position. A series of trenches, mounds, and ditches populated the middle, while the rear was protected by dense rows of infantry—the last line of defense protecting Telmun.

Only a fraction, a tenth of what had marched on Shuruppak,

came prepared, properly armed, physically trained, and prepared mentally for the carnage of war, a tenth of millions. So many had come, wanting to fight, wanting to be a part of history, of helping forge their own destiny, but make no mistake, few, in their hearts, were soldiers, many more would reflect on this day in the years to come, and say how they had stood, bravely, in opposition of the greatest force Eridu had ever known—all the while skirting around the question if they had ever cast a blow in anger against the enemy.

Holindrian had committed everything, or very nearly everything. Two hundred thousand, far and away the bulk of his revolutionary warriors were now engaged on the Fields of Ezinu. They were an army representing every culture and people of every continent; blonde Antelmari woodsmen, Laurentian westerners, Trovian sailors, Volzari farmers, Hundaren desert dwellers, Audentican herders, Norpian southerners, Gerpedon plains folk, and even Ginnons—a people long since thought to have bred out violence, as one had not ever been known to harm another human being, let alone speak impertinently of another. Only the realms of Anshargal and Melammu contributed none to this fight for freedom, in fact, the opposite was true, a great number of Etlu reservists came from these lands.

Occupied Obenia was otherwise preoccupied.

Massive stones were flung into the air, soaring, arcing, and then smashing into the wheat fields. Craters, huge holes in the ground, became graves for advancing rebels as the boulders—spherical works expertly carved—rolled over fragile fleshy bodies. Though not advancing as a single mass, a mob, many a good man and woman died crossing that field, more still doomed ahead, at the stone wall.

Congested by the narrowness of the Traveler's Road, as it was the only possible means of their travel, it took a long while for help to come to the revolutionaries. Having had to make so much of the march without support, what was always going to be a march of certain death for some was made all the deadlier. But now, the first column of Liberation artillery was breaking from the tree line. Horse drawn flatbed wagons, towing ballistae and catapultae, tied down and skewed, aimed in such a way so as not to murder their locomotion, funneled out on to the battlefield and began opening fire at the Etlu line.

The stonewall became assaulted by rock and javelin, ahead of the first infantry assault. The Etlu had great difficulty in targeting the artillery chariots. Their crossbows and new harquebuses were unable to touch those inflicting damage as they retired beyond the range of the Etlu weapons when they happened to stray too close.

White markers, erected in the fields, denoted to the Etlu when they might unleash a sanctified hell upon the rebels. Those armed with repeater crossbows engaged first, at sixty yards. In an endless stream of bolts, they sprayed the thick throng, and the revolutionaries fell to the ground in droves.

But the charge continued. Over the dying screams and cries, the revolutionaries sang, yelling the lyrics to Etienette's song:

Sing with us and free the mind!
The men above are not divine!
The awoken hearts now form a line,
Their discourse cannot divide!

Ten more yards. Puffs, fog, clouds of gray smoke hid the stonewall. Flashes, sparks, sudden burst of flame. A deep rumbling roar, an alien sound, similar but decidedly different than thunder. Repeaters continued to shoot down rebels, but it was this new weapon, firing invisible projectiles, tiny metal missiles, that cast a horrendous feeling of dread on Holindrian's army. The harquebus had made its presence known, claiming a high toll in sacrificial blood.

Those on the frontlines were decimated, and, as their bodies were violated by lead, following divisions hunkered down, their stomachs pressed against the earth, prone. Despite the support of their artillery chariots, doing what they could to hamper the robust Etlu line, they were incapable of breaking the stone wall or silencing elements of the Etlu catapults, safely stationed too far behind, near the protection of the forts.

Conotocarious, as if by the shoulders of each individual man and woman under his command, forced his regiment into the pockmarked field, lying flat as can be. He had been leading his regiment as part of the First Corps, positioned in the first division to come under enemy fire but in the second brigade. That first brigade, under the command of a fellow Westerner by the name of Rufus, had been reduced to a handful of men, their commander among them—though wounded.

Bolts from the crossbows continued to fly low, zipping inches or less right over their heads. Hearing the "poof" of the fire sticks, everyone did their best to get some protection from those metal pellets, piling the bodies of the dead, stacking them so that they might hide, letting the bodies absorb the worst of it. They tried to return fire but loading and then firing a crossbow from this position was proving immensely difficult. The archers, whose short and long bows were a less mechanical process, gave a marginally better effort.

Lying on the ground offered some protection from the Etlu infantry, but not their artillery. It was plain enough. Conotocarious knew they, he and his regiment, could not remain there, cowering, using the dead as shields, indefinitely. Even with their numerical superiority, fear was a powerful weapon, and, currently, the Etlu wielded an unlimited supply.

Apsu was paralyzed by inaction. He did not know; he could not fathom how to respond. His back was against a wall—literally, he stood there, pressed firmly against the back wall of the Pantheon, beside him, the altar and on it, the Burden. *How did we get here? How did we fall so far?* There was something else on that altar, something they had prepared but he had hoped, he prayed he wouldn't actually have had to use... it was a syringe. It was full of taratum extract, but, this time, refined to its most potent form, lethal, but, Holindrian had manifested a tolerance, an adaptation to a more conservative dosage... Melammu assured it was the only way to subdue him. Apsu stared right at it.

Mummu fell, hard to the ground and seemed immobile for a moment. Shi nursed a purplish-black and yellow mark against the right side of her face where she had been struck. Turning, she saw Holindrian.

Swinging low, where his abdomen had been just half a second earlier, the pointed tip of Melammu's haladie carved out a path through Holindrian's shadow underneath him as he leapt backwards, into the air, arching his back. He landed on the palms of his hands and he sprung himself upright—only to be hit, square in the chest, by a kinetic blast. Striking the column to his rear with the force that would have shattered the constitution of a mortal man, Holindrian slid to the floor, delirious, pain radiating throughout his body. A trickle of blood ran down the back of his neck. Shaking his head, opening his eyes, blurry, he saw a figure vault towards him, arms held high over her head...

He flinched. Gritting his teeth, he braced himself. Expecting to be impaled any second. He heard something. Away. Off to the right. Opening his eyes, he saw why death had not claimed him. Death had taken another.

Shi was crouched, kneeling over Melammu, the retractable wrist daggers dripping with a rich, dark blood, a crimson not native to the body of the common man. Her wounds were oozing, gushing, flowing uncontrollably. Shi was trembling. Her hands stained with the red color as her robes drank their fill of the stuff, becoming soaked in it, drowning in it.

There was a scream, a shrill, the unmistakable howl of a banshee. Then a snap and a soft thud.

Unsure of what had just occurred, Holindrian called out for Shi. There was no answer. Grunting, he pushed himself, rising, and as his sight returned, he very nearly fell once more to the ground. Shi was lying on her back, legs folded underneath. She had this look on her face… one of profound sadness. The tear she shed for Melammu, for what she had done, still fresh in her eye. He reached out to her. He heard nothing. Her heart was silent, lungs drawing not even the weakest, subtlest of breaths. Touching her neck, he felt it. Broken. Her neck was broken.

Mummu was gone, but not far. He could hear sobbing, back down the passageway. In all honesty, Holindrian did not even notice Apsu there, and he would not, not for several moments more. Out on the edge of the cliff, he appeared with hardly enough time to witness a so thoroughly, a so absolutely grief stricken Mummu turn her back to the sea, close her eyes, and…

He did not know how long he sat there. Feet plopped out in front of him, grass beneath him, eyes staring out at… the sea? Nothing. Most likely, he was staring at nothing. He was trapped inside a bubble. Isolated. Alone. He did not hear Maaschuel leading a charge of marines up the Fishermen's Steps nor did he notice them hurry by, seizing control of the gates and engaging the Etlu behind their own lines. The cheering of the Hundaren cavalry, who had routed the Etlu and taken control of the harbor, was lost on him.

At some point, he summoned the strength to, once more, rise. Stumbling, drunk with an anguish and heartbreak he had not known since the First Age, he managed to guide himself back inside the Pantheon, bracing himself, dragging his hand along the corridor's wall. He stopped. Mouth agape. Apsu. He was sprawled on the floor, cradling the Burden in his arms, an empty syringe lying beside him on the mosaic, the sleeve of his robe pulled up high.

3.12 GODS MUST DIE

The Battle of Telmun concluded as follows: Shortly after securing the beachhead and docks, ensuring the Etlu navy would have not a single friendly berth, dock, slip, or stretch of shoreline to return to, Fajr gave chase to the retreating Etlu, desiring greatly to prevent them from reforming new positions on the higher ground in which they fled towards. Turmoil disrupted the Etlu outside the Gate of Titaan and Zigor was caught entirely by surprise when Maaschuel broke his lines with a few hundred revolutionary marines. Zigor attempted to regroup, ordering the army to fall back to the trenches surrounding his fort so as to make a proper last stand. Conotocarious, whose keen abilities of perception did not fail him this day, rallied his regiment and charged the stone wall bringing with them, hot on their heels, the whole of Holindrian's army. Finding himself between two prongs of rapidly advancing rebels and without the ability to maneuver now that his Etlu were fighting from the trenches and earthworks, Zigor, at long last and reluctantly, surrendered to Maaschuel once he felt that he had exhausted all possible avenues of victory. He contemplated not giving the order, of fighting to the last man, himself if need be, but Zigor, devout as he was, as much as he believed in the cause, in the Baltutu and everything they stood for, he was a pragmatic man. He saw no value in committing what remained of the seventy thousand Etlu stationed here to die in the face of overwhelming, assured defeat. A commander does not needlessly throw away the lives of those under his command, not if there is no advantage to be gained, not if the battle cannot be won, and Zigor knew this battle could not be won… not now. In the harbor, victory here, too, was found for the rebels, but the formidable Etlu fleet was not destroyed, far from it. An island, near the eastern entry, housed a fort not easily taken, and in fact, had failed to be taken. The channels around this island provided the fleet cover from which they set sail to the east.

As dusk settled over the Shuruppak, it was the juxtaposition of unbridled jubilation and the utmost melancholy. The deadliest single day of war drew to a welcomed close. It would be some time before there any real certainty emerged as to how many had been sent from this world and on to the next.

Holindrian's army, that band of two hundred thousand that had marched courageously and audaciously into a maelstrom of bitter resentment and scorn, tonight in their moment of triumph, gathered to bury the 59,000 souls who had given the last full measure of devotion in their bid for freedom. Ox carts, wheelbarrows, and the flatbed wagons that only hours ago had carried revolutionary artillery into battle hauled the dead from the place where they had fell to the place where they would sleep forevermore.

The Etlu under Zigor suffered losses of an even greater magnitude, with respect to their numbers. Of the seventy thousand redeployed to Telmun in the wake of the Baltutu defeat near Virescent, a score fewer than eighteen thousand had survived the day's carnage. Much of the twenty thousand routed by Hundaren cavalry (not even quite half that number) would live out the rest of their days until taken by old age or some affliction in later years.

The sea claimed the Etlu who plummeted into the dark blue depths, anchored to the ocean floor by their heavy plate armor. Bodies of Laurentian and Trovian sailors covered the sandy beaches, leaving hardly a spot for those recovering the remains to set their foot without stepping on some part of human anatomy. Galleons and triremes rested on sandbars and rocks; the keels shattered, masts splintered, and sails torn to tatters, rags tugged by the wind.

Seagulls, vultures, and other scavengers spared not a moment in searching the site for a banquet of dead flesh ripe for consumption.

The dead were buried together in Ezinu's Fields, Etlu and Amurru—soldier and rebel. This should be, in whatever world is to be born out of the ashes of this one, considered, without exception, hallowed ground, consecrated with the blood of men and women who died, no matter their side, with unwavering fealty to what they believed to be not only true, but right.

Never, in the Age of the Baltutu, had so many died in one solitary contest. More would die in the days to come, succumbing to the wounds suffered or infections contracted. It is better, I should think, to be counted amongst the dead or the living than lost, fates never recorded and loved ones set at ease. There were others of an indeterminant number who may never be seen again, heard of again, for they disappeared in the aftermath of a great battle. Families left unsure whether to mourn or hold out hope of seeing long departed loved ones. A pain extending well beyond either distance or time.

The fate of many would never be, unfortunate though it is to say, truly known.

A city of canvas and campfires was founded by the time night's grip was well and firm, covering the land as far as a mortal could see. After an initial raid on Telmun by an ardent faction of rebels, Maaschuel ordered the gates sealed and charged Conotocarious to bar further entry. Artifacts from all human history was contained within Telmun's vaults—with some trinkets preserved from the all-but forgotten First Age. Irreplaceable treasures from peoples no longer remembered by their descendants. Knowledge of things beyond description, beyond the comprehension of people of my time. It had been decided well before the launching of this campaign that Telmun would not fall to gangs of wild men, scarcely better than feral animals.

It was the opinion of some, numerically insignificant but disproportionally vocal, that no victory would be complete while the cornerstones of Baltutu rule persisted. Their shackles, as they argued, would never truly be shed, freedom never truly achieved, if the new world retained the conventions of the old one. As a wildfire cleanses the forest of debris, stifling vigorous and essential growth, so too must the very foundations of civilization be upended so as to infuse the soil with nutrients to once again be fertile and befitting the common decencies and sensibilities of humankind.

This faction of radical revolutionaries believed in Holindrian's word with evangelical fervor. They would have gladly seen Telmun razed. Wrecked down, its wondrous architecture struck down brick by brick. Plundered what was of obvious use, then burned the rest. Destroying a library whose volumes were greater in number than all the stars in the observable sky.

The deaths of the four Baltutu only served to intensify their zeal. Theirs was a revolution of blood more so than of ideas.

Their leader was a man by the name of Drust. His home was the little island of Castroniphinae on the far side of the world. In his previous life, he had been a cobbler, an important occupation, though, given the testimony of those who had known him since adolescence, Drust never found it particularly gratifying. It had been because of Drust, and his likeminded fellows, that the island state was freed from Apsu, but it had been a bloody affair. In the years that followed, many who believed in the cause would say his methods were brutish and unnecessarily violent. The temple, magistrate's office, and all symbols of the Baltutu were cast down, destroyed. The killing, by and large, was indiscriminate—if you were found to be on the premises, even there only to conduct menial business, mercy would not stay their hands in cutting down their victims for freedom's sake.

A bloodlust or sickness, again, in the years since the end of the war, has been attributed to the man. Surviving members of his family have refused to speak, to offer clarity or further perspective of any kind, defaulting the judgment of their kin to others. It is difficult to positively distinguish truth from supposition, rumor, and intentional revision of memory to suit the accepted narrative.

The historian's challenge is only compounded when one realizes Drust was a man of action and not of words, thus, no record exists or is known to have ever existed containing the man's thoughts as he perceived them. An overreliance on hearsay then becomes inescapable.

It was well past midnight. Cold. Dark. The clouds had not subsided. No starlight tonight. Few campfires continued to burn, decaying into coals. The body collection was finished for the night and a quietness settled in over the fields. A quietness of rest. A quietness that was equal parts permanent and transitory.

A tent, hastily assembled, sat atop the cliffs. The opening flap parted and the indisputably impressive sight that was Telmun commanded the view. It was an austere way to live, a piece of canvas draped over poles—sticks gathered from nearby, a single bedroll covering the ground. Five of these such tents were arranged around a shared fire holding out their palms to the flickering flame. Most were sitting, all in fact, save for one. Drust. He stood, staring, not at the fire for it would make it difficult to see in the dark, but at Telmun and the Pantheon's moon-lit dome.

"He had orders, Drust."

"...that's the rub, isn't it? 'He had orders'." Drust shook his head, the glow from the fire never illuminating more than half of the man's face. "Nothing is changing. Not really. We're trading one master for another."

Clisson spoke, echoing Drust's sentiment, "this priest, this officer… Cono'carious may wear a soldier's cap but we ain't fooled. We won't be fooled. Those who ruled over us all before they'll do so again. Some of 'em already are!"

Drust's face flushed with loathing. The priest in his town on Castroniphinae had been among the first to die. And the Ethics Officer. Then the administrators. He had experienced a VET camp before. "Rehabilitation". The time he had spent in that place fueled the anger burning inside.

He had been a fine shoemaker. Best in all Castroniphinae, he would say. People would let their shoes turn to rags, let their feet grow raw, before they would accept a pair of shoes not fashioned by his hands. In an effort to make certain that people from all over the island could distinguish his shoes from those of lesser makers, he created a mark and engraved it on the heel. Drust thought he was doing right by his community, just as he had always been taught. The Ethics Officer did not see it that way, nor the priest. He spent three months locked away in a decrepit place, a dark hole barred away from the rest of the world. There would be lectures—the priests were always lecturing. Interviews followed by beatings—especially if you gave answers the priests or administrators did not like. Just enough water to survive. Meals reduced to a gelatinous substance. No sanitation. They stood and slept in their own filth. When the priests were satisfied with the progress of recovery, they would release you, on the condition you reported regularly to a designated Ethics Officer.

The only lesson Drust had learned was to distrust and despise. Watch what you say around people. Let them hear what they want to hear, never let them see who you truly are, what you are truly thinking, what you are truly capable of. They will underestimate you and lessen their suspicions.

Clisson was still talking. There was a general murmur of agreement around the fire.

"What even be the point in all this fightin' if we just goin' be slaves to some other?"

"Yeah! What's stopping these 'officers' from keepin' all this authority they've been given in this here war? Sure looks to me like they say we're a doin' ourselves a favor, but when we really be doin' them a mighty favor!" Clisson said, and again, there was nodding from the men.

"When it's all over, we goin' go back to whatever was we doin' before. Won't be no different. Mark my words. No different at all... not in ways it counts."

"I bet if that Laurentian feller keeps up what he doin', they'll get him his own kingdom!"

Hearty laughter broke out round the camp.

"It isn't the leaders of this army we need to be worrying 'bout. Conotocarious. Maaschuel. They's just men. I reckon we can handle a few men," and Drust jerked his thumb back towards the killing fields. "Men can handle the ambitions of other men. Stop 'em before they get too corrupt. Tyrannize us."

"We ain't just been fightin' men, have we now? Uh nah, no. We been fightin', well, I ain't too sure what they are, but... we ain't never gotten this far without Holindrian," Clisson said, drinking from a bota bag full of wine plundered from Zigor's fort.

Drust smirked. "Don't you see the problem? Right or wrong... it wasn't our idea to start this war. One day we just found ourselves in a war and had to take up a side. We still just followin'. Now it's just one instead of six. Don't you see it? It's so clear to me! Nothin' we do matters a lick while *he's* still alive. We never gonna be free to do and choose as we want long as even one of *them* is breathin'. Holindrian's done good by us, but none of us really *believe* life is gonna change. It can't... 'cause we just followers followin'."

Under better light, the passion in his cheeks would have been as impossible to miss as it was in his voice.

Drust continued, taking a step closer to the fire, chest heaving, locking eyes with each man there: "Now, before yesterdee, I wasn't gonna say anything. I mean, we never would have gotten this far without him. I admit it. I admits it! He taught us what freedom *is*, what our lives might *be*. So, you know, when I say this, there is no malice in my heart… but we know what he's capable of. Look what this one's done. Holindrian's stirred up a war all by himself. If—*if* he ever wanted to, he could seize up power anywhere, conquer us all just like theys done before. He talks 'bout makin' man free. Says we outta be able to rule ourselves. Make our own laws. Live our lives the way we wants to. Tell me, how are we ever gonna be free when at any time he could just take it all back, just like that?"

The other men were quiet, but they were a captive audience, listening to each word he spoke with reverence.

"It's too much power, for any man. Don't matter at all how good of a man he may be. It's too much! But now, we know they can die—just like us! They can be killed! Boys, I believe in the Cause too much to risk it all. To risk us becoming slaves again for someone else…" his voice dropped suddenly, and they all leaned forward, turning their ears to him so that they might hear what he was about to say next, "if we really wanna win this revolution, well, I'm afraid, Holindrian is gonna have to die."

Not another word was spoken that night. The fire was put out. The men saw themselves to their tents and fell asleep.

The ideologically pure do not debate the validity of their beliefs, but the fallacy of all others. When they argue, it is not whether they should act, but how far they must be willing to go. And there are never any limits. Not really. In their minds, no one (save for themselves) is above reproach, no one is above damnation, no one is deserving of compassion. Violence, rape, murder, torture—all the evils which are in direct contrast to the proper nature of man, evils that would seek to plunder all value from human experience, those are their tools, and terribly effective they can be.

Clear on the other side of Telmun, on that small hill near the ruins of the Margidda, beside three ancient headstones, Holindrian finished shoveling the last of the soil on to the caskets he had fashioned hours earlier. Four bodies cleaned and wrapped. Four graves dug. Four caskets built. Alone. He had labored alone, dismissing repeated offers from Maaschuel of help. Alone. This he had to do alone. He laid them to rest in no special order, and if he did, he was not conscious of it. Standing there, alone in the dark, with only the faint torchlight to offer him any semblance of comfort, he thought much but said nothing. He tried to apologize to Enkirus and Esh but could not. He tried to curse Uilliam but could not. He wanted to. He wanted to say something… but he could conjure up no fine words, no words worthy of uttering in remembrance. He even contemplated digging a fifth grave, drawing a sword, and ending his own life, but could not (even though he had carried out with him a sword to do the deed). It was lying just over there, yet Holindrian could not muster the strength to do that, either.

But, perhaps, that fifth grave would not have been for him, but rather, a part of him. He had thought *Holindrian* was born the day he was shut inside the Kurn, poisoned and betrayed. He had thought that was the day Maramurru had died. He had been wrong. Maramurru had been living inside him, remaining a part of him over these past months, but no longer. Maramurru was a part of the old world. Holindrian, by contrast, existed because of the old world's failings and he would help right them.

Anshargal would hear what had happened here today. Holindrian's mission was not yet complete, but it soon would be.

3.13 THE PROMISE OF A WORLD DEMOCRATIC AND FREE

"Is this it?" Maaschuel asked; he and Holindrian sifted through Maramurru's chambers.

His belongings had been packed into wooden crates and the two men pried them open, one by one, searching through a variety of artifacts, some of them from the Baltutu period but many more from before. Rummaging through boxes haphazardly piled in a corner, Maaschuel pulled out from one of them a granite bust gifted to Maramurru by the Sanahj, under whose rule the greatest of all the pyramids, the Kurnugi, was constructed.

Looking up, Holindrian saw it, breathed a sigh of relief, and smiled. "Yes! Yes, that's it." Setting the bust back down inside the box, he moved over towards Maaschuel. "Thank you."

It was a book, a bound treatise of some kind, but in a language Maaschuel was not familiar with and certainly did not recognize, but was obviously of great importance or sentimental value; he was not sure yet of which.

"*The Mouse That Roared*," Holindrian said, waving the thin hardbound book, "you remember once asking me what 'democracy' was?" He flipped through the pages, skimming their contents before finding the one he sought. "*Democracy here is more than a minimalist definition. It is and ought to be more than the minimalist definition of free, fair, and competitive elections; democracy may, necessarily, begin as such, but it is a living and maturing entity, one that has grown, in the appreciation of modern society, to incorporate ideas of procedural and civil rights, the protecting of minorities from tyranny, the separation of governmental power, installation of institutions and societal norms, and an impartial bureaucratic system.*" Holindrian's eyes returned to Maaschuel, smiling, only to see that the meaning of these words were altogether lost on the man. "Ah… well, we'll have to revisit this chapter, to be sure," and, closing the book, he slipped it into his jacket.

Maaschuel stared at something else, his gaze low, aimed at a disorganized pile of things. Moving towards it, he shoved back the stuff until what he saw was free. Taking hold of it, he could feel a distinctive shape within the folds of cloth. Chuckling, he passed it on to Holindrian.

"I wasn't sure I'd ever see it again," he said, as Holindrian took possession of the parcel from him.

Wrapped in a heavy cloth, the slender bundle was tied with leather straps. Pulling the ties loose, he unfolded the wrappings. Holding the grip with his left hand, he removed the scabbard. Tracing the fuller with the tip of his middle finger, he felt a shudder as goosebumps erupted all over his body at the touch of the alien steel.

"I thought surely Anshargal would have taken it. At the very least, never would have thought they'd have buried it." He flinched at his poor choice of words. "…that they would have packed it away in here with the rest of your effects."

Holindrian gazed upon it; almost in a sort of trance. "It is a painful memory in and of itself…" he trailed off.

"What is it?"

"She said something to me once. She said, 'if you want to know how humans are supposed to live, how they are supposed to behave and treat others, look no further than to a child. Look to that young, gregarious, inquisitive, empathetic, unafraid child who knows nothing of society's labels and ills, and you'll know how we are all supposed to be.'"

"She went before her time."

Holindrian's head bobbed. "Indeed. *Hmm…* I've had so much of it. I have seen and done and learned things—I am grateful…."

"But?"

"…but, for all that, there are days where I'd give it up gladly just to experience the world as you do."

Maaschuel frowned. "Holindrian, you are the most human man I've ever known or could hope to know. *I* shouldn't have to say this to *you*, but it doesn't matter how long or short one's life is. Has no bearing whatsoever on the quality of your human experience. What matters is how you lived. How many lives you've touched? How loved you are by those who knew you. What they remember of what you leave behind. If, you felt so inclined, however, and wanted to make me immortal… I wouldn't turn you down. A blood transfusion, perhaps?"

"Long life may not be as appealing as it first sounds. Besides, it doesn't work that way."

"A short life might not be so great either." Maaschuel surveyed the courtyard as they stepped out from the chamber. "What will become of this place?"

"I don't know. I suppose that will be up to you. I'm leaving it to you, to all of you, and all its contents. Though I earnestly hope you choose to preserve what is here and not reduce it to rubble, the choice doesn't belong to me."

"Leaving it?" Maaschuel didn't particularly like the sound of that. "What does that mean? Going somewhere?"

"We all have to go *somewhere*. I go to the east."

Maaschuel liked that idea far less; his heart feeling like a great weight had just been attached to it. "But, why go after him? Surely, he recognizes that it is over. There can be no turning back now."

"This isn't about politics or the future of humanity anymore. *This* will be vengeance. And he won't just stop with me—he can't. He will come for you, and anyone he believes is responsible, no matter how far removed, for the deaths… in their deaths. His retribution will be terrible. It will be absolute. Anshargal will bring about the Apocalypse; unleash Hell itself on to the people of Eridu. It would be the first and foremost of all calamities, the epitome of foolishness to hold on to hope that sense and reason, or the Burden we have so long endured will stay his hand. If anything, if he does reflect on the old lessons, I fear, it shall only serve to spite him. He will end the world. That is why I must go. Any chance we have now depends on me stopping him."

If Maaschuel had been of another temperament, he might have struck Holindrian for holding such an absurd notion. "You know you're not going alone, right?" But, before Holindrian could offer some clever rebuttal, he said, "it is hubris for you to think that you alone can do what you propose on your own. Holindrian didn't achieve victory here nor at Virescent or anywhere else in between. The people… *the people* achieved victory. If this fight has been about their future and their wellbeing, they have earned the right to see it finished. And, if Anshargal is as dangerous to that future as you say, you better damn well believe we'll be marching to face him—not behind you, but beside you. You can't expect them, or me for that matter, to not see this through. Let's go win it, together," and he held out his hand.

Maaschuel's voice carried his impassioned plea, and those within the walls of Telmun paused in their task to listen. There was a sizable crowd surrounding them when Maaschuel's voice reached its crescendo.

"They could all die. We could all die," Holindrian said in a hushed whisper, meant for only himself and Maaschuel to hear.

Maaschuel shrugged. "Then, we'll do that together, too."

Holindrian could feel the hundreds of pairs of eyes fixed upon him, bating their breath.

3.14 A WAR OF WRATH

"…I see a fire consuming the whole of the world. Inside mountains and over oceans, a relentless burning leaving only ash, turning all to blackened coals. That is what I see.

"A great loss has befallen our great civilization. The igno-rant, those weak in their faith, have risen up, taken arms against their Gods and their countrymen. Families torn apart, turning the home into a microcosm of war. These heretics, these infidels have made our lands unclean with their very presence, adulter-ating all they touch. Fertile farms now salted wastes. Holy places now cursed with violence and blood.

"You here represent a people who remain pure and unconta-minated. Your faith remains undiluted; your souls are prudent, modest, pious, equitable, and just. Thus, be assured, you are blameless. See that your obligations are forevermore satisfied in the eyes of your Gods, and your Gods vow to never forsake you or your eternal spirit.

"None of you can nor will be held responsible for the crimes of others. Your God knows your worth, but this heresy cannot be tolerated. Not by the sacred laws of the Baltutu. If a hand of cruel intention seizes a priest, let the hand of the wrongdoer be removed so as to assure he may never do so again. If a house of worship should be besieged by betrayers, know that in doing so, they have damned for all eternity their souls, feel no remorse for sending them into the dark void. Expel from your homes and your communities incendiary persons, anathematizing before neighbor and God.

"Disorder will end. This time of troubles will end, this I promise to you with divine assuredness. But it cannot end, it will not end, my blessed people, unless you heed your Lord's call. Together, we must restore peace and harmony to this world. They have killed and captured many of the faithful. They occupy lands rightfully yours. They have devastated our holy empire. Go forth, seek out the heathen craven wherever they may lurk and fulfill your duty to self and God by hastening them to their inevitable end, affirming their place in Hell so that you might affirm yours in Heaven alongside the Anunna-Ki lords.

"Should any of you suffer death at their hands, go willingly, knowing any sins or trespasses of yours are duly pardoned. This, by the high position I hold in the eyes of our Lords, I grant you. Come, let us aid in their repentance."

These words so masterfully spoken by Anshargal upon his arrival in the east, at a place deep within Humare by the name of Bahram, inaugurated an inquisition, a crusade sanctioned by Heaven's own prince. A day after addressing the crowds from the south-facing Steps of Anur (a series of monumental steps, numbering, in total, 105, a single step representing a year, from the Anunna-Ki lords coming to Enkirus to the end of the Second Age) Anshargal received thousands, of all ages, answering their Lord's call for men and women of fighting age and ability. More came in the days after that, until the ranks of his army had swelled to more than eighty thousand by the middle of October.

These fresh recruits would spend the remainder of the fall and much of the winter training and preparing to engage the rebels in battle just before the start of spring in the new year. He had left an entire corps in defense of Telmun under General Zigor, a man he knew capable of withstanding the probing attacks and skirmishes Holindrian's rebels were conducting along the fortified border.

Anshargal might have been more concerned for the safety of the capital were not so much revolutionary effort being concentrated to the east. The border country between Hundare and Humare was deteriorating rapidly, with heavy casualties on both sides. Brutal fighting. He could not—would not jeopardize the thirty thousand Etlu who had followed him into the scorching eastern desert, where temperatures of a hundred degrees threatened his wounded soldiers with dehydration, heat stroke, and other sicknesses.

Hundaren cavaliers clashed with those of Humare, staining the sands under the shadow of the mountains with red. Humari warriors had held on to the border country dividing their ancestral lands from the Hundaren, even managing to push back the revolutionary line, capturing a natural harbor. More important than the harbor, however, was the securing of gates along the Eastrun (eastern road). A swath of land, about 34 miles wide, separated the transcontinental mountain range from the coast where the climate was hot and dry in the summer but cool and wet in the winter. The Eastrun was a major artery connecting the continent and would be invaluable to whoever controlled it. For Anshargal, it guaranteed a means for him to return to the west, without having to rely on more perilous mountain passages.

To underscore the significance of what his dedicated Humari had achieved, Anshargal deployed ten thousand of his Etlu (those in recovery) and commissioned a network of defenses to be constructed to better hold the road.

Late November was marked by disaster. For this Baltutu Day brought not a feeling of thanksgiving and solidarity, but anarchy and transgression. His realm remained largely undisturbed by the phenomenon of violent upheaval and civil disobedience sweeping the planet, as nearly all those with a propensity for dissension had, one way or another, been satisfactorily removed from his society. The same could not be said elsewhere. Anshargal felt pressure on his borders. To the east and southeast, Ginno and Ginsup, provinces of Mummu, became infected. Military action preserved the territorial integrity of the realm, but it was made known that believers, true believers of the Baltutu, would always be welcomed in lands where the Red X flew.

Shi's Gerpedon collapsed and was reduced to a buffer zone between, unleashing a floodgate of refugees and attackers alike, adding increased risk to the precious mountain passes. Barumgal, who had been conducting a moderately successful campaign against the Antelmari from Ohlin, withdrew through one such pass once his supply lines were obliterated amongst the ensuing chaos.

In the face of these misfortunes, Anshargal remarked firstly, "I am greatly disturbed. Deeply agitated," but then, went on to say, "I will kill or have anyone killed, governor or farmer, who not only does not swear fealty to the Baltutu, but fails to convince me of their sincerity!"

Anshargal's temperament was tested more directly half a week later when news reached him concerning the return of the Obenian king, who had taken up arms, not as a leader of men, but as a common soldier, fighting alongside them in an effort to reclaim their country.

"We should have had that miserable swine killed."

Had he the troops, the proper troops, not these... conscripts... Anshargal would have set out posthaste for Telmun so that he might hunt down Holindrian and end this war. He said as much when last he spoke with Melammu, in the days before the capital fell.

"I underestimated the enemy before; I will not make that mistake again. We will show him no quarter. Their rebellious breed will be purged from the current stock. The black flag, Melammu, the black flag! If Holindrian is to triumph, it is not alone that our Empire should fade into obscurity. It is the triumph of anarchy—we can clearly now see this is but a prelude. Civilization. Government. Fraternity. All will be extinguished if each individual man should be his own king. The black flag is our only defense against the harbinger of our Armageddon."

Melammu agreed firmly, *"our brother and sisters are too timid to recognize what it will take to end this war, to win this war."*

"The history of the mortal race is full of such wars. It may be of value if we reflect on bygone days. I assure you, under the black flag such terrors will be unleashed that the rebels will be brought to their senses. Quickly! Holindrian will have no choice but to submit."

The most trying news by far would come a few days early in December when the remnants (a significant portion if truth be told) of the Etlu navy arrived in Humari waters, taking advantage of the safety the Gulf of Humar provided. Anshargal learned of the fall of Telmun. There were rumors, gossips, and all manner of revolutionary propaganda claiming the deaths of four of the six Baltutu. Frustration mounted as all attempts at contacting them or sensing them yielded only disappointment. It would not be for some weeks, not until some 2,500 defeated Etlu that he would hear, definitively, of how Melammu and the rest had died —at the hands of Holindrian, whom Anshargal bestowed the title of Betrayer.

As a cold winter night settled in, the people of Bahram shutting themselves in behind closed doors and around warm fires, Anshargal died... only to be reborn, with the aid of sacrificial blood, harvested from the veins of the luckless Etlu soul who had delivered the foul news to his Lord, his mission not yet complete. Anshargal disrobed, embracing the hypothermic desert night stark and bare.

3.15 THE ROAD TRAVELED

"We are nearly at the end!"

Holindrian stared curiously at the speaking glass. "What is that supposed to mean?"

He sat on the edge of the cliffs, feet dangling over, the ground cold against his bottom (even through his heavy trousers). It was cold, but he could almost feel the warmth of spring in the wind. It would be here soon enough, and when it came, they would be at it again. One last battle.

"Well, that's precisely it," Uilliam said, feverishly; Holindrian assumed he could read his thoughts from wherever he was, "we are coming up on the end of the road I started you on," he sighed mightily, "and not a moment too soon. I can't promise you that I will be here at the end."

Rubbing his palms together, Holindrian breathed hot, heavy

air between them. "If this is an attempt at humor... know that I am not in the mood for jokes." When Uilliam did not respond, he continued, "this is as much your revolution as anyone's. Now you say you're just going to, what, *leave*? Uh nah... you got me into this...."

"You got yourself into this. Four thousand years ago. You and your siblings lost your way. I returned to help you regain your footing."

"Where are you going?" Holindrian said after a while, crossing his arms, silver eyes squinting in the face of the wind.

"Away—if things are really as bad as they seem," there was a quiver in his voice that had not been there before, not in all these years, a sense of panic, uncertainty.

Holindrian straightened up a little. "What do you mean, 'as bad as they seem'?"

"Ah. *Hmm.* Uh um..." He was struggling to choose the exact words. "Know that the struggle for freedom—to resist the yoke of tyranny is not exclusively a human concern," gulping again, louder this time, he said, "the universe is a very dangerous place, Holindrian. We are presently being reminded of that fact."

"Aliens?" Holindrian asked, ignorantly, benightedly—though, it was to be expected given the context.

Uilliam groaned. "Everything is alien to something, but yes. 'Aliens'."

"Are you losing?"

"Too early to say. It is not we who wage war neither it is we that war is waged against. Anyway, I don't want you worrying about me—not to say that you are, of course—or what may be happening on the other side of... yes, well, concentrate on the task at hand. I know this particular road has not been easy nor should it, but I trust you understand the significance of this burden. You have done beautifully! This will be the most important fight of your life. Succeed, and let them take it from there."

Holindrian shook his head. "What am I supposed to do when this is all over—should I survive it?"

The light was dimming fast. "I, if I were you, I would remember to kindle once more humanity's light."

3.16 THE EMPTYING OF TELMUN

Everyone had gone, returning to his or her homes. Everyone, that is, except for some eighty thousand volunteers pledging to stand with Holindrian to the end—any end. For many, the war was over. The Baltutu were defeated, Telmun had been sacked, and the Etlu had dispersed, fleeing into the distant east. It was the end of February, and in this coastal climate, that meant it was time to march; it was as much the season of renewal as the season of war.

In southern Hundare, where the fighting had been among some of the worst during the war, they prepared themselves and their homes for the coming campaign in the shadow of a wall. From the sandy shores of the gulf to the rocky mountain bases, a wall of stone and earth had been erected with far-fetched speed and the full wealth of resources of man and nature. Milecastle fortlets, 34 in all, each home to a quarter regiment—two hundred men—divided the east from the west. A twelve-foot-wide gate regulated entry at the flagship fortress of Haurvatat right there on the coast.

Before the war, Haurvatat had been a prosperous Hundaren border town, controlling the western point of access to the Eastrun (known as Westerline in the west-facing countries), the primary continental highway, as well as being home to some of the best well-preserved examples of proto-Hundaren ruins in the region. In a previous age, the Huthar, antecedents to both the Hundaren and Humari, cultivated the coastal and sparse desert climates, thriving for thousands of years, amassing architectural wonders as impressive as any civilization before it. Few had survived into the Age of the Baltutu, and of those that had, none were so magnificent as the Palace of Kings.

A hypostyle construction, a colossal portico on each side, the columns were of such fine craftsmanship that, even at their exceptional age and centuries of neglect, the decorative carvings had refused to be eroded by time or weather. It remained in superb condition.

Present day Haurvatat, that which was constructed in more recent memory, was less glamorous. The Baltutu, upon seizing power, could not bring themselves to wreck the remnants of the Huthar, but situated new settlements closer to the coast, encouraging the people to profit from trade on the road and seas. Under its current masters, the wall sealed old and new Haurvatat behind it, locked behind the gate.

As Haurvatat had been a Hundaren city, a number of its population had taken up rebellion against the Baltutu. Their lives were forfeit, from that moment on, in the eyes of the Humari invaders. With the sanctioning of high Heaven, the sentence of death for their crimes was dutifully executed. Blood ran thick, ankle deep through the streets, a red band staining the stone foundations unlikely to soon fade (nor did it fade in the decades which followed, and it persisted as a scar to be borne forevermore). Lynchings. Burnings. Evisceration. Decapitation. Exsanguination. People were killed in a variety of awful ways.

The Hundaren poet Anaitis's most renown work, the *Musif Avaz*, sings of the atrocities suffered by lovers of mixed origin as the Revolution's worst atrocities wrecked Haurvatat and is ardently recommended by this author. Similarly, the *Sangha*, of Humari fascination, is an amalgamation of sanitized tales recorded and compiled by a VET priest that, from a revolutionary perspective, was tantamount to fiction.

When the Etlu finally arrived, the massacre was not yet complete. Survivors were rounded up and crucified on the cross, limbs bound tightly with rope. For more than a mile, on either side of the road, their bodies failed, decaying under the sun, all along the Westerline-Eastrun road. The scarlet "X" became a symbol of their God's wrath. In hardly any time at all, it was painted on the western face of every fortlet, and boldly across the main gate.

Holindrian stood on the crown of the tallest hill he could find; the present terrain limited his options. Stroking his unshaven chin, the telltale signs of a goatee sprouting through the bronze skin, he stared off, best Maaschuel could discern as he trudged up the mound, at nothing. Everything bled together— blue above the horizon, brown below. But Holindrian had spectacular visual acuity and could perceive what a mortal man could not.

"What do you see?"

"Well… they've built a wall. Looks to me that it runs from the shoreline to the base of the mountains," he replied, biting his thumb.

"Damn! Here I was hoping they'd just given up."

Maaschuel came and stood beside him, imagining that he could see what Holindrian saw. "Forts about, what, a mile apart? Pretty standard positioning, really." He gestured vaguely in the direction of where the wall ought to be.

"Any ideas how to get us on the other side?"

Maaschuel shrugged. "*You* could probably knock. I bet they're dying to see you."

He was probably right, Holindrian thought. "Any word from Oda?"

"No. Not since turning and riding farther north. She and her Wildcats are fast, but it'll still be seven days, perhaps more, before they can scout the pass and report back. Hot, arid, and rough country. We Antelmari don't much like the heat."

"I can't think they'd leave any of the passes left open and unguarded." He sunk his hands into his pockets. "As it stands, we are facing a siege, Maaschuel. How he does love his sieges...."

"He does. He is good at them, too good. Holindrian, if Anshargal is here, it's because he wants us to attack." He moved so that he was now standing directly in Holindrian's line of sight. "He knows there is no way we can deprive his army of supplies."

"After the gate has been broken, I will commit what remains of the navy to an assault on the beach, perhaps draw some pressure off the infantry." Holindrian squinted over the shorter man's head.

"Won't be enough." Maaschuel drew himself straight as he could, standing as tall as spine and legs would permit. "That gate might be tall, but the road is narrow. The terrain challenging. They'll have erected barricades, traps, and other obstacles. You'll be marching four men abreast. All enemy fire will be concentrated on a single point. No eighty thousand men and women ever made are going to take that gate. Not that way."

When Holindrian said nothing in response, his silver eyes remaining fixed, Maaschuel said, "it would be like Virescent, in a way. The enemy is going to have elevated, fortified positions. I agree that we need to be the ones who strike, but not this way. Not on this ground."

A strong gust smacked the side of his head, the folds of his jacket caught in the wind.

"How do you propose to draw him out from behind his wall? I should not want to engage him here." He swept his hand over the flat, rocky, and parched earth west of the wall. "We know that he has at least one corps of Etlu present. One corps would reap untold devastation against us on open ground."

Maaschuel agreed with this assessment as well. Attacking Etlu directly, without some sort of tactical advantage, was suicide. He placed great faith in the troops—they had seen and weathered combat and death—but there were few among them who could hope to stand against that sort of raw power.

"Let's see what Oda has to say about the condition of the mountain pass. It would take some work; we'd want to be careful and smart about it, but it might be worth clearing those roads."

Holindrian's head swung to the left. The mountains, large and majestic, were snowcapped. The tallest were as giants in the far distant background, a blur in the haze.

"We could screen our movement behind the mountains. Come up, over, and behind and attack Haurvatat from the north," he said, massaging the tightness in his hand.

Maaschuel refrained from exclaiming the full breadth of relief he felt. "*Phew...* that'd be quite the march—but an opportunity to fight on ground of our choosing. We'd be in enemy country though. Have to take almost everything with us—provisions that is—and it would be hot... even within sight of the coast."

Holindrian continued to massage his hand, right at the base of the thumb. "Could we do it?"

"What you mean to say is, 'can *you* do it?'" Maaschuel said, correctively, "I believe so. Death and disaster at least aren't assured."

Holindrian made an exceptionally poor imitation of a frown. "Can you do it?"

Maaschuel couldn't help but laugh. "Yeah, sure. I'll just add this to the list of nigh impossible tasks you've asked of me. *Maaschuel, help me start a revolution to free all mankind. Maaschuel, sneak across the river in the dead of night, secure a bridge, and hold it against a guy who can kill you with his mind. Maaschuel, signal the marines when it's time to attack... but to do that, you're going to need to come with me, unarmed to Telmun.*"

"When this is all over, there will be but one last thing I ask of you."

Maaschuel nodded, clearing his throat. "The big one. We win this, we survive this, I'll get it done."

"I've asked so much of you, Maaschuel. I have always been able to count on you."

"Always. Oh, before I forget," and he rummaged underneath his cloak, "they made something—the troops—thought you might fancy a look."

Unfolding the bundle of cloth, it was a navy banner not too dissimilar from any number of blue banners draped throughout his realm, but there was something different about this one, something special. Holding up the cloth, a corner in each hand, revealed a white laurel that had been sewn with a coniferous tree, also white (possibly a spruce) at the center. In the upper right were two white suns, and the larger of the two had rays reaching out towards the tree. At the bottom was the word *liberty* stitched in argent.

"The consensus was we were due for a new standard."

When Oda returned to the revolutionary camp days later, she told them of the condition of the mountain pass. The nearest cuts were blocked, either by ancient erections of brick and mortar or those of rocks and boulders stripped from further up the mountain. Precious time and labor would have to be expended to clear the obstructions if an army were going to pass through. The risk that Anshargal's scouts would locate and report Holindrian's intentions to their master would be a near certainty before the task was complete. Waging war in the mountains would be disastrous and could only benefit Anshargal and the status quo.

"There is another possibility. Ve encountered follovers of Shi. They told us of not a road over the mountain but a tunnel through it. A man-made cavern braced vit brick valls."

Her northern Antelmari accent had diminished noticeably these past eight months, much unlike that of Folcher's, her uncle. The "V" and "W" sounds still gave her some grief, the former sounding like an "F" and the latter a "V".

Holindrian and Maaschuel traded glances. "Can you show me on a map?"

Rolling out a leather-bound scroll, Oda jabbed her finger at a point between two labeled and frequently used passes. "There!"

While Holindrian massaged his temple, Maaschuel asked, "did you ride through it?"

"Ja. The Shi-lings led us to the other side. Fery rocky. Offergrown. But, ja, it is passible."

"How can there be a tunnel… *through* a mountain… we've never heard of? It's not listed on this map or any map."

"It may date back to the Fourth Age. Their collapse wasn't sudden, but prolonged and arduous. Societies sealed themselves off from one another. Shrinking, eventually becoming totally isolated. Knowledge was lost through attrition."

Maaschuel looked to Holindrian. "Did they know of it—the tunnel—in the last age?"

"Not to the best of my ability to remember," he said, shaking his head.

"How did the Shi worshipers find the tunnel?" Maaschuel asked, now looking back at Oda.

"They said they found it."

"How?" Maaschuel pressed.

Oda pointed to another location on the map, this one marked, "the shrine. They vere priestesses before, and the shrine is built offer the riffer. They vere collecting vater when one of them tripped and tvisted her ankle. Seeking shelter for the night, they found a caffe, but vhen they came inside they saw it vas constructed, not eroded and shored vith fired brick."

Maaschuel's hands were covering his mouth. "I think we may have found our way in, Holindrian."

"Anshargal has to be expecting we'll come at him laterally. Maaschuel, if they know about this tunnel, they will be able to contain us. The Etlu will keep us bottled up at the tunnel's exit and hit us with endless artillery."

"He knows we're coming. He's dug in. He expects some trick or deception on our part, but I don't think he cares. He knows *we* have to come to *him*. I can hurry the troops through. *I* can do this! I won't let you down."

"Maaschuel," he said, sighing, "it's not a matter of letting me down...."

But Maaschuel was as chipper as ever. "I know, I do… but, Holindrian, I can do this!"

Reluctantly, Holindrian consented. "What is this junction here," he said, pointing to a town just northeast of Haurvatat on rocky hills.

"…Gathbiyya," Maaschuel said, hunching over the map.

"This is where we will converge."

The next morning, the suns seemed like they had forgotten to rise. The camp was broken down, tent canvas rolled up, a quick meal prepared by the cook was chewed on, and battle dress donned. Holindrian took to the top of that hill once again, his back to the east.

"Good morning," but his voice was hoarse and hardly carried passed his own ears, "*uh ahem*… good morning!"

A hushed silence fell over the camp.

"In just a few moments, we are going to head north in what will be the first of our last actions to end this war. You know, we began this journey nearly a year ago, when the wheat begins to turn that lovely golden color. Look how far we have come. Eight months later, we have come so far; we have come so close, because of *you*. And now, we have to push a little harder, we have to work a little longer—we can't afford to let up, not now, not when there is so much at stake. I'm asking of you what I have only ever asked of you: I'm asking you to *believe*! In yourselves! In your dreams! It's too easy to become bogged down in fear and hopelessness and cynicism, but what I've seen in you, in *each* and *every* one of you is hope. Hope! Believe in there is hope. Believe in the human spirit. Believe in the capacity of others to do good works. That's what this revolution is about. *That* is what we are fighting for! Maybe it's fate that today is the start of the new year, and you will be fighting to do what has not happened much in the history of the world… You will be fighting to set others free. This is it—*this* is the end. If you are willing to stand with me and fight with me, one last time, I promise you, we are going to change the world! Freedom… it's *yours*! It has *always* been yours!"

Maaschuel waited for him at the base, sword on his hip; untamed blonde hair tied back in a bun. "You know, for a revolutionary leader, you make a lot of speeches."

"Last one, I swear," he said, holding up his hands penitently, "how long until you're ready to march?"

"Soon. We'll be gone well before the suns are high." He observed the columns struggling to form in their early morning grog.

"Did you load the wagons?"

Maaschuel groaned, "you're not leaving yourself much." When he saw Holindrian wasn't satisfied with his answer, he continued, "yes, they're loaded… including the weapons recovered from Telmun. How well this lot is going to handle them is another matter. *I* wouldn't mind a month more of practice and drills—for my own benefit. Getting all that artillery through… haven't quite figured that out. Need to see the terrain. Are you alright?"

Forward. Everything forward. Seventy-thousand men. Cavalry. Another nine thousand. One hundred pieces of artillery. Forward. It all moved north with Maaschuel. There's high ground there, overlooking the city, good ground. Anshargal will have to relieve men from the ramparts on the wall, disperse from urban Haurvatat. The triremes escorting the rest of the fleet will punch a hole in the blockade. Every ship, every captain must commit entirely to the beach assault. Yes. He would still hit the beach. The galleons will then form a new, defensive blockade, a picket line, behind the Etlu navy. Force them to meet us in shallower waters. Once the triremes have let loose their marines, they will rejoin the main fleet. All too few of us, eleven including myself, will stay behind. Anshargal will not know from where the attack will come because it will come from everywhere, every direction.

"Holindrian?"

He had not heard Maaschuel speaking.

"Are you alright?" Maaschuel asked, insistently this time.

Holindrian nodded. "It will be far easier for us to remain supplied along the Westerline than it will be for you in the mountains. You will be in hostile territory for more than five days. You must be exceedingly cautious. There are few villages in the high desert, but we simply do not know how things might have changed. We don't know the terrain, beyond these maps. We certainly do not know all of the enemy's movements and positions. It is fortunate that you should be undertaking this march now; snow will have already begun to melt. Water sources should be plentiful."

Maaschuel held out his hand; he knew what this was about. "I'll see you on the other side."

"In fifteen days," Holindrian said, taking hold of the hand firmly.

"We can march quicker than that."

"Don't tire them all out. We need them standing and fighting not lying and sleeping. *Fifteen* days. I'll look for your signal, then we blow the gate."

3.17 GATHBIYYA – THE FIRST DAY

Skirting along the shadow of the mountain, a brigade of revolutionary cavalry had come upon a ridge, due east of the town. Parched lands, soaring temperatures, and strong winds out of the south raised a brown screen of dust thousands of feet high. It was dreadful weather. Hot. Dirty. Thoroughly uncomfortable. Perhaps the worst Eridu could muster. Sand and rock whirled about, biting like chips of glass, but the rebels knew they owed no small degree of their continued survival to that storm.

Judging by the positioning of the suns overhead, midday had only just passed. It was a rare occurrence, surely, for temperatures to be as stifling, as oppressive, as tiresome as they were this day. On this, the ides of March, nature conspired to punish both the attackers *and* the defenders—revolutionaries and soldiers of the false gods.

The wall was in sight. Could not have been ten miles from Gathbiyya. The town was barely distinguishable from any other Baltutu village save for the nature of the building materials, indicative to the region. The most pronounced feature of the town was that, because of the local geography, the town was butted up against a steep, but traversable rocky hill. The town itself constructed on top a mesa with rocky slopes. Organized in a semicircle, the magistrate's office and other bureaucratic buildings flanked the central temple—a temple that a year ago would have spread the word of Maramurru, now, more probable than not, had been converted into a place of worship for Anshargal. Irrigated farmlands, producing cotton by the looks of it, covered the ground between the temple and the homes. The agora ran along the Cardo Maximus, as was the custom. A quaint stone gate greeted returning residents and visitors.

Something else was in sight as well. Moving closer, dust swirling in the air, the forward cavalry could glimpse the battle underway in the gulf. Triremes, had to be triremes given how they moved, were charging, a southern wind lending aid. Larger ships, galleons, retreated further out to sea, inserting themselves as a barrier, a long wooden wall.

"Send vord to Maaschuel. Tell him that the naffy's attack has begun. Ve are moving to engage at Gathbiyya. He must come vit all possible speed. Go!"

Oda dismissed the messenger. Her teeth sank into her pink, chapped bottom lip.

"Standard radial settlement," said one of her riders, Nersle, steering their mount alongside.

"Standard? There can't be fife hundred people down there." Oda's eyes had counted and found Gathbiyya's population to be markedly lower than it should have been for a settlement of its size. "Look to the road," and her words refocused the rider's gaze and the crucified remained lining either side.

"The Harrying!"

"Ve need to clear out anyone still there. March 'em out! Ve need to draw pressure off the beach."

With a sudden jolt, Oda and her horse spurred towards Gathbiyya, two thousand cavaliers and their wagons following close behind, a cone of dust emanating in their wake.

Three quarters of the town's population was gone. Those who remained were evangelical in their praise of the "Saperon" an epitaph of such ancient origin none now alive were familiar. Some, on seeing cavalry advancing under a blue flag they did not recognize, threatened to take up arms against the invading rebels. These partisan civilians could not contest the veteran cavalry for long and soon, after dozens lay dead, their resistance collapsed. Flocking to the Cardo Maximus with all the speed they could derive, the last inhabitants of Gathbiyya fled.

"Nersle, find a vay up this hill. This rocky one." Oda gestured behind her to the hill dominating Gathbiyya. "Place a scout up there. Ve don't vant them flanking from the north. Tell them to watch for moffement on the wall."

Nersle led a band back around town, carving a path in the rock, and on towards the summit.

There was not time to cut down the wretched dead. Dried corpses, hanging by ragged wrists and ankles, their heads slumped halfway down their chests. Skeletons with thin, decaying, green, blistered flesh over bone. It was a shame, a damned disgrace, but there simply was not the time. They would have to fight with the dead bearing witness.

Oda moved her cavalry into a defensive posture, taking advantage of the stone gate and picket fences to offer some protection. She had with her a single battery of ballistae. She deployed them where they would have the greatest visibility of the Etlu, which she knew would be coming.

The main bulk of the enemy would come up the road. They would have to, Oda thought. The ground on either side was rugged, loose sand with great big boulders strewn across the landscape, the aftermath of a volcanic eruption predating humanity's arrival. It would be difficult, nay, impossible to keep intelligible lines of battle. The Etlu would march up the road and come at her straight. Oda would hit them on the road and hold until Maaschuel arrived to take the high ground.

Peering through a spyglass of Laurentian make, Oda watched the triremes ride foaming waves to the shore. There were wild cork and olive trees interspersed with palms of all different types, fan, date, and dwarf, too. The sand on these beaches had a powder-like quality to it, soft as could be beneath bare feet, and it was black. Oda had never seen black sand before. The Etlu had laid wooden fortifications. Soldiers, Etlu and conscripts (from what Oda supposed judging by their mismatched uniforms), rushed to counter the coming assault. She turned away just as the triremes let loose, unleashing a tumultuous clamor of artillery: the clunking of ballistae and catapultae gears with each discharge.

Now she followed the fleeing residents of Gathbiyya so recently evicted. They had run straight into Haurvatat, into the arms of Anshargal's army. Even from here she could hear the alarm being raised. Bells were ringing, rousing soldiers to the feet and to arms. Perfect. *Perfect*! The marines may yet have a chance. She and her cavalry now had to do their part.

· · ·

"Maaschuel, sir!"

Oh, how he hated when they called him "sir".

"Oda reports that the navy is engaged in the harbor. She has assumed a position in Gathbiyya and requests infantry support."

Maaschuel quickly tried to account for each of the past days, then decided against it. The fight was here. The war did not give a damn about timetables and plans.

"Fajr, all forward! Courier, inform Oda to limit her engagement with the enemy. No aggressive movements. She is only to hold until help arrives. We are proceeding with all haste," and he dismissed the messenger.

He had debated which cavalry brigade to allow as vanguard. Fajr would have been the wiser choice. Their destination had once been a part of Hundare, her native land. But he could not explain it. Not objectively. Oda was a gut feeling. He trusted her; he was more comfortable giving her this level of responsibility. It did not make sense, but it would not have changed anything. Fajr very likely would have done just as Oda was doing.

"Double quick! Double! Quick!" he shouted, breaking out into a jog ahead of the columns.

Cursed climate! The suns were not even at their zenith any longer, yet, somehow, inexplicably, the heat seemed to defy nature and the temperature felt as though it continued to climb. How did people manage to live here, with little water, in this damned heat, little else but sand and rock far as the eye could see. They should have been on the verge of escaping the desert, though he could not say he believed it. From how the Hundarens talked, it was normal for the heat to persist all the way to the shoreline. Unnatural. That is all there was to it. There are just some places not meant for humans to live.

There was no conceivable way Maaschuel and the seventy thousand men and women of the infantry would reach Oda before dusk. He had ordered the quickening of their pace, but many had succumbed to the heat. Maaschuel feared half of those who remained to complete the journey would be ready to fight. It was up to Oda, Fajr, and their cavalry to hold Gathbiyya, just for tonight.

At this moment, two thousand marines, exclusively Laurentian and Trovian Coasts persons, were storming a foreign beach, plunging into waters they may or may not have ever sailed before, abandoning the safety of their triremes for the uncertainty of an amphibious assault. How many of Anshargal's defenders were they now charging headlong? Did rock and fire rain down on them? Was the full might and attention of the War God fixed solely upon them? He did not know. It was impossible to know. What Maaschuel did know was the only chance those brave souls had was with Oda and Fajr—and if he could get there with any sense of promptness and the strength to fight, he could lend aid to their survival.

3.18 DAWN OF ANGUISH

Twilight was upon them. As they set out, Skivia, the third most distant planet from the sun, was becoming visible. A green, static light, and a hallmark of the coming of night. The dark purple curtain was falling. It would be a long trek through the night. The threat of daylight would be urgent before they were in sight and within striking distance of their target.

"Holindrian? *Holindrian.*"

Someone tapped the back of his arm. It was Clisson.

"Yes? What is it?" he spoke in a hushed voice; they were crawling, flat on their stomachs, a decent size ceramic pot strapped to his back, one identical to those carried by the others.

Visibility, at this time and this distance would be poor indeed, but their mission demanded every precaution. Once night truly fell, they would be free to move more freely and more expeditiously.

"What does ya suppose happen to Maascule?"

For being Castroniphinites, their accents did not harken back to their homeland, sounding rather, to Holindrian's well-traveled ear, to be an amalgamation of disparate coastal peoples.

Holindrian could see a dome of light far to the southeast. Haurvatat. The shore. How he hoped they were not too late. That Etlu patrol boat had very possibly spoiled the whole thing.

"Holindrian?" Clisson said again, but it would be the Universe, not Holindrian who answered him.

There came a whistle, high and shrill. A blue, twinkling dot racing up, arcing over the city, wheezing, then, a sudden burst and shower of blue glimmering sparks. Another one, this time in the direction of the beach. By Fortune! They had made it! The band of eleven, with the exception of Holindrian and Drust, whooped and hollered—in muffled tones—unable to stifle their relief. Their pace quickened.

"*Shh*! Quiet… we gettin' close," Drust said, following in Holindrian's tracks.

Voices carried from the fortlets evenly spaced along Anshargal's Wall. Flickering orange light from warm fires and lit torches reflected off the walls, some stone, some wood, others earth. You could see them from many miles away when the conditions were right. Thirty-four bastions of light. Beacons guiding them towards their target: The main gate. Tonight, the conditions were right.

They stuck to the north side of the Eastrun, where the ground was rockier but also more generously covered with shrubbery and trees that broke up the otherwise featureless landscape.

A trench had been cut, abrupt, at nearly a vertical pitch. If they went up a little farther, they could cross at the road, but eleven skulking about people, doubled over, might draw the unwanted attention of the watchful guards. Four two-person teams split from the main group, leaving Holindrian, Drust, and Clisson to approach the gate. To reach the wall opposite the ditch they were going to have to slide down then climb, use picks to scale the other side, place their ordinance, and repeat the process in reverse before taking cover.

Once up and over the embankment, with all the guile the three men possessed, they crept towards the gate, Holindrian in the lead, hugging the stone slabs as best he could, staying out of the torchlight, but daybreak was only a few hours off.

Slinging the ceramic pot from his back, he crouched. From the pocket of his coat, he retrieved a length of twine and a fire starter. Stacking their pots alongside Holindrian's, Drust and Clisson then retreated down the ditch.

"Ah! There you are! There you are...."

Holindrian froze, a shudder running down his spine; he could feel a pair of eyes bearing down on him.

"I was wondering where you had concealed yourself. You are close now, brother of mine."

Tying the fuses together, he looked back over his shoulder. Drust and Clisson scrambled over the top.

"You've led your friends, and all those who believe in you, to their deaths."

Grabbing the fire starter, he clicked it a couple times. Sparks. There was a hiss as the fuse caught fire. Dropping the fire starter, he leapt up, pushing off the embankment hard, arching his back, he rotated high into the air just as the fire met the gunpowder.

As the ground rushed out of sight beneath him, a flash, then heat washed over him. Landing, some thirty feet back from the wall, he caught just a glimpse of it as the explosion spread along the mortar, super heating the fragments, launching great sections into the air. In a single, fluid motion, Holindrian dove behind the dike, a concussive wave impacting on the other side, shooting up bits of dirt and small pebbles over his head, the rush of air ruffling his hair.

Four more explosions came next. He could see the furthest one well before he could hear it. Plumes of dust, wall, and Etlu were ejected into the night sky. They could hear the ensuing chaos their work had caused, confusion, shrieks of pain. Great holes now pockmarked the wall leaving fire and smoke where before there had been unmovable stone and concrete.

"Come then, Enkirus's wayward son, have your resolution!"

Drawing his sword, Holindrian rose from behind the dirt mound. Saying nothing, offering no final words of encouragement, he dashed forward, a one-man stampede into the thickest cloud of debris. He was determined to end it. He would end it.

3.19 GATHBIYYA – THE SECOND DAY

Gathbiyya was quiet. The fighting had fizzled out well after dark, but no one could be sure of what the exact time was. Maaschuel's arrival, at the head of seventy thousand revolutionary infantrymen, broke the counterattack. The punishing hours before had threatened to drive Oda and Fajr's cavalry off to the heights overlooking the town. They had been hit with an entire division of energized militants, reinforced by two regiments of Etlu later in the battle. The fanatics gleefully sacrificed their own lives, charging into a hail of arrows and bolts and artillery bombardment again and again, paying no attention the dead piling at their feet. More than once, they had breached the frontline. By day's end, Oda and Fajr had fallen back, fighting through the town, down the agora, until they reformed, their backs to the temple.

Maaschuel smashed into the enemy's lines, flanking them, and pushed them off the mesa and out of the town altogether—at least for tonight. Oda's Wildcats were shattered. Oda set up on the top of the rocky hill, the center of the revolutionary lines where they entrenched themselves on that hill. Fajr's cavalry had fared better and was now back at the rear of the column, protecting the supply wagons as they rolled up over Gathbiyya.

Collecting the dead took the rest of the night. The Etlu did the same. Pyres would be burning soon, on both sides. The militants did not retrieve the bodies of their dead. They were left, disturbed only by the languishing residual heat. A bloody sacrifice to their god Anshargal.

When Maaschuel, Oda, and Fajr could at last rest, lying their tired heads down on stiff bedrolls, sleep did not come quickly nor stay for long.

For Maaschuel, his mind was consumed with planning the coming battle. He doubted how long Gathbiyya could be held if Anshargal attacked in force. The right would be hit hard. Only a narrow strip of the hill on that side was worth defending, as everywhere else was a precipitous drop. Impossible. The left was gentler, wide, and relatively flat, open enough to march an army, but exposed to artillery every step of the way. Accordingly, Maaschuel commanded most of the artillery to reinforce the left. Rocks were stacked forming a knee-high wall the length of the line.

Oda laid there, staring up at the stars, trying not to think. Nine hundred casualties. More than four hundred of whom were dead with more, perhaps, likely to pass before the rising of the suns. The survivors, herself included, were down from the heat exhaustion. Those militants, the people Anshargal or Saperon (whatever he took to calling himself) had corrupted… she hardly recognized them as human. More like feral animals, beasts, frothing at the mouth with bloodlust and eyes dripping with hate. They were abominations. She could not be sure whether she detested them or pitied them, and she did not know which was worse.

Fajr dozed, slipping in and out of consciousness, without the faculties to reckon how, if any, time elapsed between spurts of sleep. Guarding the convoy had been dull work, but it gave her riders a chance to rest. Most would fall asleep in the saddle, trusting their mount to follow the caravan onward. Someone would alert them if there was trouble, even if it was the jarring of being knocked to the ground by a rearing, frightened animal.

Sentinels kept an eye on Gathbiyya, watching, listening for movement.

Indeed, though dawn approached with due haste, the victory that should have belonged to the suns to bring first light was robbed from them by that of a third, newer suns. With a violent upheaval, the whole of the earth lurched in a great quake. A steady rumble—a horrible, terminal groan followed in its wake. Flames, like menacing tentacles reaching from the deep towards the ends sky, licked and lacerated the air. A cloud of smoke, monstrous in its size and composure, raced across the flat country. The light of the fireball was slow to be out shown.

Whole sections of the wall were gone. Rubble, charred bodies, mangled fragments, and smoldering debris was all that was left in some places. The alarm bells sounded once more. The second day of battle had come.

3.20 THE COURAGE OF CONOTOCARIOUS

The suns had risen with a zealous haste and heat unknown in other parts of the world. A breakfast of dehydrated meats, fruits, a bowl of piping hot oatmeal was had by all. For some, it would be their last. The fighting resumed at once.

Peering through his spyglass, down a way, perhaps four hundred yards but surely not more, there was Barumgal overseeing final preparations. The brunt of the attack would be on Maaschuel's left. He was strongest there. Entrenched. The conscripts and Etlu would have to slog up that hill, all the way to the top, but it was the sensible place to attack. They would need to in order to press his right where Maaschuel was weakest—Barumgal would see it. The poorest soldier could see it. He would need to protect it, desperately, but his numbers, already stretched across the line, were all too few.

Barumgal's soldiers were already entering Gathbiyya, encountering minor resistance, intended to do nothing more than slow his procession through the town. Five thousand rebels were dug in on the ridge above town. The Etlu would struggle to climb it in their armor. To this enterprise he entrusted Dalibor, one of two Ohlinine commanders who had journeyed with him across a continent. The conscripts would scale it like ants descending on a good meal. Maaschuel's right was weak. Here, Barumgal would come at him with six thousand Etlu—these were the best-rested troops at his disposal. Miroslav, the second Ohlinine, would be responsible for breaking the rebels' right flank and taking the army from the rear.

Easing back in the saddle, Barumgal folded his arms in his lap. The anticipation, the prospect of destroying the rebels here, on this field and in this battle was inebriating, almost to the point of excess. He gave the order to begin the attack.

On the hilltop, Maaschuel waved Conotocarious and his regiment over, vigorously, keeping an eye glued to the ring of enemy artillery that surrounded the mesa. They came at a good pace, dashing, holding their weapons up against their chests, though stumbling in the uneven dirt.

"I'm placing you here." Maaschuel kicked the ground, drawing a line with his boot. "Form your regiment to the right of this line, but keep your left close to Sanoris. No gaps."

"Yes... sir," and he gave the order for his regiment to move into lines of battle from Maaschuel's line in the sand.

"Conotocarious, you are the end of the line." He pointed out beyond the troops where there was nothing. "You are the extreme right." He looked very stern, somber. "You cannot retreat. You cannot withdraw. Not for any reason. Do you understand? They will hit you hardest, but you must hold your ground. If you don't, this army will be flanked."

"Yes, sir. I understand."

Maaschuel patted his arm. "I'm sorry, but I won't have any help to send."

A boulder came hurling towards the hill, crashing, cratering the ground. A plume of dust in dramatic fashion. Maaschuel grabbed the reins of his horse, mouthed a farewell, mounted, and rode off, signaling their own artillery to return a volley.

Conotocarious surveyed the ground. Rocks, the size of grown men, jutted out of the hillside like daggers. It was worse to his far right where the drop was effectively a cliff, a straight, impassible bluff. No, the Etlu would have to come at them from the left, covering a large swath of exposed hillside and charging towards the flank and his regiment without abandon.

"How are we fixed for munitions?" he asked, wiping the dirt off his face.

"Reckon thirty arrows and fifty bolts per bowmen. Some held in reserve. Handing them out now," Mr. Davos responded, a frightful yet ready look about him.

He nodded. "Pikes in front. Longbows to the left, they'll have better line of sight here."

"Here they come!" shouted a voice Conotocarious did not have time to identify.

Barumgal's ring of artillery, after hammering the mesa for over an hour, ceased, a horn blared, and six thousand Etlu advanced out from behind the cover of the aqueduct channeling fresh water from the mountains to the crops. Advancing past their catapults and trebuchet units, clad in their red cloaks and bright, shining steel plate armor, they began to scale the mesa.

Revolutionary artillery intensified and peppered the slopes. Arrows were let loose, flung high into the air, plunging down from above. The Etlu climbed faster than one might have thought possible, given the angle of the slope, the weight of their armor, and the adversity of the heat. Either they were not bothered by it or removed it from their minds, because when the first wave came within crossbow range, both sides exchanged a hail of bolts.

Hunkering down behind broad shields deployed as cover, the frontline of the Etlu provided masking fire with crossbow repeaters as their second wave marshaled forward. A third edged to their left, on a collision course with Conotocarious and his regiment.

"Pour it into them!" he heard himself shouting, bow strings plucking, crossbow crannequins clanging.

Ratcheting back the tension, Conotocarious reloaded, aimed, and fired. Puncturing the steel, the Etlu soldier staggered as his lung deflated. Gasping for breath, he crumpled and fidgeted in the dirt before his body became motionless.

They were still coming. Twenty yards. The power of the longbows imbedded the missiles deep in the chest like spears made to skewer a wild boar. Through the dead and wounded, through the cries of pain and prayers for deliverance, the Etlu continued to press the attack.

"Don't let up!" he yelled, a bolt whisking over his ear, so close he could feel the tail smacking the side of his head.

Fewer stones were raining down on the Etlu. The artillery was shifting away.

"Keep up the pressure!"

Finally, the Etlu began retreating down the hill, falling back behind their shield wall, assuming a tortoise formation. The longbows lessened their rate of fire but remained poised.

Conotocarious mopped the sweat off his brow with the back of his hand, tugging on his loose sleeve, using it as a rag. Running his other hand over his close-cropped hair, he looked to the regiment. The extreme right had not been hit at all, but the left, the bowmen there had taken a number of casualties, men and women were lying slumped over their meager rock wall, while others had been pulled off the line, bolts and arrows sticking out of their flesh, especially on their left-hand side.

Someone shouted, "here they come!"

Conotocarious raised his crossbow and fired. "They're coming again! They're coming again!"

The ensuing attack mimicked the first. Etlu came charging up the hill, breaking out of their defensive position, repeaters spraying his line in an endless stream of deadly iron bolts. This time, the Etlu had moved further down and targeted the center of the regiment. Then, just as before, the Etlu pulled back. Resuming the tortoise, their shields held in front and above.

A total of five times this attack was made against Conotocarious's regiment—an unrelenting force colliding with an unmovable object. The line held, but each wave whittled away at their strength. The wounded laid on the ground. Medics tended to as many of them as they could, but with the suns now glaring straight down, it was as though all of their fiery intensity was concentrated in this one rugged spot.

Catching the eye of Mr. Davos, Conotocarious waved him over as the latest wave of Etlu slunk back behind their broad shields. "How are we doing?"

"Well as can be expected, I should think. Everyone is putting up a solid fight."

"That they are."

"We doled out some of the reserve munitions, however. We cannot do this all day."

Conotocarious scratched the scruff around his mouth; he wasn't used to having a beard, for priests were to remain clean-shaven. "We can—and we must. Tell them all, everyone, to make their shots count."

Mr. Davos pointed his index finger down the slope. "Sir, they are coming!"

The sixth attack managed to be halted by the pikemen, who skewered the Etlu, driving their pikes into the vulnerable necks, arms, and legs. The seventh saw the Etlu breach the rock wall, trampling over the stacked stones, hacking, stabbing, and slashing Conotocarious's people in droves. The line was reformed into the shape of the letter "U", the crest flush with the wounded. Conotocarious's bowmen fired, full draw, mere feet from their would-be murderers. With no time to reload, Conotocarious grabbed a repeater from a fallen Etlu and led an advance that pushed the Etlu back down the hill once more.

Mr. Davos now laid on the ground, a gash across his left arm. "*Argh*! I'm alright, sir." A medic was tying a bandage around it. "Uh," he groaned, "not as bad as it looks, I assure you. Bolt. *Uhm*... cut right through. Certainly, not the downstairs of Telmun," he quipped as he was helped to his feet.

"Nor the Shrine of Amurru," Conotocarious said, surveying what was to come.

"Truth be told, I cannot think we will survive another attack such as that."

They could not.

"Mr. Davos, see that rock there? *There*! Yes, *that* one. We are going to refuse the line. Place two hundred on the far right at that point. When you get to that point, we are going to make an angle." He held up his hands perpendicular to each other, representing what he wanted done. "Do you understand? We'll fire into them just as they come up."

Mr. Davos acknowledged that he understood.

"Alright, go! Quickly, before they come again. You there, Tem, are you injured? Hurt, are you hurt, son?"

The soldier shook his head.

"I need you to carry a message to Maaschuel. Tell him... *ask* him, if he has any of Holindrian's explosive powder held in reserve... Conotocarious requests that he urgently discharge it on the enemy position." He steered Tem to the edge of the hill, pointing to the aqueduct. "You see that? Tell him to aim there. Do you understand me, Tem?"

The young man, hardly more than a boy, nodded before setting off at a quick pace.

Conotocarious just managed to give the order to expand the line to twice its present length when the eighth wave of Etlu came roaring up the hill, beating their shields. Though they were visibly exhausted, they were also visibly committed to the cause.

By the time it had been repulsed, another twenty of his men were had been struck down by the zealots' war lust.

The reformation had worked. The crossfire created by the right-angle formation had trapped a number of Etlu in an impossible to defend against onslaught of arrows. Their complement, for the whole right flank (some three hundred and fifty thousand arrow and bolts) were now depleted. The right would not be able to hold much longer; when it fell, the whole of the army would be at risk of being overrun.

Sanoris, a Gerpedonite stonemason by trade turned regiment commander, held Conotocarious's left and offered what munitions he dared spare to assist the struggle to defend the right flank. The far right was pressed harder and harder with each successive attack, relieving some of the tension further up the line. Additional reserves of arrows and bolts trickled to Conotocarious's position, but not enough to prolong the fight much longer. It was then that Tem returned.

"He says there isn't much, but he'll direct what little there is to the… um…"

"The aqueduct," Conotocarious said, lending the word.

"Yeah. The aqueduct. Says the artillery will be waiting on your signal."

He clapped his hands together. Sanoris was perplexed.

"Sanoris, can you hold?"

The Gerpedonite observed his own regiment. They looked ragged and miserable. Slouching, they leaned on one another, their bodies utterly spent. Every now and then one would peer over the piled rocks and search for signs that the enemy was preparing to charge again. The tiredness in their eyes was seen clear enough. They were hungry; they were thirsty, so desperately thirsty under the glare of the suns on this hottest of days. Their munitions were all but gone, their swords and spears dulled so as to be worth less than a butter knife. For as wretched as they appeared, dirty and blood soaked, that glimmer, the fire

Holindrian had ignited within them, still burned in their hearts for they longed for freedom. For all the things they were, they were not yet broken, and they were not beaten. They would hold.

"I reckon I can. What's this about explosive powder?"

"We're going to blow the aqueduct. Destroy it. As they come up. They're going to keep coming, I'm sure of it—so, we're going to charge down the hill after the aqueduct comes down!"

Sanoris's mouth was ajar. "Ch-cha-charge? You want to *charge* Etlu?"

Conotocarious nodded. "No… They must be tired. We are. They're still only human. They're tired. So, I say, we charge! We'll have the advantage of moving down the hill. We'll push them… all the way back down."

Sanoris said not a word and Conotocarious continued: "We don't have the arrows to repel them again. We can't keep taking losses like we have. I don't know what else to do. If they come, I'm afraid we're going to break…"

Burying his face in his hands, Sanoris said, "alright. I'll give the word. We'll go on your order," and he departed to prepare his regiment.

Conotocarious saw the Liberty Banner fluttering in the wind. He exhaled deeply. The breeze felt refreshing on his sweat soaked skin, a reassuring kiss.

Mr. Davos was back. "We are going to have to start throwing rocks at them," he said.

Conotocarious dispatched Tem. "Go! Tell Maaschuel to rain fire now!"

"Now?"

"By the time you reach him, the Etlu will be more than halfway up the hill. So, *yes*! When you get there, you tell them Conotocarious says to fire right now."

As Tem departed, Conotocarious informed Mr. Davos of what was about to happen, to which the former master-servant clicked his heels then hobbled away.

The Etlu broke free of their tortoise formation once again, a mass of brawn and steel; Conotocarious could see their eyes as clear from atop the hill as if he were standing mere feet away.

Drawing his falchion from its hilt, summoning a voice he scarcely recognized as his own, he bellowed the order: "Draw! Your! Swords!"

The firing of arrows trickled then stopped altogether.

"Right wheel… charge!" he pointed with his free hand at Mr. Davos far down the line.

Watching as the extreme right swung forward, like a door, Conotocarious then looked to his left; Sanoris and the other regiment commanders were all waiting his final instruction.

"CHARGE!"

With the flag waving behind him almost like a cape, he extended his right arm fully, sword gripped tightly behind white knuckled fingers. Conotocarious led his regiment over the side of the hill, just as a low whistle, fast moving shadows, and three brilliant explosions tore out the support columns, bringing an entire section of the aqueduct down, drowning the Etlu general and their artillery in a tsunami of cascading water. Those Etlu at the forefront of the retreat were, too, carried away. When they reached the bottom of the hill, or more accurately, where the water line had risen as the valley below was thoroughly flooded, less than 2,500 revolutionaries captured a comparable number of depleted Etlu troops, for whom the war was now over.

"Surrender your arms. Remove your armor," Conotocarious ordered, one hand ushering his regiment to halt, the other holding his sword at the ready.

The Etlu were strung out in a line. They seemed to be just as poorly off as the rebels. Their crossbows were out of bolts, but many were still armed with short swords. A melee contest would decimate both sides though the rebels would have surely faired poorer. The Etlu were not troubled by that fact, rather, they embraced it. They preferred it.

"…don't," cautioned Conotocarious as the de facto leader took a step forward, raising his own sword.

Conotocarious could feel his nails cutting into his palm. The Etlu captain seethed with anger but was present of mind enough to recognize that even should he and his soldier kill these rebels, they would be robbed of the strength to collapse their line still perched on the hill. So, he stopped and dropped his sword. He was not looking at Conotocarious, but over him, at the hilltop. Turning, Conotocarious saw why. Oda and what remained of her badly beaten cavalry had come to the edge of the slope, lances upright, horses resolute. Following the suit of their captain, more Etlu swords were thrust to the ground. Morion helmets and plate armor, too, were discarded.

As the disarmed Etlu were led way, Conotocarious knelt, his knees giving way under him. Scooping water with his hands, he splashed it across his face and closed his eyes.

They had held the right.

3.21 HAURVATAT

The fighting in Haurvatat was unlike anything seen since the Fifth Age. Urban. No fields. It was like fighting through a forest. Nine thousand Etlu and untold hordes of conscripts—every bystander on the street a potential enemy in waiting. Under their master's will they were altogether transformed from ordinary and calm to fervent and maniacal. They pursued with a relentless hunger, bloodthirsty, and wailing. With cleavers and clubs and bare fists, they attacked. A commandment had been issued that they take the life of a rebel by whatever means were necessary to force the life out from your veins, to silence your pounding heart, to thrust the deliverance upon you.

Holindrian had not seen the likes of this for some time. Their corruption was absolute, minds twisted. No discernable traits of humanity, aside from their physical form, remained. What was left were vile, deranged husks. He thought, he told himself as he slayed them, that he was doing them a mercy by releasing them of this world and setting their minds free of Anshargal's wickedness.

Drust and Clisson shadowed him throughout the night and into the morning. Skilled fighters though they were, there was an uneasiness about them. The feeling of being watched was ever present. The weight of their eyes a burden he had not agreed upon to bear. He put it from his mind. He could not afford to be troubled by spying gaze now.

Fires burned uncontrollably. Between the wooden stalls in the agora and the timber construction of the many homes and buildings, fuel was plentiful. Everything in the immediate vicinity of the harbor was wrecked by savage artillery bombardment. Scorched and pulverized by fiery stones. A black cloud hung over the city; anchored by pillars of fire, it could not be moved by even the strongest wind. Thus, the air was thick with smoke and ash. Choking those ensnared it was a poison to be inhaled and which burned the lungs with every breath.

"Do they know this is the future you have promised, Holindrian? Anarchy. Violence in perpetuity. You have led them to their destruction as a race."

Twirling the hilt of his sword between his fingers, Holindrian brought the blade down on the extremist on his left. A single gash shattered the sternum and exposed the entrails. The second, an identical wound, befell to the attacker on his right. Both succumbed at once, their legs swaying out from under them. Dead. Sheathing the sword, Holindrian continued. He would not be stopped.

Drust and his man Clisson kept to his shadow. Holindrian's followers rapidly increased. Every straggler who caught a glimpse of him felt the power of his presence, was drawn to him. Hundreds flocked to him. Dripping with red. One even clung to a Liberty Banner blackened with soot, charred at the edges, and torn in many places, but that word "liberty" remained clear and legible.

An agonizing groan, then a crash. A building, gutted by fire, collapsed. An impenetrable gray mass of smoke and dust spilled into the street, acrid and abrasive. Glowing embers filled the air like summer fireflies buzzing through a midsummer's field. With a flick of his wrists, the wall of fire ahead parted and a traversable tunnel permitted him and his companions' safe passage.

On the other side, what remained of the marine assault force fought a bitter and overwhelming detachment of Etlu soldiers sent to stop them. Beyond that, the steps of the Palace of Kings. Anshargal was there. He could feel it.

"With your death, this rebellion will falter in short order. At last, this rebellion will be no more."

Holindrian drew his sword once again. "Forward! All forward!"

Leading the charge, Holindrian scampered over the barricade, a hodgepodge of whatever the defenders had scavenged; furniture taken from empty homes, benches off the streets, cabinets from stores, and more. Marines followed Holindrian's lead. Scaling the irregular structure, they lobbed bolts and lead bullets from hand cannons and the flag bearer waved vigorously so that all that might see that the revolutionaries were storming the palace.

Leaping high into the air, Holindrian dove into the thicket of Etlu defenders; landing, he rolled, cutting down soldiers as though they were wheat to be harvested with a sickle.

A malevolent voice pierced his ears: "You wanted to show them a new world? Very well, come and claim it!"

He had just enough time to react. Deflecting Anshargal's attempt at lacerating his abdomen. Holindrian countered and drove into him with his shoulder, knocking him back, stumbling.

"…Anshargal," he wheezed.

But Anshargal shook his head with malice. "Like Mara-murru, Anshargal is no more. Saperon alone stands before you," under the echo of his morion, the pitch of his voice sunk to low, rumbling bass.

The imprint on the mask was sadistic and inspired great fear even within Holindrian. A golden faced, bearded man personifying vengeance. Flaming jewels burned within the sockets of his eyes, his whole body was radiating intense heat, and he seemed to glow in his armor, a rageful glint to him.

Stomping, Saperon towered over Holindrian like a brooding bear. He bared down upon him, leveraging his size against his enemy. His next blow was parried, but he struck Holindrian hard with the back of his gauntlet, sending him to the ground.

Blinking, Holindrian became momentarily entranced by Saperon's broad chest plate. Forged by Melammu herself, it was as much a work of art as a defensive instrument. Her skill in the crafting of things had been unrivaled. Had the Baltutu nurtured and advocated the advancement of the arts, it can hardly be said a better patron might have existed in all human history. Comprised of steel and other metals whose properties have still not yet been rediscovered, she set out to create plate armor exceeding the abilities of mortal man either to reproduce its minute architecture or fathom its exacting elaboration. It had the look of bronze but far surpassed the common metal's protective properties and was further adorned in gold.

She placed upon it, directly over the place where the heart should have been, an engraving of Earth (referencing the old images housed within the mysterious and ancient halls of the Ziggurat), replicating the long-lost home precisely. Every peak of every sky-touching mountain. Every last fjord and river. Every wide spanning plain and expansive forest... The accuracy of her work was impeccable. The oceans and clouds, just as they had been captured in a still frame, were transcribed in ever-lasting steel. The Earth was recreated, even possessing the quality of rotating on its axis, should the eye linger long enough.

Encompassing the Earth, Melammu wrought the ages of the Erestun man. First, born from nature's womb, an infant sprung from the branch of an ash tree. So, life like it was, the ear searched in vain trying to detect its whimper. The hubris of man came next. Man's ambition spread across the globe dominating the natural world, impressing it into servitude. Animals found themselves caged for sport and entertainment. The soil developed for the cultivation of man's insatiable hunger. Forests plundered for all their great worth and the land laid bare. Third, the tragedy of man. The very nature man had repeatedly, aggressively, and relentlessly raped, the very nature that had born man unto the world—that nature turned on man; smothering man under a black cloud of death, covering the whole of the world. Man was left to fend for himself, eventually, however, he would succumb to starvation and pestilence and at last, the world would be rid of him.

The fifth series portrayed the benevolence of the Anunna-Ki, who, with one hand, saved humanity, plucking it off its doomed homeworld and, with the other, showed them a new world where they might make their home. With Enkirus at the forefront, the people held hands in thanks, while his Anunna-Ki lord presented man with the opportunity for a future: Eridu. All of the same skill that brought Earth to life could be found again in Eridu, where the binary suns' rays bathed humanity's second home in everlasting warmth and affection.

The birth of the Baltutu was next. Wrapped in Esh's tender embrace, the faces they had long since grown out of, those childhood faces stared back with wonderous, toothy smiles.

Humankind must be an addict to calamity, incapable of reform or recovery. The seventh panel was a record of the failures of the five previous civilizations. Beginning with the protracted stagnation and decline of the Age of the Settlers followed by Cy's raid on Erestu-Ur with his army of tamed Gudanna. The causal descent into barbarism and madness that characterized the Third Age came next before the plundering of the pyramid builders by unlettered scoundrels; only to be succeeded by the most terrible destruction humanity could yet muster—fueled by vain ambition and insatiable greed. The final frame depicted the Baltutu helping lift a man and a woman rise from the ruin.

The Age of the Baltutu. This panel showed the domestication of man. Worshipping of the six was central. From this act of fealty, the knowledge of farming and rearing livestock, the ability to subsist in comfort in a world where violence and humanity's many vices; theft, murder, and cruelty foremost among them were extinguished.

So was Saperon's bronze hued armor.

"Do you expect the Aurora of Ida to sparkle in shades of placid blues? No! See red—blood red scarlet shall forever shine down on Eridu!"

Holindrian tasted metal, iron, on his busted lip. Blood trickled down his chin. Saperon encroached, black clouds billowing behind him. Ash and live coals swirling around him, caught in a cyclone. Shielding himself behind his arms, Holindrian turned up his palm, aimed square at Saperon's chest, and pushed.

Saperon was launched a dozen feet into the air, yanked hard and expectedly by an unseen force—a hook ripping him away. Legs flailing as he rocketed upward, he fell back towards the earth, but he did not crash nor impact hard on the palace steps, he just came to a stop. Frozen in midair inches above the ground. He levitated! Holindrian had never seen anyone, not even his own kin, levitate before.

Shrinking back into the shadows of the palace colonnade, Saperon's Etlu folded in around him. Holindrian could feel Saperon's angry eyes spewing hate.

"To the palace!" Holindrian commanded with great authority, for he had already charged ahead, his mind possessed by a singular thought.

3.22 CONFRONTATION

In Gathbiyya, the fighting returned with devilish fervor. Though overwhelmed at the start, Dalibor's conscripts had formed a zealous in their defense. The dead piled like a wall among the stained fields of cotton, alfalfa, olives, dates, bean stocks, and varied palm.

On the eastern slope, Maaschuel's defensive line had not broken, but it was so battered so as to be beyond recognition. Barumgal had sent wave upon wave of conscripts, fodder sacrificed to expend revolutionary munitions and resolve to fight. Now, as a brown cloud of dust stirred in the distance and the evening suns cast a purplish orange light on the field, the two viceroys clashed, wrestling for ultimate supremacy and neither willing to fail those who entrusted them so dearly.

Barumgal slashed; the cutting edge of his curved blade scraping down the front of Maaschuel's cloak. Gold and azure fibers expelled like dandelion seeds drifting in the wind. Maaschuel struggled to keep as much distance as possible between them for he was the shorter of the two. The heavy broadsword he used more like a club. Gripping the central ridge, he countered Barumgal's next attack. Locking the blade against the cross guard and hitting Barumgal with the pommel. Staggering, a cut just over his left eye, blood streaming down his cheek.

"*Argh*!" he cried, wrapping his arms around Maaschuel's midsection.

The pair fell. Maaschuel landed hard on his back, but he rolled and somehow ended up on top. He swung at Barumgal's bleeding face. With blood oozing from his mangled nose, Barumgal seized Maaschuel's wrists and head-butted him, leaving a black and purple welt under Maaschuel's right eye. Then, Barumgal jabbed his knee into him; one, two, three times! Gasping, his every breath labored, Maaschuel sunk, clutching his ribs tightly. Pushing himself up, Barumgal retrieved his sword and came at Maaschuel again.

Vaulting to one side, Maaschuel forced Barumgal to miss, his blade chopping into the parched soil. Wobbling, sword in hand, he held it as firmly as he could and spaced his feet evenly apart. Barumgal hoisted his blade high over his head, hissing as a viper does. The curved sword sliced through the air, but Maaschuel stood as resolute as a godwood tree and parried, deflecting the tip of Barumgal's sword to the ground. Following the arc down, Maaschuel dragged the sharpened edge of his sword across the man's thigh.

Dropping his sword, falling to his knees, Barumgal pressed his hands to the wound. Dark, oxygen rich blood flowed between his fingers, pooling in the reddening dirt. Face flushed with pain, eyes watering, he stared up at Maaschuel with a quivering lip.

Wincing, the sweat soaked Maaschuel held the point of the sword inches away from Barumgal's vulnerable neck. He was prepared to thrust the tip through to the spine and send Barumgal into the inevitable: "It's over, Barum. Finished! Call them off—end it!"

The dead and dying were trampled as the battle raged on around them. The two camps exchanging artillery, lobbing flaming stones at one another. The air was thick with odor of blood and sour sweat; a music composed of foul curses and curdling screams accosted the ear. There was no longer any sense to it, no order. There was only a mob, a maddening melee, an undefined mass of men and women beating one another to death.

"Barum... surrender... *please*." His hands were beginning to shake, and it was becoming more difficult to stand.

But, Barumgal said nothing.

"Ugh… end this! You can be a free man!"

"Look around," Barumgal spat, "look at what your… quest, your obsession for freedom has wrought!"

Sweat dripped from his nose. Licking his lips, Maaschuel grimaced at the taste. "I am. It doesn't have to be this way. Please… *Azad*… please!"

3.23 ENKIRUS AND A PLANET CALLED ERIDU

Enkirus fell to his knees on the ground amidst the wild, untamed grass and wept. Wide open spaces. Gentle hills. Cliffs of white and black, volcanic beaches, and the bluest waters one could imagine. He inhaled deeply… the rush of life he felt course throughout his body! His lungs had never tasted air so sweet and pure. Birds soared, birds he had never seen the like of before! They flapped their wings, paying no attention whatsoever to those with whom they would be soon co-habiting this world. Everything seemed so much more vibrant… It was as though a filter had been placed over his eyes, hiding the true beauty of things all his life, and only now was it removed.

Turning his head towards the sky, he saw not one, but two, *yes*, two suns, one orders of magnitude brighter than the other. He was surprised how, to his amazement, it actually felt a little cooler than on Earth—more temperate. Comfortable, yes, *very* comfortable!

Enkirus closed his eyes and he listened to the splashing of the ocean on wet rock. He could hear the ocean spray; taste the salt on his lips. Joyful tears rolled down his cheeks.

Uilliam smiled at the old man. "The others are waiting for you." He gestured to a stepped tower just visible over the top of the forest. "We have provisions and shelter to help you acclimate to your new home, but you, Enkirus, I need you to enter that Ziggurat your people have built."

"What will I find there?"

"Why, the future, of course."

The Margidda was nestled on the crest of some cliffs. An old and wide forest stood before him with trees so tall he could barely make out the direction Uilliam bid he travel. But the summit of the Ziggurat was visible. In all his years and his many travels, there were monuments constructed by his kind of such impressive stature. Though not yet completed, Enkirus could see enough to press on. *Forward*. That would be his direction. Forward.

Those who, like him, had been among the very last to leave the Earth, followed him to set foot on alien ground and breathe alien air and be warmed by two beautiful, alien suns. Suns! Animals, too, were venturing forth. A mechanized arm deposited a host of animals to which humans were familiar: horses, oxen, pigs, goats, hens, sheep, dogs, and many more. They would also make Eridu their new home.

"And take the boy with you," Uilliam said, preparing to leave.

"...thank you," was all Enkirus could manage, but it was enough.

"Welcome home, Enkirus," and in a flash of radiant light, he was gone, lifted up passed the clouds.

3.24 SAPERON'S SUICIDE

Sounds, incoherent and distorted echoes, reverberated through the palace's walls of stone. Each one tickled Holindrian's ear, straining the bones inside as he prowled and hunted Saperon, who had disappeared within darkened corridors. He was still near, that much he was certain. Holindrian could feel him... sense his presence. Saperon had not fled; he would not flee, not now, at the end of all things.

Bursting through a locked door, it shattered into thousands of splinters; Holindrian found himself exited on to the roof, the third tier of the palace. There, just there, was Saperon, a level below him. He was traveling along the balcony which overlooked the courtyard.

Taking more than a few steps away from the ledge, Holindrian ran, a superhuman sprint. He dashed through the doorway. Hurling himself forward like a shot, Holindrian soared over the courtyard. Like a squirrel or a cat, his eyes remained fixed on the precise place he sought to land. In a flash, his brain calculated what his body needed to do: His hips lifted, his head rotated underneath so that it followed the lead of his shoulders, and he was grace personified. Holindrian landed on a weathered stone floor, and it cracked beneath his boots. Gladius drawn, he cut down the Etlu guards with ease. His momentum carried him on to Saperon, who greeted him with a heavy-handed chop of his kopis.

The blow nearly forced Holindrian to his knees, but he commanded the muscles in his thighs to rise. And so, he did. He rose. He pushed back against the full brutish force of Saperon. Sparks ignited as their blades scratched the granite walls and pillars of red marble. The clanging of their swords unleashed a whirlwind gale through the palace; cracks and fissures vandalized the ancient wonder because of their fury.

Driven backwards, Saperon waved his hand behind him and, with his command of the natural elements, thrust the double doors behind him open with such force that they tore their hinges from the frame, nail and all. He drew Holindrian into the great hall. To their right, Etlu, armed with crossbow repeaters and harquebuses, shot from behind overturned tables. On the left, Holindrian's rebels, reinforced by Drust and Clisson, returned with a volley of their own, unleashed from fire lances, hand cannons, and clunky, manual crossbows. White smoke hung in the air, thick and foul. Rounded balls of lead and pointed iron darts ricocheted off the ancient stone walls. Bodies of the dead were piled three high, and it seemed as though the whole of the war had converged on this place of communion.

Floating onto the central table, Saperon swung and hacked at Holindrian. In turn, Holindrian responded forcefully. He jabbed angrily. His fist connected hard with Saperon's helmeted face. With a second blow, Holindrian smashed the morion faceplate and imprinted upon it his bloody knuckles in a sizable dent.

Bullets, intended for neither, came perilously close to curtailing the lives of Holindrian and Saperon. Pivoting, Holindrian dropped back and rotated his gladius downward. Two weighted and hot spheres of black lead were deflected away from Holindrian's exposed side. A third that would have lodged itself in his throat was slapped away with the point of his sword. Saperon more elegantly repulsed the bullets that entered his proximity with nothing more than sheer will, scattering them in an instant.

With the grip held between both of his perspiring hands, Holindrian came at Saperon as though he wielded an axe. Countering, Saperon seized Holindrian's sword hand, while Holindrian did the same to him. Wrestling with each other at the head of the table, Holindrian knew he would have been reduced to ash at that very moment if only Saperon possessed the ability to spew fire from his eyes.

"We were building something beautiful!" he cried, pitching Holindrian through the stained glass window of such gargantuan size that both men of some stature were dwarfed before its radiance.

Disintegrating into a hundred million pieces, shards of glass flew out in a thousand different directions. Tumbling, Holindrian hit the roof tiles below hard. Weakened by his sudden impact, it collapsed a moment later. Sinking through the hole, a downpour of glass, sand, weathered timbers, and chunks of clay fell upon him. Glass imbedded itself in his tangled mass of hair and coat so that the sunlight cast a saintly sheen about him.

Descending, Saperon hastily and furiously resumed his attack. He slashed and hacked at Holindrian once more. "But, like a serpent in the grass, lurking, you lashed out. First with a forked tongue," Holindrian parried again, and the dust and glass were expelled from his person by a wind with the strength of a hurricane, "tempting them with knowledge you know they were incapable of comprehending."

Saperon swung. Holindrian ducked. But Saperon's needling words persisted, "then, you wrapped your coils around them, losing them in a snare of hyperbole and false promise!"

Holindrian elbowed him, and Saperon stumbled. "… condemning them needlessly to agonizing judgment!"

Holindrian let out a cry which chilled Saperon's very bones and curled his blood. A fleeting moment of hesitation from Saperon was all Holindrian needed to seize control of their fight. With a power not drawn upon since his smiting of Cy thousands of years before, Holindrian dismantled Saperon's withering defense. He chopped and hacked at him, over and over. Sparks shot out with each blow like lightning, the clash of steel the thunder. The gladius burned bright with cobalt hued flame. Waving his sword back and forth, each swing hit Saperon like a stiff kick in the chest by an unbroken steed. Saperon fell back. He made one final, futile effort to regain control of the fight, but Holindrian was relentless in his persecution. At any moment, the kopis of Saperon might break, cleaved in two.

Pressed to the ledge, his back to the marble railing, Saperon declared, his voice a frightening shriek: "When we are finished here, *I* shall resume our most noble work!"

Knocking the sword from his hands, Holindrian struck Saperon with such force the marble behind him was vaporized, reduced to a fine dust. He fell, the full height of the columns, onto his back. Clambering to his feet, he watched with stunned eyes as Holindrian leapt down into the courtyard. Saperon summoned his kopis. He was not yet beaten. He would not be beaten while he still drew breath.

Deflecting the next blow down to the left, Holindrian used what energy he had to launch himself. Extending his leg outward, he wrenched the deformed morion off Saperon's head. The bearded faceplate shattered into a dozen pieces. Blood surged from his mouth, jaw fractured, the tissue already bruising in a sickly yellowish green. Falling to a knee, Saperon gawked at Holindrian with dampened eyes, his stylized jet-black hair matted with sweat and hate.

"…do you hear that, *Saperon*? Do you hear the people sing?"

It was at that moment that many voices came together—many voices, but a single, harmonious sound.

Sing with us and free the mind!
The men above are not divine!
The awoken hearts now form a line,
In Victory's arms…

"They. Will Abide! The war is over. They will put down the sword, pick up the plow, and live in a garden of their own creation. The Age of the Baltutu… is over."

The lids of Saperon's eyes fell—he was so very tired. "Thank you." He sounded… relieved.

Before Holindrian could process what was happening, Saperon took hold of his wrist, bringing the edge of Esh's sword against the flesh of his exposed neck, and, in one motion, ended his own life.

Holindrian did not know how much time passed, but when his awareness did finally return, he found himself slumped on the ground holding his brother's corpse in his arms. Upon Saperon's… Anshargal's face was a most unexpected expression… a smile? Yes, a smile. He had died smiling.

Holindrian looked up. He was not sure why, but he did. Something, someone disturbed the black smoke setting over the courtyard. Lacking the cognitive desire or interest as his body was so thoroughly exhausted, he let the figure approach him unchallenged.

"Hello there, little brother."

His heart could bear no more; he thought it on the precipice of ruin. How? How could she be here? He mouthed something, but there was a disconnect between the movement of his lips and the thoughts swirling in his brain. He felt a numbness all over and there Holindrian succumbed to paralysis and disbelief.

Esh knelt down beside him, taking him into her arms. "…I know. I *know*. It's going to be alright." She stroked his hair. "Everything is going to be alright."

Holindrian did not have energy left to cry—and how he desperately wanted to cry, to bawl uncontrollably and to spend the rest of eternity weeping. A semblance of peace crept back into his being in the presence of his long-departed sister. He would have lingered in her grace were the decision his. Whether she was truly here or a manifestation of his grief and guilt, Holindrian could not say, but he nonetheless was grateful for the respite.

After several moments, he realized they were not alone. There was another figure, a sprite, standing just behind her, but it was featureless and transparent.

"A friend," Esh said, noticing where Holindrian's eyes had wandered off to.

He mouthed, "Uilliam?"

Esh, placing his grungy face between her pristine, soft palms, smiled. "No, but you will meet them one day. As for Uilliam, he will see you soon," she whispered, and she made to leave.

"Wh-Where are you going? Can… *please*, take me with you!"

"I can't, little brother. How I wish I could," she said, with a shake of her divine head. "Know that you will rest… one day… when your work is done. There is still much you must do."

Holindrian frowned. "I don't wish to stay here. This world… I fear it's not where I belong."

Esh and her sprite companion began to diminish. "Then go. Find the place where you belong."

Her visage faded; his long dead sister was gone once more.

Maaschuel approached unsteadily. The jubilation outside the palace walls had grown so loud that even Holindrian's ears mistook the coming of his friend. Maaschuel waved his arms franticly. His voice, hoarse from the day's long battle, did not carry and particulates so pervasive in the air obscured his mouth from sight. But Holindrian heard the crack of the gun only after his eyes detected the flash of flame and the bullet sped towards him. Drust and Clisson emerged from behind a veil of black smoke cloaked in betrayal.

Releasing his brother's body, he ducked as another shot whizzed by, fluttering his hair as it passed. Stretching out his hand, he discouraged Maaschuel from coming any closer. He was not exactly sure what was about to happen—he did not even know if it would work—but Esh's words alone guided his actions now.

The next shot was low. Holindrian looking up at the sky and said, "for you we fled, for you we fight, to kindle once more humanity's light."

A blinding, technicolored light burrowed through the black smoke, a shimmering light that engulfed Holindrian completely. He felt a gentle tug. Lifted off his feet, he dangled for a moment, suspended above the ground. Maaschuel was watching, jaw dropped.

"Goodbye," Holindrian said, not sure if Maaschuel could hear him, as he held up his hand.

Then, he was gone. Holindrian disappeared into the clouds as the rainbow of light vanished.

"Where's he gone?" Drust exclaimed, rushing forward, spit dangling from his chin, searching wildly for his target.

Maaschuel hobbled over, neck craned up at the sky. "A place where we cannot follow."

Drust sauntered, back to Clisson, bewilderment still etched on his face.

Maaschuel watched as the pair exited the palace. Later, he would deal with them later. There was something there, lying on the ground, amongst the rubble, inches from Saperon's body, at the place where Holindrian had been standing only seconds before. Kneeling, he claimed it, dusting it off. It was a book. *The Mouse That Roared*. Holindrian had left it behind. Opening it, Maaschuel saw that in between the ancient lines, Holindrian had scribbled in the translation of the book's long-lost knowledge.

"*A place where we cannot follow*," he thought, "*...not yet.*"

3.25 THE CATALOGUE OF BATTLES

The fourth and final Obenian-Baltutu war began on March 15, 7,529, when Anshargal's army of Etlu sailed to the northern coasts of Laud on ships constructed by Maramurru. The bombardment of Mattiyahu and surrounding cities, harbors and ports, and outlying defenses, began on April 5, and lasted seven days. King Matthiolus surrendered to Anshargal and Maramurru on the eighth day.

Maramurru was imprisoned inside the Kurn for 83 days, 57 of which were spent in complete isolation. His imprisonment began around the third week in May following his and Anshargal's hastened return from Obenia, where they did not linger following their victory. Though difficult to precisely date, it can be argued that while the Human Revolution began in earnest soon after Maramurru was betrayed, actions undertaken by him in the preceding two centuries certainly made the Revolution both possible and inevitable.

During his absence, unrest broke out in the fishing communities of the Trovian Coast 35 days before Maramurru (styling himself as the Holindrian) freed himself, the deposed king, and many Obenians from lifetime internment inside the old pyramid. This was violently put down. Maaschuel's rousing of the Antelmari and his duel with Barumgal on the road marks the classical start of the Human Revolution.

The Antelmari-Ohlinine War begins shortly after Maaschuel departed to rescue Holindrian from the Kurn. These engagements are often nameless and poorly documented by the combatants. Hostilities grew increasingly unrestricted, including the purposeful targeting of civilians, constant, and with little respite through December of the following year. This war would continue 29 years after the signing of the Charter of Free Peoples.

The battles of Virescent and Mercod occurred on the second of September and lasted two days and nights. Anshargal retreats to his eastern province of Humar to rebuild his army.

The Hundaren Campaign and the gathering of Holindrian's allies would carry on well into late autumn and the first frost.

Matthiolus returns to Obenia in November, prior to the Baltutu Day uprisings, which happened on November 20 and was traditionally the day, during the Second Age, where newborn Baltutu were introduced to the people.

No formal military engagements but widespread sectarian violence erupts on the borders of the Shuruppak. Erestu-Ur is overrun immediately preceding the Battle of Ezinu's Fields as the Etlu ready defenses around Telmun in anticipation of a siege. There is no siege. Telmun is stormed by throngs of rebels on November 30, overwhelming the Etlu defenders. Telmun falls on

December 1. One hundred thousand persons, if not more, are killed. Apsu, Melammu, Mummu, and Shi are among the dead.

The Battle of Atlantaries Harbor occurs concurrently and secures the Shuruppak for the Revolution with a withdrawal of Etlu naval forces to the east.

The Harrying of the Revolution is considered to have started as early as October but more earnestly in the wake of the sacking of Telmun, well before Holindrian's army crossed under the Rowen Mountains by way of a Fifth Age transcontinental tunnel. This event was geographically focused on border regions with particular emphasis in Hundare, North Volz, and Polpedon. The Harrying waned somewhat as the New Year approached and Holindrian crossed into enemy-held territory.

The Battle of Gathbiyya, the death of Anshargal (Saperon), and the disappearance of Holindrian occurs on March 11 in the year 7,530 SE. Much of the Etlu navy is destroyed or captured during the battle whilst trapped in the Gulf of Humar.

King Matthiolus dies in the Fifth Obenian War around this time.

The island of Castroniphinae attempted an invasion of the Audentica mainland but is rebuffed on the slopes of Rey's Shield sometime prior to June 7,530 SE.

The Blood Rest lasted from Saperon's death through the first half of summer of 7,531 SE when the Etlu broke the Revolutionary blockade around Obenia. Most evacuated to Delma Vorta but an estimated two legions, approximately twelve thousand soldiers, raided the island territories of Ilias and Troas before pushing into Laurentia. There, the Shrine of Amurru is razed in October 7,531 SE.

The latter half of 7,531 SE saw rapid Etlu advancement across all fronts; the continents of Byrnes and Duerre are seized as the bulk of the Etlu army penetrates deep into Ephezion, east of the Rowen Mountains. The islands Ginsup and Sarpo also fall. By December of that year, the Etlu are marching into the lands of

Ginno. In concert with their allies from Humar, the Etlu drove the Democrats (a term applied after the fact to describe the rebels) out of Gathbiyya and back across the Fold. The fighting between Hundaren and Humar along their shared peninsula is among the most ferocious of the entire war, rivaled only by that in the north by Antelmari and Ohlinine.

By the start of 7,533 SE, the Democrats had recovered from the previous years' losses. With the Etlu unable to replenish their losses and increasing numbers joining the Cause, the Battle of Naris, the furthest point of Etlu penetration into Hundaren territory, proves decisive. The Etlu advance is halted on May 8, 7,533 SE.

By June of that year, the Democrats laid a daring siege to the fortress city of Bahram.

After a protracted battle, an agreement to the cessation of military conflict between the Etlu and Democrats was signed on August 19, 7,533 SE.

On December 26, 7,533 SE, the heirs of the revolution Holindrian began, met in the Pantheon at Telmun to inaugurate the start of a new age, an age of freedom, the Age of Democracy. The Charter of Free Peoples, the culmination of the Human Revolution and the first document of democratic governance to exist between the humans of Eridu in more than five thousand years, was signed.

3.26 THE EULOGY

The war would continue, but not forever. Skirmishes on the periphery. The crux of Saperon's crusade had been broken. In time, the rebels would sack Bahram, the heart of Saperon's remnant empire, after a lengthy siege, and that December, on the 26th of that month, the leaders of the revolution gathered in the Shuruppak to fulfill Holindrian's promise when this all began.

Assembled together in the Pantheon, Maaschuel addressed

the assembled crowd as they prepared to restore democracy to Eridu and sign the Charter of Free Peoples:

"Remember the lives you have lived. Remember the reasons why you fought. Remember all those who sacrificed to give you this moment. *Remember*.

"He didn't wish for worship or tribute or monuments. His wish for us was simple: Freedom. It's what he wanted for us—all of us. He wanted us to be free—now and for all time. That was his one hope. That future generations might live and die never knowing oppression, that they may live out their days untouched by despotism and maltreatment, that they may live in a world made free. Tell them, he said to me, tell those with sons and daughters yet born, tell those friends yet met, that we fought and persevered and died so that Eridu might be free. All of it. From here to the ends of the earth. *Here*, by our law, the law of freemen, we live.

"Barely three years ago... When he began this campaign, I knew it was likely I would never see *this* tomorrow. Victory, in my mind, seemed unattainable. But I followed him, like so many of you, because in spite of what I knew, I *believed*. Time has proven our friend wise. I am surrounded, this day, by men and women (who ought to have been free by birth) released from their shackles and made free by their choosing.

"Now, here on this hallowed ground, we have come, bound by common purpose, to see that dream fully realized and to fulfill the ancient promise this world holds!

"I ask that you give thanks—to yourselves, your families, your comrades. Give thanks to the glorious dead! Give thanks to those who fought to deliver us from mysticism and tyranny! Give thanks to all who sacrificed to usher in a future brighter than anything we could have imagined! But, most of all, give thanks, you free people of Eridu, to HIM!"

PART 4

THE CHARTER OF FREE PEOPLES

In order that we may profitably emulate the wisdom and preserve the sacrifice of all those who have been lost in attaining our freedom, the persons here assembled declare and solemnly affirm to establish and promote these principles of civility, governance, and common decency in their respective lands for however long they shall remain a signatory to this covenant between all men, the ruled as well as the rulers.

The right of full citizenship belongs to all persons of an established jurisdiction who have matured to the age of 18 and were born in the jurisdiction in which they claim the rights of citizenship. A person who is at least 16 years, or is declared to be 16 years by their community for the purposes of law and order, or should they reside in the jurisdiction of another, may put forth an application of full citizenship under that regime. The right of full citizenship may not be extended to any person currently the recipient of that right by another jurisdiction, unless it is made plain that the aforementioned person seeks to forfeit his or her previous grant of full citizenship. Persons of less than 16 years or determined to be of less than 16 years in their capacities, are either to be considered wards of their families or their communities, and as such, are entitled to certain protections as to guarantee the bonds of fraternity between all.

A person possessing only citizenship is entitled to all the protections and provisions of this Charter, and may not be abridged by the laws of their jurisdiction, save for the barring of participation in the selection of representatives and officers of government and the holding of the same in government. Citizenship exists from the moment of birth in a jurisdiction or petitioned as the result of residing in a jurisdiction.

The right of full citizenship may further be forsaken as a condition of punishment; however, no one may exist nationless, so as to ensure the base protections for human consideration.

The particulars of the following reside with the independent nations that have hereto signed, but it is made known here, that the institutions of government be consistent with the doctrines democratic or republican governance as have been handed down to us. The lawmaking assemblies are to be composed of full citizens, selected in a manner accommodating the right of all full citizens to participate in their selection. The administrative entity is responsible for the dutiful implementation and enforcement of all laws passed by the lawmakers, in accordance with the standards established by the same. The chief administrator may be selected either by the full citizenry themselves or by their chosen representatives by any set of requirements established in addition to the condition of being a full citizen. The judiciary is charged with the interpretation of law, and it is upon their word alone to determine when a law has been violated or is valid at all, with respect to the charters governing the intricacies of each state. The conditions of the former categories are equally applicable to the judiciary with respect to who may hold office.

As the use of war and the implementation of violence as a means to achieve desired ends has been made known and further precipitated the establishment of the new order, we resolve, as signatories to this Charter, to make the exercise of war the last refuge of the state. An obligation is now placed, were it nonexistent before, for all who place themselves in the service of their nation, to make all efforts at resolving disputes through diplomatic and peaceful means. A responsibility exists as statesmen to preserve the peace and avoid war where practicable, in order to spare posterity of the horrors we have so recently witnessed and the horrors inflicted upon one another.

Cognizant that wounds of our recent struggle will be long in their waning, no government, here abiding, may, for any purpose, deny the rights of citizenship or full citizenship to any petitioner on account of their place of origin, creed, or occupation. Any person or group who sincerely believes a nation party to this Charter has unjustly discriminated against them in breach of this prohibition may entreat the Council of Free Peoples for restitution.

The determination as to what constitutes an offense resides with the government. The judgment of offenses in the interests of justice is advised to be held in public forums, presided by an authorized person of the judiciary, a solicitor for the state, and a qualified advocate for the accused, with an assemblage of citizens selected by lot, to participate in the trial, charged with deciding the innocence or guilt of the accused. Any person who sincerely believes a nation party to this Charter has not satisfied their obligation under this provision may entreat the Council of Free Peoples for restitution. Dissatisfaction with the nature of the verdict alone is not cause for a petition.

All signatories hereby agree and affirm that no laws or prescriptions or other methods of prior restraint shall be instituted or be permitted to be propagated by government to the detriment of expression, art, or denomination. Censorship is a power that exceeds the bounds of participatory governance, reserved exclusively for the individual or the familial unit. Any person who sincerely believes a nation party to this Charter has not satisfied their obligation under this provision may entreat the Council of Free Peoples for restitution.

The Council of Free Peoples claims no authority over any nation beyond that granted for the adjudication of petitions filed on behalf of those who perceive maltreatment with respect to their rights as delineated here. The Council is to be made of emissaries, one from each nation, and is permitted to serve no more than three two-year terms over the course of their sponsorship by their nation. Should the nation of a sitting emissary be accused, they are required to recuse themselves for the duration of the hearing, acting only as an advocate in the defense of their government. A simple majority vote, by all remaining emissaries will determine the verdict. The Council is to meet no less than once per annum, at the Shuruppak, and then otherwise as necessitated.

This concludes this, the Charter of Free Peoples.

AFTERWORD

Maaschuel

After presiding over the congress establishing the first democracy since the Fourth Age, Maaschuel returned to Antelmar, with Oda. He spent his nights staring up at the stars, peering through Holindrian's telescope, in part because he longed to see his friend, the man who raised him, one more time. His observations of Earth and the cosmos would be invaluable to future generations as they planned to journey to the stars. Living in the northern forests until his death at the age of 83, he served as general in the numerous wars with the Ohlinine following the end of the Human Revolution, eventually brokering a peace that would not be broken until decades after his death. He succeeded Oda's uncle, Folcher, as lawspeaker of their people. When, at long last, he passed on, after being visited by Azad, he is rumored to have said, "by Fortune, may at last I be able to follow once again."

Barumgal

With their defeats at Gathbiyya and Haurvatat and the death of his lord, Saperon, Barumgal chose not to flee to Bahram, stating to those imploring him to do so that he did not believe their cause could be won. He was pardoned for his crimes by Maaschuel, who welcomed him to Antelmar, offering him sanctuary, as not even his homeland of Humare desired him within their borders, considering him the great betrayer. For the rest of his days, walking with a limp, he sought to repent and redeem himself in the eyes of his new community. During the wars with the Ohlinine, he graciously served as Maaschuel's right hand. Dying only hours after his friend Maaschuel had passed, his last request was that he be remembered by his birth name rather than the one given to him by the false god. The marker on his grave reads: "Here lies Azad, a free man."

Conotocarious

Serving alongside Maaschuel at the Siege of Bahram as general, he was wounded severely, but surprises all, when he not only refuses to be taken from the battlefield until the engagement had ended but survives his injuries as well. Weakened though he is, with the aid of a cane, he and Maaschuel accept the unconditional surrender of Dalibor—the undisputed end of the war. His signature is the first to adorn the Charter of Free Peoples. Upon his return to Laurentia, with the priesthood abolished, he converts the grounds of the Shrine of Amurru into the first college open to all citizens of the new, independent Laurentian state. During his former life, priests had been discouraged from marriage and raising a family, but, with the founding of a new world, he and a priestess, for whom he had long harbored secret affection, wed. At the age of 97, he passed quietly, while asleep in a rocker. To honor the memory of this most famous of all

Laurentians and a hero of the Revolution, the capital city is named.

Oda

Finishing out the remainder of the war, she returns to her native land with Maaschuel, only to find Ohlinine invaders a year before had razed the village. Prolonged warfare delays any possibility of marriage and children, but at her uncle's urging that, if something is important, you make the time for it, she and Maaschuel at last wed. It is with the birth of their first child that she works tirelessly to help in ending the seemingly endless conflict between the two peoples. For her work in securing peace, she, like her husband, ascends to the highly respected office of lawspeaker.

Fajr

Wars of retribution between the Hundaren and the Humari continued for more than a generation after the end of Holindrian's War. Fajr and her desert cavalry never again know peace in their own borders, but because of her actions, the Hundaren are spared from certain conquest. The price, however, for saving the fledgling Hundaren nation from assured destruction is her own life. Leading the largest cavalry charge ever known, she was felled by a Humari arrow. When news of her death spread, allies she had made years prior arrived, in force, and put an end to the conflict.

Drust

Though initially spared by Maaschuel, Drust's radical views continued to degrade, becoming more and more militant. Any semblance of authority or central government was perceived as a threat, as, he believed, anyone, no matter how good or pure at the start, could, in time, become a vassal, a vessel for corruption and abuse. Commanding a small band of like-minded people, he set out to destabilize all governments. Within ten years of the end of the Revolution, Drust had made himself an enemy of all the free people of Eridu, and a coalition was organized to hunt him down and destroy him. He died alone and forgotten after having been captured, tried, and sentenced to life imprisonment.

Matthiolus

He would never again sit upon the Obenian throne, though he would be more fondly remembered in death than he had in the later part of his life. With much of the Etlu navy bottled up in the gulf near Humar half a world away, the soldiers of the Baltutu were trapped—one hundred thousand, a third of all Etlu—in hostile Obenia. The former king served alongside a number of subjects and generals who emerged to lead the insurrection. Killed shortly after the defeat of Saperon, he would never hear of Holindrian's victory nor see his lands freed of foreign occupation, but he would be immortalized as the king who stood shoulder to shoulder with common folk, joined in common cause.

Folcher

After the Battle of Virescent, his return to Antelmar was characterized by perpetual war. Wounded six times by the time the Baltutu Civil War ended and once more before his participation in the wars against the Ohlinine was quickly punctuated, he divided much of the remainder of his time between helping with reconstruction efforts and playing with his great nephews and nieces.

Etienette

She never returned to her bakery. Discarding her apron, she participated in the Battle of Telmun, and was among the first over the stone wall. With the war concentrated in the east, she attempted to march with the army on the eve of the Battle of Gathbiyya but became so sick and weak due to the heat, she and others were evacuated back through the tunnel. She would spend the rest of her life traveling unrestricted across the globe.

Dalibor

Within three years of his surrender at Bahram, burdened with the weight of his failure, he never again took up arms, not even in the wars between his Ohlinine and the Antelmari. He did not seek revenge against Maaschuel or Barumgal, not out of any sense of forgiveness, but because of intense self-loathing. He died shortly thereafter, of causes unknown, and, at his own request, was buried in an unmarked grave in the Ohlinine wood.

Panayiotis

My father, Panayiotis, lived long enough to see the Human Revolution concluded, but, in the winter after the signing of the Charter of Free Peoples, he contracted pneumonia. Weakened from his worldly travels and his advanced age, he had just enough strength to return to our homestead and the place of his forbears. He had one request of me, that I chronicle the lives of those who participated in shaping the future of Eridu, and so I have. This afterward is my own work, done to fulfill a father's dying wish. My name is Panayiota, and there is a new world whose stories I must tell.

MACAULAY CHRISTIAN

Macaulay Christian is a project manager for a commercial construction company. He graduated with a degree in political science and holds a master's in legal studies. Macaulay and his wife live in Dallas, Texas, with their two dogs. When not writing, he enjoys cooking in the kitchen and baking sourdough.

Thank you for reading

Leave a review on Goodreads

Follow on Facebook

Instagram: @mlchrist1241
Threads: @mlchrist1241
TikTok: @mlchrist1241

Author Website

Author Store